Pieces
FOR YOU

BY

GENNA RULON

Pieces For You

Copyright © 2013

Genna Rulon

The Cataloging-in-Publication Data is on file at Library of Congress

ISBN: 0615928854

ISBN-13: 978-0-615-92885-2

Cover design by G. Relyea

© Genna Rulon, 2013

Cover Images Copyright

Used under license from shutterstock.com

Dedication

To the women—the survivors—of violence,
Your strength and perseverance are an inspiration,
and a testament to the profound courage of your soul.
I pray each of you finds your happily ever after!

Prologue

Samantha

"The phoenix hope, can wing her
way through the desert skies, and
still defying fortune's spite;
revive from ashes and rise."
~ Miguel de Cervantes

Journal

May 29th

Since I refuse to speak, the big boss, Shelly, has given me a journal with a promise that I don't have to share the contents, as long as I write down my thoughts each day. I've never kept a journal, but it seems to defeat the purpose of not talking.

I am at The Phoenix Centre (TPC) for the next two months because I was brutally attacked. I know I'm here to "heal," but I don't want to talk about it. I don't want to see the pitying looks I know I would receive if I share my story. I don't want to return to that night and relive the torture. If I don't talk, I can try to pretend it didn't happen. That it was just a nightmare I have yet to wake up from. If I open my mouth and say the words it becomes real, and if it's real, then I can never escape it. Is it real if I write it down?

Everyone here keeps tossing around the word "recovery" as if it is an achievable goal. Can someone recover from meeting the devil in person, being violated and beaten by him, and then left for dead? Is it possible to heal after being betrayed by the man who promised to love you, knowing his choices led to your destruction? Maybe some people can...maybe some of the girls here can...I just don't think I'm one of them

May 30th

They wheeled me into a group therapy session today. I would have objected, but then I'd have had to speak. They said I didn't have to talk, just listen. I think they hope that listening to other girls who suffer like I do will make me feel less alone. What they fail to realize is I want to be alone. I don't want to understand the other girls' pain. I don't want to bond with them or feel compelled to share the details of my attack or how I'm feeling. I don't know these people and I don't want to. I am sure they are all lovely—it's not them, it's me. I don't want to be understood and seen. I want to disappear. If no one can see me, no one can hurt me.

The hits just keep on coming. I had my first physical therapy session. What did cause me other than excruciating pain? I can wiggle my fingers and shrug my shoulder now. As if being emotionally crippled wasn't cruel enough, I am physically crippled too. At least the physical wounds will heal, or so they tell me. I still can't walk or use my left arm because of the casts, and my face continues to look like a boxer after a long, unsuccessful career. My doctors are thrilled with my progress. They act like I reinvented the wheel. I want to feel their excitement and hope, but all that is left is pain and numbness. I prefer the numbness.

Word of my continued silence and lack of participation must have found its way to Shelly's ears because she showed up at my door a little while ago. When she failed to engage me in conversation, she whipped out the big guns, reminding me of my promise to Everleigh to try, to participate...to get better. It was a hit below the belt—Shelly plays dirty. If I wasn't on the receiving end of her emotional blackmail, I would have applauded her resourcefulness.

So now I feel selfish and guilty, as if I'm not lugging around enough guilt-colored baggage. Beyoncé doesn't even travel with this much luggage for crying out loud.

As much as I hate to admit it, Shelly is right. I made a promise to Everleigh and I will keep it...even if it kills me.

June 2nd

I spoke today. Shelly's guilt trip proved impossible to shake. I owed Everleigh so much for taking care of me when my parents wouldn't. I have never broken a promise to her and I didn't want to start now. I thought about how much it would mean to her if I actually told her I was okay and that I was getting better. Maybe if she heard the words she would worry less and be able to start living her life again. So I did it. I spoke. Nothing monumental—I asked someone to pass the coffee at breakfast. The room fell silent for several seconds before everyone resumed their conversations as if nothing unusual occurred. I was grateful they didn't make a big deal about it. I knew it was a big deal, but I didn't want any additional attention. I'll admit, it was nice to be included in trivial conversations. It made me feel less alone. And my conscience is no longer nagging me...that is a small weight lifted.

June 4th

I shared today in group—really shared.
I've been participating since I resumed
speaking two days ago, a few comments
here, a fact there, but nothing
specific...nothing too deep. I planned to
continue that way until they finally
released me out into the world, but my life
rarely goes according to plan.
A new girl came this week. She's really
young, maybe fourteen. She shared
about her rape, dissecting everything she
did wrong, why it was her fault, and how
she didn't fight back hard enough. God,
she broke my heart. Her tears were like
a knife in my chest. I knew that
pain...I'd lived it...I was still living it.
But she was so brave, letting the truth
and pain and tears pour out of her with
such raw honesty. This girl was

practically a child—I didn't want her to feel alone or to blame herself, so I opened my mouth and let my story spill out. All I could look at was her big brown eyes, filled with compassion, understanding, and...relief. So much damn relief. Relief that someone understood and had experienced the same hell. After group she came over and hugged me, the first physical contact I willingly allowed with the exception of Everleigh, and I was okay. As I left the room, Shelly nodded to me from the doorway and mouthed the words 'I'm proud of you.' I was proud of me too, and for the first time since the attack, I had a second of happiness. It was gone before I could even fully appreciate it but it was there— the promise that I might be able to feel joy again someday.

June 12th

I met with Shelly and TPC's head
physician today to discuss my pain
management plan, as well as my difficulty
sleeping. I want off all pain medication
because I'm scared of becoming dependent
like some of the other girls. I'm not
judging them, everyone's recovery is
different; I just don't want to fight an
addiction along with everything else. I
legitimately needed the narcotics to deal
with the pain until this point, but now
Motrin keeps my pain at a manageable
level. Both Shelly and the doctor
supported my decision, but there was one
issue that had us gridlocked.
The pain medication helps me fall sleep,
which has been an epic struggle. Every
time the meds wear off, the nightmares
come, and I relive that night in gruesome

detail. I can hear the leaves crunching beneath my body, smell his overwhelming cologne, hear his sick laughter, feel his hands on my skin...Every. Single. Time. I wake up a shrieking, sweat-soaked mess—hysterical and irrational. It doesn't matter how tired I am, I can't fall back asleep because I am afraid of the terror that awaits me.

The doctor keeps insisting I need to take medication that will force me to sleep. She says I need the rest to continue to heal physically. She tried to scare me into agreeing by explaining that prolonged sleep deprivation would negatively impact my physical and psychological recovery. But I'm adamantly against taking sleeping pills. My mom pops Ambien like candy to help her sleep. The woman can't sleep without them, and she doesn't remember anything that happens while she is under their influence. She sleepwalks and has whole conversations that she doesn't remember the next day. I refuse to depend on drugs that could leave me vulnerable while I sleep.

No. Thank. You.

Shelly tried to find a middle ground, suggesting a low-dose anti-depressant to help me sleep and combat the effects of the night terrors. We spent over an hour debating before I finally convinced them it was my way or the highway.
I will not bend on this. I know millions of people take them with success and that's great for them, but I know myself. Pay me now or pay me later. I'd rather face the nightmares now and learn how to deal with them. Fortunately, in the end I got my way. My body, my choice.

June 19th

WooHoo!

I got my casts off today. In celebration, we took physical therapy poolside and I was able to do my exercises in the water. Olga, the gigantic German therapist (I couldn't make this up), worked the shit out of my arm and leg. I think she may be a closet sadist because every time I grimaced in pain, she smiled. I am trying not to focus on how much flexibility and range of motion I've lost. It's not permanent...or at least that's what they keep telling me. I even took baby steps while holding onto the side of the pool—all by myself. It was a small victory, but it felt huge. The weight of the casts and being confined to the wheelchair were constant reminders of what he had done, as if he could reach across the 3,000 miles separating us to retain his hold on me. When the plaster was sawed off, it felt like his grip had been pried free, too. I was so relieved I cried like a big, fat baby—I had no idea the weight I had been carrying, both physically and emotionally.

When I shared these feelings in group, Shelly suggested we celebrate. I had no idea what she had planned, but when we all gathered on the beach, she lit a fire in a huge barrel and handed me the pieces of my casts. Then I understood. I threw each piece in with deliberate slowness, imagining each as a bond no longer tying me to him. I watched as they withered and burned, disappearing to ash. It took hours before they were all gone, and when they had finally dissolved in the flames, I breathed a sigh of relief.

There is still so much that needs healing (inside and out) but I'm no longer tethered to him. I am free, and for the first time I know it deep in my bones. He may have beat me, scarred me, shattered me in a million pieces, but I'm not under his control anymore...now I get to decide.

June 26th

I'm so freaking excited!
Everleigh and Hunter arrive today...not
that I'll get to see Hunter (no boys
allowed at TPC), but I feel better
knowing he's here for Everleigh. I've
missed her so much. As wonderful as all
the girls are here, it's not the same as
having your bestie/almost-sister around.
There is no one in the world I trust more
than Everleigh. I hate that I've been
missing all the exciting new-relationship
gossip about her and Hunter. Even
though we speak several times a week, I
still feel disconnected being so far away.
I need the comfort of someone who has
known me my whole life—who knew me
before. It's irrational, but I need proof
that someone who loved me before can still
love me now. I'm realizing how much

that asshole took from me—my choice, my power, my sense of security, and worst of all, my self-worth. The therapists tell me these feelings are normal and common for rape victims. I'm starting to believe them—intellectually—but it doesn't stop the feelings.

It also doesn't help that my parents only came to visit me once in the hospital while I was still in a coma. They haven't even tried to contact me since I awoke. They were never candidates for parents-of-the-year, but their complete abandonment during the worst time in my life hurts. Are they just self-absorbed and incapable of love, or do they blame me for what happened? As if I don't already blame myself enough.

I need to see Everleigh. I want to spend a little time with her just being normal; sitting around in PJs, eating ice cream, and watching a movie while painting our nails. I'm craving that simple, familiar routine...any proof I'm still me.

July 6th

I walked into breakfast today and the room fell silent. I thought something happened behind me to capture their attention so I turned around to see, but there was nothing but empty space. I guess I was the attention grabber. It took me a minute to figure out why they were staring, then I realized—I got dressed for breakfast. I've been wearing clothes every day (of course), but this morning I actually got dressed—today I wore my Sam clothes. I wasn't sure how to interpret their silence, and then it began...catcalls, hoots, and whistles. There was an entire room of women cheering my transformation. Geeze, I didn't think I looked that bad before. Okay, that's a lie. I looked like shit before. I had broken every fashion rule I previously lived by, wearing baggy t-shirts and yoga pants as if they were acceptable attire for public viewing.

I told myself that the comfy clothes were practical for physical therapy, but in truth, I was still trying to fade into the background. Last night I realized something. By forcing myself to break my cardinal rule against wearing loungewear in public, it was just one more way he was still controlling me. I decided to dig through a suitcase of clothes Everleigh packed for me and planned an outfit for the next day. Once I was dressed, I felt another small piece of myself click into place.

Of all the pieces of the Old Sam, I might be most grateful to have regained the fashionista shard—it's one thing to feel like shit; there is no excuse to look like shit, too.

July 16th

Over the past few weeks, Shelly has been taking several girls off-premises to help them ease back into the real world...and men. The girls who went on the "field trips" have been at TPC for a while and are showing "marked progress." I am happy to say that includes me! Today we went to the mall and I was in heaven. According to Shelly, it's the perfect location to start becoming desensitized to large groups of strangers, and the attention of men. I was thrilled to have a chance to shop with the excuse it was for therapeutic purposes; it takes the sting out of looking at the credit card bill at the end of the month.

We were all sitting at a table in the food court, sipping coffee and comparing purchases, when a group of twenty something guys approached our table. We must have looked like a perfectly ordinary group of girls hanging out at the mall, open to pick-up attempts. The guys failed to wow us with their played-out lines, bragging about their expensive sports cars and listing their various attributes. A few of the other girls were visibly uncomfortable, but the guys were not taking the hint. Shelly tried politely to end the conversation, subtly encouraging them to leave, but they were not picking up what she was putting down.

With a mix of frustration, shock, and humor, I decided to take matters into my own hands. I sweetly advised the guys that while I was sure they were very appealing to most women, they zeroed in on the one table that had no interest in hooking up.

Clearly unhappy with my dismissal, the spokesman said, "What are you, a bunch of lesbians or something?" As if not wanting them could only mean we didn't want any man. Ha! I tried to do it the nice way with no success, so I decided I'd do it the Sam way.

"No, we aren't...but with the lines you've been using, I bet at least half of us are debating the merits of switching teams. Congratulations, you just witnessed the birth of a new flock of lesbos. Good job, boys."

As the group walked away—calling me a "bitch" under their breaths—the girls applauded. I took my bow before returning to my lunch with a smile on my face. It was a good day. Not only did I spend the day in public with only minor discomfort, but also I got to shop, break out some sass, and school a group of inflated egos. However, the main reason for the smile still painted on my face was because I stood up to a group of big-ish guys, without fear they would hurt me. I was brave today. I said 'no' and they listened. They may have called me a "bitch," but that was the worst thing that happened...I've never been so happy to be called a bitch in my life.

July 25th

Tomorrow's the big day. I'm going home.
I'm excited and fucking terrified.
After two months, I'm leaving here
stronger. I've conquered most of my panic
attacks and anxiety. I've learned to
accept that the devastating horror I
endured was beyond my control and no
fault of my own—I was simply in the
wrong place at the wrong time. I didn't
ask to be hurt, I didn't invite the
abuse, and I sure as hell didn't deserve
what happened to me. It had nothing
to do with me—it was him. He was the
problem, he made the wrong choices, and
he was the one to blame.
It took me a long time to stop looking for
an explanation for why it happened. I
now understand how counterproductive it is
to search for reason in a senseless act of

violence; it only leads to an endless cycle of blame and 'what ifs.'

When I finally stopped asking myself 'why me,' I was able to focus on finding the small joys life still held. It's become a healing game for me, always searching for the little blessings hidden in the mundane. Sometimes I share them but often hoarding for myself the little hidden treasures others have missed. It's silly but it allows me to find beauty in a life that seemed to turn against me for a time. I've also found the humor I thought I lost. I regained my comfort in expressing thoughts flitting through my mind without censoring myself—in other words, I discovered the pieces of Old Sam that were inappropriate, irreverent, and overshared...god, I missed her.

Tomorrow, I rejoin society. Not completely healed, but definitely healing. I know I still have a long road ahead of me. The obstacles and bumps are going to suck, but I believe I can make it to my destination and enjoy the ride getting there. At TPC I found healing and hope, and I will hold them close on my journey.

Chapter One

"While we have the gift of life, it seems to me the only tragedy is to allow part of us to die—whether it is our spirit, our creativity or our glorious uniqueness."
-Gilda Radner

I couldn't breathe, couldn't see. Something was wrapped around my head, clinging tightly to my face, blocking any traces of light. The strange fabric was moist around my mouth and nose as I panted, struggling to draw oxygen into my burning lungs. I could feel wetness gathering around my eyes where tears were spilling freely. I opened my mouth to scream, but terror seized my vocal chords and no sound escaped. Something hit me—hard—so hard my head rang and I immediately felt warmth oozing down the side of my face. I tried to raise my hand, hoping to stop the flow, but I couldn't move. Oh my god—I was tied down—this couldn't be happening to me. I don't want to die. "Please."

"Sam."

I heard a voice calling me as if through a long tunnel, echoing in my mind. I tried to answer, but the words died on my lips.

"Sam, wake up," the voice commanded as my world began to shake turbulently.

"Dammit! Samantha Whitney, you open your eyes and look at me right this minute or so help me God—"

Everleigh.

I recognized the voice of my best friend. I was safe—I must be safe if Ev was here. I fought to raise my unwilling eyelids, desperate for the reassurance her voice promised. I was trapped in my own body, merely a passenger unable to control the vessel containing me.

"Sam, please, you have to wake up now, it's not real—none of it is real. Open your eyes for me—you're safe. I promise you're safe," she pleaded, her voice thick with tears.

Ev's desperate pleas were a rope lowered through the black abyss in which I was trapped. I grabbed hold and tried to pull myself out, hand over hand until glimmers of light appeared. Finally, my eyes opened and I stared into the pain-etched face of my best friend. I had to avert my eyes momentarily to avoid her suffering; I hated to be confronted with the agony I caused her...again. This proved to be a mistake when my vision was unexpectedly filled with Hunter's sympathetic expression.

Shit, it just kept getting worse. It was bad enough when I thought Ev was here for another one of my fits, but her boyfriend was witness too.

"I'm okay," I croaked unconvincingly, even to myself. I was anything but okay; I was as far from okay as a person could get without NASA and a space shuttle's aid.

Ev's arms wrapped around my shoulders and I desperately wanted to shrug them off, still unprepared to be touched after the dream. But I knew the gesture of comfort was also for Ev's benefit, so I tolerated her embrace...barely.

I focused on my months at TPC and began the breathing techniques I had learned during my stay—my "recovery." Slow, even breaths until my lungs were at capacity, hold it for three-count, slow and controlled exhale. I repeated the process five times before I began to feel grounded again. I raised my hand and patted Ev's back, communicating my gratitude and reassurance.

She reluctantly released me as Hunter stepped forward to wrap his arms around her waist from behind. She leaned her head back against his chest, and I felt a prick of jealousy for the ease with which she accepted his physical comfort. Guilt swamped me for begrudging Ev and Hunter the happiness they deserved. What was wrong with me? I was not a covetous, bitchy person—at least I never used to be. I'm not sure who or what I was anymore.

"Babe, I think I'm going to sleep in here tonight," Ev said to Hunter.

"Okay love, I'll get your pillow and some blankets," he said as he left the room.

I sighed, wanting to decline but knowing I would never fall back to sleep if left alone. I returned from TPC six days ago, and Ev had slept on the floor next to my bed for several hours each of the nights. I don't know how Hunter—or her back—could stand it night after night. Hunter was as much a prisoner as Ev to my ridiculous fears. He may not be camped out on my floor, but I was unable to sleep if he wasn't in the apartment. I needed the security his gun-toting, FBI presence provided.

Hunter returned with blankets, a pillow, and a thick foam pad that I had seen in camping commercials...that was new. He shrugged as if all of this was perfectly normal as he quickly made a bed for her. He tucked her in and placed a sweet kiss on her lips, telling her he loved her. Then he stopped by the side of the bed and placed a swift kiss on the top of my head while whispering "sweet dreams."

Hunter was the only man I could stand to touch me or be near me. He was a friend and a brother-in-law of sorts, if you discount the fact that Ev and I were not sisters by blood nor were they engaged or married. Regardless of the technical correctness of his honorary title, the sentiment was 100% accurate. Hunter had been by my side, supporting me and Ev, every step of the way.

"You okay?" Everleigh asked quietly.

"No," I answered honestly...for a change.

"You're going to be," she said with conviction.

"How do you know?"

"Because we won't let it be any other way."

I clung to her confident determination in the absence of my own. Before I fell back to sleep, I mouthed a quick prayer, hoping she was right.

I couldn't breathe, couldn't see. His weight was pressing down on me, trapping me, forcing branches and rocks to cut into my bare back. I hurt—everywhere. I could no longer discern between the various sources of pain; it was a tidal wave of agony I could not fight. The sounds of his grunts echoed around me. His smell, even through the hood, churned my stomach until I became ill. I don't want to die. "Please."

"Sam, wake up."

The voice called to me—sweet, like an angel. Was I dead this time? Was it finally over?

"Sam, you need to wake up. You can do this...fight your way back."

Everleigh. I could hear her calling to me. I tried to find her but all I could see was pitch black. I wheezed as my panic increased.

"Dammit, Sam, you have to breathe. Don't you do this to me, you are stronger than this."

The world shook and shards of light pierced the darkness.

"There you go, open your eyes. You are safe, in the apartment. Take a deep breath."

Ev's face appeared above me, concerned but not terrified—that was an improvement.

"Hey," I whispered, my throat burning.

A glass of water appeared before me and I readily gulped the cooling relief. I must have been screaming again. She put her arm behind my back to support me as I continued to sip. When the glass was empty, Ev took it from my shaking hands.

"Are you okay alone for a minute? I want to refill the glass and grab my blankets."

I nodded, unable to speak.

"I'll be right back. I'll leave the lights on for you."

She slipped from my room and I heard her speaking with Hunter in hushed tones.

I lay back down and concentrated on isolating and relaxing each muscle, one by one. Tension still held my body as tight as a guitar string. The remnants of my panic were tangible, like boulders weighing down my limbs and restricting my breathing. I despised my inability to control the episodes. Rationally, I understood they were a normal reaction, even months after the attack. But I resented myself for succumbing to the incapacitating fear—it was like he could still control my body...shit, not going there. I would not think about him, about what he did...dammit! I clenched my fist and hit my bed with the full force of my frustration. I wanted to howl my anger, but I didn't want Ev and Hunter to know the truth. I couldn't let them know how much effort I was exerting to cling to my sanity and claw my way back to normalcy. The struggle required for me to suppress my panic, forget the night terrors, and project the illusion that I was the same girl they knew and loved was mentally exhausting. That girl had been destroyed, shattered—not cracked or chipped, but completely obliterated into millions of tiny specks. I had regained pieces of Old Sam, but I knew I would never be able to collect all of the fragments. I would never be whole again, and I had no clue what could fill the gaps that remain.

I grunted as the ache of my fingernails piercing my palms registered. The pain was grounding, but I had learned not to court the fleeting comfort of pain to alleviate my inner turmoil.

When Ev returned, she must have thought I was already asleep because she silently arranged her pallet on the floor at the foot of my bed. Soon after, her soft snore filled the room, and I listened to the strangely comforting sound for hours before finally drifting to sleep.

I couldn't breathe, couldn't see. A loud crack, the only warning, seconds before excruciating pain exploded in my abdomen. Again. Again. Oh god, make it stop—I'll do anything to make it stop. A whoosh of air and the world began to fade, my mind and my body both shutting down. I don't want to die. "Please."

"Sam, wake up."

The world shook and my eyes popped open. I blinked against the jarring light, trying to focus on Ev's face. She was wearing a slight smile tonight.

"It was better this time, easier to wake you up."

"That's good," I said without enthusiasm.

"It's been three nights since the last one—you're getting better. Be patient with yourself."

She hugged me tightly and stroked the back of my head, just like her mother used to when I was hurt. There was nothing I wouldn't give to have Meme here. She'd know how to make me feel better, if only for a little while.

"I miss Meme," I shared softly.

"Me too. She would be able to help you so much better than I can."

"Ev, you have been better than any friend or sister could ever be. I just...sometimes I just want my mom, even if she wasn't really mine."

"Oh, Sam. She was your mom just as much as mine and loved you with all her heart. She chose you as a surrogate daughter—that is how special you are."

We both wiped tears from our cheeks. It had been a while since we talked about Meme, about how much we missed her. As much as I wished she was here to hold me and mother me, Ev must wish she was here to share the burden I had become.

"I'll go get my blankets. Be right back."

"No." I grabbed her arm to stop her. "I'm okay tonight. I think I can go back to sleep alone."

"Really? Are you sure? I don't mind staying."

"I'm positive, but thank you. You are a better friend, a better sister, than I deserve."

"Don't be stupid. I'll remind you of what you once said to me: 'I've done nothing for you that you haven't or wouldn't do for me. You have been my shoulder to lean on enough times—it's my turn.'"

With a hug and a kiss on the top of my head, she left me with the impact of my own words from when her mom—our mom—died.

Everything I endured during the past few months of suffering, at least I had someone to blame. I could point a finger, seek justice. He would not go unpunished for what he had done to me and the others. I would fight back the way I couldn't last time—fight to keep him from ever hurting another human being and fight to regain every piece of me that he destroyed. There was no justice for Meme, however, nowhere to point the finger of blame. It was her own body that betrayed her. She never had the opportunity to 'fix' herself. She would miss every milestone and celebration she ever looked forward to sharing with us: college graduation, weddings, and children. She was denied the opportunity I had been given—a chance to live—so I would do it for both of us and be there to share with Ev every single joy Meme would miss.

I quietly cried myself to sleep, not because of the terrors or the reminder of the tragedy I suffered, but because I missed the only mother I had ever known.

I couldn't breathe, couldn't see. His laughter was causing me to shudder; my fear so pronounced it had a taste, smell, color. I don't want to die. "Please."

I shot upright in my bed, trembling and coated in a sheen of sweat. I was okay. Safe, I reminded myself. Freakin-A! I had done it, managed to wake myself up—drag myself out of the nightmare. My therapists at TCP had promised the day would come where I would have enough control to do just this, but I never believed them. I didn't dare to hope. I was actually getting better.

Physically, I was almost back to normal; the scars that remained were mostly hidden and the few more obvious markings could be easily erased with minor plastic surgery. I was lucky. The wounds on my mind and soul were still healing, but those were invisible—I could choose to whom I revealed them. I scrubbed and cleaned, dressed and protected, exposed and let them breathe, until they finally began to scab over and heal. For the most part, they were simply scars, no longer festering wounds making me ill and spreading toxicity throughout my body.

I smiled a small, self-satisfied smile. That's right, bitches...I can do this. You don't control me—I'm in charge here.

I snuggled under my comforter and identified the unfamiliar feeling bubbling within me—hope.

I couldn't breathe, couldn't see. I don't want to die. "Please."

"Sam, wake up."

I opened my eyes, shaking my head to dispel the dream. Ev and Hunter's faces smiled back at me. Ah, I was being double-teamed.

"I'm sorry I woke you," I said.

I was disappointed to have broken my record of five consecutive nights of peaceful sleep. Dammit, I was doing so well. Why tonight?

"Don't be ridiculous. There's no reason for you to apologize. Besides, if you hadn't woken me, Hunter would have with his snoring," Ev placated.

"I do not snore. If you want to relieve her of the unnecessary guilt, then invent your own shortcomings, don't drag me into it," Hunter teased while squeezing her against him. "And Sam is well aware that *you* are the one who snores."

"I do not snore! I just breathe very heavily when I sleep," Ev countered. This argument had become familiar in the weeks since my return.

"Angel, I've heard you breathe heavy many times, much to my delight, but the sounds you make while sleeping cannot be classified as anything other than snoring."

"Don't be an ass. I. Do. Not. Snore."

"Sorry Ev, but Hunter is right. You do snore when you are sick or completely wiped. Loudly," I contributed to the debate.

"Well, thank you for your uninvited opinion, Judge Judy. I see how it is. Everyone is just going to gang up on me since neither of you can take me on your own. It's pathetic really, but I accept the shallow victory nonetheless."

Hunter raised an eyebrow at Ev. "Victory? That is a stretch, even for you. I don't recall seeing any points on the board under your tally."

"You keep it up, Mr. Charles, and you'll be finishing out your night on the couch."

"Ev, if you've taught me anything, it's to never make idle threats. You and I both know there is no way you are making that fine man sleep on the couch. Just look at him...all shirtless and drool-worthy, with those tantalizingly low pajama pants." I pretended to eye the portion of Hunter's body not obstructed by Ev's.

"I am not a piece of meat, Sam," Hunter feigned insult. "And my eyes are up here."

"You're eyes are lovely, Hunter, but they have nothing on your abs."

"Sam, stop ogling Hunter. I'm the one who has to live with his inflated ego when you're done feeding it," she scolded. "And his butt is way better than his abs, if we're taking stock."

"Dear Lord, women, have you no shame? I'm right here."

"Of course you are, baby, now turn around and illustrate my point for Sam," Ev joked.

Hunter shook his head and moved toward the door—walking backward to conceal his mouth-watering tush. Such a shame. I may view Hunter as a brother, but he wasn't my actual brother and I wasn't blind.

"Goodnight, Sam. I hope you enjoyed objectifying me," Hunter huffed but had a difficult time containing his smirk. "Women."

Once we were alone, Ev sat on the edge of my bed. "Are you really okay?"

"I'm fine, this one wasn't that bad. I'm surprised I even woke you. I just feel a little high-strung, but you two gave an impressive performance to distract me."

"Then our mission was accomplished for tonight."

She squeezed my hand and I squeezed back, then Everleigh left the room to return to her own bed and Hunter. I was thankful that she no longer needed to sleep on the floor to help me get through the night.

As I relaxed back into my mattress, I realized that my room was dark—completely dark. My nightlight bulb must have burnt out during the night and for the first time, the absence of any light didn't bother me. I gave myself an imaginary pat on the back.

I had found several significant pieces and puzzled them together in some semblance of the original. I was feeling like Old Sam more frequently and for longer durations. Progress. Even Ev and Hunter had noticed my improvement. They never came right out and said it, but it was obvious in their actions and reactions. Since I returned home, they had slowly stopped hovering and the lines of worry creasing their faces began fading. Hunter didn't hesitate to stand close to me or hug me now. For a while, he was taking great care not to be left alone in a room with me, as if I might panic. Of all the men in the world, Hunter was the one I trusted most to keep me safe. Ev became confident that I was comfortable enough having Hunter around and began purposely leaving us alone. The excuses he provided to make an exit were hilarious. When he finally caught on to our game, he turned the tables on us by refusing to ever leave a room either of us was in. It led to "the great bathroom showdown," where neither Ev nor I could use the bathroom because Hunter refused to stop tailing us. We finally 'fessed up to our shenanigans so he would relent.

In the last few weeks, they even relaxed enough to talk to me like they used to—like I was just Sam, not an over-sensitive time bomb. Their return to normal helped to fuel my own. I found inappropriate comments sliding from my lips more frequently and I loved it. Ev even had to tell me 'too much information' several times this week—now that was proof-positive Old Sam was alive and well.

While much was still unaccounted for, a fact I was learning to accept, I was acutely aware of one key piece still missing in action. My libido was still on extended vacation in Bora Bora, sunning herself on the deck of her overwater bungalow with a fruity drink in one hand and a book in the other. She had an open ticket and clearly had no intention of booking her return flight in the foreseeable future...bitch. I don't think I was ready to explore that facet of New Sam yet, and it would take a mountain of trust for me to make myself that vulnerable to a man again, but it didn't make my complete lack of sexual interest any less disconcerting.

I watched the movie 'Magic Mike' yesterday and felt nothing...not a damn thing. Sexy, built male strippers with killer dance moves and packages that could steal a girl's breath—yet it did nothing for me. Six months ago Old Sam would have been scrolling through her phone searching for viable 'repeat performance' contenders to put out the fire—New Sam went to sleep alone, not even a steamy dream to keep her company.

I looked at the clock and shook my head at the time. I should be asleep instead of dissecting my inadequacies. Tomorrow was going to be a challenging day. I had my first therapy appointment with Dr. Cynthia Veritus, which was sure to be a fun and uplifting session. NOT! It wasn't that I objected to therapy, I didn't. I knew it was a vital part of my recovery and it was nice to have someone emotionally objective whom I could toss my shit at without fear of upsetting them. I have had video sessions with my therapist from TPC over the past month, but face-to-face sessions pushed me more toward absolute honesty.

My dread centered on the necessity to recount and relive what had occurred and my state immediately following the attack...that would inevitably be the focus of the first few sessions, which was going to suck. By the time I left TPC, I was comfortable with all of the counselors and it was easy for me to share. They helped me process and heal, but they understood my triggers and slowly helped me to stretch my boundaries. I didn't know what I would have done if approached with the 'battering ram' therapeutic approach...yes I do, I would have walked—well, wheeled, since I was still stuck in that stupid chair—the hell out of there and never looked back. Now I have to start from scratch, building a level of comfort and trust with someone new. It's like training a new boyfriend, but without all of the butterflies in my stomach and lip locks—in other words, all the work and none of the rewards.

I yawned, finally feeling the weight of my exhaustion pulling me under, and then surrendered, closing my eyes with a prayer for another night of dreamless sleep.

I awoke in the morning feeling rested and ready to face the day. As I entered the bathroom, I noticed that the recent nights of rest had helped to banish much of the purple shadows beneath my emerald green eyes. My auburn hair was also finally growing out after being hacked off by my attacker. Luckily, my skin was still sun-kissed from my months of recovery in San Diego, which helped distract from my still slightly gaunt frame. I regained most of the weight I lost following the attack, so I was no longer the leading contender for a walk-on role in the latest zombie movie. Unfortunately, with my tiny five feet one-inch frame—okay, four feet eleven and three-quarter inches, but I always wore at least a kitten heel so I had earned the extra inch and a quarter, dammit—even being down seven pounds from my pre-assault weight was substantial and unflattering. I simply couldn't pull off Kate Moss' 'heroin chic' look, so I was not going to miss looking like the walking dead.

After a quick shower, I brushed on some blush and mascara to encourage a "healthy" appearance, before braiding my hair over my shoulder, Katniss-style. I returned to my room and opened the door to my walk-in closet. There were many reasons I loved my small, luxurious condominium, and the number one on my list was this expansive closet. I was not OCD about anything *except* my wardrobe; my clothing was organized by type and color, and then sub-categorized by textile and/or attitude. My shoes and accessories followed the same neurotic pattern. I created each outfit, worn layer by layer, with great care, each communicating a message and theme to the world. Through my clothing I was able to control how the world perceived me, which was a reaffirming prospect to someone whose choice and control were violently taken from them. Yes, I even viewed clothing with therapeutic intent—it also didn't hurt that I could refer to shopping as a healing activity now.

I visualized the outfit in my mind. A white bohemian shirt to emphasize my tan and mask my too-thin body. Navy cuffed shorts that lent seriousness to my casual Indian Summer look, and a pair of navy espadrilles with a floral ribbon at the ankles to add a playful element. A pair of white feather earrings for whimsy and a collection of thin, gold bangles finished my look. Perfect. From the outside, I was the picture of stability and normalcy.

I made my way to the kitchen where I spotted Ev perched on Hunter's lap as he fed her an omelet. I grabbed a Greek yogurt from the fridge before joining them at the kitchen table.

"I think I liked you better when you were all reserved and aloof...this touchy-feely Hunter is kind of freaking me out," I teased.

In reality, I was overjoyed to see my best friend finally receiving the affection and love she deserved. Ev and Hunter's journey to couplehood had been fraught with secrecy and delayed gratification. At one point, I had debated drugging them both and throwing them into bed together to speed up the process. I was getting sexually frustrated just watching their self-denial...I'm not sure how Ev didn't combust.

"You are just jealous you don't have one of Hunter's famous omelets. My man has *many* talents—big, impressive talents."

"Are you offering me a sample of Hunter's impressive talent?"

Hunter nearly spit the coffee out of her mouth.

"Paws off lady, I don't share."

"You always did monopolize all the good toys when we were kids, never sharing your Malibu Barbie."

"For the hundredth time, you had the same freaking Malibu Barbie, along with her Malibu mansion, convertible, coordinating wardrobe, scooter, and whatever other accessories Mattel had marketed that year. There was no reason for you to want *my* Malibu Barbie," Ev returned with exasperation. This was an ancient debate, which may pre-date the conflict in the Middle East.

"But *your* Malibu Barbie had a couture hand-sewn wardrobe and Meme painted Barbie's nails with that little marker—so stylish...so me."

"And then mom sewed a coordinating wardrobe for *your* Barbie and painted her nails. There was no difference."

"But *your* Barbie was the first, the trendsetter. *Mine* was just a copycat wannabe."

Ev threw her hands in the air dramatically. "I give up! Fine, you want my Malibu Barbie? We can switch. Will that make you happy and finally end this ridiculous debate?"

"No need, I switched them during a sleepover one night. I've had the innovative fashionista for the last thirteen years."

"Are you freaking kidding me? You stole my Barbie? What is *wrong* with you?" she asked, no longer pretending to be annoyed by our age-old dispute...oops, I probably shouldn't have 'fessed up to that particular truth.

I shrugged. "Sorry, but you really didn't appreciate her. You didn't even notice when I made the swap—what kind of mother are you?"

Ev lunged across the table and would have caught me if Hunter's arm hadn't locked around her waist and hauled her back into his lap.

"Why you—" Ev didn't get the chance to finish what was sure to be a scathing reprimand because Hunter's mouth was on hers in the blink of an eye, distracting her with what I can only say was impressive technique. When he finally broke the kiss, Ev was glassy-eyed and breathless.

"Would you like an omelet, Sam?" Hunter asked as if he had not just laid a scorching kiss on my best friend seconds before. Bravo, Hunter, bravo.

"You are not preparing breakfast for that...that...Barbie snatcher. Come on, Mr. FBI Man, can't you drag her down to headquarters and charge her with something? She may have even departed the country with Barbie at some point. That's a federal offense—do something useful with that badge of yours."

Hunter rose, somehow managing to hoist Ev over his shoulder, and started down the hall.

"Excuse us, Sam. Your best friend evidently needs a reminder of how useful I can be."

I could hear Ev's half-hearted protests as Hunter shut her bedroom door. I laughed aloud at their antics. Ev was one of the most determined people I had ever met. She could easily steamroll over most adversaries. It was divine intervention that she fell head over heels for the one man who could best her. He challenged her and she loved every minute of it. They were a unit, stronger together than their individual halves.

Ev had been like a sister to me for the last fifteen years and now I had gained Hunter, who almost instantly became like a brother—a really hot older brother who would hopefully parade equally hot friends through the house. I may not be ready for a man right now, but that wouldn't last forever and Hunter was my golden ticket into the sex-on-a-stick buffet. When my appetite finally returned, I intended to stuff myself like a half-starved contestant at a hot dog-eating competition.

I finished my breakfast and headed out to my car. Dr. Veritus' office was not far and I arrived in less than fifteen minutes. I practiced my relaxation breathing as I gathered the courage to face a history I would prefer to forget. Confident I had done all I could to prepare myself, I entered the office suite. I was comforted by the refined elegance of the space. There was minimal clutter and several flowering plants, adding both color and life. I settled myself in a comfortably stuffed chair and waited.

A few minutes later, the door in front of me opened and an attractive woman in her early fifties emerged. Dressed in a colorful sundress and ballet flats, she conveyed warmth and acceptance. I wondered if she had done this deliberately or if she just thought the floral pattern was pretty on the hanger.

"Sam?" she asked in a strong, clear voice.

I nodded.

"Hello, it's nice to finally meet you. I'm Dr. Cynthia Veritus, but please call me Thia."

"Hi Thia, it's nice to meet you, too. I have heard great things about you; I'm hoping they're all true."

She laughed at my joke, which set me at ease.

"Come in, Sam—let's get this over with."

I followed her into the adjoining office, confused by her choice of words. It wasn't the most encouraging opening statement, but perhaps I had misheard. I sat down on the comfortable, tan loveseat and noted that her office matched the style of the waiting room. Thia sat across from me in a navy wingback armchair and offered me a kind smile. I returned her smile and waited for her to begin. She continued to smile at me but said nothing, which was becoming exceedingly uncomfortable. My own smile began to fall and she smirked knowingly. I rededicated myself to what was apparently a staring/smiling contest, determined to emerge victorious. She smiled even wider and I caught a glimmer of laughter in her eyes, but she was rock solid and unwavering.

Son of a bitch! I was going to lose this contest...I'm not even sure what that meant, but it couldn't be a good sign.

"Fine, I give," I acquiesced with a sigh.

Thia smiled before raising her hand to muffle what I can only imagine would have been a chuckle if permitted to escape.

What the heck? She was laughing at me...how unprofessional!

"What gives? Aren't you supposed to be asking me what brings me here? The details of what I experienced? What dysfunctional ways I have coped with everything thus far?"

"Is that what you want to talk about?"

"Hell no! That is the last thing I want to relive for the umpteenth time," I virtually shouted.

"You don't want to talk about what is past and I'm not asking. So what is the problem?"

Well that took the wind right out of my sails. I had no idea how to respond, so I resumed our staring contest. It was juvenile, I know, but it felt really good being defiant.

This time she did laugh aloud and I glared back at her. Was I actually paying her to laugh in my face?

"Okay, so what is your biggest concern right now?"

She finally asked a question...thank god!

"I'm not sure. I've been back almost two months and I think I have kept it together—for the most part. I've been having night terrors occasionally. I'm still a little uncomfortable out in public when alone and I find myself looking over my shoulder. The deep breathing exercises help to center me, but I wish I could get rid of the paranoia completely."

"It definitely is *normal* after what you have experienced, but I think you are ready to conquer this particular fear."

"Okay, what do I do?"

"We will get to that in a little bit, it's a part of your homework assignment."

"Homework?"

She nodded in reply. Dammit, I thought I was done with homework. Oh well, I would try anything once.

"What else?" she prompted.

"My parents have requested I come to dinner next week."

"And?"

"I don't want to?" I asked, as if it may be the wrong answer.

"Why not?"

"Because they never make time to see me. They only came to visit me in the hospital once after the attack—and I wasn't even conscious! They never bothered to visit me when I was at The Phoenix Centre and I haven't actually spoken to either of them in over six months, since before the attack. The only communication I received was an email from my father's secretary reminding me to use the Platinum Amex for any medical expenses. Trust me, whatever they want, it's not going to make me happy."

"Are you certain? Maybe they had an epiphany after almost losing you and want to work on improving your relationship."

"Spoken like a rational person who has an empathetic bone in their body. There's a reason I am an only child, Thia. My parents thought having a kid would be a great addition to the illusion of their Rockwell portrait life. Once I arrived, they handed me to the nearest nanny and resumed business as usual. My mother was horrified by the effects pregnancy had on her previously impeccable body, and spent well over a hundred grand to repair the damage I caused. Ultimately my cost exceeded my value, so they determined children were a bad investment and a hindrance to their quality of life. These are not the type of people who have sudden moments of introspection—nothing good will come of this dinner," I finished with conviction.

"Well, I'm convinced. Next?"

"Are you mocking me?" I asked, confused by her quick dismissal of my mommy and daddy issues.

"Not at all. You seem to comprehend that their issues are theirs, not yours. While you're understandably apprehensive about the dinner, you aren't harboring any unrealistic expectations and have already developed healthy coping strategies to process your feelings concerning your parents. Unless you begin to exhibit inappropriate emotional responses to their behaviors or indulge in self-destructive coping mechanisms, I see no reason for us to explore this any further. Do you want to analyze the minute details of every disappointment you have ever suffered at their hands? We can do that, but I'll need to grab my calendar to schedule all the additional weekly visits."

"Sarcasm much?"

"I am happy to waste your time and money by exploring every little facet of your past and psychoanalyzing the myriad ways each has shaped your psyche...if that would make you feel better," she deadpanned.

"You should grab coffee with Everleigh some time—you two would have a blast out-snarking one another."

"Since Everleigh is your best friend, I will take that as a compliment," she countered, successfully turning my poke around.

"Two peas in a freakin' pod," I muttered.

"Next?"

"Geeze, I might as well be waiting my turn at the supermarket deli counter, holding a little ticket with a number on it."

"Sarcasm much?" she parroted my earlier barb.

"I'm not sure if you are the best therapist ever or the worst."

"I get that a lot," she offered without concern, causing me to laugh. "Don't worry, I'll grow on you."

"If you have a magical solution to cure my night terrors, I will commit to providing you an organ of your choice should a transplant ever become necessary."

"Now that is a tantalizing offer. My patients are far more biddable when I drug them..." she paused and I stared at her like she was a complete lunatic. "*Kidding.* Of course I could prescribe a sleep aid if you don't currently have one, but that would not be my suggested course."

"What do you suggest?"

"Homework."

"Such a dirty word to be throwing around so casually. Okay, lay it on me."

"I want you to find a part-time job in an environment you feel safe to help increase your comfort level in public—consider it exposure therapy. Plus, you need something to do besides shopping," she said as she eyed my outfit, correctly pegging my current method of passing time. "You should attend the dinner at your parents' next week. At the very least it will clear them off your list of worries. I also want you to establish a regular exercise routine. Sign up at a gym and use it. It will aid your sleep and possibly help reduce the number of night terrors you have been experiencing. Not to mention, it's another public venue for you to build comfort and confidence."

"I can handle those assignments."

"Oh, one more—eat! The Italian in me is dying to shove heaping piles of carbohydrates into that scrawny little body of yours."

I laughed at her exclamation; it was clear she wasn't exaggerating for effect.

"Will do, Chef Boyardee," I teased, glad to be ending on a positive note and with several manageable tasks to focus on. "It's been...strange, but good...I think."

"Excellent. You handled me better than most do on their first visit."

I didn't think she was kidding, which gave me an odd sort of pride at the unexpected accomplishment. As I departed, I couldn't help but wonder if I had just found a guide through the minefield of recovery or if I was being "Punk'd" by Ashton Kutcher—if it was the latter, this would have made for some great TV programming. I glanced around to make sure there were no cameramen hiding in the bushes. Nope. Thia was a therapist unlike any I had encountered thus far. I resolved to follow her directives and get a jump on my homework assignments.

After a stop at New York Sports Club (NYSC), I was officially a card-carrying gym member and planned to institute my workout schedule beginning tomorrow. I had been to the gym at Hensley with Ev before, but all we ever attempted was the treadmill, elliptical, stair-climber, and stationary bike—the rest was a complete mystery to me. Most of the equipment in the gym looked like it belonged in Christian's "Red Room of Pain." I didn't think NYSC was a front for a BDSM club, so there must be another purpose behind the various contraptions; I was just clueless as to what that purpose was. While there, I was tempted to explore some of the machinery, but felt uneasy with the vast number of shirtless men, all grunting and sweaty. I didn't know these men and felt unprepared to put myself within arm's reach.

I took a deep breath to calm myself and tried to survey the room with Old Sam's eyes. The selection of man-candy was spectacular. I was mentally stripping off a wide array of tank tops and exercise shorts—from a distance. A glimmer of hope shined, despite my initial panic, and there was the slightest stirring, a twinge really, which registered in my neglected lady bits. Hell yeah, it may only be a twinge, but it was the first sign of life from her royal highness in five months. As I left the gym, I pondered my response—was there hope? I feared my goodies had dried up, petrified from lack of use. My relief at the possibility of reanimation was palpable. I indulged in a brief parking lot happy dance, only to find a snickering couple approaching me.

"What? You'd dance too if you just realized your years of kegels weren't wasted."

I left them in open-mouthed shock, a smile painted on my face and extra bounce in my step.

My added confidence spurred me to bite the bullet and call my parents. Elsa, their housekeeper, advised me that they were not available, so I left a message confirming my presence at the family dinner the following week. Homework item number two completed.

I needed time to consider employment prospects where I would feel secure and enjoy the work—well, if not enjoy, then at least not despise.

I stopped at Chipotle for a spicy chicken burrito—food consumption. Homework item number four accomplished. Then I headed to the mall to acquire new gear for my athletic intents. I had no problem working out and sweating, but you can be damn sure I was going to look my best doing it. I struck gold with a selection of outfits from Heidi Klum's workout line. One of the pieces was even featured on "Project Runway," a show my DVR was programmed to always record and never delete without my prior authorization.

When I was satisfied I had appropriately rewarded my homework initiative, I finally headed home. Ev arrived shortly after and rushed to the bathroom to shower before Hunter arrived for dinner.

Chapter Two

"I make mistakes, I'm out of control, and at times hard to handle. But if you can't handle me at my worst, then you sure as hell don't deserve me at my best." -Marilyn Monroe

I was organizing my new purchases in the appropriate dresser drawers when the doorbell rang. I could hear the shower running, leaving me to answer. Hunter had a key to our apartment, but he usually rang the bell so I was forewarned of his entry, a lesson learned the first time he walked in on me fixing a cup of coffee dressed only in my bra and panties. I've never seen Hunter about-face with such speed; he nearly vaulted over the dining table to close himself in Ev's bedroom. I was fairly certain I caught the hint of a blush before he bolted. Ah, good times.

I raised up on my tippy-toes to peer through the peephole in the door, a recent addition courtesy of Hunter, and saw nothing but a wall of black. I paused for a moment, wondering if the person on the other side placed their thumb over the glass, but dismissed the idea when I noticed the contours of the black abyss before me. I verified that the security chain was engaged before unlocking the deadbolt and opening the door.

Jiminy Crickets! The black void was a shirt, specifically a t-shirt undergoing durability testing as it strained to contain a scandalously muscled chest and shoulders most NFL linebackers would envy. I found myself confronted with a decision that no woman should ever have to make; do I look upward to assess the face attached to the scrumptious MMA pecs or go downward to find what other gifts God had bestowed on this specimen. Who was I kidding; there was only one right answer. As my gaze headed south, I was greeted by a mid-section that was clearly well tended and hard as stone. Despite his sinfully tight shirt, I couldn't make out his abs, but I suspected the shirt was covering a defined six-pack. Would it be rude to ask him to remove his shirt before inviting him in? Continuing my exploration, I discovered distressed denim, bulging in *all* the right places, draped over long, thick legs. Hot damn! Hunter was finally paying off with the hot guy friends. I knew this day would come, it was inevitable, but I was still overwhelmed with gratitude—Ev would be getting an extra nice Christmas present this year.

I slowly raised my gaze, verifying that the sight I beheld was not a mirage, and it happened...finally. There was no tingle or twinge, not a whisper of desire or hint of arousal—no, the floodgates of my previously dormant libido opened and a tsunami of lust swept through me. My breath caught and I was forced to grip the doorframe to prevent melting into a puddle on the floor or climbing this tree of man-flesh like the primate I had been reduced to. I gathered the remnants of my cognitive function—the miniscule part of my brain not dedicated to making an erotic laundry list of the many naughty activities I wanted to enlist this man's help with—to prepare for the possible disappointment, should the face accompanying this god-like body be one that sent children shrieking in horror. On the other hand, guys had practiced the "bag over her head" technique for years. I needed to do it, rip the Band-Aid off and accept the possible disillusionment. I reinforced myself, inhaled deeply, and raised my eyes. You've got to be kidding me!

"Griffin?" I accused more than asked.

"Hello Sam, good to see you too," he returned wryly. "Shall I turn so you can get the 360-degree show?"

I reached up to unlatch the security chain, allowing the door to swing open.

"Since I've been busted eye-fondling you already, I don't see the harm," I called his bluff.

Surprise registered on his face before he slowly turned, stopping when his ass was perfectly presented, going so far as to put his hands on his hips, emphasizing his biceps and back too. I suspected he may have even clenched his glutes for maximum impact. Never one to look a gift-butt in the mouth, I took my time perusing every inch of him. Once again wildfire devoured my previously dormant netherworld, scorching me with need. What the hell had happened to him over the past five months? Griffin had always been hot, six feet four inches of toned muscle, with a halo of light blonde hair and pale grey eyes—but this man would inspire legends. Women would whisper his name reverently for decades, never exaggerating because the reality needed no embellishment. And here he was, standing in my doorway, wreaking havoc on my body. Damn, damn, damn—he could *not* be the man to light me up. He was my friend and a very, very close friend to Ev and Hunter. Why was I even considering the possibility? I wasn't ready to ride the bucking bronco just yet.

I heard the slightest chuckle and watched massive shoulders shake. Instinctively, I swatted his butt in retaliation. Rock. Freakin'. Solid.

"Get in here, you Neanderthal."

"Bossy little thing, aren't you?" he teased, as he turned to face me once again. He stepped forward then hesitated, clearly analyzing his method of approach. Sometimes I felt like a skittish mare everyone was afraid to spook by approaching too quickly or touching too soon. I hated that those who knew what had happened treated me differently, as if I was fragile and damaged. As if he could read my mind, he leaned down and swept me into a hug that engulfed my whole being. My feet were dangling at least a foot off the ground, and I could have very easily felt like a ragdoll flailing in a child's arms, but Griffin cradled me carefully, bracing an arm across my lower back for support and cupping the back of my head in his enormous palm. He squeezed me tightly for several seconds as if reassuring himself I was real, before returning me to the ground. His tenderness and concern surprised me. I knew he cared about me, we were friends after all and he was one of the good ones, but we had never had a "touchy-feely" friendship. I knew he had been spending time with Ev and Hunter outside of the apartment, but they had kept most of our friends away since I returned, giving me time to adjust and settle in.

"Some things never change—but some do. Have you been eating your Wheaties while I was gone? Geeze dude, are you planning to dress up as Thor for Halloween?"

"I've been working out more frequently. It helps to relieve stress and frustration. You can mock to your heart's content, but don't forget I was there a few minutes ago when you were appreciating my efforts. Not my original goal, but a very welcome by-product," he said with a smirk.

I slapped his chest in punishment for speaking the truth, but his warm hand trapped mine against his rock hard body.

"I'm glad you're back, Sam. I missed you," he ended the unexpected confession with an equally unexpected kiss on the top of my head.

After he freed me, he entered the apartment and shut the door. We stared at each other and I tried to puzzle out what was different. I was on the verge of placing the missing piece when Ev exited her bedroom and another knock sounded on the front door.

"That has to be Hunter with the food. Griff, can you get the door? Sam, can you get drinks while I set the table?" Ev directed without waiting for acknowledgement. The girl was a force to be reckoned with.

"Griff, good to see you, man," Hunter greeted while giving a one-armed man-hug complete with the required back slap.

Hunter walked by and ruffled my hair with a smile, "Good day?"

"Yes, productive."

He nodded his approval before continuing into the kitchen to slip behind Ev, wrapping one arm around her waist and using his other hand to turn her head until he gained access to her mouth, which he proceeded to kiss as if he was a soldier returning from war. Ev was helpless to resist, hands loaded with dishes and silverware; not that she would have put up a fight. She was content to play her role as the long-separated newlywed elated by her hero's return. When she placed the tableware on the counter and spun in Hunter's arms to face him, I took my cue to avert my eyes. "You'll have to forgive them. Months of pent-up orgasms before they got their shit sorted out really did a number on them. It's like living with rabbits...or teenagers," I offered the obligatory apology to Griffin that Hunter and Ev's mouths were too occupied to supply.

"If you knew the effort I invested in forcing those two to acknowledge their feelings, you'd understand how happy this peep-show makes me. Besides, I've been around them enough that I don't even notice anymore."

"That's right; I forgot you and Hunter have reached BFF status in my absence. If they keep turning me into an unwilling voyeur, I'm afraid I may actually become one. Do you think they will learn any impulse control in the near future?"

"Doubtful," he said. "How are you, girl? I wanted to come by as soon as you got home, but knew you needed space. Hunter finally gave me the 'okay' this week to come for Thursday night dinners again."

"I'm doing really well, happy to be home where I belong," I answered, my standard response to anyone other than Ev, Hunter, or my therapist.

Griffin grunted, a short quick dismissal. "I don't believe a single word that just left your pretty little mouth, but I'll leave it be...for now."

"Is that a threat?" I joked, slightly off-balance by his ability to see through the image I projected.

"No, just a statement of fact. I've been accused of not letting a matter rest until I am satisfied I have the truth—or my desired outcome." He nodded toward the kitchen, letting me know exactly who had made the accusation.

"Funny enough, I recall hearing that about you. Ev calls you Mr. Neosporin behind your back because you are always picking at her scabs."

"If you don't flush the wound thoroughly, it'll become infected and the scab will only serve to trap the infection and prevent healing."

"Aren't you a well of wisdom? Have you considered writing fortune cookies for extra spending money?"

"Nah, those little slips of paper are too small to fit my wealth of wisdom. Besides, the pressure to make sure each insight could have 'in bed' added to the end and still make sense would drive me insane."

I laughed at his unexpected joke. I had never seen this funny side of Griffin before. I liked it.

"Okay Hugh Hefner and Bunny #1,378, get in here before I throw cold water at you and break up your fun," I warned, not at all kidding.

Hunter and Ev groaned in unison, displeased with my interruption and the reminder of their audience.

"Come on, lovebirds—" Griffin began, but I cut him off.

"I think you mean horn toads."

"The pretty lady has a point. Come on, horn toads. I'm hungry."

They finally peeled apart and joined us at the dining table. Griff and I sat on one side, while Ev sat across from me and Hunter across from Griffin.

"What did you get tonight, Hunter?" I asked.

"Sushi," he replied, and all three broke out into fits of laughter.

Sushi was not innately funny; clearly there was a backstory I hadn't heard yet. They exchanged a few more barbs, which made no sense to me, before dissolving into hysterics. It was obvious that Griffin had officially become a member of our clan. I embraced the addition, but I wished I wasn't left on the outside of their inside joke—I had missed so much while I was gone.

Griffin looked at me and quickly composed himself. He leaned in close, closer than I had been to any man other than Hunter since the attack. I tensed momentarily but relaxed as he whispered into my ear.

"I hate fish, completely and totally despise it. I usually bring the take-out to our Thursday night dinners, but one week Hunter did the honors and brought sushi. I didn't want to be a pain in the ass, so I tried to eat around the fish...but it was freaking sushi. I spent the meal picking rice off the inside-out rolls with chopsticks—I am useless with those things, so I ended up stabbing more than anything else—and guzzling miso soup. When Ev and Hunter noticed my pile of naked seaweed-wrapped fish, they blew a gasket. I received a ten-minute lecture on the sanctity of Osh Sushi and how my waste was an abomination. Ev stormed into the kitchen and threw a frozen pizza at me before announcing that it was more than I deserved. After the two devoured my massacred sushi, they forgave me, but they still love to torture me about it."

I could picture the whole scene perfectly, the tiny wooden sticks in Griff's hands as he abused Ev and Hunter's favorite food. Ev verbally spanking Griff for said abuse. Her subsequent pizza Frisbee. I am sorry I missed it, but at least now I felt like I was there and was *in* on the joke. Griffin smiled down at me and I knew he understood. He had recognized my moment of loneliness and reached out to pull me into the circle. I leaned my head into him, taking the comfort he offered until silence registered.

Griff and I broke from our private moment and were trapped by Huntleigh's (yes, I gave them a cheesy couple name in my mind) astute gaze. Not interested in being the Petri dish sample under their microscope, I took evasive action to distract them.

"I had my first session with Dr. Veritus today," I cast my bait, knowing Huntleigh would bite.

"How'd it go?" they asked in stereo.

It was like shooting fish in a barrel.

"Good...I think. She was different than any of the therapists at The Phoenix Centre, almost rude."

"She was rude to you?" Ev demanded, ready to head into battle for me.

"Rude isn't the right word. She was sarcastic and dismissive, but not in a bad way."

Ev looked at me skeptically, not ready to lay down her sword.

"For example, she didn't want to talk about the attack or my mini-breakdown afterward. When I told her about my parents she

listened and then didn't explore it further. It was just...different,"
I said weakly, aware my explanation did little to clarify my point,
but how could I explain what I didn't understand?

"That sounds completely unprofessional. When I spoke to
her on the phone after your attack, she was so nice and dedicated.
She even recommended TPC, which was incredibly helpful," Ev
said.

"That's what you needed, Ev. Sam's needs may require a
different approach. Treating her as if she is fragile could be more
harm than help," Griffin said, shocking Ev and I both. "Think of
it as triage; she needs to address the most pressing issues that are
still open sores and hindering her ability to heal. The portions that
are already scarred over may not be pretty, but they are not a
danger to her. At some point she may want to revisit those scars,
see what can be done to remove them or reduce their impact, but
they are not the primary concern."

"I never said she was fragile," Ev said, barely above a whisper.

"No, you didn't say it," Griffin returned, his implication clear
but free of accusation.

"Is that how you think I'm treating you? Like you are
damaged and fragile?" Ev asked me, voice full of concern.

"A lot of the time, yes—but I know it's because you care. I'm
not 100% and I still have a ton of work to do, but I am not going
to resort back to the catatonic mess I was before—I promise, Ev. I
am going to be okay, you don't need to hover and worry. You're
going to drive yourself nuts."

"I know," she groaned, "but I just want to fix it, make
everything better. I hate what happened to you; it killed me to
watch you suffer. I don't want either of us to have to go through
that again."

I reached across the table and grabbed her hand in mine as
Hunter threaded his arm around her shoulders, kissing the side of
her head sweetly.

"You won't have to—nothing like that will ever happen to me
again. It's like being hit by lightning, shit luck but the odds of
repeating the experience are infinitesimal."

"I hear what you are saying, Sam, and I agree, but be patient with Ev. You have no idea how much she missed you and worried every day you were gone," Hunter added.

I sighed, regretting all the pain they too had suffered alongside me. "I know. I'm not complaining, but it is a tiny bit discouraging to feel like you are on suicide watch—I am not, nor have I ever been in danger of hurting myself. Look how far I've come already...I use words and everything," I joked, trying to lighten the mood. "I do have one complaint."

"What?" Huntleigh asked in unison, eager to accommodate me.

"You two haven't read to me once since I've been back. Do I have to be in the hospital to get your dramatic performances of my favorite smexy books?"

Griffin burst into laughter while Hunter and Ev both blushed.

"At least we found our after-dinner entertainment. I was worried I was going to have to sit through another one of Ev's girlie shows," Griffin teased.

"For the last time, Grey's Anatomy is not a freaking girlie show. It is riveting entertainment and a study of human behavior. You should love it, psych-boy."

Griff turned to Hunter, "What concerns me is that she actually believes that load of crap. If the doctors in a real hospital spent as much time as the TV ones do getting down in on-call rooms, the death-rate in this country would be through the roof."

"They need to blow off steam somehow; it's a very stressful job. Besides, how do you know? You don't work in a hospital!" Ev said emphatically.

I leaned into Griffin and he lowered his head so I could whisper in his ear. "You are about to enter the red-zone. I suggest a strategic retreat before she goes thermo-nuclear...even *I* am not allowed to criticize Grey's Anatomy."

He nodded and shot me a smile I am sure was meant to look grateful but instead was sexy as hell. My body tingled in response and I nearly jumped out of my chair from the long-lost sensation. What was this man doing to me?

"*Anyway*, Thia gave me homework before our session next week," I said, saving Griffin from Ev's wrath.

"What kind of homework?" Ev asked.

"Accept the dinner invite from my parents—check. Eat more—check. Join a gym and exercise—part one, check."

Griffin interrupted me, "Which gym did you join?"

"The NYSC around the corner. I'm going to start working out tomorrow."

"Hmm, that's where I work out, if—"

"I thought you belonged to Bally's by the mall?" Ev interrupted.

Griffin shot her a look. "I used to, now I'm a member at NYSC."

"Really, I just saw you at Bally's on Monday. When did you switch?" Hunter asked with a smile.

"Recently," he grumbled.

Hunter chuckled.

"What other assignments did she give you, Sam?" Griff brought us back on topic.

"To get a job. I was planning on it anyway, so now is as good a time as any. I need something to do while I wait for December to come back around so I can make-up the final I missed after everything happened last semester. I would like to wrap that up and officially graduate from Hensley. I feel like it will provide some closure."

"Don't you think it's a bit soon?" Ev said with concern.

"You're doing it again, mother hen."

"Fine," she huffed. "Wait, I have a brilliant idea. Come work at Higher Yearning with me," she exclaimed as if she had discovered a cure for cancer.

"I don't know anything about making coffee."

"I taught you how to make coffee for me—it took two years, but you finally got it right. The timing is perfect. We lost several baristas when school ended. I was able to steal Meg away from Cup O'Joe at Hensley since she is a local, but I could still use another person. You would be doing me a favor."

While Ev may in fact need another barista for the coffee shop she was managing until she officially gained ownership, I doubted that was her sole motivation; she wanted to keep an eye on me to reassure herself. There was nothing I wouldn't do for her, and her for me—as she proved a few months ago when she pulled me back from the edge of insanity and forced me to get help. That said, her constant worry was shaking my limited confidence.

"I agree with Ev, it's the perfect solution. You would be helping her out and fulfilling your assignment. Is there something else you had in mind? I know you love fashion, but I can't see you working at a clothing store. You would spend your time searching for yourself instead of helping customers," Hunter piped in, proving how well he knew me.

I sighed, still apprehensive.

"What do you think, Griffin? Aren't you going to weigh in?"

"I'll give you my opinion, but be sure you want it before you ask for it."

"Hit me big guy," I answered, undaunted.

"You've made incredible progress from what I've been told—your strength and determination are inspiring."

I smiled at him, pleased.

"But," he continued, "you've survived a trauma most people could never imagine, let alone overcome—it will leave its mark. There are going to be days when you struggle; Ev will understand and be supportive if you need to take a 'mental health day'."

I was surprised by his frankness. I also wanted to punch him for noticing and calling attention to my 'marks'. So I did...I punched him in the arm as hard as my little balled fist could hit.

I was nearly paralyzed by fear, unsure of how he would react to being hit. I wasn't a violent person. I had never hit anyone in my life. I braced myself for his anger; instead he laughed, full and deep. It permeated every cell of my rigid fear-soaked body, and at once I relaxed.

"Lo, you are going to have to try much harder than that to hurt or anger me," he finished with another chuckle.

"Lo?" I asked, confused.

"Lo—L. O.—as in little one."

That did it. Something foreign and enraged washed over me and I hit him again. I was so angry; angry about the truth in his words, angry he could see the weakness I tried to hide, angry he told me he could see my scars. I was angry I had been hurt, damaged...raped. I stood, pivoted towards him, and used both my fists to pound on his chest. The only noticeable result for my efforts was a slight staccato rhythm to his laughter.

I heard Ev gasp at my outrageous behavior, as Hunter rose to help contain me, but nothing penetrated my violent fit. Griffin held up a hand to stay Hunter. I battered his chest until my fists ached, but, as if I was possessed, I couldn't halt my movements. Ev began to object but Hunter stopped her, whispering, "Let him, angel. He's probably better equipped to help her right now; at least he's trained to deal with these types of episodes."

Tears welled in my eyes, spilling from the corners, my body needing another route to expel the pent-up anger and frustration. I sucked in a raged breath when two hands engulfed my own more gently than seemed possible given their size. A sob escaped me despite my efforts to suppress it. Suddenly I was airborne, cradled carefully in steel-banded arms. Griffin walked to the den and positioned himself on the loveseat with me in his lap, nestled in his arms as he stroked my head soothingly. I could feel his heartbeat against my chest—my own struggled to calm, desperate to match the cadence of his.

"Shh, beautiful girl, it's okay—let it out," he whispered softly in my ear, offering comfort I wasn't sure I deserved. "That's my girl."

I tried to stop my tears, but they continued relentlessly. I clutched Griffin's shirt like a lifeline tying me to the rational part of myself that was currently missing in action, as if he alone had the coordinates to its location.

He began to hum a song, barely audible. As if he had administered a sedative, the turbulent sea of emotions began to calm and my tears receded. Unfortunately, the rivers of snot pouring from my nose continued and I was forced to sniffle loudly rather than use Griff's shirt as a Kleenex.

I remained in his embrace, feeling protected and safe for the first time since before I was shattered. In Griffin's arms, I felt whole. I couldn't explain why it was him that sparked the deep level of trust and reassurance I was unable to find in anyone else, allowing me to completely fall apart, or why I was finally permitting myself to show and release my anger. I didn't search for an explanation, I just basked in the relief he provided.

When he finished his song, I realized that in my distress I hadn't absorbed what melody he had hummed. I was about to ask when he tilted my chin with his finger until our eyes met. Eyes I thought were grey, I now saw were marbleized with countless shades of blue and slate, light and dark, complex like the man himself.

He dried the tears from my cheeks with his thumbs before kissing my forehead tenderly. My head was bracketed with his hands, which blocked out the rest of the world, creating an intimate sanctuary where only the two of us existed.

"Feeling better?" he asked gently.

"I think so—I feel...lighter. It's weird."

"You dropped a few pieces of the baggage you've been hauling around."

"I'm so sorry, Griff. I've never hit anyone before, I have no idea what came over me. You didn't deserve—"

He silenced me with a finger on my lips.

Unexpectedly, I wanted more. I wanted his lips to replace his finger.

"Shh," he said softly.

I was struck by his tenderness and understanding, this gentle giant holding me while I lost it. He didn't run in the face of the ugliness I held inside me. He didn't belittle my anger or pain. He just held me and offered a safe place to let it out and a soft place to land when I was spent. For that alone he would always hold a special place in my heart.

Chapter Three

*"Every morning I jump out of bed and step on a landmine.
The landmine is me. After the explosion, I spent the rest
of the day putting the pieces together." -Ray Bradbury*

I awoke the next morning thrilled to have slept through the night without a single nightmare. I was blissful and ready to conquer my new position as HYB—Higher Yearning Barista. Knowing Ev would be where the coffee was, I walked into the kitchen to pour myself a cup before joining her at the dining table.

"Sorry about my meltdown last night," I said, deciding it was best to shine light on the pink elephant in the room.

"Don't be, you have nothing to apologize for...well, maybe you should apologize to Griffin for attempting to beat the shit out of him, but other than that, no harm done. Are you okay? I was concerned you might lose it when he picked you up, being restrained by a man and all. Especially one the size of a Mack truck. I was about to intervene when Hunter dragged me into the bedroom and told me to let Griffin handle it. Can you believe the man had the audacity to tell me it wasn't my place to interfere? The nerve! I was about to tell him just how out of line he was, but he distracted me. He always cheats when he knows I'm going to win."

"No, he always cheats when he knows you aren't going to give in. I hate to state the obvious, but you have yet to officially win."

"*Yet*, but I'm close. I can feel it in my bones. My day is coming," she predicted with a certainty I didn't quite share. "So you're okay? Griff didn't cause you to panic?"

"Not at all, it was the opposite. I don't know what's changed. I was never as close to him as you were and I hadn't ever thought of him as anything more than a casual friend. Suddenly my non-existent sex drive is acting like a spring breaker at Mardi Gras. If he had pulled out a string of beads when he came to the door last night, I would have happily earned them. I don't get it."

Ev giggled either with me or at me, I wasn't sure.

"You *noticed* Griffin before—there was one night at the bar when that psycho grabbed me and Griff saved the day. Unfortunately, you were with Robbie the Coward at the time and weren't in the market for a replacement. I don't know if you are in the market for anything right now, but there is nothing to blind you to the glory that is Griff."

"Preach it, sister. Did he always look that good? Because I gotta tell you, the man here last night made me want to suffer a long-neglected Brazilian," I said, suddenly eager to call the salon and schedule a desperately needed appointment.

"You really have an obsession with those damn Brazilians—it's hot wax dripped in places no wax should venture before being yanked off, along with every hair and peach fuzz that was unfortunate enough to cross its path. You should bring this up with Thia. You may have masochistic tendencies."

I shrugged, unconcerned. "I think I just like the results, not the process of getting there. I mean, when you are bald down there, every nerve ending is ready and waiting for attention. When a guy gets the right angle, you can really—"

"Ding, ding, ding. I'm calling a time-out for excessive detailing of unnecessary information. Besides, I never said I wasn't familiar with the benefits of a Brazilian, I simply find your method of achieving the end result unimaginably painful. There is more than one way to skin a cat."

"Oh, no you didn't. You did not just say that...you dirty, dirty girl. I don't think I have ever been so proud of you." I wiped a crocodile tear from my eye.

"Okay, your bid for the Oscar has been duly noted. Can we get back on topic now? Griffin was always hot. He's been working out, which could be part of it, but he has also gained an edge since the attacks. I'm not sure what's up with him but something is simmering beneath the surface, and the vibe he's giving off is 'don't fuck with me.'"

"Yes, that's exactly what it is! There is a new depth to him. Not going to lie...I'm digging it."

"Are you going to make a move?" Ev asked innocently. "I think he would be receptive if you flashed the green light his way."

"You are not nearly as subtle as you think you are. I know you and Hunter are playing matchmaker. It is tempting, don't get me wrong, but I'm not sure I'm ready to slap bellies with anyone yet. There's no way a guy like Griff is going to want a sex-free relationship—the women at the bar must be throwing themselves at him every night, especially on the nights he sings."

Ev tsked her disapproval. "Don't jump to conclusions. I think Griffin would be open to whatever you are able to offer him. He may have barflies and fangirls throwing their panties at him, but that doesn't mean he brings them home. Just because they want him doesn't mean *he* wants them."

"I don't know if I can do it. . . open myself up that way. I want to, but what if I freak out? I would be humiliated and then I would still see him all the time."

"I don't want to push you. I am not saying you should jump into bed with Griffin—or anyone else for that matter—but if you are going to try, I can't imagine anyone who would be more understanding than Griff. He cares about you, Sam. He was devastated by what happened to you. He texted me every freaking day looking for updates. I'm positive you can trust him."

"I'll think about it. Right now I need to get dressed and head into work before my new boss fires my ass."

"You better hurry up—that bitch has a zero-tolerance policy for tardiness," she teased.

I strutted into Higher Yearning ten minutes early, proud of myself. I had visited Ev at work countless times, but this time I paused to study the space with the eyes of an employee. The décor was chic with exposed brick walls, grey damask armchairs, vibrant red couches, espresso-colored bistro tables, and crystal chandeliers. The vibe was cool and inviting, and the smell was heavenly—working here was definitely the right choice. I smiled at the girl behind the counter on my way to the break room. After I had stowed my purse, I returned to the front to officially announce my arrival.

"Hi, I'm Sam. You're Meg, right?"

"Yep, nice to meet you. Ev mentioned that you were starting today, too. I know this is your first time working as a barista, but don't worry, I'll show you how everything works. Higher Yearning has the same machine as the campus coffee shop, so it's familiar to me."

"Excellent. Ev is a tyrant with coffee and I would rather not have her be the one to teach me," I confessed.

Meg laughed, clearly familiar with Ev's addiction.

"I presumed as much after years of serving her on campus. I actually brought her a gigantic gallon-sized mug as a joke—a thank-you-for-hiring-me gag gift."

She pulled the mug from under the counter and showed it to me. It was beyond gigantic, and on the front was written: "I don't have a problem. I can stop anytime—I just don't want to." I laughed so hard I nearly dropped the priceless mug, wrecking all the fun.

"Okay, butter hands, hand it over. If you're jealous of my cool gift, just say so. I'll tell Ev it's from us both—no need to destroy it," she teased.

Oh, I liked her sass; we would get along just fine.

"I don't need your suck-up gift—I have nepotism on my side."

"Touché!"

"Hello, coffee warriors!" Ev greeted, entirely too chipper.

She was in a good mood when I last saw her this morning, but something must have happened to turn her into the uber-giddy girl walking toward us. Ah, Hunter must have stopped by on his way to work to 'wish her a good day.' If that wasn't code for making the bed dance, I didn't know what was.

Ev gave us a tour of the shop, highlighting the location of supplies and reviewing procedures. She asked Meg to make her three different beverages—a test—and of course the show-off aced it. Meg even served Ev's favorite coffee in the surprise gift she had brought. Ev squealed with excitement like a child in Toys 'R Us as she received it. After asking Meg to teach me the machines, Ev headed to the office to take care of paperwork and orders.

Six hours flew by, and along the way I managed to master most features on the monster coffee machine. When I got stuck, Meg would help me with the patience of a saint. She was easygoing and funny and, if I had my choice, I would work all my shifts with her.

I planned to exercise after my shift so I changed into my workout clothes in the bathroom before saying goodbye.

"Exciting plans?" Meg asked, spotting my cool new workout attire.

The black capri leggings and racer tank were skintight with green seaming that matched my eyes. For activewear, it rocked.

"I'm headed to the gym—day one of my new workout regimen. I have no idea what I'm doing, but I'll figure it out."

"Dressed like that, you can count on it," a rich, sexy voice spoke from behind me.

The unexpected contribution scared the shit out of me—I levitated several feet off the ground and shrieked like a banshee. Without thought, I spun around and raised my hand to protect myself.

"Whoa, Lo," Griffin said as he caught my arm, "easy. I didn't mean to startle you."

He clasped my hand in his and pulled me in for a comforting hug.

"Sorry, you caught me off-guard."

"Your guard seemed pretty spot-on. If I had been any slower to respond, you would have hit me...again. This is becoming a nasty little habit," he teased.

"Maybe you should stop doing things that make me want to hit you. I'll have you know that no one else has ever caused me to strike them. Maybe it's you."

"Or maybe your subconscious is looking for excuses to touch me," he returned with a wink.

I'd like to say he was wrong, but at that moment I would have taken any available excuse to rub up against him. My hormones were in hyper-drive. Damn, was it hot in here?

"Umm, I'm just going to—" Meg stammered as she slinked away.

"See what you did? You overwhelmed poor Meg and she ran away."

"Are you going to attempt to hit me again as punishment?"

"Wiseass—you're lucky you're hot," I said as I poked his chest.

"So you think I'm hot?" he said and smirked with satisfaction.

"Fishing for compliments—really? Your hotness score just dropped a point."

"You headed to the NYSC?" he asked, evidently unconcerned with the penalty point.

"Yep. I'm going to kick some gym butt, as soon as I figure out how to use all those fancy machines."

"You're in luck, I was heading there myself. I'll show you the ropes and teach you how to use all the scary machines."

I eyed him dubiously. His fitted jeans and blue polo shirt—although exquisitely displaying his assets—were not regulation gym attire.

"My gym bag is in the car," he volunteered as if psychic.

"What exactly is in your gym bag? I'll need specifics before I commit."

He smirked at my challenge. "Black shorts and a tank. Do I pass inspection?"

"Assuming the shorts ride low on your hips and the tank is tight, I guess you'll do—especially since you're cheaper than paying for one of the gym's trainers."

"Be careful, Lo, you keep flirting with me and I may start to think you mean it."

"You're a hot guy, Griff. I flirt with hot guys, it's instinctual. Don't read too much into it."

"So that's all I am... just another hot guy, same as the rest?" I looked into his eyes and saw that his question was sincere. "You're special," I said, squeezing his forearm to emphasize my point. "Come on, I've fed your ego enough for one day."

We exited Higher Yearning and I attempted to walk to my car, but Griff stopped me.

"Why don't you ride with me? It'll be dark by the time we're done. I may even feed you afterward; help you fulfill another homework assignment."

I paused, uncertain. I knew Griff wouldn't hurt me; he didn't have it in him to hurt a woman. Ev and Hunter trusted him implicitly. I trusted him too, but an irrational part of me objected to the risk of being alone with any man. I wanted to say yes, to overcome the misplaced fear, but the compulsion to distance myself from all possible threats was so strong.

"Samantha, look at me." He cupped my cheek and guided my face upward until our eyes locked. "I will never hurt you. I would give anything to take away the pain you've suffered, but that's impossible. I don't expect your unconditional trust; I'll earn that over time. Once you're comfortable enough to drop your guard with me, you can relax and enjoy life for a little while, knowing you are protected."

He hugged me to his side, asking for nothing, only offering comfort and support. The realization allowed me to do as he said, relax and enjoy the moment without fear—I was safe with Griffin. I knew it deep within, as if my soul recognized the truth in his words.

He led me to a black Dodge Ram 3500 pick-up. The truck had fancy sport wheels that added a few extra inches, making it a challenge for me to climb in. Griffin placed his hands on my waist, lifting me in, while I struggled to contain my laughter. His hands were so large compared to my small frame that they encircled my waist like a belt.

"I love that sound—your laugh. Do I want to know what has you so entertained?"

"You're so big and I'm so small—we are walking extremes, and side-by-side it's comical. The top of my head barely reaches your chest."

He laughed and responded by resting his elbow on top of my head.

When we arrived at NYSC, Griff went to change while I stored my purse in the women's locker room. I was waiting for him outside the men's locker room as he exited. Holy sweet mother of drool-worthiness—this was the reason God had given women eyes, so we could witness the perfection before me. My mouth went dry but other areas did not. As promised, his black ribbed tank molded to every contour of his defined chest and abdomen. His shoulders and arms were bared to my greedy eyes, sheer power obvious in every corded muscle. His black basketball shorts hung low on his hips, allowing his tank to mold to the masculine 'V' pointing the way home. I had never before seen physical perfection and it was almost too much to absorb. He was huge in every sense of the word without becoming a neckless, puffed-up body builder whose arms were so augmented they couldn't be lowered past a 45-degree angle to their bodies.

"Lo, as much as I enjoy your appreciation, you need to stop before you get me kicked out for indecency."

"If you're going to display the merchandise, you best be prepared for window shoppers. Suck it up."

"Don't I wish," he said to himself. "Come on girl, let's get you on a machine."

I laughed at his choice of words, conjuring my previous image of the "Red Room of Pain."

"Will it hurt?" I asked, a subtle joke for my own benefit.

"Only if you do it wrong," he returned with a knowing smirk.

"If I do it wrong, it's your fault—you are the teacher."

"I am a very thorough instructor. I'll ensure your form and quality of movement yields the desired results."

"What if I can't do it?" I asked, unsure if I was referring to the actual topic of conversation or the sub-text.

"You can do it—if you believe you're ready and you trust your teacher, I have no doubt you will excel."

"But, what if I disappoint you?" I whispered, certain I was addressing the sub-text this time.

He wrapped his arm around my shoulder and pulled me into his chest before waiting patiently for me to meet his eyes. What I saw there told me that Griffin was done pretending to discuss the gym and I braced myself.

"Lo, you could *never* disappoint me. If you're honest with me and yourself, you have no reason to worry. No one's unblemished, we all have our scars—some are just easier to hide. The right man will navigate the minefield and bring you to the other side safely. He will find a way to give you the pleasure you deserve, no matter what it takes. You are worth any effort."

If that wasn't a confidence builder, I don't know what was. He made it sound like a great honor.

"You really like putting it all on display, don't you? No editing."

"I'm not playing games with you, Sam. I have no intention of hiding what I want; I won't make that mistake again."

"At least you're not one of those super intense guys who says exactly what he thinks and leaves a girl at a loss for words—that would be overwhelming," I said with a smile, trying to lighten the mood.

"I'm not into lying, it's a waste of everyone's time. Now, let's see if you are as beautiful when you are dripping sweat."

I smacked his arm playfully. "I always look good. And I don't sweat...I glisten."

After a quick tour of the gym, Griffin walked me through the various exercises on the circuit training machines. He knew as much about the equipment as any of the trainers would and instructed me on the proper form to ensure maximum results while preventing injury. By the time we were done, I was feeling the burn and the time had passed quickly with his company.

In a classic male move, he grabbed the bottom of his tank and lifted it to wipe the dampness from his face. My ravenous eyes snapped to his stomach. I was greeted by one, two, three...eight, eight perfectly chiseled abdominal muscles. The elusive eight-pack—I had heard rumors of its existence, seen pictures even, but

I'd never encountered the phenomenon in person. I reached up and pinched my arm to ensure I was not dreaming. Ouch! Nope, not dreaming. My fingertips itched to touch him, to trace each and every line and crevice—suddenly a black wall of cotton obstructed my view. Son of a bitch, it was criminal. The man should not be allowed to wear a shirt...ever.

His expectant look greeted me. He must have asked a question while I was plotting how to accidentally slide my hands under his tank and cop a feel.

"I'm sorry?"

"How about we end with thirty minutes of cardio?"

"You're a freaking slave driver. I'm going to ache all over tomorrow."

He cast a challenging glance at me then shrugged.

"I understand if you can't handle it."

I narrowed my eyes, wanting to dismiss his challenge but unable to do so.

"Bring it on, big guy. You may have more muscles but running with those monster feet has to put you at a disadvantage."

His satisfied smile was my only warning of the ass whooping I was about to be handed. Thirty minutes later I clung to the side of the treadmill. As I dismounted, I was praying my legs would continue to hold my body weight. My competitive streak had reared its ugly head, encouraging me to keep pace with Griffin. I successfully matched his pace for the full thirty, but I was gasping for air and dripping with 'glisten.' Griff, on the other hand, was breathing as if he had taken a leisurely stroll through the park and was only slightly damp. The kind of damp that made you want to trace his exposed biceps with your tongue to taste the salt of his skin.

I released the hand rail and nearly collapsed to the floor, but I was off my feet and ensconced in Griffin's strong arms before I could blink. I considered protesting but ruled out the prospect once I admitted to myself I wasn't confident in my ability to walk— I didn't acknowledge the fact that I was enjoying this particular mode of transportation.

He smelled so damn good, clean with a hint of masculine sweat, a temptation I couldn't resist. Beyond my control, my tongue darted out of my mouth and covertly tasted the section of chest exposed above his tank. Oh god, he tasted even better than he smelled, like a chocolate-covered pretzel—sweet, salty, and addictive.

"Did you just...*lick* me?" he asked, sounding both shocked and amused.

"I have no idea what you're talking about."

"You licked me. I felt it," he accused, but I noticed he wasn't complaining.

"Your imagination is running wild because of all the workout endorphins."

"It wasn't a complaint. In fact, you're welcome to have another taste."

"Fine...I licked you. But it was an involuntary reflex—hot guy, exposed chest...you know how it is."

"Mmm," he replied, his eyes darkening with lust. "I am familiar with the temptation, but it's not a hot guy who's testing my self-control...it's a petite, auburn-haired vixen."

We suddenly stopped and he placed me on a floor mat in an empty aerobics studio. I was too curious to feel apprehensive about being alone with a man who could easily overpower me.

"What are we doing in here?"

"Your muscles need to be massaged after the strain you put them through. You pushed yourself too far on the treadmill, especially after the weight and resistance training. Deep tissue massage will encourage blood flow to the muscles, which will break down the excess lactic acid trapped in the tissue—you'll have horrible cramping otherwise."

I placed my hand on his forearm to stop the physiology lesson.

"You had me at deep tissue massage. Show me that those humongous mitts of yours are useful for more than serving drinks and playing guitar."

He didn't need to say what else his hands were good for, his lethal smile spoke volumes.

I turned my back to him while twisting my ponytail into a bun, providing him unfettered access to my neck and shoulders. When his nimble hands kneaded the tense muscles at the nape of my neck, I groaned in satisfaction. He worked my neck, shoulders, and back masterfully, the size of his hands enabling firm, consistent pressure, which felt so good it verged on painful. He dedicated the same attention to my arms, all the way down to the tips of my fingers, paying extra attention to my palms—a newly discovered erogenous zone.

"Lay on your stomach...I need leverage for your lower back," he commanded.

I was putty in his hands, willing to comply with any request, as long as he continued to manipulate my body. I flopped to my side and rolled onto my stomach gracelessly—I was too relaxed to care about my ragdoll flop.

He knelt beside me and pressed his thumbs into the dimple at the base of my spine, circling before dragging his fingers up and out in an arc. He adjusted his position several times trying to gain a better angle, clearly unsatisfied with his current technique.

"Lo, I want to try something—I am going to kneel above you with a knee on each side of your hips. I won't rest my body weight on you or restrain you in any way. Do you think you can handle that?"

"I...I think so. You can try," I stuttered. The visual painted by his suggestion was both erotic and terrifying.

"You *will* tell me if you feel any panic or anxiety. And you *will* tell me if you feel uncomfortable for *any* reason. One word and I'll move, understand?"

"Okay," I consented, equally unsure if the position would rocket me into a full-blown panic attack.

I began breathing deeply, hoping the technique I'd learned at TPC would help relax and prepare me for this experiment. I heard the rustle of his athletic shorts and felt the air shift as he settled into place. Nothing...no contact whatsoever. He had positioned himself so precisely that his shorts didn't even brush against me. If I didn't *know* he was straddling my body, I would never have known. I exhaled my relief, overwhelmed with joy that the position did not trigger any anxiety. It was a small victory, but one I relished.

His hands returned to my lower back and I could immediately tell the difference. The new angle allowed him to penetrate my muscles more deeply, effectively releasing knots and stretching my spine. I moaned in pleasure as he coaxed a particularly resistant knot into submission.

I heard his sharp inhale as his hands froze against my ribcage.

"Are you intentionally trying to drive me insane?" he asked tightly.

"Hmm?" I asked dazedly. "What are you talking about? I didn't do—"

"Sounds like you're auditioning for a porn movie. Not helping me here," he said without censor.

"Oh, was I making noises? Sorry, it just feels so good."

"I got that," he said with a laugh.

I looked over my shoulder to scold him for mocking me, but was too struck by the image of him hovering over my vulnerable body to speak. A tremor ran through my body. I wasn't afraid—I believed Griffin would never intentionally hurt me—my response was automatic. My body shook, recognizing a position I had never seen but was familiar with nonetheless. I wheezed while adrenaline pumped through my body.

Griffin leapt to the side, positioning himself beside my head. He cupped my face as he leaned down and trapped me in his gaze.

"Look at me, Lo...it's me—Griffin. You're safe. No one is going to hurt you. It was just a memory...not real."

"Oh god, Griff. I'm so sorry, it's not you. I trust you. I'm sorry—shit!" I rambled, a potent mixture of embarrassment, frustration, fear, and anger.

"What do you have to be sorry for? We both knew it was a possible trigger. We stumbled on a landmine when you saw me looming above you. I would be concerned if you didn't have triggers, if you were repressing everything. You are fighting your way out of a nightmare. You are pushing forward, staring down your ghosts, and reclaiming the parts of you they were haunting. I am awed by your bravery—by you."

He leaned down and placed a kiss on my lips, so soft I wasn't certain he had actually made contact.

"I should do your legs, but we can quit now if you want," he offered passively, giving me the choice to either face my fear or call a time-out to lick my wounds. There was no judgment or opinion in his words, only support.

"Do it!" I ordered, more sharply than I intended. "Sorry—I mean, please let's finish. It felt really good and I don't want to be hurting tomorrow."

"My brave girl," he whispered against my ear, causing me to shiver.

He scooted back and drew my left leg into his lap, working every muscle with excessively delicious care. I sank into the floor and floated on the cloud of sensation he created. The residual fear and adrenaline dissipated, and somewhere between my right and left leg massage I realized I had faced yet another demon and won. When he finally finished, we returned to our respective locker rooms to gather our belongings.

I was waiting for Griff to exit the men's locker room when a gym rat approached me from behind, nearly causing me to wet my pants when I discovered his body within inches of mine. He leaned against the wall next to me with his arm resting above my head. I felt caged and uneasy.

"Hey sexy, haven't seen you here before. Need me to show you how it's done? I know the manager—I can hook you up with a free month...in exchange for dinner?"

I was about to—I didn't know what—run, scream, panic, tell him I wasn't interested in his 'free month' if he was the last man on earth. Then I heard it—a growl. A deep, menacing *growl* was coming from behind me, about a foot and a half above my head. I slapped my hand over my mouth to stifle my snicker.

I couldn't see Griffin and he didn't say a word, but whatever his body language communicated, the dumbass in front of me clearly got the message because he turned tail and left, practically running.

I spun, hoping to catch a glimpse of 'scary Griffin,' but his face was devoid of all emotion, his eyes tracking my visitor's departure.

"Excuse me," I said to capture his attention. "Did I just hear you *growl* at that moron, or am I hallucinating now, too?"

"I didn't growl, it was a deep exhale."

"Oh, an audible exhale that reverberated in your chest...like a growl," I said before dissolving into giggles.

"I love that sound—you laughing."

"Should I start calling you 'Tony the Tiger' now? Wait...how about 'Harry the Hippo'?"

"Hippos do not growl."

"They absolutely do! I took a zoology class for my science requirement sophomore year, and hippopotamuses, my growly friend, most definitely growl."

"If I growled—and I admit nothing—but if I did, it was not a damn hippopotamus growl. It was a tiger growl...no, a bear...I want to be a bear."

"Alright, Yogi it is. Come on, my furry friend, you promised me dinner."

"Despite your torment, I do keep my promises. Let's go."

"Do you have the picnic baskets in the car?" I teased, enjoying watching him squirm.

"No picnic baskets, I'm afraid."

"Oh, is Boo-Boo bringing them?"

He shook his head and grabbed my hand, leading me to his truck, where he opened my door and hoisted me in. We drove to Five Guy's Burgers for a quick bite, and I spent most of the time finding various ways to work 'growl' into the conversation. His cheeks tinged pink every time, which only encouraged me to continue. By the time he dropped me off at my car, I was glowing. I hadn't felt this many 'good' emotions since before the attack.

He helped me down from the truck and walked with me, pulling me in for a hug when we reached my car. I laced my arms around his neck and pulled him until his lips were firmly against mine. His hand rested on the small of my back, pressing me into him with the slightest pressure. He nibbled on my lower lip, nipping then soothing artfully. His mouth drifted across mine to kiss the corners of my lips, as if he needed to lavish attention on even the smallest corner. I licked the seam of his firm lips with the tip of my tongue, instigating him to explore me more fully. I felt his groan more than heard it. In a moment of reckless abandon, I pressed my body against his more fully, but was unable to obtain the pressure I sought because of our extreme height difference. Frustrated, I locked my fingers behind his neck and pulled while I jumped, intending to climb him. He instinctively caught me, but only permitted momentary contact before he lowered me back to the ground, slowing our kiss. With a final press of his lips, he broke free and cupped my face.

"As much as I love being the telephone pole to your service technician, I think we better call it a night before this goes any further."

"Spoil sport," I said, disappointment coloring my tone.

"I want you too much to rush this and ruin my chance. You're worth waiting for."

He kissed my lips gently, pulling back before I could tempt him further. Dammit.

He helped me into my car and shut the door, waiting until I pulled away before walking back to his pick-up.

Griffin was funny, insightful, instinctive, smart, kind, badass, and sexy as all hell. I wished I was whole and could offer him everything he deserved, which was so much more than the jagged pieces I had to offer.

Chapter Four

"For anything worth having one must pay the price; and the price is always work, patience, love, self-sacrifice."
-John Burroughs

Griffin

I watched her tail lights melt into the night as I dragged the cool evening air into my lungs, futilely attempting to ease the discomfort in my chest...and pants. This waiting—giving Sam the time she needed to fully trust me and to heal–may kill me, but I would suffer anything to have her.

Pulling the breaks when her body and lips were begging me to continue was a Herculean feat, one I deserved a goddamn medal for. Hot and sweet, she was the embodiment of temptation. She drugged me with her taste until I was senseless, an animal instinctively claiming its mate. Her little arms clung to me with a desperation that called to my heart...and one of my less honorable organs. I had to stop; her mind was not ready to process what her body was begging for. I knew I made the right decision when I saw both disappointment and relief in her eyes. She *wanted* me, but lingering fear of physical intimacy was still there. Until I proved she could trust me, that fear would remain a shadow in her eyes. If it took every day of the rest of my life, I would earn her trust—

and then her love. There was no doubt in my mind that Sam was *it* for me. My certainty was soul deep. She was mine...made for me. I didn't care what the requirements were, how much patience was needed, nothing would deter me from her. I had wanted her for so long and waited for what felt like a lifetime. I first noticed her more than a year ago when she came to The Stop to celebrate her twenty-first birthday. It was a Saturday night and the bar was packed, but I heard her laugh above the music, drink orders, and drunken conversations. Sam's laugh captured my attention and when I finally saw her, I was done. She was gorgeous, one of the most beautiful women I had ever seen— and so tiny, it called to my primitive instincts to protect her. Even from twenty feet away she radiated a joy and confidence that couldn't be overlooked. I walked away from a customer mid-sentence and shouldered another bartender out of the way to get her drink order just to talk to her. When she leaned across the bar to tell me what she wanted, I almost snatched her up and carried her out of the bar. Her eyes were a vibrant green that shined with mischief in the dim bar lighting. A curtain of wavy red-brown hair spilled down one shoulder and all I could think was how that hair would look spread out across my pillows—so damn sexy. I set her drink in front of her and waved off her credit card, telling her it was on the house as my birthday present to her. She placed a quick peck on my cheek and said, "Hot *and* generous. Where've you been all my life?"

She spent the rest of the night living it up, dancing with her friends, and celebrating. I couldn't take my eyes off of her; I was so mesmerized I screwed up more drink orders than the greenest bartender. Unfortunately, her friends fetched her birthday drinks for the rest of the night and she left before I had a chance to talk to her again, which was for the best. I was in a relationship at the time and couldn't have made a move even if given a chance. My girlfriend at the time, Kimmie, began commenting on how distant I seemed within a few weeks of my meeting Sam. I hadn't seen Sam again, and nothing actually happened beyond me doing my job, but I couldn't shake the memory of her. Kimmie was dull and lifeless compared to the vibrancy of Sam. Our relationship puttered out as I lost interest. We ended amicably enough with my excuses of needing to focus on finishing my Master's and settle into the new position of managing The Stop.

I suspected Sam was a student at Hensley and found myself looking for her every time I was on campus. When I randomly saw her, I would nod or smile, but I never approached. I wasn't afraid; I knew women sought out my attention, but I wanted to stand out to her the way she did for me. With the attacks on campus plaguing every woman's mind, I didn't want to approach as a virtual stranger and spook her.

Every time she came to The Stop after her birthday we would exchange brief pleasantries, but she was always surrounded by friends and I was working, limiting our interactions. I realized how strongly I wanted this girl, but wasn't sure the timing was right to start a new relationship. I was overwhelmed with the responsibility of managing a business on my own after my parents dropped it in my lap, announcing their sudden retirement and relocation to warmer climates. I loved my parents, but they were of the mindset that their parental obligations were complete after you became an adult at the all-knowing age of eighteen. Part of me was surprised they "let" me finish undergrad and most of my Master's before hanging up their aprons and flying south. They viewed my education as an exercise in discipline and possibly a hobby, but in their minds, my future always lay in The Stop.

With all that was on my plate, I decided to focus on my final year of classes. Once finished, my reward for a job well-done would be my pursuit of Sam. With the pressures of school behind me and The Stop running smoothly, I could dedicate complete attention to the intriguing siren and invest all the time necessary in the early stages of a relationship. My decision to wait to pursue Sam would always remain one of my biggest regrets in life—a mistake that I may never forgive myself for.

Six months after our first encounter, I watched as Sam began dating and subsequently fell in love with Robbie. He was weak and pliable—completely wrong for her. She might have been happy then, but I knew in the long term her life with that pushover would be filled with disappointment. My hands were tied, so I sat back and watched as the girl I wanted drifted further and further away. And as further proof of life's irony, once Sam was no longer available, she began to appear everywhere I looked. She even started to engage me in short conversations on slow nights at the bar, letting me see exactly what I was missing. Each piece of her I discovered only intensified the invisible cord binding me to her. Yet Sam was clueless, with not even the slightest inkling of how much I wanted her. I couldn't find it in me to take away the temporary happiness she was enjoying. Instead, I continued to bide my time and wait for the inevitable break with Mr. Right-For-Now.

Unexpectedly, Everleigh and I developed a friendship while I was lying in wait for her best friend. She discerned my feelings for Sam right away and repeatedly warned me not to set my hopes on her. Ev was convinced that Robbie and Sam were destined to walk down the aisle, but I knew it was only a matter of time before he screwed it up. So again, I sat back and practiced patience.

When Ev and Sam suddenly disappeared, I was concerned. They were regulars, rarely deviating from their scheduled visits to The Stop. Everleigh surfaced without Sam after six weeks—yes, I counted the weeks—and I was confronted with my worst nightmare. Sam, the girl I was already half-in-love with, had been brutalized, hospitalized, and was now recovering 3,000 miles away. All of this occurred without my knowledge. I hadn't been given the opportunity to support her, to tell her she would survive this, and to assure her that I would do everything in my power to help her. I was absent when she needed me most. My anger was a living breathing creature possessing me. I spent hours dreaming of the ways I could kill the bastard that hurt her. I fantasized about finding Robbie and wrecking him for allowing it to happen and then abandoning her, only to come back and break her heart with his cowardice.

I never told Ev how livid I was at her—furious she didn't contact me when she knew I would have been by Sam's side every minute. At the same time, I knew it wasn't my place and that Ev was struggling to balance her own grief with Sam's care, but it remained a difficult pill for me to swallow. When the initial shock wore off, I saw reason and forgave her for not reaching out to me during the crisis. My wants were not what was important, Sam was...and I vowed to do anything necessary to help facilitate her recovery. Sam was at TPC for two months, and during that time, I focused my energy to find justice for her. I promised myself and Sam, though she didn't know it, that I would never fail her again, and that her needs would always come before my own.

My promise was tested the minute I found out Sam was coming home from TPC. Ev and I both agreed she needed time to acclimate to being back, outside of the safe haven of her therapeutic environment. I never imagined the wait would wind up being another two months. They were the longest months of my life.

I shook my head, remembering how I lost my damn mind knowing Sam was home, yet having to keep my distance from her. I was also deprived of my closest friends, Everleigh and Hunter, who had dedicated most of their time to being by Sam's side. I didn't want to take their time if it meant taking them away from Sam, so I poured myself into work and increased my already excessive number of hours at the gym. The gym had become my go-to location after Sam's attack. I was in agony trying to stay away from her throughout the two long months after she returned. I could have given the biggest guy I could find at the gym a set of brass knuckles and let him go to town and it would've been less painful than waiting.

Finally being able to see Sam, even if only as a friend, was an answer to my prayers. Her fire and spirit still burned brightly, despite her pain. I was awed by her strength, resilience, and determination to survive.

I have had no interest in any other woman—zero—not for the past year. My Calvin Kleins hadn't so much as twitched at the sight of another woman. I didn't want anyone else, so Thor's unwillingness to swing his mighty hammer for any other woman wasn't a problem. I knew when I finally had access to Sam, there would be a long road ahead of us as she healed. It would take time to build a relationship, but I was in no hurry—I was in for the long haul. I didn't mind waiting if I could at least see her and be nearby to support her. Sex was the least of my concerns—well, that wasn't entirely true. I wanted Sam in my arms and in my bed, nothing had changed in that regard, but the physical connection was a long way off. I was willing to give Sam all the time and patience she needed before attempting sexual intimacy. I knew it was a vital part of her healing and needed to be handled carefully. The choice would have to be hers, without any pressure. Sam needed to reclaim her power and when she was ready, I would be there to show her how loved and desired she was.

Chapter Five

*"The abandoned infant's cry is rage,
not fear." -Robert Anton Wilson*

"Where the hell have you been?" Hunter asked, his deep voice snapping me out of my food coma.

"Don't you bark at me, Hunter Charles—Ev may let you get away with it because afterwards you throw her over your shoulder and take her to the bedroom, where the two of you make sounds usually reserved for zoos. Since I will not be screeching like a chimpanzee, you don't get that privilege. And FYI, I was at the gym, which Ev knew."

"You left Higher Yearning to go to the gym four hours ago—you scared us to death," Ev scolded, as if I was an errant child.

Hunter wrapped his arms around her from behind. They were a united front, ready to go into battle—God help their future children.

"I'm sorry, *Mom*, I guess my phone was on silent. You do realize I am a grown woman; I didn't know I needed to text my every move and ask your damn permission. I was at the freaking gym."

"Your car never left Higher Yearning, and you left the gym over an hour ago. We were worried, and you weren't answering your phone," Hunter complained.

"How do you know when I left the gym?" I asked incredulously.

"I traced your cell," Hunter said as if it was a completely normal answer.

"And I called the gym," Ev added.

"That's not stalkerish—not at all," I answered snidely. "I appreciate your concern and I understand it, but you have to relax a little bit. You're going to make me even more paranoid than I already am if you keep freaking out. I can't live my life waiting for the next tragedy to strike, and neither can you two."

"She may have a point," Ev said to Hunter, as if I was no longer a part of the conversation.

He grunted in reply, not convinced, but not pushing the issue either.

"Where did you go after the gym?" Hunter asked.

I sighed. They were still missing the point. Oh well, at least they cared.

"I went to the gym with Griff and we got Five Guys after. Mystery solved, no sinister danger lurking."

"Ooooh, that's nice. Isn't that nice, babe?" Ev asked Hunter, trying to hide her excitement but failing miserably.

"He didn't answer his phone either...asshat. He and I are going to have a conversation about answering 911-texts," Hunter grumbled.

"You sent a 911 text? Are you nuts?" I shrieked, shocked by the extremity of his actions.

Hunter shrugged guiltlessly, undeterred by my reaction.

"You're home safe, time to move on," Ev said dismissively, her previous concern forgotten in light of a juicier story. "Tell me about your date. Now."

"It wasn't a date, we were just hanging out. He was showing me how to use the equipment at the gym and we grabbed some post-workout protein, nothing too crazy."

"Sure...and Hunter just wanted coffee all those times he came into Higher Yearning," she said while tossing a sassy smirk at her man.

"What? You make a delicious cup of coffee," Hunter objected unconvincingly.

"You're so full of it. I had you completely enchanted and you couldn't stay away. Admit it, you didn't even know there were different types of coffee beans. Just goes to show how lost you were before me."

"The best thing about being with you—I no longer have to drink coffee. I get a caffeine fix every time I kiss you."

"Keep it up and you'll be back on the mug!" Ev threatened.

I burst out laughing at the absurdity of her threat.

"I would pay to see that! You can't keep your paws off each other for fifteen minutes. The *only* thing you crave above coffee is Hunter's co—"

"That is not true. I have excellent self-control, don't I, babe?" she asked Hunter.

"I have to agree with Sam on this one, angel. You are firmly in the easily persuaded category. But don't feel bad, I put myself in the same category—it's a good place to be and the company is spectacular."

"Just because you are a caveman and can't control your impulse to throw me on my back at every turn doesn't mean I am too. I'm just...accommodating."

"You sure were *accommodating* this morning, but I don't recall you being the one on your back."

Ev gasped. "I can stop anytime, just you wait."

In response, Hunter kissed her collarbone and dragged his lips up the column of her neck until he nipped her earlobe. Ev visibly shuddered from the pleasure. Hunter then whispered something in her ear and Ev blinked before nodding rapidly.

"Sorry Sam, we have to go organize my DVD collection," Ev apologized as she pulled Hunter down the hall.

Hunter looked over his shoulder and winked at me. Another point for Hunter—Ev was never going to score...but who cares, with the amount she was going to be scoring in the bedroom tonight.

Over the next few days a pattern developed. I worked nine to five at Higher Yearning, and at 4:55 Griffin would show up to get a cup of coffee before the gym. By the time I was done, Griff had finished his coffee and was ready to accompany me—I had unofficially obtained an official workout buddy. He was the perfect partner, ensuring proper execution of each exercise, encouraging me to push myself, and supplying an entertaining distraction to pass the time. After each session he administered a quick massage to keep me feeling limber and pain-free. I'm not going to lie, most days it was the promise of a massage that provided motivation to get my butt to the gym. *And,* the previous position that triggered a negative reaction was no longer an issue when I looked over my shoulder at Griffin—another victory.

By the following Tuesday, I was actually a halfway decent barista, thanks to Meg's help. While mildly sore after my workout, the ache in my abused muscles was significantly less than the previous week—I had Griffin to thank for that. I found myself looking forward to therapy with Thia on Thursday so I could brag about my homework successes. Since it was nearing the end of my shift, I brewed Griffin's new favorite—Colombian with a shot of espresso and a shot of steamed milk, dubbed the "super charged"—so it would be cool enough for him to sip when he arrived.

The chime of the door alerted me to a customer. When I turned to greet him, I was rewarded with a man worthy of the cover of GQ magazine, dressed in a stunning single-breasted suit. His brown hair was styled in the perfect 'I'm professional, but I don't try too hard' tousled look. He stood six feet tall with a lean, fit build. His model-perfect face, boy-next-door smile, and warm caramel eyes contributed to the 'I need a second look' package.

I returned the smile, but before I could ask for his order, he presented me with a business card. I looked at him quizzically while accepting the card—Westly E. Black, Attorney at Law. I eyed him suspiciously. It was my experience that an attorney visiting your place of work—or anywhere, actually—was a harbinger of bad news.

"Would you care to join me for a brief conversation, Miss Whitney? I have a proposition for you."

This was definitely not going to be a light-hearted chat.

"Are you with the District Attorney's office?" I asked, my last glimmer of hope.

He looked down at his attire as if it was all the answer I needed. Dammit! No one working at the DA's office would be outfitted in Ralph Lauren Black Label.

"Let's get this over with," I groaned.

I followed him to a set of wingback chairs located as far from customers as possible. I sat down, uneasy, my posture rigid and defensive.

"I'd offer you coffee, but I have a feeling I will be asking you to leave before it's finished brewing."

"Are you always so pessimistic, Miss Whitney?" he asked blandly.

"When it comes to attorneys, Mr. Black, yes I am."

He sighed as if put out by my generalization. I would have felt guilty if I believed there was even the slightest chance I was wrong about the assumption.

"Miss Whitney, I represent the Varbeck family—"

"Get the fuck out. Now," I hissed at him, blessedly keeping my volume at a respectable level despite my profanity.

"Now, now, let's not be hasty. I have a mutually beneficial offer I think you would be wise to consider. The Varbeck family is willing to provide you a significant sum of money—with a signed non-disclosure agreement, of course—if you decide not to testify as a part of the county's case against Heath Varbeck, should it ever reach trial. Which is doubtful, I might add."

Was he saying the name of the sick bastard who raped me to screw with my head? If so, it was working. My body began to shake uncontrollably, making it difficult for me to speak.

"Yyyou nnneed to lleave. Now!" I forced out with great effort.

"You're upset, which is understandable, but you need to calm yourself and think about this rationally. Do you really want to sit on a witness stand and have your life opened up and examined under a microscope in public? We all have secrets we would rather keep in the dark recesses of our minds. Do you really want a defense attorney shining a light into those dark places? Do you want to subject your family to that ugliness? Sam, take the money and move on. Nothing will undo what you've been through. Testifying will not bring comfort or healing—you will only be exposing yourself to further suffering."

"Was that a threat?" a voice, unrecognizable in its fury, asked from behind me.

"Sir, this is a private conversation. I'll thank you to mind your own business."

"I asked you a question; don't make me repeat myself."

"I have no need to threaten Miss Whitney, I was simply bringing to her attention facts she may not have previously considered."

"Since we are stating facts, here's one for you—if you don't remove yourself from the premises in the next ten seconds, you will no longer be capable of doing so. And to save you the trouble of threatening *me*, I am prepared to deal with the consequences of putting you in the hospital. I have my own set of lawyers in overpriced suits."

Westly rose to leave, but Griffin stopped him with a hand on his chest.

"Approach Samantha again and you will find out just how far I am willing to go in order to protect her...from any threats," Griffin said, barely above a whisper—not a threat, a vow.

The attorney held Griffin's eyes. He didn't appear afraid, which made me question his sanity. With a quick nod in my direction, he departed unhurriedly.

Griffin was at my side with surprising speed, scooping me into his arms and sitting us on the nearest couch. He positioned his body so I had the illusion of privacy while I gathered my senses. Distress receded and anger rose to take its place.

"Who the fuck did that piece of shit think he was to come to my place of work and shove a ridiculous bribe in my face like I was a corrupt politician? To embarrass me, to threaten me! I should have stomped on his ridiculously expensive Ferragamo-clad feet and kneed him in the balls—put those self-defense classes to good use. Maybe he would think twice before threatening another innocent victim...if nothing else, his threats would be delivered several octaves higher, lessening their impact."

Griffin's chest rumbled as he chuckled. I looked up, confused by his mirth, when realization dawned.

"I said all of that out loud, didn't I?" I asked.

"Yeah, but it tamed my desire to follow him to the parking lot and reiterate my message without words."

"Violence is never the answer," I said, not meaning it. Sometimes a good ass-whopping was exactly what the doctor ordered.

"That's true. I wouldn't want to do something like stomp on his foot and kick him in the balls. Such physical displays of anger are simply barbaric."

"Ha, ha. You think you're so funny."

"No, *you* think I'm funny, and you happen to be right." He kissed the top of my head while rubbing my back soothingly. "You okay?"

"Yes. It was an overload of competing emotions: shock, offense, sadness, anger...lots of anger. There were too many to process at once, and he just kept saying *his* name over and over. I know I will have to face worse at trial, face *him*, but I'll be prepared—this was just a sneak attack."

"I'm sorry I didn't get here sooner. I feel like I am always arriving too late where you are concerned," Griffin confessed, as if anything that had occurred was his fault. Men! Why did they insist on ignoring things that were actually their responsibility (like putting down the damn toilet seat), but jumped to claim responsibility for something they had no control over?

"Seriously, what's wrong with you...forget to pay your psychic cable bill? Is your reception fuzzy?" I asked, heavy on the sarcasm.

"Don't be stupid, you big lug, you showed up exactly when I needed you."

He said nothing, not wanting to argue but clearly not conceding.

"I guess we know why so many of the witnesses have backed out of testifying at trial. The DA contacted Ev last week to reconfirm she and I were both still on board. I couldn't understand why he would even ask—now I do. The Varbecks must have systematically bribed or scared the others."

Griffin growled, causing me to laugh.

"Oh, yay!" I clapped my hands and bounced like a child, "Yogi is back."

"I do not growl. But I guess I should be grateful that you went with a bear, the hippo was just...wrong."

Despite my teasing, I was annoyed with myself for turning into a stuttering mess at the mere mention of *his* name. Before the attacks I would have had Mr. Westly Black walking out of here with his head bowed and tail between his legs. I had progressed enough that I could sling a scathing retort at a random stranger, but where *he* was concerned, I lost my confidence.

"I hate being this weak girl," I said, giving voice to my troubled thoughts, " I just want to be normal."

"What is normal, Lo? Is that the goal—to blend in with everyone else?"

"I'm not sure. I want to be me, but sometimes I'm not sure who that is anymore. I don't want to be a basket case, riddled with triggers and anxiety at the slightest provocation. I know I don't like *that* girl."

"You have the patience of a four-year-old on Christmas Eve. It's been five and a half months. You've survived, healed physically, and are facing your fears daily. What the hell else do you expect? There is no magic pill, and if there was, it would be a temporary Band-Aid—not a true fix. Keep doing what you've been doing and you'll get to where you want to be, even if you aren't sure where that is yet."

"You make it sound so easy."

"Not easy, definitely not," he said with conviction. "When walking through hell, most people try to hide...feeling fucking hurts, healing fucking hurts. That's why so many people avoid experiencing that level of honesty with themselves. Where do you think addictions stem from? Why do so many relationships fail? Where does all the anger and violence in the world originate? People desperately trying to avoid experiencing exactly what you are facing head-on. They search for quick fixes, substitutions, temporary releases—but there is no easy route through hell. You've been dealt one of the shittiest hands imaginable; most will never be challenged with a fraction of what you have. You are one of the few with the bravery to walk through the fire, let it burn you to ash, and rise again, changed but all the more beautiful for it."

He kissed my lips tenderly, exploring their texture and contours with his own and causing my eyes to drift closed at the pleasure and intimacy. His lips left mine as he placed a kiss on the tip of my nose, followed by both of my eyelids, and finally my forehead. It was both comforting and tantalizing. I wanted more...needed more, which led me to entwine my fingers through the hair at the back of his neck and pull his lips back to mine. I didn't allow a gentle caress or tease, I demanded heat and power. I wanted to explore and be explored by this man. I traced the outline of his lips with the tip of my tongue before licking the seam. His ensuing groan provided the opportunity for me to slip my tongue into his mouth and begin my expedition—I was Columbus and, holy shit, I had found the New World. He was delicious, minty and warm with a hint of something dark and rich...he reminded me of an Andes crème de menthe chocolate. I loved those freaking things. I couldn't get enough of him, discovering every nook and cranny of his mouth as if it was my life's purpose. I nearly stamped my foot and pouted like a two-year-old when someone cleared their throat behind us.

"I hate to interrupt, but that is not a pay-by-the-hour couch, so knock it off. You are making my customers either jealous or uncomfortable, neither of which is encouraging sales," Ev said sternly, but I saw the twinkle of pleasure in her eyes. She was getting what she had hoped for, even if she wasn't pleased with *where*.

Griffin blushed—actually blushed—which was positively adorable, and caused me to laugh.

"Love that sound," he said under his breath.

I made a move to rise but Griffin held me firmly in place.

"Uh, Griff, I'm going to need you to release me before Ev puts us in time-out."

"She's right. I will revoke your coffee privileges if you don't keep it PG."

I attempted to stand, but again Griffin prevented me from doing so. I turned my body slightly to make eye contact and discovered the problem. Griffin was excited, as in really, *really* excited—nice to know I still had it. I was thrilled. Not only did a man—one who knew what had happened to me—find me sexually appealing, but I had been so engrossed in our make-out session I didn't even notice the shockingly large effect I was having on him. Furthermore, now that I was conscious of the effect, I realized I was not freaked out by the contact.

Hallelujah! I clapped my hands and did a little happy dance.

"Not helping," he warned.

"Oops! Sorry, I'm just really excited."

"No, I'm pretty sure that's me," he groaned.

"But *I'm* excited that *you're* excited and your *excitement* is doing nothing but good things to me. You get me?"

"Despite my limited mental functions at the moment, I actually understood that," Griff said with humor.

Ev cleared her throat again, not hearing our whispered conversation about Griffin's predicament.

"Ev, geeze! Griff needs a moment to...um...coax the bear back into hibernation."

"Aww, hell," Griffin grumbled as Ev replied, "Overshare."

"What? I censored."

"You need to talk to Thia about this animal fixation. It's really starting to concern me," Griff said while shaking his head.

"Hey, I could have said 'tame the hippo'...be grateful."

"Keep talking about hippos. It helps."

"Like the big grey kind wearing a pink tutu and dancing around in Disney movies that are more appropriate for hippies on an acid trip than children?"

"Yes, exactly like that."

He rewarded me with a quick peck on the check before finally allowing me to stand. Ev rolled her eyes. I couldn't help myself; I leaned in close to whisper in her ear.

"Forget a horse...like a damn elephant."

"Hello, queen of indecency, he's my friend. I do not want or need that visual."

Griffin stood and Ev looked him straight in the eyes, fighting the natural urge to search for evidence of my claim.

"I expect this from her, but you Griffin?" she said, before spinning on her heel and walking away.

"Well, I may not be able to look Ev in the eyes for a month, but it was worth it. Ready to work off some of this pent-up energy?" he asked, unconcerned.

"Lead the way."

"I intend to."

After our workout and highly anticipated rub-down, Griff brought me to California Pizza Kitchen for a famous BBQ chicken pizza with extra cilantro. Yummy!

"I have to skip the gym tomorrow, I have dinner with my parents." I made a face as I said the word 'parents' to emphasize how much I was looking forward to the family powwow.

"Sounds like fun. Ev gave me an overview of your situation. I heard they're a whole new breed of special. Do you need back-up?"

Did he just offer to suffer dinner at the Whitney estate? Either Ev did a piss-poor job of explaining the realities of my family or the man was a candidate for sainthood.

"I like you too much to subject you to the joys of a Whitney family dinner."

"Okay, but it's a standing offer. If needed, I've got your back."

"Thank you, but I'll find another way to take advantage of you...I mean, of your kind offer," I said with a saucy wink.

"Good." He cleared his throat, stalling. "I wanted to invite you to dinner."

I looked around the restaurant, at the food on our table, and then at him.

"Isn't that what we're doing now?"

"No. I want to take you to dinner as my date. Preferably when we've both had time to shower beforehand and aren't wearing gym clothes. What do you say?"

"Yes." The word was out of my mouth before my brain had any say—pure instinct.

"Are you free Saturday?"

"I'll have to consult my calendar; I'm incredibly busy, you know." I thumbed through my imaginary calendar. "Saturday is perfect. Dressy or casual?"

"I know spending a fortune on dinner won't impress you, but I would love to try Maroni's. The food is supposed to be spectacular and I've never had anyone I cared enough to try it with."

"I've heard about it, but haven't been either. Can you get a reservation? I heard they're booked at least three months in advance."

"I'll take care of it," he said with confidence.

"Okay, it's a date."

After dinner he drove me back to my car. When we arrived, he came around my side to help me get out.

"You need stairs for this monster."

"No, *you* need stairs, I have no problems. Besides, I like having the excuse to help you get in and out."

"Playa," I accused without heat.

"Back in the day, maybe. But I'm more interested in quality versus quantity these days."

"Isn't that exactly what a *player* would say?"

"I guess you'll have to judge me by my actions and decide for yourself."

"Smooth."

"Call me after your parents' tomorrow if you need anything."

He said goodbye with a sweet kiss on the top of my head that did nothing to satisfy my desire for him.

Wednesday was business as usual at Higher Yearning. Ev arrived midway through my shift with Meg.

"Meg, do you try to upsell customers by offering additional items like pastries or a bottle of water?"

"Absolutely, I've even been cutting up a muffin before rush-time to offer a small sample, which increases sales of baked goods," Meg replied proudly.

"Great idea. I love that you took the initiative to try something new. Just be sure that your sales tactics respect the integrity of our products and the decorum of Higher Yearning."

Meg looked at Ev, her confusion evident. "Did I do something wrong? Oh my gosh, was there a complaint about me?" she asked, horrified.

Ev chuckled. "No, you have been amazing, Meg—one of the best employees ever. Let me give you an example of what I'm talking about. As I said, I value initiative, but there are limits to how far we should push the envelope. Yesterday, an employee—who shall remain nameless—decided to entice a customer by shoving her tongue down his throat. It may ensure the customer's return, but we are not a coffee brothel."

Meg stared at me with her mouth hanging open. She had been working yesterday but didn't catch my lip-lock with Griffin.

"Don't listen to her, Meg. She's messing with you," I said, hoping to erase the shocked look on the poor girl's face.

"So you didn't make-out with a customer on the couch yesterday?" Ev challenged, clearly having fun paying me back.

"You, my friend, have a big mouth. Yes, I kissed Griffin on the couch yesterday, but there were extenuating circumstances, and I didn't kiss him to persuade him to buy more coffee."

"Wait, the huge blonde hottie?" Meg asked, her shock replaced by envy.

"One and the same," I answered, gloating.

"Sorry, Ev. I believe in professionalism, but who wouldn't kiss that gorgeous creature if given the opportunity? I would have revoked her woman card if she had passed that up. He is definitely the sexiest guy I have ever seen."

"Hey, what about Hunter?" Ev protested. "He's drop-dead gorgeous. Plus, he's a total badass."

I was convulsing with laughter at the ridiculousness of Ev selling Hunter.

"Oh, Hunter's hot, too. I guess I just prefer blondes," Meg consoled.

"Clearly you haven't had enough time to appreciate the wonder that is Hunter. He's supposed to stop by later. After you study him more closely, you'll see your mistake. Trust me, there is no one hotter than my man."

I leaned into Meg's side and stage whispered, "Just tell her you made a mistake and Hunter is your favorite. She won't let it rest until you agree with her...believe me."

Ev threw her hands in the air and headed toward her office.

After my shift, I changed clothes in the restroom—God forbid I showed up for dinner in jeans and a Higher Yearning polo. I slid into a tailored Fendi pencil dress in cream with nude Louboutin pumps and a pearl necklace. The outfit screamed 'innocent and unsoiled.' Maybe the clothing would help my parents see me that way, too. As I exited the bathroom, Hunter was entering the shop.

"Any idea what the emergency is that required I get here by 5:00 pm?" he asked as I greeted him.

"It's going to be so much better if you're surprised," I said and checked my watch. "In fact, I can spare ten minutes and still make it to my parents' on time for dinner. Let me tell Ev you're here."

Ev darted from the back and grabbed Hunter's arm.

"Don't talk to her, she's the enemy," Ev scolded Hunter as they approached the counter.

He turned back to me and raised one eyebrow. I only shrugged and positioned myself for optimal viewing. Let the show begin.

"Meg, you've met my boyfriend Hunter, haven't you?"

"Yes, we met last week. Hello, Meg, nice to see you again."

Ev wrapped her hand around Hunter's bicep and 'oooh'-ed. "Have you been working out more than usual? You feel extra ripped. Feel this Meg, the man is rock solid."

Meg and Hunter both looked at Ev like she had lost her mind, which of course she had.

"That's not necessary, I believe you," Meg said in a placating manner.

"Did you know Hunter saves lives for a living? He is a real-life hero!"

Hunter stared at Ev for a moment before turning his gaze to me.

"What am I missing?" Hunter asked me, unable to puzzle out Ev's agenda.

"Oh, no, you'll get no help from me. I am enjoying this way too much," I replied.

Ev elbowed him in the ribs, demanding his attention. "Wow, you're wearing the new jeans we bought last weekend. Your ass is spectacular in these. Turn around and show Meg."

"Okay, you need to explain why I feel like a pooch from 'Best in Show.'"

"Evidently Meg hasn't had an opportunity to really see you up close and personal because she claimed Griffin was the hottest guy she had ever seen earlier today."

"And you are defending my honor by parading me around like a coiffed poodle to prove I'm hotter than Griffin?"

"Yep."

Hunter shook his head at her, accepting her craziness for the compliment it was.

Hunter turned back to Meg and hit her with his megawatt smile, dazzling her. Meg's eyes widened, breathless at the sight.

"You don't have to believe it, but if you could tell her what she wants to hear I would appreciate it. Ev is so much happier when she wins and I don't give her the chance very often."

Turning to Ev, Meg said, "You're right, Ev. Hunter is the hottest guy I've ever met...and I'm not even lying to make you happy."

Ev turned to me and stuck out her tongue.

I had full confidence Griffin would reclaim Meg's vote without even trying. With a wave goodbye, I left for the hour-long drive to my parents' home.

By the time I arrived at the main gate of the Whitney estate, my spirits were high. I was ready to square off against Ev in the hot-guy battle and face whatever my parents had in store.

I clicked the remote to open the front privacy gate and drove onto the familiar grounds. The property was meticulously manicured, as always, and the great lawn particularly green despite the New York fall. I followed the meandering hedge-trimmed driveway around a replica of the Fontaine de la Concorde in Paris, finally arriving at the front entrance. Up until four years ago—when I last lived here—I would have pulled around the left side to the garages. Now I parked in front like the visitor I was. The Whitney estate had never been my home—merely the museum in which I slept.

I rang the bell and waited for Thorngood, the current butler, to answer the door.

"Miss Whitney, welcome. Your parents are awaiting your arrival in the drawing room. Shall I show you the way?"

"No thank you, I remember how to get there," I said dryly.

As I walked through the house, the setting sun caught my eye as it reflected off the bay, showcased by the expansive windows. The beauty and warmth of the scene was a stark contrast to the cold, sterile feel within the house. My heels clicked against the marble floors, effectively announcing my arrival as I entered the drawing room. For the life of me, I could not explain why it was referred to as the 'drawing room;' none of us drew or were artistic in any way.

"Father, Mother," I greeted as I entered.

They both rose as I approached, offering the customary air kiss near each cheek. I can't remember the last time I had experienced physical contact with either of my parents. It was no longer something I expected or needed from them. Any hope of connecting with them died after the attack, when they abandoned me to Ev's care because it was too real for them to deal with.

"Thank you for joining us, Samantha. Dinner will be served in an hour, but your father wanted to have a word with you first," my mother said formally.

"It has come to my attention that you are considering testifying for the District Attorney in regards to the incident that occurred at Hensley," my father stated without preface.

I inhaled deeply, hoping to calm myself. The first time either of my parents deigned to talk about what happened and my father refers to a heinous attack as 'the incident,' dismissing it as if it were nothing more than a drunken indiscretion between consenting adults. I was in a coma for almost two weeks, underwent multiple surgeries, had over twenty broken and fractured bones, nearly lost an eye, still had two scars on my face that required plastic surgery to repair, and if that wasn't enough, I was violated in every possible way. I wanted to scream and rant, but it was no use expending energy that would not change them or make me feel better.

"Yes, I am going to testify," I said, trying to appear calm, certain I was failing.

"Have you considered the ramifications of exposing the sordid details as a matter of public record? Our friends, potential employers, future suitors...everyone would have access to your testimony. Furthermore, you would open yourself to cross-examination from opposing counsel. Are you certain you want to invite such scrutiny to every facet of your life, considering the potential embarrassment for yourself and our family would be substantial?"

"What concerns you more, father? The further indignity I will suffer or that your friends at the country club will know I was violently raped?"

My mother gasped at either my blunt accusation or use of the word 'rape,' but I couldn't be sure which was the source of her distress.

"There is no need for histrionics, Samantha. You are needlessly upsetting your mother," he reprimanded harshly.

"Answer the question," I challenged, unwilling to back down. I was determined to force him to acknowledge the truth.

"I personally have no interest in assigning blame. You cannot be so naïve that you don't understand the way such matters can besmirch a family like ours. As a member of this family, you have a duty to protect the Whitney name at all times."

"Or else?" I questioned, surprisingly shocked despite his expected reaction. "I am fairly certain I heard an underlying threat in there."

My father sighed as if I was an unbearable burden. "Why do you insist on having every detail spelled out? Do you enjoy our discomfort?"

"*Your* discomfort?" I asked in astonishment.

"Yes, our discomfort! How do you think your mother and I feel having to discuss this distasteful matter simply because you don't have the discretion to deal with your difficulties in a more private and respectful manner? I paid a fortune to have you treated by the facility Everleigh suggested. I was led to believe they would fix you, saving us from such unpleasantries."

"I'm sorry I can't pretend as well as you, or be content to medicate myself to the point of oblivion like mother. I guess I'm selfish like that."

My parents completely ignored the jab, pretending not to understand my accusation, in effect, proving my point.

I thought I was blessedly numb after so many years of disappointment. I had hoped when they injected their acid of disapproval into my heart that it would no longer burn—god was I wrong. The small part of me that still loved my parents for their basic genetic contribution to my being was incinerated—excruciatingly and irreversibly reduced to ashes. In that moment, the final piece that tied me to the last name I shared with them died.

"You will not testify or discuss the subject in any way...ever. Do not defy me in this, Samantha; you will not be pleased with the consequences," my father barked.

"I can assure you that I *will* be testifying and I *will* speak about the attacks, my suffering, and anything else I damn well please to whomever I want, whenever the fuck I want," I screamed, my restraint finally snapping.

"As you wish, Samantha. But if you will not protect the Whitney name, then you will not benefit from it. As of now, you are cut off—financially on your own—without the protection or clout your name has previously provided. You will find out exactly what it means to be without family. Perhaps after you have truly suffered, you will come to your senses."

"Money. Ha! I never gave a damn about the money. You may have been my father and mother, but you were *never* my family. Family doesn't desert a member during times of crisis. Family doesn't coerce to the detriment of another. I would tell you a family loves, but it's an emotion of which you are incapable, and therefore you wouldn't comprehend the significance of the word."

I rose on shaky legs, snatched my purse, and walked to the door.

"Goodbye," I whispered, knowing it would be the last word I ever spoke to them.

I made it to the car and out of my parents' posh waterfront community before the dam of emotion broke, forcing me to park in a nearby strip mall. Once the car was safely in park, the tears came and didn't stop. I sobbed for the parents I never had. I sobbed for the loss of Meme, the only mother I had ever known. I sobbed for the little girl who desperately sought her parents' love, not comprehending I was chasing something they didn't understand and could never give. Finally, I sobbed for the woman I now was, devastated by their abandonment during the lowest point of my life and the knowledge that all they felt for me was shame.

My phone rang and the call automatically connected through
my car's hands-free system. I tried to hide my tears but I suspected
the caller heard my despair.

"Where are you?" Griffin's voice came over the line, a balm.

"Oyster Bay," I croaked.

"What are you near?"

"I...god, how could they—"

"I know, baby. I'm on my way, I just need you to look around
and tell me what you're near."

"Eleganté Spalon, but you don't need to come. I'll be fine by
the time you get here, it's an hour away."

"What happened tonight?"

I told him everything, every blistering and trivializing word.
Silent rivers of disgrace coursed down my face. That man—I would
never again call him 'father'—exposed one of my deepest fears and
callously reinforced my insecurity. Blame—was I to blame for what
happened? Should I be held accountable? The rational part of
my brain screamed the word 'bullshit' at the notion, but a small
destructive voice within me whispered he was right...if the man
who created me held me responsible, wasn't I?

"I'm here, baby," he soothed as my car door swung open,
causing me to levitate out of my seat. "Just me, Lo. You're safe,"
he said as he reached in the car and unbuckled my seatbelt,
scooping me into his arms and removing me from the driver's seat
in one smooth movement. Before I knew how it happened, I was
cradled in his lap in the backseat of my Mercedes.

I wanted to be strong, for once be master of the feelings that
commanded me, but today was not that day. In the security of
Griffin's arms, I unleashed a raw display of anguish and betrayal.
He held me together by offering his strength when I did not have
my own. He listened to my senseless ramblings, grief-laden wails,
outraged screams, and tormented whimpers. He soothed me with
simple words and validated my feelings, providing empathy and
compassion in each judgment-free tender caress.

When there was nothing left and I was completely empty, he
still held me.

"How can you stand to be around me? I have a meltdown once a freaking week and you have the shit-luck to always be nearby. Aren't you ready to run yet?"

"If there was anywhere else I'd rather be, I'd be there. The only thing I can't stand is *not* being around you."

"I'm...I don't...okay."

"There is no response required, Lo. Tonight the jackass who never deserved the privilege of calling you his daughter decided to tell you how *he* sees you. You need a second opinion, so you got mine. You choose which to believe. And for the record, I am not an emotionally stunted, self-absorbed narcissist—making me a more reliable source."

We sat in silence for a while as I processed everything he said and accepted that most of it was spot-on. The ugly, spiteful little voice in my mind that tried to keep me chained in a prison of torment was barely audible for the moment, and I experienced a second of blissful peace.

"By the way, how did you get here so fast?"

He cleared his throat. "I was in the neighborhood."

"Really?" I asked doubtfully.

"Yes."

"Why were you in the area?"

"Ev and I may have discussed our concern about the dinner with your parents. There was some debate over who would spend their evening killing time in the area, but I ensured I was here should you need back-up."

"What did you offer her in exchange for the honor of being my human Kleenex?"

"Ev can't be bribed."

"Then how are you here alone?"

"Distraction. I enlisted help from the only person I know who can manage that spit-fire."

"Ooooh, Hunter is in so much trouble. It's going to be a fun couple of days at home."

"He's only in trouble if he didn't do his job right. If his shock and awe campaign was a success and you return home in reasonably good health, he'll be fine."

"Wrong. She will see this as yet another time he outwitted her, which will lead to retaliatory measures. Trust me, the condo is going to be better than an episode of 'Survivor' after this stunt." I felt his smile on the top of my head, accompanied by a small kiss. I'm not sure why or how he always managed to show up when I needed him lately, but I hoped it wouldn't stop.

Chapter Six

"Every heart sings a song, incomplete, until another heart whispers back. Those who wish to sing always find a song. At the touch of a lover, everyone becomes a poet." -Plato

Thursday morning I awoke exhausted from a restless night's sleep. I dreamt of myself as a child lost in a maze and unable to find my way out. It was the first time I'd dreamt of anything other than the attack and, regardless of the dream, it was good news.

I joined Huntleigh at the kitchen table and helped myself to the pancakes and bacon that could only have been made by Hunter. Blueberries exploded in my mouth, making my taste buds sing. The man's cooking abilities may be limited to breakfast foods, but with his skill I could eat breakfast for every meal. I vocalized my approval with unintelligible grunts and moans, my mouth never empty long enough to form actual words.

When I had finished my first round of deliciousness, their odd silence registered.

"If you are just going to sit there like statues and watch me eat, make it authentic—strike a ridiculous and unnatural pose...maybe hide an arm behind your back to make it look like it's missing, at least that way I can pretend you're art and not feel creeped out."

"Ha, ha. Tell me what the heck happened last night. You could have woken me when you got home," Ev chided.

"First, you were *not* asleep when I got home," I said, grinning at their guilty faces. "PS, the neighbors called and said you need to keep it down, you're working their dogs into a frenzy."

"I was worried...Hunter was distracting me so I wouldn't obsess over what arrows your parents might sling—it's his job to keep my mind occupied so I can stop being overbearing," Ev said.

"It's a tough job, but I'm *up* for the challenge," Hunter said cheekily.

"Oh god, you are spending way too much time around Sam," she muttered.

"I love Sam, but more importantly, she tends to be where you are, which is where I want to be," he countered with a look of genuine adoration on his face.

"Awww, stop it you two, you're making me misty."

Ev kissed his lips sweetly, the same love shining from her eyes. They were disgustingly perfect for each other, the ideal balance of independence, challenge, and devotion. Despite my fear that I would never be 'fixed' enough to find happily ever after, I was content to live vicariously through theirs.

In an attempt to give them privacy, I relocated to the couch where they joined me a few minutes later.

"What happened at Chateau Moneybags last night?" Ev asked, her distain apparent.

I groaned, unsure if recounting the events would lead to another emotional vomit-fest or if I had really exorcized some of the demons last night. I steeled myself and delivered the blow-by-blow to my rapt audience.

I still felt anger and sadness as I relived the showdown, but the devastating pain that had overwhelmed me the night before was markedly absent.

By the time I finished, Hunter had laid himself across Ev in some complicated martial arts position to restrain her. She was raging, prepared to fight—out for retribution. She struggled against Hunter's ironclad hold, desperate to get to a phone and enlighten the people formerly known as my father and mother regarding their many failings as parents and human beings. Eventually I tried to persuade her that a call would be a waste of breath—my parents would not hear her words and spontaneously gain self-awareness. Perhaps I was cynical, but I wouldn't allow such hope to take root. I had been devastated and disappointed by them too many times.

When he finally loosened his hold, Ev proved her merits as a self-defense student by flipping an unsuspecting Hunter over the back of the couch in an impressive Jiu-Jitsu move. He hit the ground with a loud thud, followed by a deep groan.

Ev walked over to me and I high-fived her. "Bad ass!"

She pulled me into a fierce hug, offering me the love and acceptance only family could provide.

"They are self-absorbed, ignorant assholes who never deserved you—you are better off without them in your life," Ev said with conviction.

"You guys are definitely an upgrade. My assigned family sucks compared to the one I selected myself. Proof once again of my impeccable taste."

We ended our hug with an extra squeeze and I went to dress for my appointment with Thia. So much had transpired the last week, I wasn't certain what to focus on for the session. I slid into a studded denim miniskirt and brown ribbed tank top, accompanied by my favorite brown cowboy boots and a chunky bronze medallion necklace. The outfit was fun, a little wild, and represented the Sam I was versus the cream-clad innocent I presented to my parents last night. It was me.

I rushed to my car, not wanting to be late. Safely belted in the driver's seat, I was about to pull out when I noticed something tucked beneath my windshield wiper. Annoyed by the physical equivalent of SPAM emails, I lazily rolled down my window and clicked my windshield wipers into motion. After several rounds of playing 'catch the fluttering paper,' I successfully snagged the offending advertisement. Unless this was a 50% off coupon for a designer outlet, I was going to be pissed.

EMBRACE SILENCE, THOSE WHO SPEAK WILL COURT TROUBLE AND CONSEQUENCE.

What the—? I read the message again, ensuring I had understood correctly. Did I just receive a poetic threat on my windshield? Was this how *his* people scared off all the other victims from testifying? Maybe lyrical threats and ransom notes were the new rage in the criminal underworld. I was glad to see he was bettering himself in prison and investing his time in creative pursuits. Jackass! If he thought this would frighten me, he had another thing coming. He had already done his worst...what more could he do?

I shoved the ridiculous note under my visor and threw the car into gear. I had a therapy session to get to, and he had derailed my life enough. I arrived at Thia's office and didn't even have a chance to sit in the waiting room before she greeted me.

"Hello, Sam. You came back...a brave one."

"Brave, crazy, the two are hard to distinguish."

Thia smiled at me and I caved immediately, unwilling to endure another staring contest.

"It feels more like a month has passed, so much has happened in the last seven days."

"Tell me about it."

I told her about my parents, wanting to share the worst of my week first. She listened intently, never interrupting my stream of consciousness. When I shared about my meltdown after leaving their home, she made a note on the pad resting on her leg.

"What are you going to do now?" Thia asked.

"Nothing, they've disowned me and I disowned them right back. I have a family to love me that doesn't include them. Just because that family isn't blood doesn't make them any less significant," I answered defensively.

Thia laughed, "Retract the claws, I wasn't questioning the quality of your family unit. What I intended to ask was—how will you survive now, financially, after losing what could be considered a winning lotto ticket?"

"I understand better than anyone that money will not buy happiness. It's not the root of all evil, as far as I'm concerned, but it is low on my list of what really matters. I'll be fine without the big payday after they croak."

"But how will you live, pay rent, car insurance, food, gas, etcetera? You haven't had to worry about these realities before; it is added pressure during an already difficult time."

Oh, she was assuming I was a spoiled brat who had no clue how to survive on my own. Now I understood.

"I've had a job since my freshman year of high school. When Ev began working I was bored, and if I had too much free time my mother would try to rope me into attending random social events, so I found a job, too. I've always enjoyed working and earning money independent from my family."

Thia nodded.

"The condo was a high school graduation present from my parents, as was my car. They are in my name—no rent or car payment, just taxes and maintenance fees."

Thia nodded again, clearly expecting me to continue.

"I haven't touched a dime of my parents' money since the attacks. I didn't want their financial assistance if that was the only type of assistance they were willing to provide. I didn't want to lessen their guilt for abandoning me; I even paid for TPC myself. It's almost comical that my father still doesn't realize I haven't charged a single expense since my release from the hospital."

Thia smiled with pride. "You were well prepared for your parents' ultimatum, even though it was unexpected. You're confident you can get by with a low-wage job? You must have blown through your savings if you covered TPC."

"I'm fine. My Grandmere was an eccentric artist who left her husband and the United States once her children entered boarding school and moved to Paris. I only met her a few times, but we understood each other. She was the black sheep of her generation and apparently I am the black sheep of mine—shunning the money and the family name for real life and real friends. Of course, she and my grandfather never divorced—it was unseemly, as you know. So when he died, she inherited all his money. When she died a few years ago, she left most of it to my father, but secretly held several million in a trust for me without anyone's knowledge, except her attorney. Grandmere left a note saying it was my 'security' to ensure I could always follow my heart and be true to myself. The trust came to fruition when I turned twenty-one. I've had access to the money for the last eighteen months. TPC was my first withdrawal. It's not the obscene wealth my parents have, but if I'm sensible it could sustain me for the rest of my life."

Thia looked slightly stunned by my admission. I guess discussing four million dollars dismissively was shocking to most people. The money had already been invested, and my goal was to live off the interest. Not a bad annual stipend, but it still required fiscal responsibility.

"Oh, and I did my homework and am now employed at Higher Yearning, which will provide supplementary income."

"Well, as long as you have the supplementary income from Higher Yearning, I guess I don't have to be concerned with how you will pay for your sessions," she said dryly. "So since I don't need to kick you out, what else happened this week?"

"In addition to the parental showdown and finding a job, I've eaten at least two square meals per day. And I've been to the gym every day with the exception of yesterday, but I'm meeting Griffin after our session to resume my routine."

"That's a new name—Griffin. Tell me about him."

I gave Thia the low-down on Griffin, leaving nothing out.

"Do you want a relationship with him?"

"Am I capable of a real relationship with him...with anyone?"

She scribbled on her pad again. Shit, that couldn't be a good sign.

"What are you writing?"

"Grocery list—wouldn't want to forget cat food. My seventeen babies would be distraught."

Oh my god, was she really a 'cat lady' or was she just messing with me? I couldn't tell.

"Have you experienced physical attraction or sexual arousal since the attacks?"

"Yes!" I shouted triumphantly. "I was worried I would never be turned on again...I used to like sex. A lot."

"The return of your sexual desire is a good indication that you are making progress in your recovery. I assume Griffin was the inspiration?"

"Oh yeah, if you saw him you'd understand. If I wasn't turned on by him, then all hope would be lost."

"But you don't believe he wants you?"

"I think he's attracted to me, but that isn't the same thing as wanting to bed someone with all my baggage," I said regretfully.

"Any sexual partner, especially the first after the attack, will need to be aware of what you've been through and prepared for possible triggers. It's a lot to ask of a casual sex partner."

"Don't feel the need to sugarcoat it for me, Doc."

"That was the sugar-coated version. Do you want the ugly truth?"

"Do you charge extra for the ugly truth?"

"No, only sugarcoating incurs an additional charge, like sprinkles."

I gestured for her to continue.

"You would be the exception to the rule if you have a beautiful experience the first time you attempt sexual intimacy. In fact, most women find it takes several attempts to complete the act. Your partner will have to be patient, prepared to stop at any time. Many rape victims also report it takes time before experiencing orgasm."

She observed my horror-stricken face and laughed before continuing.

"Some men aren't able to handle the pressure of performing while concerned about triggering a flashback. Additionally, male pride tends to struggle with the inability to produce an orgasm in their partner. Many established relationships and marriages can't survive the strain in combination with the emotional baggage outside the bedroom. As you can imagine, the failure rate of new relationships is exponentially higher. It generally takes at least a year before most women are prepared to engage in more than a casual relationship."

"I liked the sugar-coated version better," I groaned.

"I'm sure you do. Time's almost up, and while I'd love to gouge you for more of your hardly earned money, I have a class to teach at the University, so it's homework time. Work on sexual stimulation by yourself—remind your body of the pleasures of sex without the pressure of a partner. Go out with your friends and push your comfort zone, a bar maybe. Go somewhere alone with a lot of people that makes you nervous...the park, a movie, I don't care where. And continue eating, you're still too skinny. I get hungry just looking at you."

"Got it; masturbate, bar hop, movie, eat. Should I take myself to dinner and a movie before I get frisky so I can still respect myself in the morning?"

"Play hard to get. It is good to have standards," she said straight-faced, but added a wink. "See you next week."

Once in my car, I withdrew my cell phone to text Griffin, only to find a text from him awaiting me.

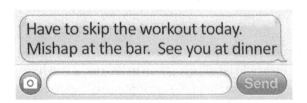

I was bummed to lose my exercise partner and my massage, but I soldiered on. It was my first workout alone, but I managed to remember everything Griffin had taught me. I kept my focus on my routine, hanging the proverbial 'do not disturb' sign with my body language. Thankfully, this time of day the gym was packed with stay-at-home moms. Not a lot of danger there.

I ran home to shower after the gym before visiting the foot spa to make up for the massage I missed. Best $28 I had spent in ages.

I would have to bring Ev back with me next time; she would love it, and we were long overdue for a girls' day.

I loved Hunter and he was perfect for my bestie, but I did miss our chick time. We saw each other every day and talked all the time, but rarely found time for the two of us to just be silly girls. My life was seriously lacking silly the last few months. Hell, it was missing fun, too. We used to go to The Spot, the bar where Griffin worked, every Thursday to sip drinks and listen to local performers. I wasn't sure how comfortable I would be at a bar now, but I missed our routine and wanted to try. Plus, it would accomplish one of my homework assignments. And I knew if I was with Griffin and Hunter, I would feel safe—even Ev could hold her own after months of Krav Maga classes.

I arrived home excited about my idea. When Griffin showed up with Italian take-out, I laughed, reminded of Thia's desire to stuff me full of pasta and meatballs. We all settled into our same seats as last week.

"Hey, Ev. Do you think the boys choose to sit across from each other so they can play footsie under the table?" I asked with a smirk.

"I was just thinking the same thing," Ev concurred.

"If I am playing footsie with anyone at this table, it's not Griffin. He doesn't have feet—those things are boats," Hunter said.

"No need to be jealous of my size fifteens, man. I'm sure your feet are perfectly—what was the word you used, Ev? Oh yeah, I remember—*adequate*."

Hunter's gaze snapped to Ev.

"What? It was during our break and I was mad at you."

He shook his head before leaning over to whisper in her ear. Her eyes widened and she nodded so vigorously she looked like a bobble head.

"Before you two get any further with your post-dinner plans, I have a request," I said, capturing everyone's attention. "I want to go to The Stop tonight like we used to, all of us."

"I'm in," Griffin answered immediately.

Hunter and Ev exchanged a look with one another, a silent conversation.

"We're in," Ev finally replied.

"Yes!" I said enthusiastically.

"Boys, you'll have to do since you don't have access to a wardrobe. Ev, I expect an ensemble that reflects the celebration of our first night out in months."

I ran to my room, nearly tripping over my feet in excitement. I flung open my closet door and surveyed my options. I wanted an outfit that was sassy and bold, something that illustrated the parts of myself I had reclaimed. The moment my eyes locked on the black Balmain leather pants, inspiration struck. I wriggled into the skintight butter-soft leather and tucked in my fitted, off-the-shoulder black shirt. As if by magic, I had curves and cleavage that didn't really exist—sultry without being slutty. I should live in this outfit. I located a stunning pair of sky-high red Jimmy Choos. A wide black cincher belt and silver cuff bracelet added a little edge. I surveyed the effect in the mirror—perfect! It was the modern-day version of Sandy from 'Grease' in the classic carnival finale.

I quickly applied my make-up, taking care so my eyes would sparkle against the blended kohl rims. I twisted my hair up and pinned it in an effortless style that exposed my neck and shoulders. Proud of my quick transformation, I exited the bedroom to get the troops moving. As I approached, all conversation stopped.

"Oh damn," Hunter grumbled.

Ev clapped her hands and squealed with approval.

Griff was frozen. I don't think he breathed for at least a minute. When he finally thawed, it was only to blink...repeatedly. He finally turned to Hunter.

"I'm gonna have to close down the damn bar...again."

"I think you may be overreacting," Hunter advised.

"Have you looked at her? The guys are going to go into a frenzy and I'm going to spend the whole night bloodying my knuckles."

I leaned into Ev's side, "Can he really close down the bar?"

"Oops, I guess I forgot to mention that Griff's parents own the bar...well actually, they retired so I guess Griff owns The Stop now. It was major drama when he decided to get his Master's in Clinical Psych, but he has managed to balance the two."

How did I not know this? Not that it made a bit of difference to me if Griffin was a guy bartending his way through school or the bar owner, but he was so low-key about it. As I thought back, the staff at the bar did seem to look to him for guidance, and he was there a lot during the day...but still. Wouldn't most men use the position to their advantage?

"It'll be fine. We'll both be there to keep it cool. It's a Thursday night, the vibe is always relaxed," Hunter reassured an unconvinced Griffin.

Griff muttered what I assumed was a string of profanities though I couldn't hear the specific combination. He studied me again, shaking his head.

"If you didn't look so damn spectacular, I'd ask you to change."

I hit him with my best smile, a blend of sweet and sexy, while gazing at him through my lashes. It was my best 'come hither' look.

"Stow that smile and the bedroom eyes before I change my mind," he cautioned me.

Yep, I still got it!

We arrived at The Stop, or The Bus Stop if you actually read the marquee, a little after eight. It was perfect timing. The dinner crowd for the restaurant was finishing their meals, and a fresh stream of people were drifting in to enjoy a relaxing night of live music. The Stop served grill and pub cuisine during the day and transitioned into a more traditional bar at night. It's been a staple in the community for the past thirty years, always maintaining a young, casual vibe. The patrons were a mixture of undergrad and graduate students, along with local, young professionals. During the week, The Stop focused on drawing a crowd with sports nights, evenings dedicated to live music, tournaments for pool, darts, and foosball, and even karaoke and trivia nights. On the weekends, The Stop focused on dance music featuring local DJs. The biggest appeal for women was that it never felt like a meat market. The owners—well, I guess Griffin—strictly enforced the legal drinking age and didn't hesitate to eject anyone whose behavior negatively impacted the enjoyment of others. There was zero-tolerance for drugs and lewd behavior that was so prevalent in other bars and clubs.

The ambiance was exactly what you would expect for an upscale pub with a hint of Irish tradition. Perfect for the upper-middle class neighborhood and neighboring Ivy League university. The Stop excelled in small details and the bar was meticulously maintained. Hedges and shrubbery decorated the front entrance and bordered the outdoor patio of the distressed brick building. While it appeared similar to many of its kind, when examined more closely, the quality of the materials used and small accents made the interior shine. The mahogany bar, leather benches, artwork, sconces—every choice was perfectly balanced. I can't remember a time when any of the thirty-plus flat screen televisions, bathrooms, or game tables were out of order. I don't even recall ever seeing a single light bulb burnt out in the funky overhead droplights. Even the lighting throughout the parking lot was carefully selected to be attractive and functional. To think Griffin held this level of responsibility and executed the daily operations with such precision was impressive.

We entered the bar and Griff took my arm, leading us to a booth near the stage that had been roped off.

"Is this the VIP section? Do we get bottle service?" I teased.

"It is tonight. There is no way the four of us are killing a bottle of anything and making it to work tomorrow, but drinks are on the house."

"Yes!" Ev cheered. My budget-conscious roommate was a huge fan of free, a by-product of growing up just above the poverty line.

Hunter chuckled at her excitement. She was financially stable now and he made enough to cover any drink she ordered, but free Stoli tasted twice as good, according to Ev.

A waitress I hadn't seen before approached our table and walked to Griff's side, resting her hand on his shoulder before leaning over to take his order, displaying her artificially-inflated friends. She'd better be careful or my claws may come out and pop those airbags. I was about to tell her to step off when Griffin gave her a look that could not be misinterpreted—back off or get out. I wanted to stand and cheer when she scrambled back several steps.

Not ready to admit defeat, she attempted to engage Griffin in conversation to the exclusion of the rest of us. He held up a hand to stop her drivel.

"Candy, this is my *friend,* Sam. Please take her order along with that of my other guests. I would appreciate it if you undertook this task with the professionalism expected of all Stop employees."

Candy? He hired a girl named Candy with floatation devices permanently strapped to her chest?

After she took our drink orders with her best interpretation of professionalism, she scurried back to the bar.

Griffin groaned quietly. I raised an eyebrow, prompting him for an explanation, words unnecessary after that spectacle.

"Candy's sister—her very normal, kind, hard-working sister who has been a waitress here for three years—broke her arm last week. She asked if Candy could cover her shifts for the next six weeks. I didn't want to replace her, but I needed the coverage or I'd get stuck working the extra hours myself. No good deed goes unpunished."

I laughed at his dilemma. I guess it wasn't easy being the boss man.

Candy returned with our drinks, placing them before us politely, with only a small look of longing in Griffin's direction before departing.

We sipped our drinks and chatted for a bit, all of us laughing and joking—it was perfectly normal, and I was delighted. Our banter was interrupted when another employee came to snag Griff for help with some urgent matter. Ev, Hunter, and I carried on with our fun, sharing stories about our day. The room grew quiet and we directed our attention to the stage, ready to enjoy the live music. We were shocked to find Griffin on stage, guitar in hand.

"Hey everyone, welcome to The Stop. For those of you who don't know me, I'm Griffin. You can usually find me serving you drinks behind the bar, but every so often an act will flake and I find my way up here. Be kind, this was a last-minute thing so I'm winging it."

Day-um, he looked incredible on stage. The spotlight was, well, spotlighting every one of his numerous assets. I'd only heard Griffin perform once before and it was eight months ago, but I remember it vividly. He seemed uncomfortable on stage last time, but his set had been brilliant. Tonight he was at ease, as if the stage had become a second home.

Ev and I looked at one another and both broke into the seated version of the happy dance. I'd always wanted an opportunity to say 'I'm with the band,' even if Griffin was a one-man show. There was just something about musicians.

Griff strummed the opening chords of one of my favorite country crossover songs, "Cruise" by Florida-Georgia Line. I bounced in my seat excitedly, thrilled he'd chosen a feel-good song to open his set. I was singing along and miming the words, having a ball. When he sang the final chorus, Griffin looked right at me as he belted the part about a pick-up truck looking better if the girl climbed inside. I pulled a total fangirl, screaming and cheering.

He continued his set with quick transitions, expert guitar accompaniment, and effortless vocals that evoked emotion with each word. He held the room captive. Each song poured from him as if he had written it himself. Like the last time he performed, I quickly jotted down his set to make a playlist the next day:

"Gone, Gone, Gone" by Phil Phillips
"If You're Going Through Hell" by Rodney Atkins
"I Won't Give Up" by Jason Mraz
"I Dare You To Move" by Switchfoot
"To Make You Feel My Love" by Garth Brooks
"Start of Something Good" by Daughtry

Griffin paused in his set to address the audience.

"I've never played this last song, but I was inspired tonight by a particularly beautiful woman. It was written as a duet, so I'll need you all to help sing the girl's part."

He strummed a chord before singing the words, "I've got," acapella-style. On the word "chills," the guitar joined him in a fantastic interpretation of the classic "You're the One That I Want" by John Travolta from the movie 'Grease'. As he sung he winked at me, and I laughed so hard I couldn't sing along with the enthusiastic crowd. Every woman in the audience was screaming the words, having a ball with a song most know by heart. I was glad my Olivia Newton-John style was recognized and appreciated.

The crowded went wild, cheering and demanding an encore. Griff smiled as he settled back on his stool, willing to oblige their demand.

"I was hoping you would enjoy the set and ask for one more song. I've wanted to perform this one for a while now, but I was waiting for the right time."

As he played the opening chord progression, I recognized the tune as the same one he had hummed to me that first night after Thursday dinner. I hadn't been able to place it at the time but I knew it immediately this time—"Fix You" by Coldplay.

He began to sing and I felt a hand take hold of mine, then another joined on top. I didn't have to look to know that it was Ev and Hunter, offering me support and echoing the meaning of the song. I was so moved by the love and support of my friends—my family—I found myself unexpectedly choked up. As Griffin sang the last lines of the song staring straight at me, I heard Ev and Hunter quietly singing along—for my ears only—as they both squeezed my hand. God I loved them, all three of them.

I finally returned my attention to Ev and Hunter.

"He was on fire tonight. I could see the emotions and energy pouring off him."

They stared at me dumbly.

"What?"

"I think everyone could see his emotions, Sam. He was broadcasting them with laser precision right at you. I don't think he even looked at the rest of the audience the whole set," Ev informed me with conviction.

"The song selection was suspiciously appropriate and I did notice him looking this way a lot, but I didn't want to jump to any conclusions."

"Short of him saying 'Samantha Whitney, this set is dedicated to you, and I want you...bad,' I don't know how he could have been more blatant."

She had a point. Still, what was I supposed to say to him? Did I want Griffin? Hell yes! Was I ready for a real relationship? I didn't know. I wanted one if it was with Griffin, but I wasn't certain I could uphold my end completely—fulfill all of the expectations of a normal relationship. I forced myself to acknowledge the biggest concern lurking in my subconscious— would I be enough for Griffin? Could he be content settling for what was left of me?

The crowd parted as he made his way toward the table. If this was a movie, I would be running across the room to launch myself into his arms, no questions, no hesitation...but this wasn't a movie. He was stopped several times as patrons paid their compliments— every second stretched out into eternity, the anticipation of his nearness electrifying my already buzzing nerves.

I wanted him. When I silenced my inner monologue and pushed aside the self-doubt, it was really that simple. I wanted him. If it were any other man I would be too afraid and abandon ship at the first sign of trouble, but Griffin knew my issues. When he stepped on the broken shards of my past, he didn't run away. Instead, he took me in his arms and carried me to safety.

I understood his worth and, if given the chance, I would treasure him. After everything I had survived, I deserved happiness...I deserved love. I had so much love to give and I knew I could fall in love with Griffin.

He finally escaped his fans, approaching me slowly, as if preparing himself for the unknown. The look in his eyes was so serious that I lost my courage for a moment.

"Yes," he said.

Huh? That was *not* what I was expecting him to say.

"What?" I asked with my own monosyllabic response.

He raised an eyebrow and studied me carefully. Did he think I was feigning ignorance to let him down easy? Avoid a messy 'you're such a nice guy, but...' conversation?

"Yes, it was for you. Every single word and note—all of it...for you."

That did it! I turned my back to him, kicked off my heels, and stepped up onto the bench, careful not to knock the table. I turned to face him, surprised to discover I was now exactly the same height as him. He looked both confused and amused by my peculiar behavior.

I placed my hands on his chest, taking a moment to enjoy the feel of his strong, steady heartbeat beneath my palms. I held his eyes as I slid my hands slowly up his chest, around his shoulders, and behind his neck. With my fingers buried in the short hairs at his nape, I slowly reeled him in, never breaking eye contact. I stopped when my lips grazed his, whispering "yes" against his mouth before gliding my lips across his. He stood frozen, receiving my kiss, as I explored the smooth firmness and shape of his tempting mouth. I tested the fullness of his lower lip with a gentle nip of my teeth, pulling slightly and teasing the bit I trapped with a flick of my tongue. I felt his body tense as he held himself in check, letting me direct the pace of the kiss. That's right, big boy, I have this under control. Satisfied I had explored the entirety of that which the world could see, I slid my tongue along the seam, begging entry to the part of his mouth hidden from view. His sharp inhale rewarded my boldness, and without resistance I entered his mouth.

His arms wrapped around me slowly, snaking about until one settled on my lower back, the other twined in my hair as he cupped my head. With the slightest pressure, he pulled me in until our bodies touched and his heat pierced through the fabric of my clothes. He smelled of forest and Tide—woodsy, clean, and masculine—it was unique and enticing. I explored his mouth slowly, savoring his taste and texture, learning every part and committing it to memory. He responded to every stroke with his own, caressing me. The kiss unlike any other built until there was no leader or follower, melding into one consciousness, clairvoyant in our anticipation and responses to one another. More than a kiss, it was an exchange of vulnerability for trust.

Hoots and catcalls pulled us from our illusion of solitude.

Uh-oh! I had forgotten we were at The Stop surrounded by bar folk, and worse yet, all of Griffin's employees. My timing may leave something to be desired. I dropped my forehead to his chest in embarrassment, trying to hide behind the wall of his body, which was a fairly successful strategy considering his size.

He nestled his face in my hair and inhaled deeply, as if trying to capture every detail of the moment we shared.

"If this is the reception I can expect, I'll be sure to perform every week."

I slapped his chest with my palm, not bothering to raise my head.

"Always hitting me. Should I be concerned?"

"Only if you insist on saying things that make me hit you," I replied, my voice muffled by his shirt.

"Fair enough."

He pulled me against him securely and then stepped back, taking me with him. Sliding into the booth, he placed me gently on the seat in the same position I began my evening. Without hesitation, he took my hand, resting it on the table in his. I was surprised and pleased by his blatant claim.

"How's it going?" Griff asked Ev and Hunter, as if nothing out of the ordinary had occurred.

"How's it going?" Ev echoed, tapping her chin thoughtfully. "It's been a rather boring night at The Stop, to be frank. My best friend serenaded my bestest friend, after which the same bestest friend climbed on the bench and kissed the daylights out the aforementioned best friend. Business as usual," Ev concluded casually.

"Angel, you forgot to mention the audience," Hunter added helpfully.

"You're right, babe. Thanks for clarifying."

"As long as you're both having a good time," Griff said, matching Ev's casual tone.

A stare-down ensued. Ev's eyes bored into Griffin's with neither backing down. When Griff raised my hand to his lips and kissed the back of it without breaking eye contact, she caved.

"Let's just get one thing clear, Mr. Evensen. You know I've been rooting for this and I am trusting you to take good care of my bestest friend. But, now that it's official, I have to warn you—screw this up, I'll kill you."

"I would expect nothing less. But just so you know, I would kill *myself* before ever hurting Sam," Griffin said, as serious as I had ever heard him.

"Glad we got that out of the way," Hunter said to Ev. "I do have one question, though. Since when is Griffin your best friend? I thought I had that job."

"Are you jealous?" she asked, teasing him. "Your title was converted to 'best boyfriend' when you finally got your head out of your ass and made a move. Griffin subsequently received a well-deserved promotion."

Hunter nodded as if Ev's insane logic made perfect sense to him.

"I accept, but based on my job performance over the last four months, I respectfully request my title be upgraded to 'bestest.'"

"I'll submit the paperwork for review and get back to you."

"Okay, but I was contacted by several headhunters today so I suggest you expedite the process."

"Excuse me? What headhunting sluts were contacting you?"

I couldn't help but giggle, which quickly turned into full-blown laughter when I replayed Ev's words in my head.

"Love that sound," Griffin said to himself.

"What's so funny, Miss PDA?" Ev asked.

"*Head*hunting sluts—" I squawked before dissolving into laughter again.

"Always in the gutter," Ev complained.

We stayed at The Stop for another hour, proving how much we enjoyed the company by teasing one another mercilessly. Griffin never released my hand, drawing little circles on top with his thumb in random patterns that I could feel all the way to my heart. As the night wore on and my energy waned, I leaned against him, trying to get comfortable. He raised his arm to provide better access, which I took quick advantage of by snuggling against his hard body and resting my head on his chest. I felt his hum of approval as he lowered his arm, wrapping it around my shoulder affectionately.

Shortly thereafter, we all agreed it was time to find our beds and began collecting our belongings. Griffin leaned to the side, swiping my skyscraper Jimmy Choos from the floor where I had kicked them off earlier. It had been a long day and I was dreading the prospect of forcing my tired feet back into the exquisite torture devices I called shoes. I may wear heels every day, but that didn't mean my feet loved me for it. I eyed the strappy instruments of pain dubiously as I hesitantly took them from Griffin's hand. Griffin rose and I scooted to the end of the bench, sighing regretfully as I raised my foot to slide it into the shoe.

"What's wrong, Lo?"

"Nothing, it's the price I pay for being vertically challenged and a slave to fashion."

He nodded his understanding with a small smile—it was a rarity that I admitted my obvious height deficiency.

I bent forward to face the inevitable feet of fire, only to find myself once again cradled in Griffin's arms, the designer shoes dangling from my fingertips.

"You've really got a thing for carrying me, don't you? Not that I'm complaining."

"I'm here so there's no reason to put those back on if they hurt you."

"Well, my feet thank you profusely," I said, placing a quick kiss of appreciation on his cheek.

"I prefer having you in my arms," he said simply, but a wealth of meaning seemed to be buried beneath his words.

"It's not your job to take care of me, Griff, although I appreciate the sentiment more than you could ever know."

"Not my job?" he asked, obviously offended.

"Nope. Why would it be your job...or anyone's, for that matter? I have to take care of me—it's my job."

"You are responsible for yourself, no doubt. But make no mistake—it's my job now, too," he replied, dead serious.

"Why's that? You afraid I'm going to fall apart? That I can't handle life in the big, scary world all by myself? I'll have you know I am a grown-ass wo—"

He silenced me with a quick, gentle kiss to my lips. I was so stunned I lost my train of thought completely.

"Hmm, effective. I'll have to remember that one. Since you're mine, it's now my job to take care of you. Carrying you when your feet hurt is a part of my job description, so drop the sass and enjoy the ride."

I felt like I should argue further, protest my own competence, accuse him of being an archaic Neanderthal...but I couldn't bring myself to say the words. It may set women's liberation back fifty-plus years, but I liked the idea of him caring for me. I knew I could take care of myself. Perhaps my rediscovered confidence was why I was able to accept his declaration. I had been self-sufficient most of my life. After dedicating the last five months to reclaiming all that was taken from me, I was ready to let someone else help shoulder the load. Lord knows Griffin's shoulders were up for the challenge.

"Okay," I chirped sweetly.

His surprise nearly caused him to trip. Quickly regaining his footing, he paused and examined my face, assessing my sincerity.

"Really?"

"Is there anything I could say that would stop you?"

"Hell no."

"Then I see no point in trying to persuade you otherwise. Besides, it sounds pretty damn good to me—on one condition."

He raised a curious eyebrow in response.

"You have to promise you will let me do the same in return. This isn't a one-way street. If I'm yours, then you have to be mine, too," I said with conviction, realizing it was what I actually wanted.

"Wouldn't have it any other way...with two exceptions."

"Are we in negotiations here? I would have brought representation, had I known."

"If there comes a time when my needs, wants, safety, or whatever conflict—yours take precedence."

"That doesn't seem fair. We should flip a coin or something."

"It's non-negotiable. You come first; I won't accept it any other way. If a madman is waving a gun, you step behind me. If we are stranded on a deserted island, you get the fresh water. If we both come down with the flu, I pick up the medicine. If we both have a crap day, you vent first. If there is *anything* you can't do, we won't do it 'til you can—regardless of how much I may want it. You get me?"

"Wow! Kind of sounds like a shit deal for you, but I'll sign."

"Trust me, I'm still getting the better end of the deal," he said, kissing the top of my head to emphasize his point.

"Wait, you said two exceptions. What's the other?"

"I changed my mind, just the one exception," he said with a smirk. "If you can manage to carry me to the car when my feet hurt, then you have my blessing."

"Dude! You're like three times my size and weight, that's never going to happen."

"Exactly!"

He placed me in the back of Hunter's Yukon and buckled my seatbelt before I had the chance. I rolled my eyes, but let it go. He leaned in, but waited for me to close the distance and initiate the kiss, which I did enthusiastically. It ended too soon, but with Hunter and Ev in the front seat pretending not to watch, it was for the best.

"See you tomorrow, Lo."

With one more swift kiss, he closed the door and was gone.

This was definitely the best day I'd had in longer than I could remember. I wasn't sure exactly what we were calling ourselves, what our status was. What is the relationship status equivalent of 'mine'? It implied more possession than just hanging out or casually dating, but it was too new to dub a serious relationship. When in doubt, keep it simple—'boyfriend' would have to do. It was strange...I was giddy and excited as if he was my first. He wasn't, of course; I had dated plenty of guys and experienced my fair share of committed and serious relationships. Everything with Griffin felt different though—like it was the first, every time.

Chapter Seven

"Nothing is so healing as the human touch."
-Bobby Fischer

My shift at Higher Yearning dragged on endlessly despite the steady stream of customers. I was excited and a little nervous to see Griffin after our transition into 'mine-dom' last night. I awoke this morning after a blissfully dream-free night of sleep. A quiet voice inside my head whispered that Griff might have reconsidered in the cold light of day. I should have known better. I hadn't been awake for five minutes when my cellphone chimed, announcing the arrival of a text message.

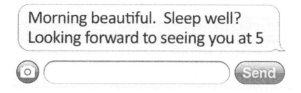

Morning beautiful. Sleep well?
Looking forward to seeing you at 5

Send

Was I broadcasting my inner thoughts on a frequency only he could hear? He answered questions before I asked them, addressed fears before I found the words to explain them, and always managed to be in the right place when I needed him. If it wasn't so damn convenient, I'd be freaked out.

I changed into my workout gear in the bathroom, returning to the front to grab Griffin's special coffee. I was about to ask Meg about her plans for the weekend when I heard my name called. I turned around to find Westly Black standing a few feet from me. I took a calming breath, not because I was panicking this time, but because my anger was rising fast.

"Mr. Black, what are you doing here?"

"I thought you might have reconsidered after our last meeting. I decided to save you the trouble of making a phone call."

"Nope, I haven't changed my mind and I won't. You're wasting your breath, which isn't really a problem because my boyfriend is going to be here any minute, and if he sees you again you'll no longer need to breathe. I suggest you leave. Now."

He didn't look scared. Was he nuts?

"The Varbeck family is willing to offer you two million dollars to focus on your recovery instead of a messy legal battle. It's a very generous offer, one I understand may be of some use to you at this time."

What the hell was he talking about? I didn't need their money, and even if I was piss-poor and living in a shelter, I still wouldn't take a dime of their bribe money. Did he think I was some materialistic heiress who would do anything for...Shit! Of course. I shouldn't be surprised, but I was. The only reason for him to presume I was desperate for money was if the Varbeck and Whitney family lawyers had conversed. That son of a bitch, formerly known as my father, was so concerned with protecting the Whitney name that he actually told the family of the man who raped me of my potential weakness (at least one he thought I had) so they could exploit it to the benefit of both families' interests.

"Mr. Black, you can tell your clients that I would rather survive on ramen noodles while living in a mold-coated, rat-infested, basement apartment in the seediest area of Long Island than take a dime of their blood money. I've bled enough thanks to the Varbeck family. And you can tell them that if I receive any more poetic threats, I will advise the District Attorney and the FBI."

"I have no idea what threats you're referring to, but I can't say I'm surprised. You are putting yourself in jeopardy, should you testify. I warned you the last time we spoke. Perhaps you should heed my warnings."

"There you go again, threatening me. Get the hell out and don't return. Griffin's truck just pulled into the lot, and as much as I would like to let him teach you a lesson, I'd rather him spend the night with me than in jail."

"Until we meet again, Miss Whitney," he said as he turned to leave.

"For your sake, I hope not," I shouted to his retreating back.

Thankfully, the asshat's car was parked in the opposite lot of Griffin's, so they narrowly avoided running into one another.

I shook the tension out of my body with spastic movements of my arms.

"Everything okay over there?" Griffin teased as he approached.

"Just shaking off the day," I said, not willing to risk a confrontation if Westly was still loitering in the parking lot.

"Bad day?"

"Nope, just a few unpleasant customers. Here you go," I said, handing him the beverage I had lovingly prepared.

"Thanks, Lo." He leaned in slowly and kissed my lips in gratitude. The kiss lingered, more than a simple peck, and expressed the depth of his appreciation.

"Mmm. You must really like coffee," I teased.

"Actually, I didn't like it until recently. It must be the barista making it; I can't seem to get enough."

"Look at you droppin' lines." I rolled my eyes, but secretly enjoyed the compliment. "Come on playa, don't want you going soft on me." I patted his concrete stomach and gasped dramatically. "One day and you're already letting yourself go."

His quiet growl drew a smile to my lips.

"Soft my ass," he said as he took my hand and slid it under his t-shirt, running my fingers along his clenched eight-pack. Never one to miss an opportunity, I took command of my hand and explored his abs more thoroughly before slithering my way up to pay equal attention to his defined pecs. Yum!

"Totally the hottest," Meg's voice declared behind me with conviction.

"And we weren't even trying," I retorted, my fingers continuing their journey, slowly descending over his bumpy terrain.

"That's what put him over the edge," she said with a hint of awe in her voice. I understood the feeling.

My naughty fingers had a mind of their own. Locating the top of that heavenly 'V,' they began to trace its inverted slope appreciatively.

"Enough of that," he said as he spun me around, "you are trouble."

He held me against him, my back to his front.

I pressed in closer and felt the indisputable proof of his desire against my back. Yep, despite everything he knew—every despicable detail—he still wanted me. Until that moment, I hadn't confessed, even to myself, the fear that any man who knew would see *that* before seeing me. Pressing into my back was evidence that this mountain of a man, one any woman would fall on her knees before, saw *me* and wanted *me*. It was a revelation and a reassurance that lightened a substantial burden within me. I was so excited by his excitement that I shimmied a little happy dance.

"For the love of God! Are you trying to kill me or just make me embarrass myself?" he half scolded, half pleaded.

It was evil, I knew it, but I bent my knees slowly, allowing my body to drift down his front before rising again equally slowly.

"Bye Meg," he croaked, before pivoting us both and then tossing me over his shoulder, quickly making his escape with his willing captive.

"Bye Meg," I echoed, offering a small wave that, in combination with my goofy smile, must have told her all she needed to know.

"Hottest ever," I heard her say to herself as we exited through the front door.

I stretched as far as my little body would allow, permitting me to paddle his ass.

"Girl, you keep this up, I'm tying you to the treadmill until you're too tired to blink."

I sucked in a harsh breath at his word choice at the precise moment he froze mid-step.

"Oh god, Lo-baby, I didn't mean...I would never...shit, I'm a fucking moron."

He reached up, gripped me gently as he lifted me off his shoulder, and lowered me to the ground, keeping a light hold on my waist for support.

His poor, albeit accidental word choice instigated a flash of memory I wouldn't wish on my worst enemy...except *him*. I didn't fly into a panic or dissolve into tears from the flashes anymore, but a tingling numbness engulfed my body and I trembled slightly.

He bent his knees, lowering himself until he reached eye level with me. Tucking a loose strand of hair behind my ear, he cupped my cheek with his warm hand.

"Forgive me."

I could hear the self-loathing in his voice. He attempted to step back, giving me the space he thought I needed, but I grabbed his face with both my hands to halt his movement.

He stared into my eyes, evidently waiting for my wrath, tears, panic...anything.

I leaned in and pressed a gentle, worshipful kiss on his lips. It wasn't sensual, rather a symbol of my appreciation and understanding. When I drew back, his eyes were wide and his lips slightly parted as if he had attempted to speak but words failed him. Now that was a first.

"Don't apologize. I'm glad you said it. The fact that it slipped through your perfect control means you are relaxing around me and forgetting to censor yourself."

He pulled me into his broad chest and hugged me fiercely, reinforcing his words with action. I nestled my head in that perfect indent beneath his chest, the spot where I knew I would lay my head and fall asleep to the beat of his heart when finally given the opportunity.

"Come on, beautiful, let's get to the gym. I'm feeling especially motivated to keep in shape after your earlier explorations."

"I can get on board with that plan," I teased, as he lifted me into his truck.

After our workout and my heavenly massage, we shared a quick dinner at a small Korean BBQ restaurant near my condo.

"We still on for tomorrow?" he asked.

"Are you kidding? I plan to fast tomorrow in honor of Maroni's...we're still going there, aren't we? I mean, I know it's impossible to get a reservation, so if we're going someplace else, that's fine," I backpedaled, realizing I sounded like a brat. It was unintentional; I was just so excited to try their famed cuisine.

"Don't get shy on me now," he chuckled, "I'm glad you're excited. We have reservations for 8:30 pm I'll pick you up at 7:45?"

I did a quick analysis. I was working until 6:30 tomorrow, but if I planned my outfit and painted my nails tonight, I could make it work.

"That sounds perfect."

After Griffin dropped me off at my car, I hurried home to plan my ensemble. I wanted to top my 'Grease' outfit from Thursday, which would be no small challenge but one I was up for.

My last customer cost me precious minutes of beautification time, much to my dismay. After he changed his drink order for the third time, I was prepared to toss him out on his ass. Luckily, Meg stepped in and took over so I could escape. Ev caught me as I was collecting my purse and wanted to chat about our plans tonight. I couldn't catch a freaking break.

"Are you ready for tonight?" Ev began what I could only assume was 'the talk.'

"If I get out of here now, I will be. I still haven't had a chance to get to the spa, so I need to shave my legs, which isn't going to happen if I don't leave now. Damn indecisive customers," I said, hoping she'd take the hint.

"Shaving your legs?"

"Yes, I decided on a dress. It is Maroni's, after all," I replied impatiently.

"*Just* your legs?"

And there it was. I didn't have time for this conversation.

"I'm taking your suggestion and doing a home-style Brazilian," I said and winked. Before she could object, I added, "Now I have a date to get ready for. I'm out of here."

After a quick exit, I unlocked my car and hopped in, about to pull out when I saw it—another piece of paper pinned beneath my wiper. You've got to be kidding me! Was this some kind of sick joke? I just wanted to get ready for my damn date in peace, but everything was trying to derail me.

I threw open my car door with more force than necessary and snatched the page from my windshield. Knowing I had to look, I sat down, buckled my belt, and unfolded the note.

STUBBORNNESS WILL LEAD YOU DOWN A PATH FROM WHICH THERE IS NO RETURN. RELENT WHILE THE CHOICE IS STILL YOURS.

He really had a flair for the dramatic. Could he be sending these from prison? The thought gave me chills—not the good kind. No, the prison must screen his outgoing mail. He must have enlisted help on the outside. I don't know which prospect was more disturbing. I briefly debated telling Hunter about the notes, but decided it would only play into *his* hand and I didn't want to worry everyone unnecessarily.

I stuffed the threat under my visor with the first and decided to ignore them, unless another arrived. For now, I had far more important matters to attend to.

I ran into the apartment like a bat out of hell and jumped into the shower before it had a chance to warm, causing me to shriek at the shock of cold water coursing down my back. I hoped Meg spit in that last guy's drink. I washed, exfoliated, and shaved in record time. If speed showering were an Olympic sport, I just brought home the gold—take that, Russia.

I slathered lotion on my body while drying my hair, no small feat, before working the best make-up magic I could in less than five minutes. I rolled the ends of my hair with a large-barrel curling iron before pulling the sides up in a 1940's pin-up style. I dashed into my room and glanced at the clock—ten minutes—I could do this. I carefully stepped into my dress before adding my emerald green Gucci crystal stilettos. Once my favorite emerald chandelier earrings were in place, I turned to survey my efforts in my full-length mirror—perfection. At first glance, my dress appeared to be a beautifully tailored Dior black lace pencil dress with a straight neckline that exposed my collarbones and cut across the cusp of my shoulders, appearing to hang on the edge as if by magic. It wasn't until the light caught my movement that a layer of emerald-colored silk peeped through, adding a subtle hint of color and elegance. But the showstopper was a deep 'V' that plunged all the way down to my lower back. It was designed to hold attention—or so I hoped.

I heard a knock and walked to the door as calmly as I could manage, considering my giddiness. I looked through the peephole to find a wall of chest that could only belong to Griffin. Releasing the security chain, I opened the door. My breath caught at the sight before me. Sweet baby Jesus, the man was the reason suits were invented. He wore a custom-made, black Dolce and Gabbana three-piece with a white shirt and emerald green silk tie.

As if that wasn't enough, in his hands he held a stunning bouquet of irises and green orchids. I had never seen its equal, exquisite and unique—the man, the suit, the flowers...all of it. He extended the flowers to me with a smile, which I returned.

"They reminded me of you," he said of the flowers. "You're always beautiful, but tonight you are beyond words."

"Thank you, they are the most beautiful flowers I have ever seen. You're setting the bar really high. How will you top this?" I teased, overwhelmed by him in the best of ways.

"Good thing I'm creative," he replied without concern.

"Just give me a moment to put these in water," I said.

I turned toward the kitchen when his sharp inhale reminded me of my backless state. Feeling wicked, I glanced over my shoulder with only a hint of a smile, my best bedroom-eyes trained on him.

"You like?" I asked coyly.

"Men have started wars over beautiful women throughout history, but none of them could rival you in that dress."

The man could teach a workshop on how to pay a compliment.

He laughed.

"I said that out loud, didn't I?"

He nodded.

"Did you want to come in? I'll only be a minute," I asked as I entered the kitchen and pulled out my favorite vase.

"I'll wait here. You are far too tempting, and I know how much you are looking forward to Maroni's."

"Suit yourself. Speaking of which, that is one hell of a suit. Really bringing your A-game tonight."

"Lo, with you, I always bring my A-game."

I finished arranging the flowers and set the vase on the dining table.

"Shall we?" I asked, excitement seeping into my words.

He offered me his arm, which I readily accepted, and wrapped his free hand on top of mine.

"Let's hope it lives up to your expectations. I'd hate to disappoint."

"You haven't yet...you've exceeded every expectation by miles."

We drove to the quaint village of Northport and entered the small bistro-style eatery. The décor was chic and modern, but still paid homage to the classic inspiration. The restaurant had several claims to fame, including a traditional Italian meatball that beat Bobby Flay in a TV 'Throwdown'. What interested me the most was their menu, or lack thereof. Diners tasted at least twenty bite-sized courses of the chef's choosing. Other than advising your server of any allergies or food restrictions, you sat back, shut up, and ate what they brought you. Unlimited wine accompanied each tasting. I loved food, all food, so this concept spoke directly to my foodie heart.

We were quickly seated and subsequently greeted by our friendly server. After providing us both a glass of Chianti, he asked if there were any food allergies.

"I don't eat seafood," Griffin advised him sheepishly.

The waiter rolled his eyes dramatically, muttering, "There's always one." He laughed and slapped Griffin on the back. "Don't worry, man, we'll take care of you, but you're missing out on some amazing food."

We chatted easily throughout our first three courses, which included mushroom soup, Kobe beef sliders, and short ribs. As the courses continued to flow from the kitchen, a few were unusual, such as the wild boar carpaccio, but most were an innovative twist on traditional dishes...the ordinary recreated as something more due to the quality of ingredients and culinary skills.

We talked for hours about trivial things like our favorite movies and music, as well as more revealing topics like families, goals for the future, and past relationships. When discussing my dating history, he growled—a growl that was so clear even he could not deny it—when I mentioned Robbie. Clearly, Griffin was less inclined to forgive my ex for his negligence in stopping the attacks at Hensley than I was—shocking, considering I wouldn't be granting my forgiveness to Robbie until pigs flew through an ice-coated Hell.

We had just been served our dessert and coffee—the quality of which would pass even Ev's formidable standards—when the conversation turned to my last session with Thia.

"I've already completed most of my homework assignments from last session. I still have to go to a movie alone before Thursday. Part of the build-comfort-when-alone-in-public campaign."

"What were your other assignments, if you don't mind me asking?"

"Because I'm so reserved I may not want to share the confidential details of my therapy session?"

"Point taken. You never have been one to hold back; I like that."

"I've been eating like a fiend," I said while gesturing to the table. "I even gained two pounds, which was one of my assignments."

"Still have several more to put back on that beautiful body."

I nodded, not taking offense to what was simply the truth. Five more pounds and I would be at my normal, healthy weight. Some might say I was ideal now, at least by fashion model standards. I like that Griffin preferred my healthy look to the 'someone get that girl a cheeseburger, stat' most men sought.

"Oh, I've also been petting the kitty every night. Not much success yet, but I'm getting closer to making her purr, I can feel it...pun intended."

My timing was all wrong. Griffin had just taken a sip of coffee as I shared my last homework assignment. He came close to spraying the mouthful across the table, but ended up choking instead. He coughed and sputtered for several minutes trying to clear the fluid from his airway and compose himself.

"Overshare?" I asked, my voice tinged with laughter.

"No, not at all. Unexpected and ill-timed, perhaps," he smiled, "but there is nothing you can't tell me. However, I am going to institute a rule that you give me warning before diving into talk of self-lovin' when food and drinks are present."

"Fair enough."

"I know I am going to regret asking this here," he said, more to himself than me, "but you haven't had satisfactory results yet?"

"No," I pouted. "Thia said a lot of women take months before they can find the elusive O again. I may kill myself if that's the case. I knew it would be a while before I would be physically, emotionally, or mentally prepared to do the featherbed jig—but to crash and burn when flying solo, that I was not prepared for."

"Just give it time, it'll come," he paused, eyes wide. "That was *not* an intentional pun."

I was feeling mischievous after a little wine and a lot of great conversation. "How can you be so sure she'll come back? She's been gone so long—maybe she forgot the way home."

Griffin groaned. "You are not playing nice, Lo. It'll happen when you're ready. Sometimes the pressure of 'trying,' especially when it's been a while, is the source of the problem. When the time is right, and you can relax, forget everything, and lose yourself, you'll fall off that cliff."

Our conversation moved on to less salacious topics and before I knew it, we were in the car on the way back to my apartment. I had offered to pay for dinner, but quickly dropped the matter when Griff shot me a look that said he was not to be argued with. It was rare that he completely shut me down without conversation, so I let it go. I didn't know the specifics of his finances but The Stop had to be making money hand over fist, and he was wearing a custom D&G suit.

It had been a spectacular night, the best date I'd ever had, and I wasn't ready for it to end. A rousing chorus of "I Could Have Danced All Night" from *My Fair Lady* was playing on repeat in my head. When I was with Griffin I could relax; I knew instinctively that he would fall on a grenade to protect me. I didn't have to worry about my safety with my own personal bodyguard in tow. But it was more than my physical well-being. He looked after my emotional and mental state with equal care. He was so in tune with my nonverbal cues that he steered us around dicey situations with ease. That being said, he didn't shy away from tough issues. He confronted them head-on, without judgment, offering tenderness and support when I needed it. He made me want to push myself to get better, not just for me, but for him too.

An intriguing idea fluttered through my consciousness. Could I do it or would I ruin everything we had built thus far? The prospect of losing him terrified me. It was too early to use words like 'love' or 'forever,' regardless of what my crazy heart may have to say on the matter. What the hell? Nothing ventured, nothing gained. I needed to push my boundaries, stretch my comfort zone.

"Hey, Griff, I have a crazy idea, but I need your help."

"That's one hell of a lead in," he said, making a small gesture with his hand for me to continue.

"I want to try something and it will probably blow up in my face, but I need to do it. Will you help me?"

"We're not having sex tonight, Lo. No matter what you think, say, or do, it is not happening. I have waited too long for this chance to fuck it up by jumping into bed before you're ready."

"Okay," I drew out the word. "That wasn't where I was going, but good to know you have strong opinions on the matter. When exactly will sex be permissible?"

"Are you ready to have sex right now?"

"No," I said immediately. I wanted him, he set me on fire every time I thought of him, but I wasn't ready to dive headfirst into those shark-infested waters...yet. I needed to ease back into intimacy with a man. Not just any man...this man.

"Then there is no reason for us to discuss it right now. Even discussing the possibility or a timeline will add unnecessary pressure. It will happen when it happens—when the time is right. When the time arrives, you will be so ready there will be no question or doubt in your mind—I promise you."

"No sex tonight, we agree. Will you help me if it doesn't involve making the beast with two backs?"

"Yes."

"I want to try sleeping with you, as in lying in bed with my head on your chest in the dark as we both sleep. I honestly don't know if I can handle it. I may freak out or have a nightmare sometime during the night, but I want to try...with you."

"Lo-baby, that I can do for you. There is nothing I would love more than to have you in my arms all night. If it doesn't work, I'll crash on the floor or the couch."

"Thank you," I whispered, suddenly struck by his level of devotion, his willingness to be what I needed. "I don't deserve you."

"No, you don't—you deserve so much better than me, but no one will ever care for you the way I do. There is nothing I wouldn't do for you."

"Then we will agree to disagree because I think you're Mary-friggin-Poppins...practically perfect."

"Just what every guy is dying to hear—I'm an umbrella-toting chick with a hat fetish," he said. "I'm not perfect. I have my flaws, my weaknesses. I'm human."

"So you say. I'm still convinced you have some tights and a cape hiding in your closet at home."

"Nope, just a man. No superpowers, and *definitely* no tights."

We arrived at my apartment and headed upstairs, hand-in-hand. When we entered, the apartment was quiet. Ev and Hunter were already asleep. Good, that would delay the inquisition until morning.

"I'm going to go brush my teeth. Be right back," I said.

Dang, I was nervous. More nervous than my first time, and we were only sleeping together. I brushed my teeth and removed my make-up before sneaking into my room to find pajamas. I heard Griffin walk down the hall to the bathroom and smiled for no good reason. I didn't have a drawer full of flannel pants and t-shirts like most girls for my night wear. I approached sleep attire with the same fashionista spirit I did my waking clothes. I decided on a navy La Perla chemise with a coral lace appliqué that added interest and accentuated my waist. The soft jersey knit was cut like a v-neck tank and fell to mid-thigh, covering me enough that it could be worn in public without being indecent. It could pass as an easy spring dress or conservative beach cover-up, but knowing I was wearing it to bed—a bed Griffin was also going to be in—made it feel slightly scandalous.

I drew a fortifying breath and headed back to the den to get Griffin. His suit jacket, vest, and tie were draped over the arm of the couch, and his shirt was unbuttoned at the neck, sleeves rolled up. He looked phenomenal. His eyes traveled the length of me, and the slowness with which he paced his examination made me feel ten feet tall. He rose from the couch and ambled toward me, but his body held too much tension, contradicting his slow, casual stride.

"This," he waved his hand to indicate my sleepwear, "is what I imagined you would sleep in, but my imaginings didn't do you justice." He took a step closer. "Any second thoughts? You know you can change your mind at any time; I'm content to sleep on the couch. Are you sure you want to do this, Lo?"

I nodded, suddenly timid.

He took another step. "This is big, sleeping next to someone for the first time. I don't want you to be upset or feel guilty if you need to kick me out. I get it. Just say the word and I come out here, no questions asked, no apologies needed. Nothing will change, the way I feel about you won't change. Do you understand?"

I nodded again with more conviction. I believed him...every word. I extended my hand to him and he closed the remaining distance to take what I offered. As we entered the bedroom, I released his hand to remove the pillows and turn down the comforter.

"Which side?" he asked softly.

"Do you mind taking the side by the door? I just—"

"Absolutely."

He stepped around me, about to climb into the bed when I noticed he was still in his slacks and dress shirt. Duh! He didn't have any clothes to change into. Having him wear only his unders was a temptation better left uncourted tonight, but I didn't want him to be uncomfortable—or so thoroughly covered up.

"Wait. You can't sleep in your suit."

"I'll be fine, Lo."

"Let me see if Hunter has any clothes in the dryer."

I scurried out of the room before he could object. I found a pair of blue athletic shorts that would work and headed back to my bedroom, anxious and excited. I "accidentally" forgot to grab a shirt for him. When I entered, he was surveying my room. I wondered what he saw. The calming green of the walls with the dark wood bedroom set was not overtly feminine, but elegant and soothing. I tossed the shorts at him. He caught them effortlessly, although I would have sworn he was completely engrossed in his study.

He held up the shorts and nodded to himself in approval. His eyes returned to mine and he waited expectantly. If he was looking for a shirt to come sailing through the air next, he would be waiting a long time...like forever. He raised his eyebrows, questioning. I mimicked his gesture, but there was a dare in my response.

"I guess I'll go change," he said as he moved toward the door.

I didn't want him to change in another room. I wanted him to strip in front of me, exposing himself physically the same way I would be exposing myself emotionally. There was a strong possibility that I would not make it through the night without incident. The reality was easier to accept when imagining he too had taken a risk. And, yes—I wanted to see more of his impeccable body, a fringe benefit.

"Wait!" I said, louder than was necessary in the quiet room. "You can change here...please."

"Do you promise to close your eyes?" he teased.

"Hell no."

He chuckled before muttering something that sounded an awful lot like, "Glad I didn't go commando." Well, that made one of us.

"You really want me to strip for you?"

I nodded.

"Will it make tonight easier for you?"

I nodded again, although I was sure having a half-naked Griffin in my bed would be a double-edged sword.

He said nothing more. Holding my gaze, he raised his hands to the first button on his shirt and slowly pushed it through the hole. He continued releasing every button slowly, revealing more of his muscular chest with each liberation. His eyes never left me, but mine drifted lower with each newly displayed inch. When the final button was undone, he flicked the sides of his shirt so it parted widely, bearing his entire upper body for my inspection. After allowing me several vertical passes, he unrolled each cuff before permitting the shirt to fall down his arms, pooling on the floor. He stood perfectly still, letting me look my fill and assessing my reaction. If he was concerned the sight of his shirtless body would be a trigger, he was dead wrong. The only thing he was triggering currently was my libido.

I realized he was putting on a show for me, pushing himself to disrobe in a way that was enticing and uncharacteristic of a man. It was my own personal strip show. No music or cheesy dancing, no gyrations or hip rolls, but it was a performance nonetheless—all to give me what I needed.

His fingers grasped the waist of his suit pants and slowly slid along the top until they met in the middle where he flicked the hidden clasp open. Unable to feign nonchalance any longer, I trained my stare to his fingers with intense scrutiny. It's a wonder his pants didn't burst into flames.

His fingers pinched the tab of the zipper and he waited...and waited...and waited. My eyes flew to his, prepared to demand he continue, but my protest died when I saw his knowing smirk. I heard the first click of the zipper's teeth. Bastard! I was missing it. Visually swan diving back to the action, I tracked the painfully slow descent of the slider. He then moved his hands to his hips, allowing his pants to gape open, offering only a hint of black cotton. This must be how men felt in Regency England when catching a glimpse of ankle. What was before me was significantly less than a bathing suit would expose, but it felt scandalous. I nodded to him, hoping to prompt action without shifting my gaze one millimeter. Finally, his thumbs hooked into the waistband and shoved. Like magic, the pants were gone and Griffin stepped out of them, freeing his feet.

He stilled for my inspection, God bless him. Black boxer briefs molded to his hard thighs and lean waist, revealing an astonishing bulge. Oh my!

He tried to stifle a laugh but failed. Oops. Guess I had said that aloud.

I raised a finger in the air and twirled it, indicating my desire to review his backside.

He complied immediately, presenting himself shamelessly. His back was a sight to behold, the breadth of his shoulders greater than the span of my arms elbow to elbow, tapering down to a trim waist. The highlight—by far—was his glorious ass, twin globes of firm muscle that reminded me of ripe honeydew melon halves, and I *loved* honeydew.

Compelled by a longing stronger than any I'd ever experienced, I walked to him silently. I skimmed the tips of my fingers across his shoulders, between his shoulder blades, down his middle back, and over the diamond indent of his lower back until I reached the waistband of his boxer briefs. I followed their path horizontally across his body, around his sides, and across his ripped abdomen, stopping when my fingertips touched and my arms were wrapped around him. I flattened my palms against his stomach and slid them upward, settling them beneath his pecs, over his heart. I laid my head against his back and listened to his ragged breaths. His hands rose to cover my own, warmth seeping into my body at every point we touched. Something was happening that I couldn't explain. We were communicating without words, connecting on the deepest level possible—soul deep, heart deep. We stood like that for long minutes, unmoving.

I was preparing myself to release him when he turned and swept an arm beneath my knees, lifting me off my feet. My arms automatically ringed his neck as he carried me to the bed and laid me down gently, tucking my legs beneath the comforter before pulling it up to cover my shoulders. He then walked toward my door and shut off the light before returning to the side of the bed. After a deep breath, he slipped in, close enough that I could feel his body heat, but not touching. I knew this was for my benefit, but it hurt—I wanted him to touch me without concern plaguing him. I wanted to feel his bare flesh against mine. I craved this man, a growing need that teetered on the edge of irrational.

I rolled toward him, landing with my leg draped over his and snuggled myself into his side with my hand on his chest. I tilted my head back to look at him, his masculine beauty stark in the soft moonlight.

I moistened my lips and watched as he unconsciously did the same.

"Kiss me," I invited softly.

He curled his arm, raising me partially onto his chest and guided my lips to his. This kiss was different than any we had shared before. It was passionate and seductive. Griffin had been holding out on me, and I would have to remember to be peeved about that tomorrow because I was entirely too busy to be concerned about it in the present. His lips and tongue explored mine with expertise. The man didn't kiss, he possessed and devoured.

I entwined my tiny fingers with his as my leg twisted around him, trapping him. I wanted more contact; I was quickly becoming addicted to his taste and touch. His muffled groan was the first clue of what I was doing. Self-awareness dawned slowly—I was languidly rocking myself against him, my body instinctively seeking stimulus. I gasped, shocked by my mindless actions and impulse to continue. And living in the moment, I did. I rotated and rocked my hips against him until I was panting, so close but not able to fall over the edge. He never stopped kissing me or caressing my back, but his hands remained in the 'safe' zone—not where I *needed* them.

I pulled back enough to catch his eye, knowing he would need to see my sincerity.

"Touch me, please. I can't...I need you to get there, I can't do it on my own."

He read the truth in my eyes, in my body. Without further discussion, he rolled us so I was on my back pressed against him while he lay on his side, his elbow cradling my head. His fingers traced my face tenderly before continuing to follow the outline of my lips. The calloused tips blazed a trail down my neck and between my breasts, where they paused as if debating an unplanned visit. I raised my hips, telling him wordlessly where I needed him.

The journey resumed, making a loop around my bellybutton before stopping an inch above where I wanted him. My chemise and panties diluted the potency of his touch as he teased me, drawing shapes and tracing the line of my pantie. Growing restless, I spread my thighs further apart, the equivalent of a written invitation by bedroom standards.

"Patience, Lo," he whispered into my ear as he nibbled the sensitive lobe.

He was asking for something I could no longer give. Desperate to spur him onward, I grabbed his wrist and forced his hand lower. Ah, yes, there...I needed him there. His skilled fingers strummed me like a guitar, causing me to moan appreciatively. I rocked with his rhythm seeking more pressure, which he immediately granted. He took my mouth, demanding everything, giving the same in return. I was so damn close, but the thin barrier of silk was in the way. I pulled my hands from his hair and grabbed the thin lace at my hips, pulling until a tear echoed through the room. Skin met skin and I sighed happily. He proceeded to prove that his skills with a guitar translated to other more carnal pursuits and I loved every minute of it—but still I couldn't get *there*.

"More. I need more," I said in frustration.

"Lo baby, relax. It'll happen, just let it be."

"More...please," I begged pitifully, desperate for release and proof I was not permanently broken.

He captured my mouth with unparalleled seduction as he slid his fingers lower and entered me easily. I moaned loudly, lucky his mouth trapped the sound.

Within seconds I was skating on the razor thin edge, my hips moving erratically, controlled only by the pressure of his palm against my clit and his fingers exploring me. And then it happened...I fell over the edge, plummeting into a sea of electricity, wave after wave crashing over me. The release was as emotional as it was physical. Tears of joy and relief coursed down my cheeks as sounds of pleasure slipped from my lips. He coaxed every last wave of bliss from me until every muscle in my body had contracted countless times.

When I was spent and limp, he rolled to his back, taking me with him and settling me on his chest. His arms wrapped around me, cuddling tenderly. He kissed the top of my head repeatedly while stroking my back soothingly.

"You," I said, suddenly aware of what must be a very painful situation.

"Are content to hold you like this for the rest of the night," he said.

"But—"

"No, I'm good. Watching you find it was the sexiest thing I've ever seen. To be the one who brought you there was fucking amazing."

I was ready...I wanted to touch him, to see him lose himself the way I had. I made several attempts to reciprocate, but the wily fox would break out a new trick to distract me until I could no longer think, only feel, leaving him forgotten. But I was determined to take the next step—it was time for me to make a new friend and offer a hands-on 'how do ya do.'

I kissed him while stroking his chest, shoulders, face—anywhere I could get my hands except my ultimate goal—until he was lost in my ministrations. I could taste victory.

Not giving him time to think, I snaked my hand beneath the elastic waistband that served as the boundary to our previous no-go zone and took hold of my target. Mother of...I couldn't wrap my tiny hand all the way around him. I'll give him this, the man was proportional; huge in every sense of the word. Undeterred, I firmed my grip and stroked him purposefully, causing him to groan into my mouth. He pressed his head further into the mattress to gain the space necessary to speak.

"Lo baby, you don't have to—"

I ignored him, continuing my up-down slide, increasing the speed and pressure based on his response to find the perfect stroke. My mouth traveled to his ear, a spot I discovered drove him wild, and sucked his lobe between my lips, gently biting and teasing.

"But I want to. Give me what I want, Griff," I whispered into his ear seductively.

His entire body shuddered, his response unintelligible thanks to the addition of my free hand.

Within minutes the last thread of his control broke, his hips joining my motion. With a final groan, his body tensed and my name slipped from his lips.

When he was once again coherent, he kissed me softly, and I could feel his grin against my lips.

"Awfully pleased with yourself, aren't you?" he asked, humor in his voice.

"Hell yeah. I earned this smile."

"You did."

We fell silent as the weight of sleep pressed down upon me. My eyes closed and I drifted off to sleep as Griffin hummed me a lullaby.

Chapter Eight

*"Children begin by loving their parents;
after a time they judge them; rarely, if ever,
do they forgive them." -Oscar Wilde*

I woke slowly, sunlight making the inside of my eyelids glow. I was incredibly comfortable and didn't want to get up—and warm, I was exceptionally warm. I curled the fingers of my right hand into my bed, but my bed was not a bed, it was a person. Griffin.

I gasped loudly, and the warm chest beneath me rumbled with laughter.

"You...you're still here," I exclaimed, crossing my hands on his chest before resting my chin on top, a huge smile painted across my face.

"I am. Good morning, beautiful," he said with humor.

"Holy shit! I slept all freaking night," I said in stunned appreciation, "and I didn't have a nightmare. Not. A. One."

"Nope. You slept like a baby, even drooled a little."

"I did not," I said, trying to subtly check his chest for wet spots.

He wiped the corner of my lips with his thumb. I launched myself at him, kissing him like he was mine, which of course he was—morning breath be damned. When we finally broke apart, wicked thoughts filled my mind.

"Oh no you don't. I know that look. As tempting as you are, I don't need Hunter barging in with the safety off."

"I can be quiet," I said, as I slid his thigh between my legs, getting started without him.

In the end, I got my way *and* I was quiet—it was an extra happy wake-up call for us both. Afterward, I left Griffin in my room to dress and headed to the kitchen with a goofy smile on my face to pour a cup of coffee. I popped as many Eggos in the toaster oven as I could fit before joining Huntleigh at the dining table.

"Good morning," Ev said, eyeing me suspiciously, unable to discern the source of my Disney-level good mood.

"I slept amazing last night, best sleep I've ever had," I answered her unspoken question.

"That's fantast—"

"And I had an orgasm!" I said, entirely too loudly. "Actually, scratch that...I had two orgasms!"

Hunter choked on his sip of coffee and Ev pounded on his back casually, accustomed to my unexpected overshares.

"I'm not going to 'too much information' you this time because I know what a big deal this is. Was it as good as you remembered?"

"Better... I swear I couldn't feel my toes for like ten minutes."

"Holy hell, I'm still here," Hunter objected.

Ev and I both waved him off.

"I'm so happy for you. You must be relieved. You didn't say much, but I knew you were really worried," Ev said.

"I was terrified I would never get it back. I swear when G—"

"Morning, everybody," Griffin said as he entered, completely unaware of what he had just walked into.

"You've got to be kidding me," Hunter lamented. "I don't need to know this shit."

"Griffin, I don't know if I should punch you or kiss you," Ev said.

Griffin looked completely lost.

"He's getting punched if you kiss him," Hunter cautioned.

"Oh, by the way, Griff stayed over last night," I stated the obvious.

"Yeah, got that," Hunter grumbled, clearly wishing he was elsewhere.

I moved to my man's side and quickly explained his less-than-ideal timing. He shrugged before kissing my lips and heading toward the kitchen. "Need coffee, Lo?" Griffin asked solicitously, unfazed.

"No thanks, I've got one but you can check the toaster oven. I threw some Eggos in there for us."

"Mmm... breakfast too. Just when I thought this morning couldn't get any better."

Griff emerged from the kitchen with a heaping plate of waffles, which he rested carefully on the table before sitting down. I moved to sit next to him, but he pulled me onto his lap—a much better seat, in my opinion. I had just taken my first bite when there was a knock at the door.

"I'll get it," I said with a mouth full of food.

I looked through the peephole to find a uniformed officer on the other side of the door. Shit! What now? I released the security chain and opened the door.

"Samantha Whitney?" he asked formally.

Griffin was at my back and Hunter at my side before I could respond.

"Special Agent Hunter Charles, FBI. How can I help you, officer?"

The young policeman looked extremely uncomfortable.

"I'm sorry to bother you on a Sunday morning, sir. I'm Deputy Sherriff Lienmieter from the Suffolk County Sherriff's office. I'm afraid I have to serve Miss Whitney with a Warrant of Eviction. She has until Wednesday to appeal the judgment or vacate the premises."

Hunter snatched the paperwork from the man's hands and scanned it.

"This states that Miss Whitney failed to appear at her eviction hearing, but she was never informed of any such hearing."

"Then she has grounds for appeal. I suggest she obtains an Order to Show Cause, which will stay the eviction until a hearing takes place. I'm sorry, Special Agent Charles. If there was anything I could do...this came from the top."

Hunter nodded as the Deputy Sherriff left us. When the door was firmly closed, I walked to the couch dazed and threw myself down in a heap. Griffin followed, sitting beside me. I wasn't falling apart, but I was definitely in shock. Hunter and Ev joined us and we sat in silence as Hunter read the details of the warrant. Before speaking a word to any of us, he flipped open his phone and sent a text message.

"Okay, here's the situation," he began calmly, obviously in professional-Hunter mode. "Your parents managed to schedule an eviction hearing without your knowledge and won by default when you didn't show. You can appeal the eviction if you have grounds. Is your name on the deed?"

"I assumed so. I am positive it's on the title to the car because I saw it when I renewed the registration and updated my address. I don't recall ever seeing the deed for the apartment, but it was given to me as a gift more than four years ago. I recall them saying something about write-offs and tax benefits once I graduated college. Maybe they hadn't transferred the actual deed to me. Can they really do this?"

"They never actually gave you the gift if your name isn't on the deed. You'll have to get an attorney to represent you and request a copy, but I'm not optimistic." Hunter sighed. "Sam, it took a lot of clout to pull this off. The Sherriff's Department doesn't usually handle eviction warrants on the weekends. You should fight this, but I think you need to prepare yourself for the prospect of losing. At the very least, you can delay the eviction for a few weeks."

"No," I said firmly. "If this really isn't *my* apartment, then I don't want to stay here. We'll find another place. I have money. I'll hire a lawyer to investigate if I have grounds, but I am not going to stay here if I don't have a chance of winning the case. No sense in delaying the inevitable and indebting myself to them further."

Griffin's arm wrapped around my waist and squeezed me, conveying his approval. He understood my need to sever these ties with my family and the importance of only fighting battles that could be won.

"I hear you, but I don't think you should sign a lease and tie yourself to another apartment until you have a clearer picture of your legal options," Ev said.

"You'll move in with me," Hunter said, suddenly very pleased, "...both of you. My apartment is only one bedroom, but I'll buy a pull-out couch today for Sam. It's not a permanent solution, but I was planning to buy a house sometime this year anyway—this is as good a time as any to start our search. It won't fix the issue immediately, but...it could become our permanent solution," he said, looking at Ev as if the sun had just risen after a year of night.

"Did you just ask me to move in with you?" Ev asked, shocked.

"This wasn't how I was planning to ask you, but my plans never seem to come to fruition the way I expect when you're involved." He held her face between his hands and kissed her lips once with devotion in his eyes. "Everleigh, I love you with all my heart. I want to fall asleep with you every night and wake up with you each morning. I want to fight with you about who used the last of the toilet paper and didn't replace the roll. I want to cook you breakfast for dinner when we get sick of take-out. I want to see your clothes hanging in the closet next to mine when I get dressed. I want to know that we are both equally tied to the place we call 'home.' Will you move in with me, buy a house, and make a home with me—our home?"

Tears filled my eyes; I was so touched by his heartfelt request. His every word expressed he wanted her by his side every day. She deserved this, the unwavering love of a good man who knew her value, one who saw her flaws and accepted them as a part of her without trying to change them.

She kissed him softly as she whispered "yes" against his lips.

I was so glad I was here to see them take the next step in their relationship, but it reaffirmed a concern that had been flitting through my conscience with increasing frequency. They needed their space, time alone as a couple. I couldn't have made it through those first two months after TPC without them by my side. They were self-sacrificing, gracious, supportive, and loving every step of the way—deciding together to make my recovery their priority. I didn't believe their relationship suffered from that choice, but it must have been difficult for a new couple that just wanted to get lost in one another. It was time for me to repay their charity by freeing them from the Sam-shaped cage in which they had willingly sealed themselves.

"Actually, I've been thinking you two need your space. I can never thank you enough for all you've done for me...but I'm better now, I don't need babysitters anymore. Save the money on the couch and put it toward the house. I'm going to stay in a hotel until the apartment situation gets sorted out and then I'll decide what to do. I may just let them have this place either way—rid myself of the reminder."

Hunter nodded, easily accepting my decision, but Ev looked conflicted.

"And if I need you, I'll come crash on the couch for the night...just not every night. Have you even considered where I would organize my wardrobe in Hunter's apartment? You'd both be forced to store your clothes in the kitchen if I moved in, because I sure as hell would be taking over all the closet space," I joked, hoping to lighten the mood. "It's time to cut the apron strings, fly from the nest—and you two need an empty nest to make the tree shake without concern of an audience."

Ev nodded, but I could see she was feeling the same way I was. As happy as she was to be moving in with Hunter, it would mark the end of an era. We had been attached at the hip most of our lives but now we were growing up—not growing apart, but growing. It was exciting and a little bit sad.

"It was bound to happen at some point," I assured her. "You found your penguin, your mate for life. It's time for you to start building your life with Hunter and time for me to live on my own and be independent. I need to prove to myself that I can do it, so one day I can find my own nest-mate."

Griffin leaned into my side, his lips kissing the base of my neck and gliding up to my ear.

"Do you have any particular Big Bird in mind to join you in the nest?"

I shivered from the warmth of his breath against the shell of my ear. Hot damn, the man could even make Sesame Street sound sexy.

"Maybe, someday," I answered coyly.

"There's no reason to waste your money on a hotel and I'm not sure if it is the safest option at the moment," Griffin said, his concern evident. "I have a guest room and my house isn't far from here. You can store your furniture and whatever else you need in my garage—you'd have to arrange for a storage unit if you stay in a hotel."

Hmm...stay with Griffin? Not live with him like Ev and Hunter were talking about, but still. Staying with him for a period of time, seeing him every day—the idea had its merits. My only hesitation was that our romantic relationship was only beginning; I didn't want him to get sick of me. On the flip side, it would certainly let me know early on if we had the potential to go the long haul. Plus, I would feel safer knowing a big, strong man was in the house with me, even if he wasn't armed like Hunter. I didn't want to admit it, but living alone scared me slightly—I needed to do it, to push myself. However, the prospect of having Griffin's muscles handy was appealing in the short term, in more ways than one. Either way it would be temporary; he wasn't asking me to move in with him. I teetered on the edge of decision.

"Did I mention the guest room has a walk-in closet that's bigger than your bathroom here?" Griffin asked with a victorious smile.

"Sold!" I said, letting him believe it was the closet that closed the deal and not the fact that he knew how much the closet would sway me.

"Okay," Hunter said, "Sam, why don't you work the legal angle and get all the information before making a final decision about whether or not to fight? In the meantime, you girls can focus on packing up the apartment so you're ready to move into your temporary homes on Wednesday."

Ev and I nodded our agreement.

"Let's go get some boxes for them, I have my pick-up," Griffin said to Hunter.

"Good plan."

After the guys left, Ev and I remained in the den, lost in thought.

"Congrats," I said genuinely. "It's bittersweet. I am thrilled for you and Hunter, but I'm gonna miss living with you. Lord only knows what fashion crimes you'll commit without my supervision."

"True. You'll have to come by frequently to make sure I haven't stocked up on flannel and tees."

"I just might."

It was hard to believe this phase of our lives was ending and we would no longer be roommates. Constant companions, we had lived together for over four years.

Ev rearranged our work schedule to give us both time to focus on packing. The apartment might not have been large, but we had acquired a massive amount of stuff in our time there. We decided to store the furniture in Griffin's garage since Hunter's current apartment didn't have the space and I was currently without a permanent address.

Griffin's house was not the bachelor pad I expected; he had a 'grown-up' house. A well-maintained colonial with three bedrooms, two-and-a-half bathrooms, and an office greeted me upon arrival. It was an impressive house with modern updates in high-quality materials, and was both clean and comfortable. My eyes swept over the heavy wooden tables, soft leather couches, and masculine bedroom set. He had all the requisite man technology like a huge flat-screen TV, surround sound stereo, gaming systems, you name it. The pictures on the walls hinted at the man who lived there and I couldn't help but smile—he had a collection of musical instrument prints, abstract in black and white with pops of color. There were others with recognizable travel destinations, and various pub-themed posters and signs decorated the walls of the office.

I cooked an extravagant dinner for my first night; field green salad with goat cheese and apple walnut dressing, Texmati rice with barley and rye berries, and zesty chicken piccata coated in seasoned homemade breadcrumbs with grilled vegetables.

"Sam, if you cook like this a couple nights a week, I'll never let you leave," Griffin said while devouring his third helping of chicken.

"I love to cook; it's a great stress reliever. Ev always joked that she ate best when I was conflicted."

"Where did you learn?"

"I spent a lot of time in the kitchen growing up. The chef at my parents' house was phenomenal and always happy to teach me."

Over dinner, I learned Griffin had worked at the family restaurant since he was fifteen and began bartending at eighteen. He carefully saved his money like a squirrel collecting acorns for winter. After graduating from Hensley University, he used his nest egg to purchase this house and handled the renovations himself. He shared his plans to manage the bar his parents had left him when they retired to Florida and open a small private practice that would be client driven. He wanted to provide help even to those who were unable to pay.

As I listened to him, I was struck by how much responsibility he shouldered. He obviously loved running The Stop and it provided a lucrative salary, but I was proud he had followed his calling as a therapist and also managed the family business he loved.

As Griffin shared the details of his life, his passions and dreams, my admiration for him deepened. I was surprised to find he could relate to the conflict with my parents from personal experience—the frustration felt when parents attempt to control your life and dictate its course. He was a man anyone would be proud to call friend; a man any woman would be honored to call hers.

After dinner we snuggled on the couch, watched a movie, and fell asleep after an exhausting day of moving. Neither of us woke until daylight spilled through the sliding glass doors off the family room.

As wonderful as it was to spend the night in Griffin's arms, it was too soon be moving in together. I wanted our relationship to have a fighting chance, and moving in together too soon could be the kiss of death. I felt like I needed to have my own place in order to maintain my self-worth. Perhaps if I hadn't been attacked, I would be more willing to throw caution to the wind. But I needed to prove to myself that I was strong enough to survive on my own before I could make a full commitment to any person.

I spent the day on the phone with my lawyer and financial advisor, attempting to sort out my options. The guest room Griffin offered me was lovely and I took my time hanging my clothes in the large walk-in closet. I did not intend to stay forever, but I would not live out of boxes and suitcases while I was there. At bedtime, an unintentional stand-off ensued. I was waiting for an invite to his room and he was waiting for my cue as to whether I was ready to try using him as my body pillow again. We stood in the hallway, straining to find random bits of dialogue, trying to figure out what the other wanted. When I asked who should be responsible for buying toilet paper, Griffin took action, sweeping me into his arms and carrying me into the master suite. I had never been so grateful to toilet tissue.

I continued to wait on news from my attorney, but my initial hopes for an easy resolution were dwindling. I found myself happy at the prospect of losing the apartment that tied me to my parents and looking forward to finding my own place, one purchased with money not associated with them.

In the meantime, it was strange to live with someone new and to learn their schedule and habits. Griffin was a considerate roommate—he would switch my clothes from the washer to the dryer, make me coffee in the mornings, and even brought me dinner several nights a week. I cooked many nights to express my gratitude for his hospitality.

However, it wasn't all sunshine and roses. Griffin was tidy but had several quirks that irritated me the first few days. For reasons I was unable to comprehend, he always managed to leave a pair of dirty socks on the floor in the family room at the end of the night. It was baffling! The man never left a glass on the table or a plate in the sink, but his discarded socks greeted me daily. I also learned Griffin despised the smell of nail polish remover, forcing me to relocate my frequent nail polish changes into the bathroom, instead of in the den while watching TV.

Ev and I would call or text one another when our men exhibited odd domestic behavior. Living together was a rousing success for Huntleigh, despite the fact that Hunter perpetually left his discarded clothes *next to* the hamper instead of putting them in their target destination. Ev even tried leaving the lid open and sliding the receptacle a foot to the right. She theorized Hunter had been throwing clothes from across the room and consistently missed the basket, but her attempt was a failure.

Ev also managed to push a few of Hunter's buttons. My favorite was when she rearranged the kitchen to place her coffee supplies in the optimal location, moving his pots and pans to a high cabinet across the room. There was also an ongoing debate about where the toothpaste tube should be squeezed—Ev, a chronic middle squeezer, and Hunter, a resolute bottom squeezer. I believe they secretly loved having new material for their ongoing verbal warfare—it was their weird form of foreplay.

On nights when Griffin wasn't working late at The Stop, I would sleep with him in the master suite, where he continued to prove that our first night together was no fluke. The man worked my body like he had written the owner's manual. Each time was better than the last and I was able to reach the big hell*O* more quickly, unless Griffin decided to tease me and make me wait for it. He was commanding and playful in bed, and I was seriously considering taking our fun all the way to home base. I desperately wanted to, but I was still afraid of not being able to complete the act. Even though I knew he would understand, it was a possible failure I was still afraid to try.

A week after I moved into Griffin's house, my attorney finally called with the news that the deed to the apartment was exclusively in my father's name. He advised I could fight for joint ownership since the apartment was a gift, but it would come down to judicial decision, which would likely fall in my parents' favor since they originally purchased the property. What he didn't say was that I was likely to be perceived as a greedy brat who was trying to mooch off my parents' affluence. If that was not enough to dissuade me, the fact that my father played golf with most of the sitting judges in Suffolk and Nassau Counties was. I was officially homeless. I had a place to stay, thanks to Griffin, but it wasn't a permanent solution.

After our call, I immediately contacted a real estate agent and provided details of what I was looking for and my budget. I was anxious to find my own home as soon as possible. Since I had been at Griffin's, I found myself imagining what it would be like to truly live there. Despite knowing it was the wrong decision, the idea of staying forever was a temptation and if I didn't move out soon, I may never do so. I was so comfortable in his house with him it felt...well, it felt like home. I knew I wasn't ready to play house yet; I still had too much to prove to myself. So I used my day off the following week to tour several townhouse condos. Griffin tried to hide his disappointment, but I could tell he wanted me to stay. I fell in love with one property, but the seller had tentatively accepted an offer, pending the buyer's mortgage approval. I was disappointed, but we scheduled several more viewings later in the week.

Two weeks after I moved in, Griffin went to my car to grab the sunglasses he had forgotten. I was on the couch reading the latest Kristen Ashley novel when I heard a very loud, very angry "what the fuck" seep through the front window. The front door slammed against the wall in the foyer as Griffin called my name.

Griffin could never scare me; I trusted him with my life. But I had to admit the sound of him stomping around was intimidating.

"In here," I called, forcing my voice to remain casual, as if I didn't notice his dramatic entry.

He strode into the room with purpose, arm extended before him, something clutched in his hand.

"Would you like to explain what the hell these are and why I had no clue they existed?"

Uh-oh. After taking a quick inventory, I concluded he had found the weekly threats I had stuffed under my visor—the ones I'd neglected to mention to him...or anyone for that matter. I weighed my options, calculating my most promising method of response before deciding on humor.

"They're poetic, aren't they? I mean, he's no Emerson, but he has a definitive style."

"You think this is funny?" he asked softly, the effect louder than any shout could ever have been.

"Not funny, ha ha, but insane funny, yeah. You gotta laugh, right?"

"No, I do not *gotta laugh*," he said through clenched teeth. "I can't believe you are turning this into a joke. These are blatant threats against you...your life." He paused to flip through the six wrinkled papers clutched in his fist and handed one to me.

THE WAVES OF SOUND ARE SILENCED WHEN UTTERED FROM THE OCEAN FLOOR.

It was the most recent threat, found on my windshield when I left for work yesterday morning. Reading it now, I could see why Griffin was upset. I hadn't mentioned its arrival, and this was the most explicit threat of the lot. Heck, I was upset by them too. I had intended to mention them to Hunter and Griffin when I received the third note, but with the move and house-hunting, it had slipped my mind. Okay, that is not entirely true—I pushed it out of my mind, not wanting to deal with the threats. It was immature and perhaps irresponsible, but I knew once I told everyone it would become a 'real' issue to be handled. I didn't want to acknowledge that I could once again be in danger.

"I know I should have told you and Hunter, and probably the police. I didn't want to deal with all the drama," I said with sincerity.

He released a long sigh, his body relaxing a degree.

"I wish you would have told me sooner. You didn't need to deal with this alone," he said, taking my hands and gathering me in his lap. "Lo, you can't hide from this. Pretending won't remove the risk. We need to call Hunter and get him involved."

"I didn't want to make a big deal out of it."

I felt his body tense again as he contained his frustration.

"It *is* a big deal. Did that bottom-feeder lawyer come into Higher Yearning before you started receiving the letters?"

"The first time, yeah," I answered carelessly, my mistake apparent when an angry growl sounded beneath me.

"How many times?" he asked in a clipped tone.

"Three...no, wait, four. But he didn't see me the last time."

He looked at me expectantly so I gave a brief summary of our exchange during his second visit. I explained that I stonewalled him on his third attempt, not speaking a word or acknowledging his presence in any way. When I spotted him walking up to the shop on his visit last week, I ducked behind the counter, hidden from view. I didn't explain why, but I begged Meg to wait on him and tell him I wasn't there if he inquired. The best part of the whole ridiculous scene was that Meg was so struck by his GQ model good looks that she became tongue-tied. First she asked, "What can you get me?" when asking for his order. Then she tried to upsell by offering a baked good, but it came out, "Can I give you something sweet?" The best by far was when she handed him an espresso and said, "Careful, you're hot." I had to slap my hands over my mouth to stifle my laughter. I thought she was going to crawl under the counter to hide right alongside me.

Griffin wasn't able to find the same humor in the encounter that I did. Maybe you had to be there?

"I'm calling Hunter...this needs to stop. Now."

I nodded, unable to deny he was right. I had waited far longer than I should have. He pulled out his phone and punched out a rapid-fire text before tossing it on the couch beside him. He held me close, as if afraid I would be snatched from his arms at any moment.

His phone rang and I couldn't hear the specific words spoken but they were clearly enraged, based on the volume and harsh tone.

"You're telling me," Griffin said sarcastically.

"You do your thing and I'll do mine." He paused, listening to the caller's response. "Yeah, it's a very good thing she is staying here."

"Okay, see you in thirty," he said before ending the call.

"Hunter and Everleigh are on their way over. Just a head's up, Hunter is not thrilled you waited so long to spill."

With that warning, he kissed my lips and set me back on the couch to await back-up.

When Hunter and Ev arrived, I was forced to recount in excruciating detail every threat I had received and all of my interactions with Mr. Black. I was rewarded with a long lecture about making responsible decisions and personal safety from Hunter. But Griffin was wrong; it wasn't Hunter who I should have spent the thirty minutes worrying over. Ev was livid, bouncing between pretending I didn't exist and yelling at me for being "stupid and reckless and irresponsible."

"I'm sleeping with a damn FBI agent. Did it occur to you at any point to take advantage of that perk? Or better yet, how about letting me know that some shithead lawyer was stalking you at work? I appreciate you are trying to be strong and independent. I'm behind you 100%, but you can't dismiss these threats as a joke...this isn't a game. You are too smart to act this stupid."

"That's enough, Ev," Griffin said firmly. "You've made your point."

Hunter pulled her into his chest, cutting off any potential commentary. I felt like the biggest asshole ever; I hated that they were so worried. It was this bone-chilling fear that led me to keep the notes a secret in the first place. I didn't want to be the source of their fear and concern...again.

Griffin embraced me, offering warmth and consolation.

"She's just scared for you," he said quietly.

I nodded into his chest.

"And worried...and maybe a little angry," he added the last with a chuckle.

I understood his humor. Ev was a sight to behold when she went off, arms flailing, face reddened. I would have been laughing had her fury not been directed at me.

Once everyone calmed down, we all sat and discussed options. Hunter took possession of the notes to have them fingerprinted, although he didn't expect to find anything. He had already called the Bureau to open an official investigation and planned to contact the warden at the prison. Everyone knew the notes were coming from *him*, but the main concern was that Heath had someone assisting him, enabling him to reach beyond the prison walls. I couldn't shake the chilling thought that perhaps he had accomplices in his crimes that we were unaware of. Hunter suspected either he or his family was paying someone to deliver the threats.

"The only good news about the last letter is that the threat is overt. Now we have a chance, given this evidence, to obtain a warrant that will let me dig into the Varbeck family. If I can connect them, Heath specifically, it will help the DA and allow us to secure a protective order for you," Hunter advised. "If nothing else, it may create enough headaches to encourage them to back off."

The mood had lightened fractionally by the time Huntleigh were preparing to leave. As we walked them to the door, Ev grabbed me, hugging me tightly.

"I'm sorry I yelled at you, but you were being stupid. Don't take chances when the risk is so high. You have people who can help, use them. And please be careful."

"I promise."

After Ev released me, Hunter stepped up and hugged me as well. "We'll figure this out, but it's important you tell me what's going on so I can investigate. You share everything that crosses your mind, whether I want to know or not... no secrets with this type of stuff."

I nodded my promise.

After they left, Griffin and I headed for bed. When we were tucked in, I cuddled on his chest, wrapped in his protective embrace.

"You need to be extra cautious until we get this all worked out. If I'm not around, get someone to walk you to your car after work."

"Okay."

"I have a few things I need to take care of tomorrow. I want to get someone in here to install an alarm ASAP. I don't like the idea of you being here alone when I'm working nights. I'll try and rearrange the schedule so I can be here most nights. I'll just run up and check in or have them call when there are problems."

"No. Griff, you can't rearrange your whole life for me. You have responsibilities, I'll be fine."

"*You* are my first priority. I'd do anything to protect you, but it would make my life a hell of a lot easier if you at least tell me when there is a threat."

"Agreed."

We held one another in silence, just being in the other's presence and listening to the duet of our heartbeats. In his arms I felt safe and found the reassurance I needed to believe everything would be okay.

Chapter Nine

*"A man does what he must—in spite of personal
consequences, in spite of obstacles and dangers and
pressures—and that is the basis of all human morality."*
-Winston Churchill

Griffin

I made my way across the parking lot with a determined stride,
fully aware I was about to push the boundaries of legal statutes and
violate several ethical tenets...I was okay with that. Actually, I was
looking forward to doing just that; my only regret was that I would
not be present to see the results of my efforts. Most people who
knew me wouldn't be surprised by my desire to protect someone
I loved. But they would never predict the retribution I had
methodically planned—the callous calculation with which I
strategized the psychological and physical reprisal. Everyone has
their launch code, the buttons no one should ever push because
the results would be catastrophic. The son of a bitch secured in
the building before me had flipped open the protective plastic
casement, keyed in the required sequence, slammed his palm on
the big red button, and then threw gallons of jet fuel on the
explosion.

I had been patient, waiting for the ideal time to exact revenge. Nothing could right the wrongs he committed nor undo the damage he wrought. I was unwilling to put my faith in the justice system; capital punishment did not exist in New York State—if convicted, the most severe sentence he faced was life in prison. After what Sam had endured, that punishment was insufficient and unjust. Her wounds had healed, but the scars remained and the memories could never be erased. My decision was made months ago, but finding his threats yesterday reinforced my choice and provoked me to act.

I was briefly searched as I entered the building before passing through the metal detector. My intended weapon was already located within the walls of the prison. No cavity search or X-ray machine would detect the threat to my intended target. I signed in and provided my psychology resident credentials before a uniformed guard guided me to one of the familiar interaction and assessment rooms. I'd spent the last four months counseling and assessing inmates as part of my clinical psych residency. Truth be told, I had completed the necessary assessment hours two months ago, but I conveniently "forgot" to turn in my log, which permitted my continued access to the prison. Today I would finally be face-to-face with my target.

Heath sat at a table in the center of the room dressed in forest green sweats, the required attire for inmates at the Riverhead County Jail. He was leaning back in his metal chair as if lounging in an oversized recliner, footrest extended, and massage feature buzzing away—not a care in the world. My fists clenched as I adopted an expression of detached indifference, a skill all therapists must master.

"Mr. Varbeck," I addressed him, curious if I would find recognition. He studied me for a moment, clearly trying to place me but failing.

"You're the shrink?"

"I'm a resident psychologist. Today I will ask you a series of questions that will serve as part of the evaluation of your mental health."

"Great. Let's finish this so you can verify that I am crazy and belong in a mental institution, not this hell hole."

I nodded, leading him to believe I agreed with his personal assessment. There was no doubt he was insane, but his crimes could not be excused by any diagnosis in DSM-5, the official psychiatric diagnostic handbook. The actions of a serial killer were not caused by a mental health disorder, rather the absence of a soul and a conscience. Heath would not be deemed mentally unfit for trial—he retained full control of his mental capacities and was able to comprehend the effects of his actions during the course of the attacks. If he was hoping for a "Primal Fear" movie-style victory where he feigned insanity to escape conviction, he would be sorely disappointed—he was no Edward Norton.

"We have yet to determine a specific mental illness, which is why I am here for further assessment," I said, summoning my most professional façade.

"Fine, ask your questions and slap a label on me."

"Mr. Varbeck, why did you assault your fellow students at Hensley University?"

"I don't believe I ever confessed to any such crimes," he returned mockingly.

I sighed at his cliché answer. While it was not surprising, it was fucking annoying.

"It is my understanding that you *did* confess to your last victim. Was I misinformed?"

"Everleigh claimed I confessed a litany of sins to her, but her own mental stability could be called into question. Did you know her best friend had been attacked a week prior to our supposed conversation? I am sure she was distraught and not thinking clearly. I can't imagine her statement will hold much weight."

I gripped the edge of the table, reminding myself of my goal. While slamming his head against the concrete floor repeatedly would be satisfying, it would prevent me from fulfilling my objective. Refocused, I continued.

"Do you enjoy hurting people, Mr. Varbeck?"

"I enjoy giving people what they secretly want and fulfilling their deepest desires."

"And you believe the girls abused at Hensley wanted to be hurt and maimed?"

"I imagine they loved every minute of the game, it was only afterward when confronted with the judgment of their friends and family that they cried foul. During the game, I imagine they would have been crying out, playing along to get more of what they yearned for."

I went through the motions of making notes on the legal pad, allowing me to hide the fury blazing in my eyes.

"What of the three girls who were murdered? Do you also *imagine* they wanted their lives to be cut short in such a brutal fashion?"

"I can't say for certain—I wasn't there after all—but I would guess anyone participating in such games understands the inherent risks. Accidents do happen."

"Are you capable of telling the truth, Mr. Varbeck?"

"I am certainly capable, but it's terribly boring—wait, maybe it's just you who is boring me," he chuckled to himself.

"Are you disappointed that you failed to conquer your last two victims? After such a long and successful run, it must be disappointing to end in failure."

I smirked with satisfaction as Heath gritted his teeth—I had found a sore spot.

"I have never *failed* at anything in my entire life, only temporary setbacks. I am a very determined and resourceful man." His smile was sinister and the resolve in his eyes unmistakable.

"Do you believe you have that kind of reach? You are behind bars, after all," I prodded.

"You still believe I'm going to be convicted?" he asked, leaning forward to rest his elbows on the table. "The influence, resources, and money my family will dedicate to freeing me are limitless."

I shook my head at his arrogance, a dangerous vice that had led to the downfall of those far more intelligent than him.

"You'll never get the opportunity to finish what you began—you'll likely die behind bars. Have you considered the possibility?"

"Who do you think you are talking to? You can't imagine the reach my family has."

"Ah, your family," I said, leaning forward, mirroring his position. "You are every parent's worst nightmare realized. You are a problem they must solve for their own benefit, and when this is over they'll pretend you never existed. How does that make you feel?"

I watched as his face reddened and he fidgeted in an effort to restrain his anger. I smiled in satisfaction.

"You have no idea what you are talking about. They'll never stop trying to free me...they believe me."

"If it makes you feel better, you are welcome to cling to that belief, but mark my words, they won't be sitting behind you offering support during your trial. Have they even come to visit you since you were indicted or have they just sent the family lawyer?"

"Shut the fuck up," he barked.

"It must cut deep that you can't even fool your own parents—the people who are supposed to love you unconditionally. It doesn't bode well for your ability to fool a jury."

"I told you, I will never step foot inside a courtroom for trial. It won't get that far. I heard the prosecution's witnesses are dropping like flies," he gloated.

"Do you believe you can dissuade all of the witnesses from testifying? Even *you* must admit some will be too committed to seek justice to bend to your will."

"Would that be the fiery Everleigh? Everyone has their price."

"You can't honestly believe everyone can be manipulated with money."

"You may be right, but I can only imagine what choices Everleigh will make if forced to choose between love and justice. Don't you think she would forgo testifying to protect her boyfriend, or maybe her best friend?"

I slammed my fist on the table without conscious thought of what the gesture revealed. Heath eyed me, assessing.

"She means something to you—Samantha. How is that lovely piece?" he taunted.

I gripped the edge of the table and locked my feet around the legs of the chair to keep myself from killing him on the spot. Fuck, this was infinitely harder than I had anticipated and my control was balancing on the edge of a razor.

"I know you, don't I? I thought you looked familiar. You're that bartender from The Stop, one of their guard dogs," Heath snarled.

"Does it make you feel powerful abusing women?" I tried to steer us back on course.

"How did you even get in here? You're a freaking bartender!" he uttered as if the word was a profanity.

"I just completed my master's in Clinical Psychology and am finishing up clinical hours today for my licensing requirements. I only have one more assessment after you....Lionel. Have you met him yet?"

I knew damn well Heath knew who Lionel was—everyone incarcerated at Riverhead knew. The man dwarfed me, which is virtually impossible. I've seen Hummers with less mass. He was the man who dictated the prisoners' social structure, and the inmate all others refrained from pissing off at all costs. You did not want to be on his radar if you weren't his ally. He was in for life on several counts of first-degree murder resulting from turf wars over narcotic distribution channels in the impoverished areas of Long Island. He should have been transferred to the state prison over a year ago, but overcrowding kept him in the maximum-security wing at the county jail—much to Lionel's delight. He'd rather be the biggest fish in a small pond. He used his time at Riverhead strategically, building his reputation beyond local lore, so that when he was transferred to state prison, he would be assured a privileged position in the prison's caste system.

Over the past months, I used our evaluation sessions to develop a rapport with the kingpin; we wouldn't be exchanging Christmas cards, but we shared a mutual respect. When he mentioned that his eight-year-old daughter struggled with reading, I found a tutor willing to assist the little girl for free. Lionel may have earned every year of his life sentence, but his daughter should not be punished for her father's choices. I learned the only thing in the world Lionel cared about above money or himself was his daughter. I had earned an ally in assisting the little girl, an unexpected boon.

"Everyone knows Lionel, he's hard to miss," Heath confirmed.

"I've met with him a few times. I helped his daughter out with a tutor."

"How touching," his retort dripped with sarcasm.

"I think we're finished. It is my assessment that you have Antisocial Personality Disorder. I'll file the report today and after it is reviewed by my supervisors, your lawyer will receive a copy," I advised as I rose to my feet, standing beside the table.

"Thank fuck, it's about time one of you shrinks diagnosed me. I told you I would never stand trial," he crowed.

"Oh no, you misunderstand. You definitely have ASPD, but that is not sufficient to have your charges waylaid for mental incapacity. It's actually considered one of the least 'curable' of the personality disorders and means you were able to process the ramifications of your actions. You are going to stand trial and if you introduce your mental state, the jury will hear that you have ASPD—like most serial killers—thus deemed unfixable. You are going to spend the rest of your miserable life behind bars upstate in maximum security."

Heath flew from his chair and lunged for me—thank God! I was hoping to incite him to take aggressive action against me so I had justification to get my hands on him. He swung for my face but I avoided contact and grabbed him by the throat, using my five-inch height advantage to secure him against the wall and suspend him by his neck so that his feet could not touch the floor. I leaned in close enough to whisper in his ear, guaranteeing the closed-circuit cameras wouldn't record any sound.

"If you threaten Sam or Everleigh in any way, I will make sure you spend the rest of your life pissing out of a tube—and if any harm comes to them, you won't live to see the end of the day." I smiled before adding, "One more thing about Lionel. He has even less tolerance for child abusers than the average inmate—he's a real sadistic bastard when it comes to teaching those deviants a lesson. I'd watch my back if I were you."

"What are you talking about? I never touched any kids," he gasped, struggling to speak with my hand still clamped around his airway.

"Oh," I shrugged, "my mistake."

I stepped back and released my vice grip, causing him to crash to the floor, gasping for breath and clutching his throat. The door opened behind me and one of the prison guards came into view.

"Everything okay in here, Mr. Evensen?" the guard inquired while eyeing Heath's crumpled state.

"Mr. Varbeck took a swing at me as I was leaving, but I managed to subdue him. His uncontrolled rage makes him a danger to others. I suggest you exercise caution."

I exited the room to the sound of Heath cursing and shouting. The panic in his voice was crystal clear, much to my satisfaction. Now he would live with a taste of the fear he had caused thousands of women at Hensley.

I proceeded to the second assessment room and greeted Lionel. This would be our last meeting. He was one of the inmates I was assigned to evaluate for the purpose of determining the impact of prison on those incarcerated and how convicts adjust to the sub-culture of prison. Inmates like Lionel were at an advantage coming from a gang society, since the dynamics of prison society offered many of the same conventions. However, everyone dealt with the loss of freedom differently, especially when that liberty was gone for the rest of their natural life.

Lionel was not a good man. He was not someone you would want to run into in a dark alley at night, but he wasn't evil. He was largely a product of the environment in which he was raised and the culture he lived. If Lionel had been born into another family and grown up in a suburb, who knows where he would have ended up? Lionel was taught early in life that his options for survival were limited, and he is a survivor. Given his massive size, joining a gang for safety and income was the best choice available to him as he saw it. The harsh realities of his life didn't excuse his actions, but in context you could see the forces that pushed him down the road he walked. There was little I could do to help him, but I hoped to leave him with a reminder of what was in his best interest for his remaining sentence, which would also benefit the prison. In many ways the warden did not run the prison, Lionel did. If he directed prisoners to lash out at guards, instigate fights, or riot, they would do as he said. It was in everyone's best interest to avoid such incidents. Controlling the climate and behaviors of the prison population allowed the guards to safely execute their jobs, and Lionel was the puppet master—he had that power. If he used his influence wisely, his remaining time at Riverhead would be relatively long and pleasant.

"How are you doing, Lionel?"

"Livin'."

"I heard the State extended your inmate transfer freeze indefinitely. Looks like you'll stay in Riverhead for a while, provided you aren't deemed a threat to the security of the prison."

"Ya, good for Lionel," he said with a gold-toothed smile.

"You know that means you need to play it cool, keep things under control?"

"Always keepin' it cool."

"We both know you're in for life, nothing is going to change that, but your quality of life will be directly related to how well you control the others. Keep them in line, ensure the guards aren't hurt, and everyone will benefit."

"Tell Lionel what he don't know."

"You've done a good job keeping everyone calm, cleaning up issues the guards couldn't address the same way you can, and have kept violence to a minimum. If you continue to do so, you will be here sitting pretty for a while, and I know that is what you want."

"Hells ya. I gots them."

After my final assessment, I advised him this would be my last visit.

"Not gonna lie, dawg, rather it be you than those otha shrinks...sorry to see ya go."

I bumped my fist against his extended one as I rose.

"I'm sorry to be leaving, but I'm glad to get away from most of the guys here. That last guy I was just with—" I paused to shake my head as if distressed by the visit. "What he did to the girls at Hensley was bad enough, but what he did to those kids..." I added a subtle shudder for good measure.

"That white boy killin' them college bitches was fuckin' with kids?" he gritted out.

"You know I'm not allowed to answer that question—I would lose my job."

I held his eyes with a hard stare. He nodded in return.

"A'ight Doc, keep on the straight."

I offered him a chin lift as I exited the room. Mission accomplished.

As I drove home, I considered the consequences of my actions. Heath was likely to be violated the same way he had violated those women before dinner was served. This brought me more satisfaction than it should, but I didn't care. I had stretched the ethical bounds of my intended profession to their breaking point, but I couldn't find it in me to regret my actions. The New York State legal system would not deliver the type of retribution Heath deserved. My justice may be vigilante but it was true justice.

I would, without question, step in to protect any woman in danger, but for Sam there was nothing I wouldn't do to protect her—to keep her safe. I wanted to destroy anything that had ever hurt her. I wanted them all to suffer as she has. Heath was the worst offender, but others had blood on their hands as well through their inaction, negligence, and participation. I may never have the opportunity to repay them all for their part in allowing the attacks, but at least Heath would be made to pay.

A part of me wished I had just killed the sick fuck when I had the chance. I may have spent the rest of my life in prison, but it would have been worth it. The only reason I restrained myself was knowing Sam was waiting for me.

As I tried to cool my residual anger, I pulled into the parking lot of the alarm company, anxious to make arrangements to protect my girl and return home to her.

Chapter Ten

"There's nothing better than good sex.
But bad sex? A peanut butter and jelly sandwich is
better than bad sex." -Billy Joel

Making dinner in anticipation of Griffin's return, I reflected on my last few sessions with my therapist. Thia had grown on me, just as she promised, but I was still on the fence regarding her own sanity. Did shrinks have shrinks? Maybe that should be a condition of licensing.

In my last session, Thia decided it was time to dive into my opposing thoughts about myself. I had made leaps and bounds in my recovery, but I still struggled with self-worth and lapses in confidence. In true Thia-style, she introduced me to a game called 'Devil's Advocate.' She would say something critical about me, and I had to disprove her comment or talk about the ways I was working to improve. I was forbidden from agreeing with anything she said.

"Ready?" Thia asked with enthusiasm.

"As I'll ever be," I responded warily.

"You're sexually undesirable to men who know you've been raped."

Okay, guess she wasn't pulling any punches with her little game.

"Not true. Griffin wants me...bad. He knows what happened to me and still wants to Humpty Bumpty with me."

Thia nodded her approval.

"You are so broken you will never be whole again."

I had a hard time disagreeing with this one. I hated that I still believed this to be true.

"Perhaps I'll never be the same, but the pieces missing will be filled with something else—new strength, love, hope, I'm not sure what exactly. I will be whole one day, just different from the original."

"Is that okay with you? Do you accept the truth of what you just said?" Thia asked, breaking from the game.

I had to think before I answered, searching for the truth within myself.

"Yes, I do believe it. I may be different from the Old Sam in some ways, walking through Hell changes a person, but that doesn't mean I can't be just as good, better even."

Thia nodded. "Ready?"

I flipped my hand palm up and curved my fingers toward my body several times, the universal signal for 'bring it on.'

"You're so damaged no man will want you as a wife and mother of his children."

I sucked in a painful breath. Holy shit, that one hurt. I'd always wanted to be a mother, to be the type of mom Meme was to Ev and me, and I had never consciously explored this fear. What if a man didn't want someone with my baggage to be the mother of his children? Did Griffin feel that way?

"I...um...I..." I paused to gather my thoughts. "Do you think that's true?" I asked, needing reassurance.

"Do you?" Thia countered unhelpfully.

"I hope not, but...I'm not sure. Will I be so scared my children could face the same horror I will smother them? Years from now, will I still be tripping over landmines that prevent me from being a good mom? Will I be too wrapped up in my own issues to support them when they need me...like my parents? Oh my god," I whispered the last words, devastated by the prospect.

"Sam, look at me. The rules of the game say that you have to argue my points, not agree. Your concerns are not unreasonable. The fact that you're already worrying about children you don't even have speaks volumes about the type of mother you will be. Now go ahead, call me a bitch and tell me I'm wrong—you're not leaving 'til you do. Time is almost up and I have no problem charging you overtime...I desperately want a motorcycle."

The image of Thia sitting on a Harley popped into my head, breaking through my obsessive worries, and caused me to laugh out loud. I refocused on her statement and strained for a rebuttal.

"No, I'm getting better every day. I'm working to be whole. My future husband and children will be lucky to have me because I will love, cherish, and protect them better than I ever could have before. They will always come first and any issues I have, my family will love me through it. I will be the type of mom Meme was to me. I will be the type of wife any husband would kill for. I will have the life I always dreamed of...*he* can't take that from me too."

Thia smiled at me with pride in her eyes.

"Good girl. I'm disappointed you won't be contributing to my Harley fund, but I'm proud of you. It's homework time."

I returned her smile with one of my own, feeling pleased with the breakthrough I had just made.

By the end of the session, I had gained a new respect for myself and an increased sense of worth. It was as if she vocalized all of the nasty thoughts that tormented my mind. I didn't enjoy the comments, but moving the conversation out of my head allowed me to see many of the thoughts for what they were—lies. It also called attention to areas where I still had work to do. The woman was a twisted genius.

I removed the steaks from the broiler and set them on the counter to rest. Hopefully Griffin would be home soon or dinner would be ruined. I had just finished setting the parmesan-and-garlic potatoes on the table next to the caramelized onions and sautéed mushrooms when he entered.

He paused at the entry to the kitchen and inhaled deeply.

"Hungry?" I asked, walking toward him.

"Whatever you made, it smells incredible. I'm starved. I had to skip lunch today."

"Good thing I made a filling dinner. Everything okay?"

"Yeah, just finished up my clinical hours and stopped by the home security store. They will be here to install a state-of-the-art system tomorrow while you are at work. I'll show you how to use it after the gym."

I shrugged. Alarm systems were the perfect item for retailers to capitalize on a guy's need to have the latest technology. It was programmed in men's DNA and I sure as hell wasn't going to fight nature.

We sat at the table where I filled his plate with the biggest of the filets and all of the trimmings. He hummed his appreciation after taking his first bite. I wasn't bragging when I said I make the best steak on Long Island. In addition to my top-secret seasoning rub, I added a pat of butter on top during the last four minutes under the broiler, adding extra flavor and moisture. No man could resist my steak.

"I viewed several apartments today," I said unenthusiastically.

"That good, huh?"

"None of them are as nice as the first one at The Glen. The only real contender today was new construction, and I'd have to wait three months before my unit would be ready."

"Three months isn't bad; it's not like you don't have somewhere to live. You can stay here as long as you like...forever if you keep cooking like this," he said while gesturing to the table.

"Thanks. I appreciate the offer and it is tempting to stay here with you, but I don't want to move in with you because some psycho is threatening me. I want it to be a decision based on love and commitment."

Oops! I dropped the L-word. Sure, I wasn't saying 'I love you, Griffin, until my dying breath,' but it still felt premature, regardless of the fact that my heart was quietly mocking my denial.

"I agree. As tempting as it is to keep you here forever, I want you to be confident in my motives behind the invite when you make that decision. Besides, it may seem old-fashioned, but I expected to put a ring on your finger before setting up house."

Okay, I guess my L-bomb wasn't too bad if he was going to mention diamonds. He wasn't proposing, but he did put me and the infamous left-hand jewelry in close conversational proximity. Maybe the idea of marrying someone with my baggage didn't scare him, as Thia had pushed me to admit.

After dinner and cleanup, we watched reruns of 'Whose Line Is It Anyway?' and spent the night laughing to the point of snorting. It was perfect. I fell asleep with my head on his chest, feeling the warmth of his body beneath me, completely comfortable.

I awoke in the master suite the following morning, sprawled across Griffin's body like a silk sheet, molding to his contours. He usually got up before I did, so I took advantage of the opportunity to examine him. He was breathtaking, a living work of art—perfectly sculpted beauty. In the peace of sleep he looked younger and unburdened, more like the man I met last year. I traced the grooves of his abs with my finger, letting it leisurely wander the paths of his body. With a mind of its own, my naughty finger found the edge of the inverted triangle and headed south from his hip until it reached the edge of his boxer briefs. I followed the cotton line, bisecting his body slowly from east to west. It was impossible to miss his body's reaction to my touch. My finger was drawn like a magnet to the soft cotton, tracing the shapes it hid from my eyes. The more I played, the more I wanted.

"You keep that up—" he said drowsily.

"And you'll what?" I responded in an unintentionally sultry voice.

"Mmm. Don't know, torture you similarly?"

If he intended his warning to be a deterrent, he failed miserably.

"Deal," I said, accepting his terms with enthusiasm.

He chuckled as his hand drifted up my ribcage to cup my breast with a gentle squeeze. My desire ignited as he toyed with me, strumming his fingers across my pebbled flesh with deliberate gentleness that had me ready to beg for more.

I was about to retaliate when his hands drifted lower, pushing me onto my back as he kissed me. His hands were everywhere, overwhelming me, as he traced my body. His calloused fingers hooked around the lace across my hips. His body slipped down mine as if he was linked to my descending panties. By the time both of my feet were freed, Griffin was biting the ridge of my hip bones, his massive body filling the space between my thighs. His shoulders were so broad I had no choice but to hook my knees over them as he circled my belly button with the tip of his tongue. He drifted lower, nibbling the line where my leg met my body until he found a ticklish spot. I laughed and convulsed from the gentle drag of his lips along the delicate flesh. He chuckled, pleased to replicate my reaction on the other side. It was a slow, sensual torture that I never wanted to end.

He turned his head, lightly touching the skin of my inner thigh with his lips while his fingers skated across my stomach, sides, and outer thighs, the combination of sensations resulting in a head-to-toe shiver. When the final minute muscle contraction of the shiver died out, another began as his mouth found the epicenter of my desire. His hum of approval reverberated across my sensitized nerves as he sampled me. The focused attention was more than my body could handle, the pleasure swallowing me whole, blotting out all thought. He skillfully teased until I was panting his name, begging. For the first time, he denied me a request and continued to push me higher without answering my pleas, keeping me on the edge in a state of pleasure I had never known. I was writhing, desperate to reach the Promised Land while never wanting his wicked torment to end. As I clutched his hair in my fists, he added the slightest suction that catapulted me into flight. I was flying through a lightning storm, the currents electrifying my body, causing my every cell to cry out with satisfaction.

When I finally regained my senses, I found that I had melted across Griffin's body like butter on warm bread, encased in his arms. He had been my rock over the past month, steadfast and unwavering, no matter what crisis or emotional outburst arose. He never made me feel less than or tainted; it was the opposite—he made me feel exceptional and precious. I couldn't imagine accepting the touch of any other man. The patience and understanding he displayed permeated every aspect of our relationship and interactions. He had insisted my needs come first and his actions proved him a man of his word. Despite all of this, I wasn't ready to make my declaration, causing my heart to sigh with impatience. Internally, however, I chanted 'I love you' with a conviction so strong no one would dare doubt.

Griffin pressed against me, doodling on my back with his dexterous finger.

"How are you?" he asked, the words muffled by my hair.

"Somewhere between 'can we stay like this all day' and 'can we do it again.'"

His laughter rumbled against the side of my face.

"Anything you want."

"Really?"

"Umm-hmm. Let's just say I've been saving up for a while and now I'm ready to go on a spending spree."

"Oh, I love it when you talk shopping...such a turn on," I said, only partially teasing.

"Is it now? Let's test that claim—Chanel. Gucci. Prada."

I loved this playful side of him and I moaned loudly, encouraging him.

"That's right, talk dirty to me."

And he did while once again proving himself a man of his word—he proceeded to rock my world again, and this time I returned the favor.

Morning dawned and I awoke in Griffin's bed, the smell of bacon calling me from the kitchen. I rolled out of bed and grabbed my robe, following my nose.

"God bless you," I said dramatically when I found Griffin in the kitchen adding bacon to a plate that held scrambled eggs, fruit salad, and an English muffin.

"Your coffee is on the table. Take a seat and I'll have your plate in a minute."

I obediently followed his directions, excited for my balanced breakfast—okay, I was excited about the bacon. Bacon was one of those foods I only ordered occasionally when dining out. It was a greasy mess to cook and I inevitably burned myself every time, a sad reality since I adored the salty, crispy deliciousness.

Griffin set the plate before me with a self-satisfied smile.

"It was my turn. I didn't want you to think I couldn't work the stove."

I chuckled because I was beginning to suspect exactly that. I didn't need to taste the meal to know the man could cook. The eggs were the perfect shade of yellow, fluffy and moist without being wet. The bacon was evenly cooked and perfectly crisped. I sampled a bite of everything on the plate before officially offering my praise and gratitude.

"I'm glad I could impress the resident chef," he said.

"Do these skills translate beyond breakfast foods or is that the extent of your repertoire?"

"Nope, this is just the tip of the iceberg. I am a master of lunch and dinner if it includes pub food or grilling. Kind of a job requirement."

Right, I had forgotten he would be familiar with the kitchen due to the bar.

"You've been holding out on me," I complained lightheartedly.

"Not exactly. My skills are limited to the menu at The Stop, and after eating the same food regularly for the last ten years, I'm sick of it. With the exception of a few seasonal specials, we have never changed the menu."

"The food is good and consistent. Customers know what to expect; it's risky to switch it up. You don't want to lose your base."

"Exactly, but it would be nice to expand our offerings and maybe grow our lunch crowd. I'm not complaining, but I don't want to become complacent."

I nodded my agreement. I would grab a menu and look at it with new eyes the next time we were at The Stop...actually, I had a better idea.

"Why don't we invite Ev and Hunter to join us for dinner tomorrow night? We can have dinner at The Stop and give you feedback. Maybe shoot some pool afterwards."

"Sounds like a plan. I'll text Hunter today. I assume you'll tell Ev at work?"

"Yep."

I helped with the dishes and hurried to get dressed (after giving Griffin my best 'thank you' kiss) so I wouldn't be late. Luckily, the fickle, often cruel local traffic was in my favor and I arrived with three minutes to spare. I ducked behind the counter while tying my apron.

"What has you so chipper this morning?" Meg asked with a smile.

"I am chipper, aren't I?" I replied happily.

A chuckle announced Ev's approach.

"She took another trip to O-Town," Ev said, certain she was on point. "Am I right? You don't have to tell me, I know I'm right."

Per her instructions, I said nothing, just smiled.

"Well, tell me!" Ev demanded. She could claim I overshared as much as she liked, but Ev was the first in line to get the dirty details.

"Oh, I wouldn't want to be too graphic. Let's just say I had a lovely morning. Then there was last night...but you don't want to know about all that," I taunted Ev mercilessly.

"Bitch, you usually say every dirty thought that passes through your head and now you have dirt I'm dying to know and you're holding out on me? Spill!"

I laughed at her determination. I had every intention of singing like a canary, but it was fun to make her work for it.

"I have officially renewed my membership to the 'O of the Century' club. Griffin's skill with his hands is nothing compared to what his mouth can do. I forgot my own name he was so mind-boggling. His body is spectacular and all those muscles...he's got the moves and the strength. I actually experienced the fabled standing 69—another item crossed off my sexy bucket list!"

"You have a sexy bucket list?" Meg asked with astonishment.

"Don't you?"

"No," she said hesitantly.

"That's it, I'm buying you a journal for Christmas so you can start your list," I said resolutely.

"You don't have to do that," Meg insisted.

"Oh yes I do. Every girl needs a sexy wish list. You just have to be nice 'til Christmas so Santa will bring you someone to be really naughty with."

Ev laughed, but I could see the cartoon bubble pop up over her head with Hunter wrapped up in a big bow.

"No, I really...don't," Meg sighed. "Can I be honest?"

Ev and I both nodded. Meg was so serious and reluctant, neither of us wanted to discourage her from sharing.

"I—" Meg began before abruptly stopping to assess us again. "I don't get it—all the hype. I've done it, of course, but I still don't get it. I used to think girls were just talking it up to be cool—like the musical 'Cats.' Everyone tells you to go see it, so you do, and when the curtain falls you're left scratching your head wondering if you went to a different play, but you tell everyone you loved it because it's expected. Is there something wrong with me if I hated 'Cats'? Does it make me a bad person? Is there something wrong with me?" she asked with desperation.

Ev and I looked at each other with the same shocked and dismayed expressions.

"Um, Meg, honey...that may be one of the saddest things I have ever heard. I doubt there is anything wrong with you other than your shit choice of bedmates. How many men have you been with?" Ev asked calmly.

"Two."

"*Really?* That's hardly a broad enough sample to draw the conclusion that sex is overrated. You just need to find the right guy...a man who *knows* what all of his parts are for and how to work all of yours," Ev tried to comfort her.

"Maybe, I don't know. The guys seemed happy and said how amazing it was, but all I really thought was 'I missed five minutes of *The Voice* for that?' I would have been closer to getting off from watching Blake Shelton's sexy ass nestled in that big red chair."

"Blake Shelton is hot," I said, as Ev chimed in with, "Screw that...Adam Levine is sex on a damn stick!"

Ev and I shot each other menacing looks over our longstanding feud about the hottest judge on *The Voice*. I wanted to stick up for Blake, but Meg needed my help more at the moment.

"Five minutes? Really? The only time that's acceptable is if you're in public," I said, now that it was clear what her problem was. Meg was one of those unfortunate women who had only encountered bedroom duds and what she needed was a stud—a tried and true stallion with a proven record.

"You *have* taken the magic carpet ride to the Taj Mah-O at some point though, right?" I asked.

"Only when flying solo," she said, a blush tinging her cheeks.

"Okay, then it's not you...you are able, your collaborators were just incompetent. Let's face it, a few in-and-outs is all it takes for men to find the Promised Land. You need a man who doesn't want to take the trip unless you are along for the ride; his pleasure needs to be rooted in yours as much as his own. If Hunter found his before me, he wouldn't rest until I was screaming his name—he just wouldn't be content otherwise," Ev said, a satisfied smile tipping her lips at the thought of Hunter's prowess.

"Same here. Griff would use every weapon in his vast arsenal to make sure I detonated. And let me tell you, what that man can do with his mouth—"

"Please, continue to rub it in. My sanity was growing tedious anyway," Meg interjected dryly.

"Sorry," I said sheepishly.

"You're a free agent right now. Are you looking for the real deal or just a little fun?" Ev asked.

"I'm taking a break from the whole relationship drama. All I want right now is a wild, commitment-free, scream-filled ride on a champion bull."

"Maybe we can run a promotion—50% off all beverages for hot, single men," I suggested. It would attract a new crop of potential broncos for Meg to consider.

"Not a brothel! How many times must I remind you," Ev scolded me. "I'll keep my eyes peeled for you, Meg. I embrace any project that requires me to scope out hot guys."

"Don't knock yourselves out. I'm resigned to a life where the hottest sex I experience is in the books I read."

Meg excused herself to collect supplies from the back—clearly ready to escape the conversation.

Now that was just sad! Poor Meg needed her own Griffin or Hunter to set her world on fire. I silently promised to look for the right man to deliver her first hands-free orgasm.

"By the way, do you and Hunter want to join us for dinner at The Stop tomorrow?"

"Sounds good. Pool tourney?" Ev asked. The pool shark in her was dying to go for a swim.

"You know it."

Chapter Eleven

"There are only two tragedies in life:
one is not getting what one wants,
and the other is getting it." -Oscar Wilde

Wednesday proved to be a continuation of the day prior at Higher Yearning. Meg and I spent our shift scoring male patrons on their overall appearance, and I enlightened her about the indicators for optimal bed buddies. I resorted to using the education degree system, in case we were overheard by customers. So far we'd had a handful with a Master's and one potential Ph.D., the rest were Bachelor's or the dreaded GED. I insisted Meg set her sights on an aesthetic eight or higher with at least a Master's degree in mattress sciences. I did concede, however, that a seven with a Ph.D. would be acceptable. Yes, it was shallow, but our goal was her satisfaction for a tryst...we weren't husband-hunting. An entirely different paradigm was necessary for life mates.

Meg felt my benchmark was set too high, which I found comical. The girl was naturally gorgeous, unassumingly and effortlessly so. Her straight, chocolate-colored hair had volume without overwhelming her beautiful face, which was a blend of the girl-next-door and a hint of exotic. Her hazel eyes shone with kindness, balancing her wide, welcoming smile. She was tall, probably five feet nine inches, and her slim body possessed curves men longed to touch—like a Victoria's Secret Angel. Yet, Meg had no clue she was naturally a nine, and with any effort she would be off the charts. She thought even an eight was too high for her. It wasn't that she was insecure, she just didn't see her appeal the way an objective observer did.

I kept my predictions to myself, but was confident she could land a ten if she exhibited any interest. Meg was the type of girl who attracted men with her outer shell, but could keep them glued by her inner beauty. She was the rare girl who could inspire a man to change because she was so damn good. However, I knew it would be a waste of my breath telling her any of that. Like most people, she would readily believe every negative comment thrown at her, but would shrug off genuine compliments. Why was it so much easier to accept the hurtful remarks? We humans were a messed up lot.

As my shift drew to a close, I realized my gym bag was in the car. I preferred to change at work rather than the gym's locker room, so I headed out to grab it. Dusk had painted the sky a myriad of pinks, purples, and oranges, so breathtaking it caused me to pause and soak in the majesty. It was these little moments of wonderment I collected to remind myself of the splendor of life.

I was still marveling at the sunset's beauty as I approached my car and therefore was unprepared for the black mass that sprang from a crouched position near my rear tire before running past me, nearly knocking me off my feet in the process. What the hell? I turned back to my car and noticed the flattened tires. Whoever that son of a bitch was slashed my tires! I rounded the far side of the car, only to be greeted by more of the same. I was going to need another ten sunsets to balance my current anger. I checked my windshield and sure enough, tucked beneath my wiper was another folded piece of paper. I snatched the fluttering page and opened it.

FEW GRAINS REMAIN IN YOUR HOURGLASS. A MARTYR CANNOT CELEBRATE THEIR OWN TRIUMPH.

Oh, for fuck's sake—were they teaching creative writing classes at the prison? This was getting ridiculous. I was too concerned with the waste of taxpayer dollars to actually be scared of *his* whimsical death threats. Perhaps that wasn't entirely true...fear had seeped in at the same moment my bewilderment at the method of intimidation wore off. I was painfully aware of what the monster was capable of. Normally I would dismiss the warnings as a pathetic joke, but my first-hand knowledge of his vile proclivities, combined with the vandalism of my car, was proof that I could not ignore the danger. Despite my desire to downplay what had just occurred, I knew I had to confess the truth to Griffin and Hunter.

I slid my phone from my pocket and called AAA. As I was hanging up, I heard Griffin call my name and I tried to shake off my anger—he would have enough for the both of us.

"Over here," I called, preparing myself to break the news.

"There you are. Meg said you came out here over fifteen minutes ago."

I walked into Griffin's chest and wrapped my arms around his waist, needing the shelter only he could provide. After a few minutes, he broke our silence.

"I'm not going to like this, am I?"

"Not one bit. I found another note on my car a few minutes ago."

"Son of a—"

"He slashed my tires and nearly knocked me on my ass when he ran. Whoever it was didn't even have the courtesy to apologize.

I know he's a criminal, but is it really too much to ask that he offer a simple 'excuse me' while making his getaway?"

"You saw him? He was close enough to touch you?" Griffin's voice was deceptively even. There was only a thread of restraint hidden in his calm and most would miss it, but I knew him well enough to pick it out.

"Yeah."

"We need to call Hunter and get him to send someone to check for prints or evidence. Okay?"

I nodded against his chest and felt him reach into his pocket. He led me back inside Higher Yearning to wait for Hunter. Neither of us said anything until Ev joined us. I brought her up to speed, while watching Griffin clench and unclench his fists, the only sign of his bridled anger.

After Hunter and a Suffolk County Police Detective finished taking my statement and inspecting the crime scene, they released my car to be towed. Det. Norse offered to bring in a sketch artist to capture an image of the culprit, but I assured him it would be a waste. The only part I saw for more than a second was his back. He was dressed in a generic black sweatshirt with the hood raised. I was too shocked to retain any memory of his face. The only description I could provide was that he was a male, about six feet tall. I thought he had dark hair, but I wasn't even certain about that detail.

Hunter sat next to Ev and wrapped his arm around her shoulder. "We'll see what the crime scene investigators turn up, but I'm not optimistic. So far, there haven't been any prints on the previous notes. I've been beating my head against a wall trying to find a tie between any members of the Varbeck family and the threats you have been receiving. It was a struggle to get a judge to grant a warrant for their financials, which are astronomical—I'm searching for a needle in a haystack. His parents swear they've had no part in threatening you, and of course they claim they didn't authorize payoffs to witnesses. I can't prove shit! If Heath is arranging the threats from behind bars, I haven't found any proof. He's had no outside visitors beyond prison staff and psych evaluators. No outgoing mail, no emails, nothing," Hunter finished with irritation.

"You're doing everything you can, babe. You'll find the link," Ev soothed.

"My best hope is to trace the bribe payouts through their attorney. If I can link his parents to the bribes, then I can threaten charges and get them to talk."

I nodded, understanding the challenges Hunter faced. I knew better than anyone the influence money could wield. Hunter had an uphill battle before him. I was mildly reassured to hear that *he* appeared to be uninvolved. Somehow the prospect of someone killing me, quickly and without torture, generated less fear than what *he* had done, and would do again, if given the opportunity. As long as he was behind bars, I could pretend straightforward death was the worst that could happen. It was a consolation, but I had learned there were things far worse than death.

I shook off my uneasiness—unwilling to let *him* ruin another night for me...for us. We were going to dinner and then I would watch Hunter find a way to beat Ev at pool while I flirted shamelessly with my man.

"Enough. We made plans and we are keeping them. I don't care if I'm dressed in work clothes and smell like Kona beans, we are going to dinner. Let's move, people," I ordered as if my chest was decorated with stars.

All three exchanged a look, uncertain how to interpret my abrupt declaration. Huntleigh seemed to defer to Griffin, who eventually shrugged.

"You heard the lady. Let's go."

We all sat in the dining room at The Stop with menus in hand, and I began to meticulously scrutinize the options. I knew the food was consistently fresh and tasty, but as I reviewed the dishes I realized how limited the choices were. Other than traditional bar appetizers, there were only two types of salads, three sandwiches, burgers, and the grill basics. The daily special (a soup, sandwich, and main course) were the only variations. Griffin was right—The Stop would definitely benefit from a revamped menu with some new dishes. Cell phone in hand, I tapped away as ideas flooded from my mind onto my notepad. Holy cow, dessert! They weren't offering any desserts, what a missed opportunity. I continued to plug away until I was confident I had a well-conceptualized menu to suggest—both lunch and dinner. I looked up to find three sets of eyes locked on me with varying degrees of curiosity, confusion, and mirth.

"What?" I asked defensively.

"Nothing, Lo-baby. You're very cute when you get excited. After the third or fourth random one-word exclamation, people stopped turning to look."

"You didn't even hear the waitress asking for your order. I decided for you," Ev added.

"Great. I hope I'm having salad and a grilled chicken sandwich."

Ev nodded; she knew me too well. After the crazy start to our night, I needed lean protein and veggies to fortify. I turned to Griffin and smiled. In return, he took my hand in his own.

"I just emailed you my suggested changes for The Stop's menu. Feel free to disregard it completely if you aren't feeling the foodie vibe. I will work on a more detailed description with general recipes this week if you want to give it a try after talking with your chef."

He raised my hand to his lips, kissing the back of it and sucking lightly. The gesture was innocent—mostly—but the sensation, combined with the insinuation of what else he might do with his mouth, had me squirming in my chair with anticipation. I caught his quiet chuckle as he returned our hands to the table.

"Evil," I muttered. It wasn't nice to rev the engines if you weren't going to take her out for a spin.

"I feel that way every time you're in the room, and sometimes when you're not—call it payback."

I huffed as if piqued, but secretly delighted in his candid disclosure. I could scarcely believe the tasty treat beside me was mine. Griffin was like the sun, bright and warm, giving strength and nourishing everything his light touched—and like the sun, he

was becoming the center of my universe, a thought that scared and
elated me in equal measure.

Finished eating, we proceeded to the game room and claimed
the only available pool table. I analyzed team options to maximize
my chance at victory. I was not as obsessed as Huntleigh with
topping their other half, but I was competitive, and really...who
didn't prefer winning? Surveying my potential partners, I
identified their qualifications. Ev was a brilliant pool player and a
sure bet. But if one thing had been proven law, it was that whatever
Ev could do, Hunter could do better—much to her chagrin. He
was a gamble since I had never seen him play, but the odds were
good. Griffin was a proverbial dark horse. Having worked most
of his life in a bar, he likely had ample practice and was the most
familiar with any quirks of this particular table. Unfortunately, if
Griffin was on my team, I couldn't tease him to distraction.
Hmm...decisions, decisions.

"I love this table, it's always been lucky for me," Hunter said
with a shit-eating grin plastered across his face.

"Me, too," Ev chirped. "Really good memories... spectacular,
in fact."

Okay, they were clearly talking about more than billiards. I
could only speculate, but I suspected this table had played a pivotal
role in "the make-up" Hunter sprung on Ev at The Stop. Those
dirty birds.

"Don't worry, I had the table re-covered shortly after their
slate-top reconciliation. I even replaced the drop light over the
table that was cracked—I don't even want to know."

"Couples?" Ev asked, apparently feeling nostalgic when
suggesting teams.

We all agreed and Hunter began to rack. Ev broke,
commencing our game with finesse. I leaned back against Griffin's
hard body and tilted my head up, waiting until he lowered his ear
to my mouth.

"Please tell me we are going to destroy them, and by 'we' I
mean you."

His only response was a devious smile. Uh-oh, someone was going to dish out a SmackDown tonight. Ev was going to be crushed if her skills failed to garner a victory.

She cleared a third of the balls in her first turn and was rewarded with a pat on the butt and a kiss on the lips from Hunter. Griffin gestured for me to proceed so I positioned myself to take the easiest shot, straight-line into the left corner pocket. I was sliding the cue between my fingers about to strike when my movement was halted. Griff came from behind and wrapped his body around mine, engulfing me. He slid his hands from my shoulders down my arms slowly until he reached my hands, where he gloved mine. The length of my body was pressed against him and I shivered, my body remembering the pleasure of his.

"You'd have more control if you slid your hand a little further up the shaft," he said as he glided our hands an inch toward the tip, "and you need to tighten your grip a little in the back. Take command of it," he finished his instruction with a kiss on my neck behind my ear, allowing his lips to drag across my skin as he moved away.

Damn, I knew pool could be a fun opportunity to flirt and lean over to flash the goods, but I didn't know it was a full-contact sport that could lead to internal combustion. Pool had just become my new favorite game outside the bedroom. I heard someone clear their throat and looked up to find Ev smirking at me.

"It's been a couple of minutes...do you intend to pull yourself out of the lust-induced fog anytime tonight?" she teased.

"Just give me another minute. My fine motor skills are still stuck on Griffin whispering 'shaft' in my ear. That is some potent imagery and I'm in no hurry to wipe it away."

They all burst into laughter. I finally took my shot and sunk the ball, but unfortunately missed the next one. Hunter stepped up and cleared several more balls for their team before finally missing. Griff positioned himself for the next shot and I couldn't resist—I caressed his ass, so perfectly presented when he bent over, nearly causing him to miss the shot. He spun to me before the ball even settled in the pocket and kissed me, hard and brief, but I tasted the promise.

The game ended with our victory on Griff's final turn. We debated another game but elected to forgo the competition, since there really was none. I was still tingling with anticipation thanks to his impromptu lesson and all I could think about was getting home, but when Def Leppard's "Pour Some Sugar on Me" played, it beckoned me to the dance floor. Griffin followed me, happy to be the recipient of my moves. I circled him like a tiger, dragging my fingers along his body as I went. I considered making him sit so I could dance for him, a newly discovered fantasy, but the promise of feeling his granite body against mine was a temptation I couldn't resist. He reached out and snagged my waist, winding me into him, my back against his front. His legs were shoulder-width apart and he flexed his knees enough so that my butt pressed against his groin. I reached my arms behind me and wrapped them around his neck, pulling his mouth to mine as I swayed my hips to the beat of the song. His tongue explored my mouth aggressively, hot and insistent. The pulsing of drums guided my body as he pressed against me, shadowing my movement. He danced like I imagined he'd make love, purposeful and commanding with no hesitancy or self-consciousness—it was enthralling. Unable to resist, I spun in his arms without breaking our kiss, allowing his leg to press between mine, stimulating me. I was practically riding his leg as we danced, both of us clinging to the other as if we were alone. It was indecent, I knew, but I couldn't get enough of him—his taste, his scent, the texture and planes of his body. This was my man and I was enjoying my rights. And when the song ended, the intensity of our connection and craving did not.

"We need to find Ev and Hunter and say goodbye, then you need to take me home...STAT. You just made a whole lot of promises I expect you to deliver on."

"I didn't say a word," he said, his voice coarse with desire.

"Your mouth may have been silent but your body was speaking loud and clear. You find Huntleigh while I use the restroom. I'll meet you near the bar in three minutes and then we are out of here."

He pulled me in for a quick kiss, whispering "bossy little thing" against my lips before releasing me with a nod. I hurried to the bathroom, grateful to find it empty. He had worked me into such a frenzy I could barely contain my impulse to jump on him and take what I hungered for with reckless abandon. I finished my potty break in record time and headed for the bar.

I was fifteen feet from my destination when someone grabbed my arm on a backswing. With a quick jerk, they forced my body to turn, and before I could react or process what was happening, I was imprisoned in unfamiliar arms as a mouth took unwelcome possession of mine. No wait, these weren't unfamiliar...I knew the feel of this body, his taste. My panic was skyrocketing, but I gathered enough of my wits to bite his lip. When he pulled back I swung to hit him, but he caught my arm before I could make impact. Standing before me, looking exactly as he did when I last saw him six months ago, was my ex-boyfriend, Robbie—the coward. Apparently, he had no qualms about taking what he wanted from an unwilling woman—lie with pigs and you'll smell like shit...the adage never made more sense to me.

"Let me go, asshole," I said forcefully.

"Sam, we need to talk. I made a huge mistake."

"What you did was more than a huge mistake. Now let me go."

"Baby, let me explain—"

"Don't you dare fucking call me that! You are a sniveling, weak, sorry excuse for a man who sat quietly by while girls were beaten, raped, and murdered. You knew what *he* was doing and never spoke up. I can smell your guilt and see the blood on your hands and I want nothing to do with you. "

He continued to keep my body locked against his, so tightly I couldn't escape. My attempts to wiggle free proved futile.

"I understand why you are so mad. You have every right to be, but I promise I've changed. We can be together again. We can move past everything that happened and rebuild our lives. We need each other...we won't ever be able to survive this alone; too many people in our circle know what happened. No woman will want to be with a man branded a coward, especially if my father pulls his financial backing, and no man is going to want a used woman."

I gasped at his cruel comment but he continued, completely unaware, "But I still want you. I don't care what Heath did to you, I still see how beautiful and special you are. Can't you feel how much I want you?" He ground an unimpressive erection against my stomach to emphasize his point.

Oh god, I was going to be sick. My head was spinning—the past and the present converging—stealing all rational thought.

"Let me go, let me go, let me go..." I screeched, "please, no...please—" I finished with an anguished whimper.

His body disappeared so abruptly I would have face-planted if another set of arms had not grabbed me from behind. I struggled initially before I heard the voice in my ear.

"Sam, it's me. I've got you, you're okay. Just breathe," Ev said, the words flowing from her in one breath, spoken with conviction.

I relaxed into her support and fought to separate from the besieging memories. As my grasp on reality returned, I became aware of angry shouting and grunts. I turned my head, unprepared for the violence that greeted me.

"No," I whispered, praying my eyes deceived me.

Griffin was perched on top of Robbie, his fists landing punch after punch on a defenseless Robbie's body and face.

"You do not fucking touch her. You. Never. Fucking. Touch. Her," he punctuated each word with a blow that would incapacitate a man far larger than Robbie. "You sick fucking fuck—you did this to her...your fucking fault." He continued to shout as he landed blow after blow.

The Griffin I knew was gone, replaced by a brutal man I didn't recognize—a man who terrified me. Blood splattered the floor, the sprays marring both of their shirts. Robbie's face was unrecognizable and he was no longer conscious, but the punches continued, accompanied by a sickening wet thud followed immediately by a harsh, cracking sound. I knew that sound...I had heard it before, only the last time I was the one laying in Robbie's place and the psychopath, Heath, was delivering the face-shattering blows. I watched mindlessly as Hunter and a bouncer tried to intervene, but even their combined strength was not enough to deter Griffin.

A piercing sound rang in my ears and all I could think was that they needed to shut off the damn fire alarm before my brain exploded. The deafening racket finally penetrated Griffin's homicidal rage and he turned toward me, looking dazed. When he gestured to me as if intending to rise, I hurled my body away from him, taking Ev with me. I was crab-walking backward as soon as I hit the ground, desperate to put distance between myself and the blood-soaked monster. The last thing I saw before Ev clutched me to her chest was Griffin surveying the carnage, a look of abject horror on his face before he returned his eyes to me.

With my face buried in Ev's ample chest, I realized that the earsplitting sound was muffled. Fuck! I was making that ghastly noise. I shut my mouth abruptly and dragged a shuddering breath past my burning throat.

I distantly heard Hunter ordering someone to call an ambulance, then instructing the bouncers to take Griffin to the office to clean him up. I never lifted my head from Ev's chest. I heard grunts and shuffling, but fortunately no sounds of him putting up a fight. The movement stopped and I heard his voice softly calling to me from a distance.

"Lo...baby," he said, his voice oozing despair.

I shook my head, never looking up.

"I'm sorry. I never...I wouldn't—I'm so damn sorry," he whispered, barely audible. The shuffling resumed and I knew he was gone.

"Go get the car," Ev said to Hunter quietly and without room for question.

We sat mutely while we waited; Ev stroked my hair and soothed me once again, like a mother would do for her damaged child. How fitting, because that is exactly how I felt: damaged and brokenhearted. I may never have spoken the words, but I had fallen in love with Griffin. And now it turned out he wasn't who I thought he was...he had hidden a monster inside of him and betrayed me with his omission.

"Can I touch you, Sam?" Hunter was already back.

I nodded, too drained to do much else.

Hunter lifted me, carried me outside, and positioned me in the back of his Yukon. Before I even processed my relocation, Ev sat next to me and wrapped her arm around my shoulders. In another flash, I was in Hunter's arms again, entering his apartment. He set me gently on the couch, which Ev had unfolded into a bed the minute we arrived.

"I'm going to check on him. You got her?" Hunter asked quietly.

"Of course, take your time. Make sure he gets home safely...I can't imagine what he must be feeling...don't let him do anything stupid."

Hunter nodded and was gone after a quick kiss. I slumped back and rested my head against Ev's shoulder; I needed the human contact to remind me I wasn't completely alone in the world. Tears flooded my eyes and the weight of losing Griffin, or at least the man I thought he was, settled heavily on my chest.

I wasn't upset he had hit Robbie; the asshole deserved it for what he had done both tonight and in the past. He was partially responsible for the deaths of three girls and the heinous rapes of more than 25 others—a thorough beat-down was exactly what he deserved.

No, it wasn't the punches that terrified me; it was Griffin's absolute and unmitigated loss of control. His fury consumed him and he lost all restraint, pounding Robbie as if possessed. I had no doubt he would have killed him had Hunter not intervened. I trusted Griffin, but I also knew he could snap me like a twig beneath the sole of his size fifteen boots. So what would have happened if I ever pushed him too far? How could I protect myself if I didn't know where *his* landmines were buried?

"Ready to talk about it?" Ev asked.

I shook my head in reply.

"Sam, I need words, just a few so I know you aren't going nonverbal on me."

"Not tonight, Ev." It was all I could muster to pacify her, but it was enough.

I lay perfectly still for several minutes, focusing on my breathing, desperate to stave off the avalanche careening toward me, but it was no use. I couldn't outrun it and I couldn't stop the inevitable, so I succumbed. Giant sobs wracked my body, grief pouring from me in unintelligible wails. I grieved for the Griffin I thought I knew; the stable man I had fallen in love with had proved to be no more than an illusion. I mourned the death of the fantasy I had unwittingly constructed in my mind...the one where we lived happily ever after. I also suffered the loss of the Sam I was with Griffin, the girl he encouraged and inspired me to be.

"It h-hurts...s-soo...bb-baad," I forced through my gasping cries. "I.ll ...llooved—"

"Shh, breathe Sam. Shh, just breathe," she repeated the mantra over and over as she hugged me.

Eventually I cried myself to sleep, but I couldn't escape my pain, even in rest. My unconscious mind taunted me with Griffin's horror-stricken expression when my screeching registered. I relived the look of self-disgust etched across his face when I crawled away from him in terror. Griffin haunted me all night, his pain amplifying my own.

Chapter Twelve

"We're born alone, we live alone, we die alone. Only through our love and friendship can we create the illusion for the moment that we're not alone." -Orson Welles

I awoke the following morning with an emotional hangover and the absolute worst stiff neck ever, courtesy of Hunter's pull-out couch—ugh, all the traditional symptoms of overindulging without any of the fun. My body hated me and was sending its message loud and clear. I lay unmoving, unable to ignore Ev and Hunter's hushed conversation filtering in from the nearby kitchen.

"How is she?" Hunter asked, concern evident in his voice.

"She's a disaster. Babe, if you could've heard her last night...god, she was in agony. She was sobbing so hard I thought she was going to be sick. It was heart-wrenching. How's Griff?"

Hunter's groan was a mix of frustration and pain.

"That good, huh?" Ev asked sympathetically.

"He's devastated, destroyed. He thinks any hope he had for a future with Sam was obliterated last night and he's not coping well. He drank himself into oblivion, but not before listing every stupid choice he's ever made to prove that nothing compared to losing it on Robbie. All he can see without Sam in his future is desolation—he always believed they would end up together for the long haul. I don't think he's able to picture a future without her...he may never be."

"Fucking Robbie! He's a tornado, destroying everything he comes near, leaving tragedy in his wake. How many more lives will he passively ravage?" Ev fumed.

"I know, angel, I know."

It seemed like the right time to announce I was wake so I made a production out of stirring, ensuring my movements were heard. I headed toward the kitchen as Ev and Hunter exited.

"Sit," Hunter ordered, "omelets will be ready in ten minutes." He ruffled my hair and squeezed my shoulder as he passed me.

I sat at the dining table as commanded, grateful not to have to decide what to do with myself. Ev placed a mug of coffee and two Advil in front of me before taking a seat. The silence wasn't awkward, but it wasn't comfortable either. I traced the grain of the natural oak tabletop with my finger, searching the wood fibers for answers I hadn't found elsewhere.

I didn't know what to say. I wanted to reassure them I would be okay, but it would be a lie. I would survive—I had learned the hard way I could survive anything—but that was the most I could promise with confidence. How could I have been so wrong, so utterly and completely blind to the darkness lurking in Griffin? I no longer trusted my own judgment; my instincts—my gut—had failed me.

I was never one to hide from harsh realities, to turn a blind eye or lie to myself. I knew *he*...Heath (there, I said it, at least in my mind)...was depraved from the first time I met him. Not the extent of his psychopathy maybe, but his pathological narcissism. And I may not have grasped the depth of Robbie's cowardice while we were together, but I did see the flaw. I just never imagined the ramifications of Robbie's weakness. Fear shaped his character, resulting in a lack of integrity and personal accountability, which would have led most others to step forward and prevent tragedy. I pegged Hunter as a man of honor and morality even during his mysterious, secret-keeping period, which Ev had since dubbed his 'Shady Phase.' Hell, I even pegged my first serious boyfriend as a cheater long before receiving hard evidence. My intuition had never failed me and to do so now was inexcusable.

I should have suspected the other shoe would drop. Griffin was too good to be true; no one was *that* perfect. I could accept flaws because we all have them, but the trick was to find a partner whose baggage matches yours. Plus, there was a difference between flaws and psychological defects. Some defects make a man dangerous, and not the sexy kind of dangerous—the scary kind. I would have bet my life that Griffin would never hurt me, but now I wasn't so sure. How long until I pushed him too far and that blood-chilling fury could be focused on me? How long before he fell into that trance, lost command of himself, and I paid the price as collateral damage? His homicidal rage was not to be ignored...oh my...I had thought about the possibility of having children with him. No, the thought was too terrible. I couldn't allow my mind to go there.

A plate appeared before me but I wanted to puke. We ate in silence—well, they ate and I pushed the eggs around my plate. None of us were prepared to confront the fallout.

I caught the look Ev and Hunter exchanged and sighed; I knew I needed to let them say their piece. They both had earned the right to be heard because of their tireless support over the last six months.

"Go ahead," I prompted, granting them the permission their silence begged.

"How are you?" Ev opened up our breakfast roundtable.

"Shitty, heartsick, betrayed. Take your pick."

Ev looked at me expectantly.

"I'm not going to have a mental breakdown, Ev, but I'm broken. I was already broken, but Griffin's betrayal has blasted me to smithereens. I feel like I swallowed a grenade that detonated inside me, annihilating the pieces I had fit back together. I am not okay, I may never trust myself again, but I *will* survive."

Hunter and Ev both looked pained by my words. I didn't have the energy to sugarcoat the truth for them. I loved them both dearly, but I was doing them no favors by pretending or offering false hope.

"I don't think Griff meant to—" Ev began.

"Don't," I said.

"But, Sam, he's hurting too. Hunter said—"

I held up a hand to halt her cutting words. I didn't want his pain to hurt me, but it did. She had to stop.

"Last night was surreal and traumatic," Ev said, evidently unaware of the torment she was causing me, "I'm sure it kicked up horrendous memories for you. I know you're scared, but he is not—"

"Stop!" I said harshly, unable to hear *his* name and unwilling to be engulfed by memories of last night or that night six months ago. What the hell was she trying to do?

"Don't...don't tell me you know. You don't know anything. You may have been almost attacked, but it is not the same—I'm sorry, but it's not. You can't understand. You can't imagine. You both have been incredible, the best family I could ask for, and I will be forever grateful. If you ever need anything— support, money, a kidney, it's yours. But however much it hurt you to watch me in the hospital and care for me when I got back, however much you suffered alongside me, you still don't know—I hope you never do. I hope you never know what it's like to be pulled from your happy life and dragged into the woods, unable to see, struggling to breathe, paralyzed by fear. I hope you never know what it's like to have a man use his strength to overpower you and force you to take a part of him inside you in a way that seeps into your soul and poisons you from within. I pray you never know what it feels like to be beaten until you pray for death, to welcome the relief it would bring." I paused to draw a ragged breath. "I would sacrifice my own life so you never know the blackness, pain so encompassing that you no longer feel human. I hope you never know," I finished on a whimper.

No one said anything. What could they say? It was the first time I had been brutally honest with them and it must be a difficult pill to swallow.

"Griffin fooled me," I said, not bothering to hide my disillusionment. "I never suspected he was capable of such savagery. He was a bloodthirsty monster last night, and I've spent more than my share of time with monsters. I don't care how strong a leash the beast is usually restrained with...last night proved the beast can get free. And I don't want to be in its path the next time it comes out to play." I sighed, bone-deep weariness settling within me. "I know you wanted us to work...so did I, more than you will ever know. I think he was my only chance at love, the soul deep, can't-exist-without-you kind, but I have to let that go now—and so do you." I rose from the table, shaky but calm. "I'm going to shower, and then I am meeting with Thia and my realtor so I'll be out all afternoon. I'll text later to see if you want me to bring dinner."

I grabbed clothes from a suitcase Hunter had brought from Griffin's house last night before entering the bathroom. I grabbed a tee, a button up, and a cardigan, hoping that I could cover myself in layers of protection as insulation from the outside world. They were still sitting mute like statues when I exited the bathroom. I walked over to them and kissed each on the top of their head before leaving the apartment.

I was relieved to find that the rental car I ordered yesterday had miraculously made its way here. I refused to consider who arranged for the change of drop-off location. Only one person knew which company I had contracted for the rental. I didn't want the reminder of how thoughtful Griffin was, even when he was supposedly heartbroken.

I called the realtor while waiting for the car to warm up and told her I wanted to buy—today. If a property was available for me to move in immediately, I was willing to compromise on my 'must haves' list. The sound of her mentally calculating her potential commission was nearly audible, so it was no surprise when she agreed to meet me at the agency in thirty minutes. Perfect.

We arrived at the same time but she didn't exit her car immediately. When she finally opened the door, she was ending a phone call.

"Good news! Let's get inside and I'll tell you all about it," she said, smiling happily. "It's your lucky day."

I rolled my eyes at her claim; given everything that had transpired in the last 24 hours, the only acquaintance I had with Lady Luck was as her prison bitch.

Once in the conference room, she shared that the townhouse I had fallen in love with, the one I measured all other options against, was mine for the taking. The other offer had fallen through because of problems securing a mortgage. It was mine if I signed the contract today! The price was reasonable, not a steal but a good investment. The seller agreed to me moving in today, provided my bank faxed confirmation of the funds transfer to their lawyer's escrow account. A quick call to my financial advisor and my bank account was officially lighter.

"How soon can we close? I have the funds available for immediate payment," I said.

"I'll set it up for next week, as early as possible. Just email me the contact details for your lawyer and I'll take care of everything else." She was practically salivating at the pain-free commission. "Here are your keys. Congratulations."

I accepted the keys and thanked her for her assistance. I was anxious to visit my new home, but knew I needed to go to my appointment with Thia first.

I arrived at Thia's office with one minute to spare. Whew! As soon as I opened the door, I heard her call me in. I crossed to the chair I now thought of as mine and plopped down, drained from the day. Thia was at her desk, typing on her laptop. She closed the cover and finally looked at me as she moved to the chair across from mine. She frowned, then she frowned some more. Uh-oh, the frowning-staring contest was far more unnerving than the standard stare-down. For the first time, Thia broke the silence.

"You look like hell. What have you done this past week, visited war-zones?"

"I see I won't have to pay extra for sprinkles today," I said dryly, "a good thing since I just spent a fortune on a new house."

"I see. When do you move in?"

"I close next week but negotiated to move in today since it was vacant. I have the keys right here," I said, patting my purse.

"What's the rush?"

"Rush? I've been looking for weeks. I fell in love with this place but it was in contract. When the deal fell through, I snatched it up. It's perfect for me; I couldn't be happier."

"You're a terrible liar...awful, really. Don't ever go into politics," Thia said with no humor in her voice. "Let's try this again—I'll be more precise and you'll be honest, yes? Why the rush to move in before closing? Last week you were staying with Griffin and on cloud nine. You were reluctantly looking for your own place. So I will ask again, why the abrupt change in course? What precipitated the rapid evac?"

"Griffin and I aren't...we're not...it's over. He's not who I thought he was. I can't...I just can't—" I shut my eyes to prevent the tears that had pooled in my eyes from falling.

"Who is he?"

"Huh?"

"You said he wasn't who you thought he was. Then who is he?" she asked, as if I could make sense of what happened.

I stared at her, unable to answer.

"Is he still caring and empathetic? Patient? Oh no, don't tell me he developed a spare tire and love handles overnight—I hate when a hot guy doesn't age well. It's such a letdown."

I sent a scathing look at her for reducing my valid concern to shallow triviality.

"Did he cheat? Hurt you?"

I winced at that one. He had hurt me deeply, but not in the way she meant.

"Getting warmer," she said to herself. "Did he abandon you?" she asked, searching my face as if to find an answer. "Did he break your trust? Did he scare you?"

I inhaled sharply, remembering his betrayal by omission. I could see the blood splatter, hear the crunch of bone under his hands. I covered my ears and shook my head, desperate to stop the instant replay.

"Samantha, look at me. You can't ignore this to avoid the pain—you know that. Tell me what happened and tell me how you felt."

I sighed, knowing it was best to relent. I was certain she could wear me down and wait me out. I told her everything in agonizing detail as she listened, never interrupting and without expression. "I swear, Thia, if Hunter hadn't intervened, Griffin would have killed him."

"Hunter? That isn't what you just told me. Think back on the moments leading up to Griffin finally snapping out of it. What stopped him?"

I grudgingly replayed the movie on the back of my eyelids, desperately trying to turn away from the violent scenes, but the projection followed my head as I moved. I heard the soundtrack of Griffin's grunts as the force of each powerful hit connected with Robbie's face, and then the sickening crack that repulsed me played in surround sound. I watched as Hunter and the bouncer tried to pry Griffin off Robbie, again and again—failing. The piercing shriek I now knew originated from me rung out and reverberated through the room. Griffin froze with unnatural stillness, his arm drawn back to deliver the next blow. Seconds passed before he angled his body toward me, meeting my eyes for the briefest connection before I skittered as far away from him as I could.

"Me," I shared the revelation with Thia. She nodded her head, indicating she already knew.

"Yes, your distress penetrated and pulled him back from the edge."

I wasn't sure if that knowledge made any difference. It didn't negate his frenzied brutality; and therefore it changed nothing.

"It doesn't matter. It doesn't change the facts."

"What are the facts?"

"He had a violent episode, verging on homicidal, in which he nearly killed someone. I never imagined he was capable of...that he could..." I shook my head, hating what I was about to say. "He was just like *him*—uncaring, vicious, and out of control."

"Is that how you see Heath? Was he out of control? It seems to me he was coherent, methodical, and very much in control."

"I...I don't know."

"Did you talk to Griffin about what happened? What triggered him? What stopped him? Has he ever done something like this before?"

"No."

"Consider having a conversation with him, if only to understand. He has been a good friend to you. If you decide to sever ties, it should be a fully informed choice, not a reaction rooted in fear. Have you considered how much of your reaction was the residual fear from Robbie's uninvited touch? Have you sorted through all of your emotions from last night? Can you determine what lay latent within you versus what Griffin's actions triggered?"

I shook my head.

"You will learn over time that your emotional responses are not always the result of the present situation. Traumas from the past *will* filter your perception for a long time, perhaps forever. Your response was natural, but you must attempt to separate past from present when making decisions if you want to live fully unchained from your past." When I said nothing, Thia continued.

"If nothing else, after all the good he has done, don't you think you owe him the opportunity to apologize? I'm not saying you have to forgive and forget, but I would be surprised if he didn't want to offer an explanation. Think about it."

I nodded, but wasn't sure I could do as she suggested.

"One more thing—while you're busy sorting this out, try employing the tried-and-true coping technique of eating your emotions. Usually I don't encourage such forms of escapism, but you can't afford to lose any weight. In fact, give me your new address, I'm going to have Alpine Bakery send you a cheesecake...oh, and one of their Tiramisu—maybe Uncle Giuseppe's can deliver some manicotti."

"Thia, I appreciate your concern, but I will eat. I promise. Don't waste your money on having food delivered."

"Oh, don't worry, I'll bill you for it. See you next week."

"No homework this week?" I asked, surprised.

"I already told you to eat. Other than that, I think you know," she said and finished with a look that spoke more than any words she could have uttered.

"Are you guilt-tripping me into self-discovery and talking to Griffin?"

Thia shrugged, "Whatever works. I'm Italian, feeding and guilt come naturally. But answer this...why would you feel guilty unless I was right, at least to some degree?"

I huffed in frustration.

"You desperately want to call me a smug bitch right now, don't you?" she laughed.

I left Thia's office, shell-shocked. I wasn't sure what I was expecting when I arrived—maybe a pat on the back for separating from Griffin, given his concerning behavior. She never said what I expected. Thia didn't say I made a mistake, but she made it clear that I acted without true consideration, allowing fear and emotion to guide my decision. I was reacting, not reflecting. Ugh! I guess I had a lot to think about.

I kept telling myself that, regardless of the motivating force, Griffin was still off the reservation last night. I had every right to distance myself from potential danger. I wasn't overreacting, I was protecting myself and being smart. But Thia made me question my conclusions. If I was so justified, then why did her words hold weight? Why was my heart screaming at me, cursing and calling me a fool?

I felt hollow inside, a huge piece of me ripped away so suddenly its absence was all the more pronounced—Griffin. My hope and faith had fled with him, their departure echoing, reiterating the loss. How could another person be a piece of you? It was fundamentally wrong. I always believed in order to be a good partner you had to be whole, not relying on another to fill the emptiness within. I believed in love, even the fairytale, but never did I consider the term 'soul mate' anything more than a literary hyperbole. I vividly remember watching the movie 'Jerry Maguire' and rolling my eyes as he emphatically told Dorothy, "You complete me."

Yet here I was, aching for Griffin...or rather the man I thought he was. He couldn't have been the puzzle piece that snapped perfectly into place, finishing the picture of Sam—he couldn't. The man I fell in love with and who fit me so flawlessly was not authentic. He contorted himself, hiding his own ugly pieces, and once the hidden edges were exposed, he no longer fit. I hated him for deceiving me, allowing me to fall in love with a sanitized version of himself and breaking an unspoken promise. Ugh! I hated myself even more than him for still wanting the illusion, wishing last night had never happened.

I needed to occupy my mind with thoughts other than Griffin...I needed a time-out. I headed to Walmart and bought an airbed with a built-in pump and the highest thread-count sheets I could find. At least it would be more comfortable than that abomination of a "bed" I slept on last night. Even hospital beds were more comfortable—trust me, I knew.

I pulled up to the guard booth of the gated community and was pleasantly surprised to find that the seller's agent had phoned to announce my soon-to-be-owner status. I drove past the beautiful clubhouse, pool area, and tennis courts on the way to my new home. I let myself in, my hands trembling slightly—this was my new start at independence. I expected to feel joyous, but the stark emptiness inside me overshadowed everything else.

The floor plan was open and spacious, high ceilings and windows met me at every turn. The wood floors and taupe walls added warmth. I peeked in the guestroom before heading to the master suite. The bedroom was spacious with French doors that opened onto a balcony overlooking the man-made lake with plume fountain. The original floor plan for the unit called for 2 bedrooms, 2.5 bathrooms, and an office, but during construction the owners converted the office that shared a wall with the master bedroom into a humongous closet/dressing room. It was outfitted with built-in shelves and clothing bars throughout. A marble-topped vanity and accessory wall was thoughtfully placed near the entry. It was a space you would find on Pinterest and immediately pin to your 'dream closet' board—but now it was mine. I hugged myself in gratitude. I entered the master bath and relished the luxurious spa-like atmosphere.

I headed back downstairs to the kitchen, my second favorite room in the house. It was a work of art. Top of the line appliances were nestled strategically in antiqued wood cabinetry. I made a list in my mind for the grocery store, planning the first meal I would cook in this chef's dream. My momentary excitement was squelched when I realized I would be cooking for one most nights.

I tried to focus on the positive by assuring myself I had indeed purchased wisely for both living pleasure and investment purposes. I texted Ev and Hunter to share the good news before I returned to Hunter's apartment to collect my meager belongings stored there. I still needed to make arrangements to get the rest of my furniture and clothes from Griffin's house. Embracing my inner wimp, I debated asking Hunter and Ev to pick up my belongings from Griffin. I couldn't see him—I wasn't ready.

The emptiness of the house echoed my mood, and I needed to be alone without an audience for my pain. I fell asleep that night feeling completely alone. My pillow was damp from the tears I shed, but I didn't have the energy to flip it over to the dry side. At least the airbed was more comfortable than Hunter's couch. I had gotten one thing right.

I awoke on a partially deflated airbed that was trying to swallow me whole. I glanced at my phone to find it was already noon, not a surprise since I had been wallowing in pain until five in the morning. Any hope of feeling brighter in the light of day quickly faded. My troubles had not flown south for the winter while I slept.

Thankfully, I had a house to furnish. I steered my car in the direction of ignorance and oblivion, also known as the nearest Raymour and Flannigan furniture store. If that didn't provide enough distraction, then a trip to HomeGoods would be my next stop.

Hours later, I arrived home, furniture ordered and a trunk full of HomeGoods treasures. Huntleigh was due in thirty minutes and I had no dinner prepared. It didn't matter, I could have had three hours and still wouldn't have been able to feed them. I had forgotten my new home was empty when I extended the invitation earlier, not a single pot or pan in sight. At times like this there was only one solution—Oshi Sushi. The food arrived simultaneously with Huntleigh.

I gave them the grand tour before we enjoyed dinner. Thankfully, neither mentioned Griffin or the break-up drama. After show-and-tell with my new home décor goodies, we exchanged hugs and goodbyes.

"The place is gorgeous, Sam. I'm so happy for you!" Ev said while hugging me.

"Nice choice," Hunter said, delivering his hug.

"Can you coordinate with Griffin and tell me a good time to have the movers go get my stuff?" I whispered to Hunter before he released me.

He kept his hands on my shoulders and held me away from him, studying me. He shook his head, denying my request.

"Sorry Sam, but you are going to have to face that one yourself. I'm not going to be the go-between so you can avoid him. I care enough to tell you 'no.'"

Son of a bitch! It never occurred to me that Hunter would decline my plea for help. Until now, there was never anything he and Ev refused to help me do. Hell, they pushed their way in when I didn't want help more than once. Great time to deploy a tough love campaign, asshole.

"Fine," I said tersely.

Hunter only chuckled at my peevish reply.

"I'm not doing it either," Ev chimed in from behind Hunter.

"Seriously?"

"Only because I love you."

"Only because you are trying to force your agenda," I seethed.

"You say poe-tay-toe, I say poe-tah-toe. Either way, I'm still not doing your dirty work."

"Fine," I muttered, as I opened the door for them to leave. I didn't exactly throw them out, and we had technically already said our goodbyes, but my displeasure was evident.

Alone again, I walked through the house, checking that the windows were locked and switching off lights. I entered my bedroom and surveyed the dark emptiness, the only light emanated from the nightlight in the bathroom. I wavered between anger and anguish as I stripped my clothes and roughly dragged my nightgown over my head.

How could they refuse to help me? They were supposed to be my family—support me even when they didn't agree. It felt like they were choosing sides and had abandoned me. They thought they were helping with tough love...well, fuck tough love. Fuck them. I'd had plenty of 'tough' over the past seven months, all I needed was the damn 'love.' I just found out that the man I foolishly fell for was harboring a monster within, waiting to go bat-shit crazy at any provocation. How could they want me to talk to him? How could they not understand how much I needed them?

I had no one.

Chapter Thirteen

"At the center of your being you have the answer; you know who you are and you know what you want." -Lao Tzu

Ev called the day after our dinner and we came to an understanding. She and Hunter wanted to support me, but they would not choose sides. After a candid heart-to-heart, Ev apologized for making me feel abandoned, and I apologized for overreacting to their refusal. They came back that evening and Ev helped me hang pictures, while Hunter was tasked with moving the family and dining room furniture as we debated layout options.

The rest of the week passed in a blur of deliveries, phone and cable technicians, and the closing of the property. The house was officially mine and it was no longer empty...even if I still was. I busied myself with work, home decorating, and, when desperate, reality TV. I was now on a first-name basis with every "Real Housewife" from New York to Orange County. Despite this, the temporary distractions were just that...temporary. My hands were busy and my mind checked out, but the oblivion was fleeting. Nothing helped, and as the void grew, blackness spread within like spilled ink.

I was still adamantly avoiding Griffin and Huntleigh were equally adamant in their refusal to get involved. Faced with no other option, I was forced to purchase a basic wardrobe and cosmetic essentials to replace the originals I had abandoned. I was lucky my new home's community center offered a state-of-the-art gym, as I was unwilling to risk running into him at NYSC. What surprised me was that Griffin had made no effort to contact me—none. Complete. Radio. Silence. A million reasons floated through my head—problems at The Stop, the flu, giving me space, too ashamed to face me—but the more time passed, the more I feared the worst...none of it had been real. Letting me go seemed far easier for him than it was for me. Did he not miss me? Was he not as desperate to see me, touch me, hold me as I was for him? My pride prevented me from asking Hunter or Ev about him. My wariness caused me to delete every text I wrote him in moments of weakness. I was a pathetic blubbering mess while he was probably sleeping like a baby without a care in the world.

By the time I returned to Thia's office, I had lost five pounds and slept no more than three hours any given night. It goes without saying that I wasn't exactly rocking the vegetarian-zombie look. I walked into her office without waiting for her invitation. She looked up and scanned me from head to toe before shaking her head with disapproval. Join the freakin' club, Thia.

She took her usual seat across from me and the stare-down commenced. The small spark remaining inside me flared and I resolved that she would not break me this time. After fifty-eight minutes of uncomfortable eye contact, she finally spoke.

"The only thing you managed to prove today was that you are stubborn and your pride is more valuable to you than your healing. Pull another stunt like this and you can find yourself a new therapist. I only treat people who want to confront the hard truths to grow and heal."

"What do you care?" I seethed, "You get paid either way."

"I have a waiting list a mile long, your money is replaceable. If you don't want to do the work, then I will invest my time in someone who will. You are special, Sam. You could be one of my greatest success stories, but right now you are poised to be my biggest disappointment."

I stared at her, mouth agape.

"You said no sugarcoating, too late to change your mind. Your time is up today. If you choose to return, you will make the effort to sleep and eat first, you will think about our conversation during your last session, and you will speak. If not, we're done. Got it?" I couldn't find words. All I was able to do was nod like an errant child.

She jerked her chin toward the door, dismissing me—it stung. I was almost out the door when she spoke.

"Sam, I hope you come back. Forget what people tell you...we have favorites, and you are one of mine."

Again, all I could do was nod. I was ashamed of my behavior, for wasting both of our time because I had refused to consider any of the issues she asked of me. I was 90% certain Thia was the best therapist money could buy; the remaining 10%, I still questioned if she was certifiable.

I spent the rest of my day cooking an elaborate meal for one and thinking. I didn't reach any enlightenment, but it was my first honest attempt to sort through the events of last week and how they connected to my feelings stemming from the attack.

I was at Higher Yearning on Monday, working my usual shift, when I saw him through the front window approaching the shop. Shit! Meg had run to the bank on her lunch break, preventing me from ducking behind the counter. The front door swung open, the chime announcing his arrival, and I watched my nemesis casually stride toward me as if he was a welcomed guest. This man had a set of brass balls the size of an elephant's.

I was tired and wrung dry. I didn't have the energy to be anxious about what his appearance meant or the threats he may direct at me. I was a woman on the edge, driven there by men, and this particular man was about to pay the price.

"Mr. Black—Westly—I have never been accused of being subtle, but it appears you require more explicit instructions than most. I do not want or need your client's money. Your threats are a waste of breath and my time. I will be testifying and nothing short of death will dissuade me. I am aware your client is considering that very possibility and you can tell him I said 'go fuck yourself.' I've already walked through Hell—trust me, death would be preferable to what your client's son did to me." He flinched at my brutal honesty, but I wasn't done with him.

"I'm going to say this one last time, really slowly so you don't miss it—Get. The. Fuck. Out. Don't ever come back. You are no better than the scum you represent. If you need to rack up billable hours, then drive here, sit in the parking lot, then leave. Feel free to charge your client double—I won't rat you out. Do not, under any circumstances, approach me again. If you do, I will hunt you down and run you over with my new Michelins."

He stared at me in disbelief.

"Was there anything ambiguous about *my* threat, Westly? Any vagueness I need to clarify, or are we finally speaking the same language?"

"Message received. You know, in the past two years as a defense attorney, I have been in the presence of criminals of every variety, including mobsters, gang bangers, and a serial killer—none of them were nearly as frightening as you were during your tirade. I'm not sure if I'm terrified or turned on."

It was my turn to stare at him in disbelief.

"For what it's worth...the only thr—" he caught himself, "cautions from my clients have come directly from me. If you are receiving actual threats you should speak to the police."

He turned on his heel and left with the same leisurely strut as when he entered.

I stared at the door, watching as he got into his Porsche Carrera and drove away. When he was out of sight, I shrugged to myself. Some people were beyond comprehension; I can't imagine how that asshat could look himself in the mirror.

When I got home that night, I called Hunter to fill him in on the latest Mr. Black visit. I knew Hunter wasn't pleased with my brazen comments, but he didn't editorialize beyond a few well-timed grunts and vexed exhales.

"Do you think he's telling the truth about the...the Varbecks?" I asked, knowing people rarely admitted criminal activities, but finding myself slightly persuaded by Mr. Black's declaration of his client's innocence.

"I doubt it. We are still poring over their financial records, but we've already identified two questionable transactions we suspect were payoffs to witnesses. Unfortunately, we can't produce a solid connection and the witnesses aren't talking. I'm not giving up, but it's an uphill battle in cases such as these," Hunter said, before pausing. His reluctance was enough warning for me to know I didn't want to hear what came next.

"You should know Robbie's family is pushing the D.A.'s office to charge Griffin with assault in the first degree. That's a felony and would likely result in jail time. Given the circumstance, the D.A. is sympathetic to Griffin, but can't ignore his actions completely. If Robbie's family backs off, the D.A. will allow Griff to plead guilty to assault in the third degree, which will only result in community service and a record."

"What do I need to do?" I asked without hesitation. Hunter didn't directly ask me to intervene, but he wouldn't have told me if there wasn't some way for me to help.

"If you talk to the D.A. and tell the police about Robbie's behavior, maybe request first degree assault charges be filed along with a restraining order—"

"So, if they back off Griffin, I will drop my complaint. Gotcha. I'll call the D.A.'s office in the morning."

"Great, thanks Sam. He would never have asked. Actually, he's going to be furious when he finds out I asked on his behalf."

"How is he?" I asked timidly.

Hunter released a long-suffering sigh.

"I don't want to step in the middle of this shit-show, Sam. You are both acting like stubborn asses. If you two want to know how the other is doing, then cut the crap and pick up the phone. I love you both, but that doesn't mean I don't want to lock you together in a room until your work this shit out. You need to have a conversation—with each other, not me. That's all I'm saying."

"I'll consider your advice," I said with sincerity.

The following morning I followed through on my promise and called the D.A.'s office. The assistant D.A. seemed relieved to hear from me, promising to contact Robbie's family and get back to me this week with an update. He suggested I proceed with the restraining order, and considering my luck with men over the past year, I decided to take his advice.

Less than twenty-four hours later, I was surprised to find the same assistant D.A. standing before me at the Higher Yearning counter.

"Miss Whitney, it's a pleasure to meet you in person. I'm Mark Stuart, we spoke on the phone yesterday. Do you have a few minutes to spare?" he asked with a polite grin.

"Sure. Why don't you order a drink and I'll join you in a moment?"

He nodded at me before turning to face Meg, a huge smile spread across his face. Uh-oh, Meg had found an admirer.

"You didn't need to come all the way down here, but thank you," I said, once we had seated ourselves in a quiet corner.

"It's no trouble. I've heard how great the coffee is here for years; it was a good excuse to try it." He took a sip and hummed his approval.

"Do you mind if we cut to the chase since I'm still on the clock? My manager understands, but I don't want to take advantage."

"Of course! I wanted to let you know that Robbie's family is amenable to Assault 3 for Griffin if Robbie escapes charges. They also promised not to protest the restraining order."

"Great."

"I also wanted to verify that you will be testifying at the trial against Heath Varbeck. We anticipate the deposition will occur in the next few weeks. I understand you have been the subject of intimidation tactics, and I wanted to ensure you weren't considering backing out."

"You can count on me. I won't be changing my mind, no matter what they throw at me. I will not allow *him* to get away with what he did. If I have to speak for all the other girls who are too afraid to testify, then so be it."

"Wonderful, I appreciate your commitment. Your testimony is key since you were both a victim and you witnessed Robbie's observation and admissions in regards to Mr. Varbeck's guilt. We will have you come in to prepare for the deposition."

"Can I ask you one question that has been bothering me?"

"Sure."

"Everleigh hasn't been threatened and she's the one *he* actually confessed to. Why do you think that is?"

"Miss Carsen was deposed and her testimony submitted during the grand jury hearing. Her account is already on record. If something were to happen to her or if she were to back out of testifying at the trial, we could move to have that deposition from the grand jury hearing introduced into evidence. It wouldn't be as persuasive, but it would be sufficient. Mr. Varbeck's attorneys will undoubtedly attempt to attack her character and the veracity of her account. That is why it is so important that we have your testimony as well. The judge and jury could possibly call into question a single account, but with corroboration, the defense will be unsuccessful."

Ah, it all made sense to me now. I didn't have any previous deposition or testimony that the D.A. could use in trial since I was in a coma and semi-catatonic during the grand jury.

He took another sip of his coffee. "Wow, this really is great coffee. The girl who served me was very helpful, too. Very sweet."

Was he fishing for a formal introduction after discussing prosecuting my rapist? What the hell was wrong with men?

"Thank you again for taking the time to come here. Please let me know when you need me to come in and I will clear my schedule."

After shaking his hand, I returned to the counter and smirked at Meg.

"You have an admirer," I said, nodding toward Mark. "He was angling for an introduction, but I didn't want to spring him on you. He's a 7.5, and I would guess he has a Bachelor's but is studying for his Master's. You could definitely do better, but if you're interested it would be a slam dunk."

"You are terrible. The poor guy—you are picking him apart like a vulture," she said, unable to completely hide her laughter.

"Hey, as your tutor in the art of selecting the guaranteed O-man, it's my job to dish the hard truths. They aren't always pretty."

Meg rolled her eyes before muttering, "You are so bad."

Before I knew it, it was Thursday—Thia Thursday. I knew I must go since hiding wasn't an option, but I hadn't made any significant progress in sorting through my emotions, separating past from present, or discerning justifiable responses from projections. In truth, I wasn't any closer to finding the clarity Thia had challenged me to pursue. I didn't want to disappoint her, but at least today I could honestly say I had *tried*. I was no longer using distractions as an escape. I spent every minute outside of work stewing in the mysteries that were my convoluted brain.

I arrived at Thia's office and settled into a chair in the reception area. Five minutes after my appointed time, I stood and collected my belongings. I was tempted to just leave, embarrassed by her rejection, but she deserved a 'thank you' for the time she had invested. I only had to knock once on her closed office door before she opened it and smiled like the Cheshire Cat.

"Come in."

"Hi. I'm here."

"So I see. Do you have all the answers?"

I shook my head, ready for her censure, but instead she laughed.

"Of course you don't, I never expected you to have it all sorted out in a matter of days. You've been trying though...I can tell."

"I have tried, but it's a tangled mess. I did gain a pound so at least I accomplished one objective."

She tssked, "You're still too skinny."

I settled into my chair and noticed a foil-wrapped plate on the coffee table in front of me. Thia sat across from me and handed me a tray with a napkin, fork, and knife before uncovering the plate and placing it on the tray. In front of me was a huge plate of homemade spaghetti and meatballs with filleto di pomodoro sauce.

"You made this for me?"

"I thought you might need a little help."

She was feeding me. She made this delicious lunch for me—with her own hands—because she had faith that I would return. She believed in me—I was totally her favorite. With a big smile, I loaded my fork and stuffed my mouth. Oh damn, it was delicious.

"We'll have to shuck social conventions for today and allow you to talk with your mouth full. Tell me about your week."

Between bites I shared the events of the week. Thia was pleased to learn that I had intervened on Griffin's behalf and that I followed through on the restraining order against Robbie.

"Are you going to talk with Griffin?"

"What's the point, Thia? It's been two weeks and he has made *zero* effort to talk to me. You were convinced he would want the opportunity to explain and apologize—looks like you were wrong."

"Have you considered the possibility that he's embarrassed?"

I thought of Griffin's face after the one-sided fight. He looked defeated and devastated. Those feelings could have transformed into embarrassment in the days that followed, once he had time to appreciate what he had done.

"Perhaps."

"You say that as if it's surprising. I'm never wrong...ask my husband, I tell him all the time."

Poor Mr. Thia. I couldn't begin to fathom what she would be like at home—he was either the luckiest man on the planet or he was karma's bitch.

"Yeah, yeah. You're the bomb, a genius among idiots, yada, yada. Even if you are right, does it change what he did? He may realize he went from psych boy to psycho, but he still has the potential to flip that switch again."

"This is why I suggested you have a conversation with him, to find the answers you need. I do not believe he is a danger to you. Based on what you've told me, I don't think he is capable of intentionally hurting you. He is the only one who can explain what set him off and if there is a risk for a repeat performance. If you want answers, you need to ask him."

I nodded, hearing the truth in her words.

"Sam, you need to understand something. You've likely heard this at TPC, but you need to internalize it. Most rape is about control and power—sex has very little to do with it. Rape, when coupled with extreme violence, is still about control and power, but the violence is often the hardest part for victims to process and overcome. Exposure to extreme acts of brutality, even if they are necessary or justifiable, may always remain a trigger for you. Even sports like boxing or mixed martial arts could trigger flashbacks. That is why I am encouraging you to try to untangle the conditioned response versus genuine concern for Griffin's potential violent outbursts. Give it some thought over this next week."

"I will, promise."

"Okay, homework time. Try to watch a boxing or MMA match on TV and see how you react, just invite Ev or Hunter to watch with you. And have an honest conversation with Griffin. Don't worry, I will permit an extension next week if you aren't yet ready to tackle that one. Write a list of things you love to do, the things that comfort you or relieve stress. Also—"

"Keep eating...I know, will do. Thank you, Thia," I said, gesturing to the now empty plate of food, "for everything...for not giving up on me."

"My pleasure. Like I said, you are one of my favorites...and you always pay on time," she said, straight-faced, but I caught the telltale glimmer of humor in her eyes.

I left feeling heavier with the amount of information I needed to consider, but lighter for having verbalized my feelings and concerns about the beat-down.

The following night I invited Huntleigh over for a dinner of veal scaloppini and spinach salad with squash, gorgonzola, and garlic-infused olive oil. Beating the crap out of the veal cutlets was incredibly therapeutic and served as my mental preparation for the night's goal. After dinner, Hunter found a channel broadcasting an MMA match—after only two punches and one kick I was shrieking for Hunter to turn it off, in the midst of a mini-meltdown. After I calmed down and talked with Ev and Hunter, we turned the match back on and I was able to watch about two minutes before needing another time-out. We repeated this process several times until I was able to uncomfortably watch five minutes of the match without losing my marbles. I was shaken and it wasn't an experience I wanted to repeat anytime soon, but it was enlightening.

Thia was right—acts of violence, even in the context of sporting events, were a trigger. Too many sensory memories resurfaced and overwhelmed me. It wasn't the same level of breakdown as the night at The Stop, but I now understood the lesson she wanted me to learn. I was still not prepared to dismiss Griffin's sheer brutality and absolute loss of control, but I felt better able to compartmentalize the effects of his actions.

That night I fell asleep alone again, but this time I positioned my pillow parallel to my body, resting my head on it as if it were a person, a man...Griffin.

I spent the better part of the following week trying to make sense of the mess my life had become. I saw Ev every day at work and while she was as supportive as ever, she refused any inquiry I made regarding Griffin. While Ev declined to give me any details, she was happy, however, to *suggest* I talk to him, hear him out, cut him some slack, try to see his perspective. Questions to Hunter were met with a simple, "Just talk to him." Despite myself, I was beginning to feel desperate to know how he was doing. Three weeks after our last contact, fate intervened, answering my questions for me.

Ev was stuck in a meeting with a supplier and I made a run to the Restaurant Depot in her stead. I was pushing a platform cart loaded with an obscene amount of chocolate and caramel sauces, exiting the aisle, when I nearly crashed into another shopper. As we exchanged the requisite apologies, my eyes saw him frozen a couple aisles down. The way he stared at me, anguish etched across the beautiful face I loved and pure agony radiated from the eyes I'd once lost myself in, broke my heart. I quickly turned back to finish apologizing for my almost collision, but in the second it took to clear my path, Griffin was gone. Had I imagined him? No, even my twisted mind couldn't have conjured the raw pain openly on display. I was haunted by our almost encounter and began obsessing like an addict.

When I arrived back at Higher Yearning, I unloaded my car in silence, hauling jug after jug of caramel and chocolate and slamming them into place in the storage room. By the time I was done unloading, my arms ached almost as badly as my head and heart.

I joined Meg behind the counter and made myself a latte.

"I'm guessing it would be a bad time to mention I just used the last of the caramel sauce," Meg said.

I shot her a death stare.

"I thought so. I'd go grab one, but I'm afraid of what you might do if a customer tried something crazy like, I don't know...order a drink."

"Someone took her funny pills today," I said sarcastically.

"What's up?"

"Nothing."

"Not according to the chocolate and caramel. I overheard them in the back saying 'puta es loca,' and you know chocolate never lies."

"Chocolate does not speak Spanish...French maybe," I argued for the sake of arguing.

"The earliest records of chocolate are from the Mokaya in Mexico—chocolate definitely speaks Spanish," she said with triumphant laughter in her voice.

"How the hell do you know that?"

"Chocolate is the great love of my life."

"That is either the saddest or smartest thing I've ever heard."

"Smartest. Chocolate has never let me down and it's brought me a lot closer to the elusive-O than any man ever has. Tastes better, too."

"Okay, that is the saddest thing I've ever heard," I said, but she made a valid point.

She shrugged as if unconcerned, which I found impossible to believe.

"Enough about my love life. What happened?"

I sighed heavily. "I just saw Griffin at Restaurant Depot and he looked about as good as I felt. He ran off before I could talk to him...not that I'm sure I even *wanted* to speak with him. I don't know. Everything is so fucked up."

"I understand why you freaked after all you've been through, but what is stopping you from working it out now that the drama has mellowed?"

"How can I trust him not to lose it again? How do I know he won't hurt *me* one day?"

"Do you really think he could ever hurt you? He looks at you like *you* are the reason he draws his next breath. It is as if he'd do anything for you—even kill to protect you," she said emphatically. Her point was not lost on me. "I know bad men, Sam...dangerous men. I know men who put themselves before anyone else. I know men who hurt for the sake of hurting. I know the darkness you are so afraid is hiding in Griffin—it's not there, I'd recognize it."

Okaaaaaaaayyyyyy. Happy, sweet, beautiful, easygoing Meg has danced with darkness. You would never suspect, she had no tells. I guess we all have our stories and our demons.

"Meg, are you—"

"Oh no you don't. I'll tell you my story one day, but you are not redirecting this conversation, lady."

"Yes, ma'am."

"Sorry, I'm not trying to be bossy. But you were so sad and skittish when you first started working here. Then you were so happy you glowed. Now you're sad and so-not-glowy again. I liked it when he lit you up and made you glow. You deserve happiness after what you've been through," she finished quietly.

"Thanks."

"Let me ask you this—if someone shot Griffin in cold blood and he almost died, then the same son of a bitch was standing in front of you, threatening to do the same thing again, what would you do?"

"I'd kill the bastard," I answered instantaneously.

Meg looked at me expectantly.

Well damn, I saw her point.

"I don't think Griffin sees a distinction between the guy who...hurt you...and your ex. He holds them both responsible. Seeing Robbie forcing himself on you, restraining you, scaring you shitless—it was as if he was there when it all happened. What man worth loving wouldn't turn into a homicidal maniac when the woman he loves is in that situation? I wouldn't respect him if he didn't do everything in his power to protect you, and he sure as hell wouldn't deserve your love. I'm not in love with you and even I probably would have tried to stab the punk."

Blood thirsty, wasn't she?

"No one can understand the scars left on your soul, but you can't believe you are the only one who bears scars from your suffering."

She was right. Those closest to me had all been changed; they had all suffered alongside me. It never occurred to me that Griffin was as marred as Hunter and Ev—that he might feel the same depth of grief, regret, bloodlust, and vengeance as they did.

Chapter Fourteen

*"Absence diminishes mediocre passions
and increases great ones, as the wind extinguishes candles
and fans fires."*
-Francois de La Rochefoucauld

Griffin

I didn't know if I was the strongest man alive or the biggest pussy ever. Maybe both. I had been obsessing over that very question for the past six hours, since the moment I saw Sam at Restaurant Depot...Restaurant-fucking-Depot. For the past three weeks I had taken every possible precaution to avoid her, including painstaking planning and inconvenience, as well as changes to my daily routine to guarantee a run-in didn't occur. One hasty decision to pick up pickles and all my efforts were wasted. Was there nowhere I could hide from her? I decided to make the Restaurant Depot trip to escape Sam's ghost that haunted me everywhere I looked at The Stop. I had practically moved into my office, sleeping on the couch because my house was filled with her memory, her scent, her belongings—pieces of her I couldn't bring myself to let go of and return to her. I was sleeping with her goddamn robe clutched in my hand like a little kid with a teddy bear—I was pathetic. I didn't deserve those small connections to her. I was only able to justify their comfort because of the pain they brought in equal measure. I welcomed the pain—it was all I had left of her. The best days of my life were waking up with her in my arms, lying in bed, lazily exploring each other's bodies. Our days together surpassed my every fantasy—well, my fantasies that didn't include sex. Thank God we hadn't crossed that final threshold; I may have jumped off a bridge if I actually knew for a fact what I'd lost in *that* regard. As it was, I was a train wreck.

My staff avoided me like the plague, afraid of my short fuse. I sent a server home the other night for dropping a tray—dropping a freaking tray—something every server had done at least once, if they were actually working. It wasn't even the poor kid's fault, a customer bumped into him. I apologized the next day and paid him for the tips he missed out on, but they all were subsequently walking on egg shells.

Hunter had been a thorn in my side since the clusterfuck. It was a struggle to remember that I actually liked the guy and not kick his ass out of my bar. He had proven useful the first week when he dragged my drunken ass into the office after six too many shots of Jack Daniels. He didn't even point out what a dumbass mistake it was to get tanked after the last customer left. It would have been redundant since Jack pointed it out repeatedly the next day. It was the first and last time Hunter held his tongue. Since my hangover from hell, Hunter had taken every possible opportunity to tell me what a little bitch I was. He started with long eloquent speeches filled with logic, aimed to persuade me that my resolution to let Sam go was a mistake. Over the past couple of weeks, his lectures had been reduced to basic phrases: "call her," "don't be a dick," "she misses you," "stubborn ass," and the hit below the belt, "she needs you."

I wanted to call her...no, I wanted to show up at Higher Yearning and sweep her off her feet, profess my love (finally), and take her home (hers or mine). I wanted her to fall asleep on my chest. I was desperate to wake up with a face full of sweetly scented hair and pins-and-needles in my arm. I wanted to hear her voice, see her smile, kiss her lips...I wanted my love back.

I couldn't do it. I might have been a selfish bastard in my lowest moments, but even at my weakest, I couldn't make her suffer ever again. I had sworn to protect her, never to hurt her, and I broke my vow on both accounts the night I kicked Robbie's ass. The look of horror on her face, her tangible fear of me...they were worse than any kick to the nuts. It stole my breath and broke my heart when she crawled away from me in terror. She was afraid of me. *Me!* With that piece of shit on the floor in front of her, I was the one she was scared of. Regardless, I would never risk making her feel that type of fear again or plunge her back into that nightmare.

I hated myself for fucking it up with her. I wish I could punch myself in the face until the external pain matched the pain inside. She was everything I had wanted for nearly two years, and the brief time with her proved she would have been worth waiting ten years. But I blew it.

I didn't regret beating Robbie until he was unconscious. He deserved every blow and more. Not only for his culpability in the attack on Sam, but for having the balls to come into *my* bar and lay his hands on her. Kiss her against her will. He deserved a beat-down every day for the rest of his life as far as I was concerned. My regret was delivering the well-earned blows in front of Sam. I knew better; I knew seeing such violence could be a trigger. I never wanted her to see me in that light, but I lost my goddamn mind when Robbie touched her. It might as well have been Heath the night of the rape—my vision went red and all I could think was that he needed to pay in blood. He needed to taste what he had so eagerly dished out. Fuck, I was an idiot! If I'd had enough sense to drag him out back, away from her line of sight, I would have been a hero. Instead, she looked at me as if I were no better than the psychotic fuck locked up in Riverhead prison.

I lost Sam because of my stupid, impulsive temper, and for that I would spend the next sixty years with only my self-loathing to keep me company. Lord knows I couldn't imagine being with anyone else. It wouldn't be fair to Miss Whoever-the-hell-she-is. She would never have been enough because I would always wish she was Sam. There was no way for that story to play out well;

both of us would be disappointed the other couldn't be what we needed them to be.

The Stop manager approached me, trying very hard to hide his hesitancy. Great. Whatever he was about to say, I was not going to like it.

"Uh, Griff...umm, well the act for tonight just called, and uh...well you see—"

"Son of a bitch! Can no one keep their mother-fucking word? That shithead made a commitment."

"Yeah," he answered cautiously.

I sighed. Dammit. I needed to pull myself together. It was not helping matters to have my staff scurrying around me like frightened mice.

"Sorry man, it's not your fault. I'll cover it," I said, attempting to smile but clearly failing. My grimace must not have been reassuring based on the way he bolted.

I glanced at my watch to find that the show should have started two minutes ago. Guess I had better get moving. I poured myself a glass of water and headed to the office to grab my guitar before taking the stage. At least I could release some of these emotions on the unsuspecting crowd in the guise of entertainment.

"Hey everyone. I'm Griffin, your unexpected entertainment for the night. It's been a shitty couple of weeks, so I hope you don't mind if I unload musically on you guys."

They cheered and clapped, excited by the prospect of my musical pain. Twisted...every last one of them. If I still had any sense of humor, I would have laughed.

I hadn't had enough warning to brainstorm a set, so I would wing it.

I strummed the first chords of "Creep" by Radiohead, the perfect start to vent my self-hatred. The crowd was staring at me with rapt expressions—women were giving me the eyes that said 'take me home.' What the hell? Were they not listening to the words I was singing?

I continued my self-serving set with "I Need You Now" by Lady Antebellum and "Tonight I Wanna Cry" by Keith Urban. I knew they were feeling it when I glanced at the bar and found it empty, everyone crowded near the stage. A few girls pressed themselves at the base of the stage, their eyes glistening with emotion. Good, they could suffer along with me; maybe I would feel less alone.

I transitioned into my personal mantra, "If Time Is All I Have" by James Blunt, letting the raw pain of the song wash over me. I imagined myself lost in a sea of happy faces on the day Sam wed a man that wasn't me. Shit, my eyes were actually stinging—the thought was enough to bring me to my knees.

I needed a song that let me release the pain and belt my regret, a song that spoke for me. Before my brain engaged, my fingers began to pick "What Hurts the Most" by Rascal Flatts—perfect. It could have been my official theme song. Hell, I could have written this damn song.

I needed to end the set and wallow in misery, preferably alone and off stage. This had been a horrible idea. I wasn't at a point where I could turn the emotion of the songs on and off like I usually did—tap into it for three-and-a-half minutes and then let it go. It was all stacking on top of me tonight, every emotion I accessed piling on top of me until I was suffocating. How to end? "Mine Would Be You" by Blake Shelton. I needed to vocalize my regret, tell our story...I needed to speak to her the only way I could. I sung the words as if she were standing before me, listening to my plea. The desperation and powerlessness seeped from my pores. I whispered the last words with a silent pledge to let her go to find happiness, even at the expense of my own. I sat in complete stillness on the stool with my eyes closed, knowing when I opened them I would have to accept the loss permanently. The audience was silent, waiting for me to move, as if they had heard more than just a song.

"Are you taking requests?" the voice pierced my brooding.

Was it an auditory hallucination? I didn't care if it was. It was the first time in three weeks I had heard her voice.

I refused to open my eyes and risk losing the real or imagined connection—so I nodded in response.

"'Hard to Say I'm Sorry'...Chicago? Do you know it?"

Again, I nodded.

"I can't sing."

I had to chuckle...no, she couldn't. She was completely tone-deaf, but I understood her message—this was her song for me, even if I had to sing it to myself.

I played for her alone. Everyone else might as well have gone home. I twisted the classic to make it more acoustic and intimate, more us. When I reached the chorus, I finally opened my eyes and found her. Sam's beautiful emerald eyes glistened with unshed tears as she mouthed the words to me. I nearly missed the second verse because I was so absorbed in her, in the dream of the moment. I would continue to play until my fingers bled and the strings met bone if it kept her here. My eyes never left hers.

As the song finished, I stressed the "can't" before speaking the words "let go." I set my guitar on the stand beside the stool and held her eyes as I descended the stage, slowly closing the distance between us. I ignored the applause and shouts of praise. Thankfully, no one tried to stop me or I would have run them over. I stopped about five feet from her, leaving the choice to Sam, asking if she still feared me without having to speak the words. How close would she come? She took a step closer then paused. I winced at her hesitation until I saw her small smirk. She was keen to my litmus test, teasing me in response—the minx. Taking her playfulness as a positive sign, I joined the game, taking a step closer to her and upping the ante by extending my arm to her. She gifted me with a wide smile, accepting my outstretched hand and stepping closer. Okay, this was really happening. I could feel her now, warm and alive against my skin. I slowly closed my fingers around hers and pulled her into my chest, closing the remaining gap between us.

I wrapped my arms around her disconcertingly slimmer frame as she rested her head against my heart. I cradled the back of her head in my palm, surprised—like every other time—how small she was; her whole head fit in my hand. So delicate, yet so strong. I didn't want to break the moment, but we needed to talk. I didn't want to make any presumptions. I hoped her acceptance came with forgiveness and another chance to be hers, but I couldn't be certain.

"We should talk," I said, my voice thick with emotion.

"Yeah. Yours or mine?"

Neither was a good option. I didn't want to be in close proximity to a bed during our conversation—okay, that was a lie. I wanted to skip the conversation and head straight for the bed to feel her skin against mine, but I had already paid the price for acting instinctively instead of using my head; I would not repeat that mistake. If this was my second chance, as I hoped, I wasn't going to fuck it up.

"I'd like to see your new place," I said, hoping the unfamiliar ground would help keep me in line until I knew what Sam wanted.

"Good," she said, but made no move to leave.

I kissed the top of her head, letting my lips linger in her hair as I inhaled her sweetness like a junkie just out of rehab. I thought keeping myself away from her was the greatest torture imaginable...I was a dumbass. Being near her and having to hold myself back was a million times worse, but I wouldn't trade a second of the sweet torment. I would suffer this punishment for the rest of my life if I could just be near her.

"Why don't you follow me so you don't have any issues at the guard booth?"

I nodded and followed Sam out the door, hand-in-hand. I caught one of my more religious servers making the sign of the cross as if a miracle had occurred...maybe it had. Lord knows she was my miracle.

When she was safely locked in her car, I jogged to my truck and hopped in, jittery from the anticipation of what she would say, what she would ask.

I had to play this smart; be honest (mostly), listen, but not overwhelm her with my feelings. For the last three weeks, I'd regretted never saying the words that might as well have been branded on my chest. She had to know how I felt about her, but speaking the words was a new level of commitment. I didn't want to blurt it out at the wrong time and have her second-guess my sincerity.

There was also the increasingly loud nagging of my conscience to confess my vengeance against Heath. I should tell her, start over with no secrets between us—if she was giving me a do-over. I argued with myself the entire eight minutes it took to reach her new house. I knew guilt would eat me alive, but I couldn't risk scaring her with my orchestrated violence. I wouldn't lose her for something I couldn't change, even if I wanted to...not that I did. I still felt no remorse for setting Heath up in prison to experience a taste of the physical and mental suffering he had inflicted.

I parked beside her in the driveway and followed her to the front door.

"Why aren't you parking in your garage? It's safer."

"I will, but it's filled with boxes and cardboard at the moment. Once it's empty, I'll park inside."

"I'll take care of it tomorrow," I said without thought. Fuck! We'd exchanged three sentences and I was already fucking this up, acting like I had a right to return as I pleased.

She eyed me for a minute before speaking, "You sure you don't mind? There are a lot of boxes in there."

"Yeah, I'm sure," I said as casually as possible. Christ, I had more game my freshman year of high school.

"Thanks," Sam said shyly, a tone I'd never heard from her before.

She proceeded to turn on the lights while giving me the *Speedy Gonzales*-style tour. At least I wasn't the only one who was nervous. We ended in the kitchen, where she busied herself making coffee.

"Good thing neither of us is feeling awkward," I joked, earning me a laugh.

"Yeah, cause that would suck."

"I'm sorry," I said, deciding to tackle the elephant before he decided to join us for coffee.

"Me too."

"You have nothing to be sorry for, Lo."

"I do. I know my reaction that night hurt you. I never wanted to hurt you...not for anything. We stumbled onto the mother lode of landmines. I couldn't control my response—it was purely reflex. What I'm sorry for, what I did have control over, was how long it took me to sort it all out in my head. I'm sorry for how long it took me to come to you."

"What did you figure out?"

"That violence was the trigger. Obvious, I know. I had to untangle all of the emotions before I could see that it was the aggression and brutality I was afraid of, the reminder of Hh...Heath. I would have reacted the same if anyone had been in your place."

"So you aren't afraid of me now?"

"No. I realized if the tables were turned, I would have done the same...worse. I don't know if I would have stopped if it had been you screaming. You stopped when you heard me, when you knew you were hurting me."

I nodded. Sam was the only thing that could have pulled me out of my murderous rage.

"I'm not sorry I hurt him," I confessed, not wanting to scare her but needing to be honest. "I could lie to you, but I won't. If given the opportunity I would do it again, but not there, not in front of you. I'm sorry I made you see it—made you relive the past."

"I can accept that. What else are you sorry for?"

I looked at her, puzzled. What else was there? I hadn't given myself the chance to screw things up any further. I shrugged my shoulders.

She shook her head as if disappointed.

"You're not sorry for pulling a Houdini? For completely removing yourself from my life? You freakin' ran away from me in Restaurant Depot!"

She was pissed. I had to explain, make her understand I was protecting her.

"It wasn't like that. I was protecting you. I—"

"Protecting me? Of all the stupid, stereotypical, jackass male explanations...seriously?"

"Lo, you were terrified of me that night. I thought forcing myself on you would make it worse."

"I'm not saying you should have come knocking on my window in the middle of the damn night, but nothing...not even a damn text. I was afraid you were done with me—that you didn't care."

I closed the distance between us and gathered her in my arms. "No baby, never that. I wanted to see you every second. I was giving you the choice...and maybe punishing myself, too."

She tilted her head back and gazed into my eyes. "Why?"

"I hurt you. I let you down...again."

"Griff—"

I placed my finger over her lips to silence the protest I knew was coming.

"You don't have to agree or understand, but I hold myself responsible for not protecting you then. My mind knows it's illogical," I shrugged, "it's how I feel. I promised you and myself I would never let anything hurt you again. I failed, and the worst punishment I could imagine was losing you."

"You idiot. Did it occur to you that you were punishing me, too? That losing you would destroy me? I need you."

"You just called me an idiot and told me you need me in the same breath," I laughed. God, she was amazing.

"Both are true."

She took my hand and guided me to the couch, pushing my chest until I was seated before crawling into my lap. "I was broken by what happened to me. I spent months digging through the rubble that was Old Sam to find pieces of myself to puzzle back together."

I nodded my understanding and stroked her back, encouraging her to continue.

"When you showed up, I didn't recognize you for what you were. I didn't know you were a piece of me that had always been missing."

I understood exactly what she meant because I felt the same. I just realized it much earlier.

"But it's more than that. You're not just a piece of me—you're the glue that holds it all together. You were made for me...or I was made for you. Either way, it doesn't matter. All the broken shards of me, every jagged edge is yours. I've put them back as best I can, and hopefully I'll continue to discover new and old pieces, but without you there is nothing there to hold it all together."

Every word out of her beautiful, kissable mouth was an answer to my prayers. I kissed her lips gently, not wanting to push her but needing to touch her in some way.

"You're wrong, you know?" I said, barely above a whisper. "It's not just a piece of me that fits you. We are both pieces, neither complete without the other. And I'm not the glue …we are like epoxy—both components necessary for adhesion. Together our bond is strong, flexible, waterproof, and resistant to heat, cold, and external exposure."

"I think you're right, even though I have no freakin' clue what epoxy is," I laughed at his utterly *"man"* metaphor. "Do you mind if your pieces are in better condition than mine?"

"I'm not flawless, Lo. I have my own jagged edges."

"I like your sharp edges," she said while dragging her fingers across my abs. I had never loved sit-ups more than at that moment.

We spent the next several hours catching up on the last few weeks, cuddling, and kissing. I didn't push for more; I didn't need it. Having Sam back in my arms, feeling her body against mine, and knowing she was mine again were more than I had dared to hope for.

We fell asleep on the couch wrapped around each other, parts entwined like the pieces of the whole we were.

Chapter Fifteen

"Being deeply loved by someone gives you strength, while loving someone deeply gives you courage." -Lao Tzu

I was warm—very warm—in the best possible way. I fisted my hand in the fabric beneath my palm, feeling the soft cotton of a t-shirt bunch against my hand. I inhaled deeply and let his drugging scent seep into my body, reassuring me that last night was not a dream.

On the couch in my family room, enveloped in Griffin's arms, I awoke after my best night's sleep in three weeks. I couldn't believe he was here...back in my life...*mine*. I rubbed my head against his chest like a cat soliciting attention and marking her territory. I couldn't get close enough. I wished humans had a pouch like kangaroos...I would happily climb in and let Griff tote me around everywhere.

His chest rumbled with laughter, startling me.

"I didn't," I said, hoping against all odds his laughter was due to another source.

"A pouch, huh? Kind of kinky, but I'd do it for you," Griffin teased, while kissing the side of my neck as he worked his way to my lips. "I've already told you, I'd be happy to carry you everywhere. You're the one who insists on walking. I'd rather have you in my arms at all times."

I was starting to see his logic and it would be a great way to gain eight inches of height, too.

"I'd love nothing more, but unfortunately I have to go to work," I said, making no effort to rise.

"Gotta pay for your new pad somehow. It's fantastic, by the way—very 'you.'"

"You haven't even seen it all...yet."

"Oh, what have I missed?" he asked with a wicked twinkle in his eye.

What a naughty man, planting ideas in my head when I had to leave.

"My closet, it's freaking spectacular. Every girl's wet dream." Ha! Take that, Mr. McTeasey.

He let out a pitiful moan.

"Maybe if you're a really good boy, I'll show you later," I added, turning the dial up on my torment.

"You, Lo, are a cruel woman. I'll have to think of ways to pay you back while I spend the day here breaking down your trash."

I had a feeling his creative retribution would be more pleasure than punishment.

"That mouth of yours is writing some big checks...I hope you're prepared to cash them."

"My mouth is more than ready to deliver," he said, his words reverberating through my body.

Oh my, I remembered what his mouth could do...vividly.

"Yes, please!"

He swatted my butt before sitting us up.

Wanting to leave him with as much anticipation as he had created in me, I kissed him like my life depended on it. We were both panting when we finished.

"Think about *that* while you play with my boxes."

I stood up and headed to my beloved closet, leaving him sputtering.

Thirty minutes later, I was dressed and out the door. I passed Griff, who had already begun breaking down the mountain of recyclables that had invaded my garage. When I reached my car, I gasped loud enough that Griffin heard me and was by my side before I had reached for the paper. He snatched the page from my windshield.

"Mother fucker!" he hissed before pulling out his cell.

I snatched the note from his hand while he was distracted and read it myself.

TIME IS NO MORE...
HE DRAWS NEAR.
OFFER YOUR
FAREWELLS...
FIND YOUR PEACE.

Mother fucker. The threats had been arriving every week, growing progressively more ominous, but this was the first that wasn't urging me to back out of testifying...there was no 'or else' this time. Previously, the notes were delivered under my windshield wiper during my shift at Higher Yearning. This time it was delivered outside my new home in a gated community. The implication wasn't lost on me. He knew where I was, where I lived, and the minimum-wage security guy was no deterrent. Shit.

My day had started so damn well. Now Hunter was going to come over here with Detective Norse to collect evidence. Maybe I could have Griffin drop me off at work and I could talk to the cops later. Part of me was terrified of the 'he' drawing near, but a larger part wanted to flip him the bird, scream 'fuck you,' and carry on with my day. I was done with letting the psycho and his family tie me in knots and derail my life. Enough was enough.

I walked over to Griffin, who paced like an agitated bear.

"Hey, babe? Can you give me a ride to work?"

He stopped pacing and turned his head toward me in slow motion, a look on his face that loosely translated to 'are you out of your fucking mind?'

"Hunter and the cops can do their thing with my car and then I'll give my statement later. You know, I don't want to leave Ev in a bind."

Griffin continued to stare at me as if I had just told him aliens had beamed me to their spaceship, impregnated me, and then returned me to earth—all in the last sixty seconds.

He was starting to freak me out a little.

"You know what, don't worry about it. It's better if you finish breaking up those boxes so I can park in the garage—safer. Definitely a better plan. I'll text Meg; she can pick me up on her way in," I rambled.

He swiped the phone from my hand with lightning speed.

"Hey," I objected.

"You. Are. Not. Going. Anywhere."

"You are overreacting," I said with an eye roll for emphasis.

"Overreacting? A homicidal maniac just told you that your death is imminent, and I'm overreacting?" he asked, barely restraining his anger.

"So I'm supposed to live the rest of my life in hiding? What, should I testify then enter the witness protection program and leave my life behind...leave you behind? Or worse, not testify at all? I won't live that way. I won't let him control my life or my decisions."

"This isn't a game, Sam, and it isn't about reclaiming control over your life. This is survival. Control is irrelevant if you're dead. You will not go anywhere without protection until we find a way to stop him. Do you understand me?"

If I had taken a moment to breathe, to think about the fear motivating his tyrannical commands, I might have been more reasonable—maybe. But I didn't take that breath; I exploded.

"He doesn't get to have that power over me...and neither do you. You're back on the job one day after ditching me for three weeks and you think you have a right to order me around? Think again. This is *my* life. Mine! So you can zip those perfect fucking lips."

"You think my lips are perfect?" he asked with a sexy smile.

Son of a bitch. I knew what he was doing, and I would not be swayed by his charm or suggestive smile.

"I did until you started ordering me around with them," I huffed.

He took a step closer to me, placed his hands on my hips, and pulled me against him. He lowered his lips to my ear, eliciting goosebumps across my flesh. Damn, he was good at this seduction stuff.

"Do you remember what I can do with my *perfect* lips or do I need to remind you?"

"It isn't going to work. No matter how tempting you are, I won't give in. I won't stop living my life." I wrapped my arms around his waist and leaned back to meet his gaze. "I'm not being stubborn. Well, I am, but not just for the sake of it. I can't live that way, not after what I've been through. If I run and hide, let him break me in that way, I will lose myself. There will be nothing left...no pieces to fit back together. I will just disappear. Please understand."

Griffin dragged a hand through his hair, frustrated. He hated what I was saying, but he understood. He was going to cave; I could see it in his eyes. Because I loved him, I let him think he actually had a say.

"I don't like this. I'm going to try and be with you as much as possible and I'll have Hunter to cover any gaps when I can't be there. Please, Lo, I need you to be careful," he said and lifted me by my waist until our foreheads touched. "I just got you back...I can't lose you."

"I don't have a death wish, babe. I'll be so careful I won't even break a nail."

"For the time being, I'd like to crash at your place or you at mine. In separate rooms if you want, as long as you're close. I don't want to take any chances."

Separate rooms, my ass. I finally had my body pillow back. If we were under the same roof, he would be warming my bed. I decided to let him sweat over my intentions...he deserved it after trying to boss me around. Alpha was hot in the bedroom, not so much in real life.

"Deal."

Hunter and Detective Norse arrived soon after and took my statement, while the crime scene investigators collected evidence. Hunter informed me I had the rest of the day off as per Ev's strict orders. I was going to argue, but after my battle with Griffin I didn't have the energy to go for god knows how many rounds with Ev, so I relented.

Griff and I spent the first half of the day taking out our frustrations on cardboard, a tedious task until I persuaded Griffin he would be more comfortable without his shirt while laboring. He was wise to my thinly veiled ploy to score eye-candy, but obliged me easily—my man liked to be ogled if I was the one ogling. Breaking down boxes became my new favorite pastime when accompanied by rippling muscles and a tight ass.

When we finished, we headed to the gym and resumed our routine. Working out was definitely more appealing with the return of Griffin's company and an extra thorough massage at the end. Afterward, we showered and stopped by the gourmet grocery to pick up ingredients for dinner. Cooking together for the first time was more fun than I could have imagined. My time in the kitchen was therapeutic, and having Griffin embrace my favorite hobby as more than the taste-tester created a new bond between us. I imagined it was how Griffin felt when I watched him perform...there was an intimacy in sharing something you loved with the person to whom you were committed.

As we shared the fruits of our labor, Griffin talked about the menu I had sent him before our hiatus. His chef was resistant to the changes and believed the old menu was fine as it was. I understood his point. The menu was good, but The Stop could benefit from adding other options and tweaking a few of their standard dishes to make them feel new. Griffin was struggling with the decision to replace the chef or force his compliance, or just let go of the idea altogether. I didn't envy the responsibilities he bore.

After dinner we cuddled on the couch and watched re-runs of 'The Office.' Both of us needed the healing power of laughter and a time-out from the darker side of life. After the third episode,

Griffin turned off the TV and turned me in his arms until I was facing him.

"Lo-baby, there are still some things I need to tell you," he said seriously.

"And I want to hear them all," I replied, as I leaned in to graze my lips across his before trailing them lower. "Go ahead, I'm listening."

"Kind of hard to focus when you're kissing my neck," he said without complaint.

"Hmmm. You'll have to try harder because I have no intention of stopping."

"I thought you should know that I've wanted you for a really long time...since your twenty-first birthday, actually. It wasn't the right time, but I knew even from the first time I saw you that you were meant to be mine. I was already crazy about you before everything happened last spring. So, when Rob—"

"Shh. Not tonight. I don't want anyone intruding on our perfect night, not even in the form of a memory."

He nodded, hesitating before speaking.

"Okay, not tonight. I'll just say that I was half in love with you before you were ever mine."

"*That* you can say as often as you like," I said, sliding my fingers under his shirt, working it up over his broad shoulders until his torso was in full view. "New rule—no shirts in the house."

His hands complied, making a beeline for the hem of my shirt.

"I meant for you," I said with a laugh.

"I know" was his only reply before my shirt was gone; my bra followed in short order. His lips explored the swell of my chest while my hands mapped him. We were exploring familiar territory, but every kiss and touch felt different, like we were touching more than just skin.

His hands drifted to my hips, pulling my body squarely on top of his. He steadied me with his grip and sat up, causing me to straddle him, his erection pressed between our bodies. I saw the question in his eyes, wordlessly asking if I was okay. In reply, I shifted my hips and pressed against him, finding the pressure I was craving. I rolled my hips and we both groaned. His fingers flexed in response, digging into the skin at my side.

"Yes..." The word slipped out with a soft moan from my lips and that was all it took. Griffin lifted me into his arms and carried me to the bedroom. We sat on the center of the bed, where I settled over him and resumed my straddling posture.

One of his hands left my hip, sliding upward until his palm supported my head and his arm braced my back. He leaned down to take my mouth, and with a kiss that held a new depth and fervor, he devoured me, his need matching my own. He then leaned me back, his arm taking my weight, as he skated his lips down the column of my neck, nipping my collarbone, and ending at my chest. Exposing me, he sucked my nipple into his mouth, working it with an expertise I'd never experienced before. I mindlessly ground against him, desperate for relief. I needed to extinguish the fire he had lit throughout my body, blazing up from my core.

I wanted more of everything...with him. I was ready, as long as it was Griffin's hands touching me, his body against mine. I was a nomad who had been wandering the desert for endless months, finally finding a wellspring. I was nearly feral in my hunger. So many months of furloughed lust crashed down on me, or maybe it was simply Griffin's effect alone. I worked myself free of my panties, the seconds of broken contact feeling like Purgatory. Griffin was preoccupied, clueless of the direction I was steering us, and I impatiently clawed at his boxer briefs, determined to get rid of every barrier between us.

I growled in frustration. Smiling devilishly, he broke our kiss and brought his lips to my ear.

"What are you doing, Lo?" His voice was hot and seductive.

"Please. Take these off."

He paused for a moment, gauging my sincerity. If he didn't hurry up and comply, he would find out exactly how sincere I was when I shredded the offending fabric with my teeth. Sensing my determination, he wisely rested me on the bed and stripped hastily, pulling what I assumed was protection from his pocket and resting it on the nightstand.

Gathering me into his arms again, he returned me to his lap, where I instantly sought the slide of skin-on-skin. My pace was frantic, as if Griffin might disappear or change his mind without notice.

"Slow baby, let me love you right," he whispered, an enticement.

"Next time," I returned impatiently, beyond reason. It was time—I couldn't wait another millisecond.

Unwilling to be rushed, he belted an arm around my hips, effectively locking my body to his, and tangled his fingers in my hair. He moved sinuously, teasing me while coating himself with the evidence of my longing. When I was on the edge and delirious, he lay back, my mouth following his like a magnet.

He angled away from me to reach for the nightstand and returned with protection. I snatched the foil packet from his hand and tossed it over my shoulder before moving to resume our kiss, but he stopped me.

"Lo, safety first."

"It's covered," I said factually. I had not missed a single day taking my pill in five years. I knew I was clean and had no doubt Griffin would have mentioned if he wasn't. He would never put me at risk. "I don't want anything between us. I want to feel you...I need to know it's you."

"You'll be the first," he said, reaffirming my confidence.

"You too," I said, moved that we could share the experience.

I tilted my hips so he was perfectly aligned, reveling in the moment of anticipation. With unhurried movement he eased into me, filling more than just my body with his painstaking tenderness. It was overwhelming, the joining of body, mind, and heart. Once I adjusted to him, he followed my lead, masterfully mirroring the rhythm and pace I set from above, aiding my rise and fall with his hands on my behind. He watched me as if I were a miracle he couldn't tear his eyes from, which I'm certain was similar to my own gaze. Our eyes never broke contact, a tether keeping me in the present, temporarily erasing the past.

I had always enjoyed sex, unashamed of my body and my desire, but this was something completely new. Intense and worshipful—an unbreakable bond that satisfied more than just the physical. He gained entry to a part of my heart previously secured, as if he held the only key and the space was his alone. Every stroke reached deeper, every nerve more sensitized, everything amplified by the depth of our devotion.

I was so close, but my legs were weakening despite Griffin's significant assistance. In what could only be described as slow motion, he sat up and leaned forward until I was on my back with my legs wrapped around his hips. My body welcomed the change in position, my tired legs grateful for the break. I closed my eyes, afraid of what the sight of him above me would do.

"Open your eyes, Lo. I want to know it's me you see."

I complied immediately, grounded by his words and the intensity in his eyes. Once he knew I was living in the second, he moved over me, in me. If I thought he was careful before, I knew nothing. He was meticulously gentle and loving, speaking my name and soft, reverential words, ensuring I never forgot where I was and whom I was with.

His eyes were intense, holding me captive. "I need to tell you," he paused to kiss my lips, "I love you, with everything I am, I love you..."

I gasped at his words and the physical manifestation of his love. "Griff...I love you, too....with all of my heart."

He took my mouth with a searing kiss and I poured every bit of my love into him, transforming the kiss from adoring to soul-piercing.

He monitored every minute response to heighten my pleasure, surpassing every sexual experience I'd ever had. He never restrained me with his body, but I clung to him like a monkey in the trees. The pressure was building, and I feared I would combust if he didn't give me release immediately. He kept me on the edge, lost in pleasure but never providing the final push I was desperate for.

"More. Stop holding back," I panted, a plea and demand.

As with everything else, I only had to ask. My order freed him of the restraint to which he had bound himself and he immediately gave me the 'more' I had requested...he gave it all to me—pleasure so exquisite it swallowed me like a riptide, dragging me in and tossing me around until I had no sense of up from down.

"Together," he ground out between clenched teeth, entwining our hands and waiting for me to join him in the fall.

With a final cry, my vision blurred and all of my senses converged, indistinguishable from one another. His name fell from my lips, full of veneration.

"Oh, Lo-baby," he whispered against my lips before kissing me devotedly, rolling us to our sides, holding me close. His right hand crossed my body to rest over my heart.

We lay together in silence as our breathing slowed and our bodies came down from the unparalleled high. I was so far beyond satiated that mere words could not describe my state. What Griffin and I had just shared was more than sex, more than beautiful. It exceeded simple lovemaking—I felt a piece of our souls had fused together and created an indestructible bridge between our bodies, minds, and hearts.

I had experienced betrayal by a man I thought I loved once before, but my feelings for him were superficial and stale compared to the profound depth of my love for Griffin. If I searched my whole life, I would never find another who I could love with the same depth and completeness.

"I love you," I said vehemently. "I love you in a way that will never ebb or fail—it will thrive and deepen every day. I don't want to experience life without you ever again; I don't want to live without those pieces of me."

"Me too, love," he said, breaking into a chuckle. "Love—I can finally skip the shorthand."

"Huh?"

"You may be my little one, but 'Lo' was never about your size, baby. I had to find a way to tell you how I felt, even if you didn't understand it—hence 'Lo,' shorthand for love."

"So you've been confessing your love covertly all this time? Very sneaky, Mr. Evensen. I kind of like Lo, too."

"You'll always be Lo, but it's nice to have options."

I snuggled into his chest and drifted off to sleep, the happiest I had been in as long as I could remember...maybe ever.

The next month passed like a dream from which I never wanted to wake up. Griffin and I spent most nights together at either my house or his. We spent our free time doing life's mundane rituals, but together they were memories I cherished. We worked out, cooked dinner, watched movies, cleaned the house, and occasionally went on adventures to explore local landmarks. We talked for hours about our lives, our dreams, our plans—even began to make future plans together. Griffin promised me a vacation of sun and sand once he officially earned his psychologist license, which should be finalized within the month. I may have influenced his destination choice when I broke out a few of my most scandalous bikinis for him to preview.

We spent long nights and lazy mornings in bed, discovering the secrets of one another's bodies, learning them better than our own. Griffin was one of those guys who was good at everything he did, but he was a super-freaking-star in the bedroom. The man could tangle sheets like a Japanese Shibari expert.

He was confident, man enough to let his love for me show in ways both subtle and obvious. He spoke words of love and reinforced them with actions, regardless of who was watching. He wasn't perfect (he was a grump when hungry and still tried to boss me around on occasion), but he was perfect for me.

The only cloud looming in our blue skies during the last month was the threats...or rather, lack thereof. It was disconcerting. I had been receiving weekly messages for several months, and then nothing since the last declaration that my time was up. You would think I would be pleased about the new quiet, but the silence felt even more ominous, like water receding before the tsunami hit, destroying everything in its wake. I didn't want to drop my guard, knowing it would be a mistake, but it was difficult not to be lulled into a false sense of security. Griffin, on the other hand, was as vigilant as ever. Despite the persistent worry, we both carried on with business as usual, enjoying our new life together.

My sessions with Thia had been broadening as she began to direct my focus beyond the past and encouraging me to look toward the future—what I wanted from life and what my goals were. I realized I had stopped thinking of the future as a blank slate of opportunity after the attack. We reviewed a list of things I love to do, things to relieve stress or that inspired me, and discussed how to translate them into a career.

"So, stress relievers or activities you enjoy?" Thia prompted me.

"I love to cook, it helps me think. Dancing definitely relieves stress. Reading helps me relax and unwind. And Griffin, he definitely helps me relieve stress," I said, wiggling my eyebrows suggestively.

"I refuse to encourage you to pursue a career in the adult entertainment industry, and you are getting a little long in the tooth for a professional dance career. So cooking and reading—let's explore those passions."

"Did you just call me old? I'm twenty-three, for heaven's sake!"

She ignored my complaint and continued, "There are ways to parlay your love of reading into a career—blogging, becoming an author, as well as traditional literary/publishing jobs. Is that something that appeals to you?"

"No, writing is not my gift and I don't think I would enjoy a traditional office environment—too confining. I just read for the fun of it, as a happy escape."

"Okay. How about cooking? Have you considered a culinary career?"

I hadn't, but now that she mentioned it, something within stirred with excitement.

"I never thought about it, but yes, it sounds like a dream job."

"Good. Homework! I want you to think about the positives and negatives of a culinary career, and research the possible routes to achieve such a career. Make lists. We'll review next week."

I spent several days considering a career in the culinary arts. The prospect was tempting, taking something I was passionate about and turning it into a career. The hours could be long, often requiring nights, weekends, and holidays...definitely a downside. I wasn't sure if I wanted to alter my entire life to attend culinary school. I also had zero experience working in a commercial kitchen, which was totally different than cooking at home.

I discussed these concerns with Griffin, trying to find clarity, when he suggested I work a few days a week in The Stop kitchen to gain practical experience before making any decisions. I hadn't considered trying the shoe on to see if it fit. Griffin was very persuasive as he emphasized the benefits of being able to "try out" life in a professional kitchen on a part-time basis while still working at Higher Yearning. He suggested working at The Stop would give me the opportunity to learn in a safe environment. He secured my commitment by promising kisses whenever I was on break.

By the end of my first day in the kitchen, my feet hurt, my back hurt, my hands hurt, and my arm especially hurt where I singed it on the stove. I smelled like food and had a thin sheen of oil coating my skin. And I was in freaking *love*. I felt alive in the kitchen—the frantic pace, the process of creating something from a couple of ingredients and spices. I loved every second of it. At the end of the day, the head chef said I had done well for a 'kitchen virgin' and that I had real potential. One eight-hour shift and I was ready to quit Higher Yearning and pour myself into The Stop kitchen. Griffin chuckled when I shared this with him, but he convinced me to continue on a three-month, part-time trial basis before making any permanent decisions. Damn his logic. I had found my Zen in the chaos of the kitchen and I wanted to lose myself in this new path, but he was right. I couldn't leave Ev and Meg in a lurch. When we arrived at my house that night, I took a shower and Griffin proceeded to massage my aching feet until I passed out.

I walked into Higher Yearning exactly one month after the last threat to find Meg staring off into space, a small smile on her face. My man-o-meter hit seven before she even spoke a word. I dropped my stuff in the back and hurried up front to pump her for details.

"Who is he and has he made you scream his name?"

That seemed to pull Meg from her daydream as effectively as a bucket of ice water dumped over her head.

"I have no idea what you're talking about," she replied evasively.

Awww, she was so cute. She actually thought she could avoid spilling the details. Such innocence.

"Look lady, we can do this the easy way or the hard way, but either way I'll break you," I said with determination.

"You missed your calling in life—totally should have been a cop."

"Nah, the uniform is completely unappealing. What's it gonna be?"

"Any chance I can distract you with juicy gossip about someone else's life?" she asked hopefully.

"Do you have any jaw-dropping gossip?"

She wanted to lie; I could see it in her eyes, but she didn't have it in her.

With a resigned sigh, she caved. "I have a date this weekend."

"Really?" I stretched out the word dramatically until it was practically a run-on sentence. When she offered no further details, I prodded, "And?"

"And I'm excited. He's hot...as in I don't even think there are words to describe his caliber of hotness."

"As in, 'stand back because your panties might spontaneously ignite'?" I offered helpfully.

She laughed, "Yes, definitely a panty-changer. God, I can't believe I just said that."

"I'm glad to know I'm having a positive influence on you. I like to do my part—leave the world a better place when I'm gone." I waited, but she didn't volunteer anything further. I elbowed her in the ribs.

"Okay, no need to get rough. I didn't want to say anything because you know him."

"Who is it?" I asked, since not one guess came to mind.

"That lawyer who came in a while back. He came in yesterday and flirted before asking me for my number. He called last night and invited me to dinner on Saturday."

Huh, I guess the assistant DA worked up the balls to come in and make his own introduction. He was good-looking. I didn't know about thong-combusting, but any guy with the right moves and confidence could increase his rating.

"That's great, Meg. I don't really know him well, but he seems like a good guy. I don't know if he's at a 'rake your nails down his back' level, but I think he could get you there."

"Are you nuts? You should have seen him yesterday. He looked amazing in jeans and a tight sweater, and his words alone got me halfway there. I'm telling you, that man has a Ph.D. in Make-Her-Screamology from Harvard."

Apparently, Mark Stuart had brought his A-game yesterday. Good job, Mark!

I was happy for Meg; she was an incredibly sweet girl, laid-back and funny. She deserved to have as much fun in bed as she enjoyed in every other aspect of her life. Good things didn't always happen to good people, but good people deserved them. Regardless of how happy I was for Meg, it didn't prevent me from teasing her mercilessly all day.

By the time my shift ended, I was ready to head home and see my own lingerie arsonist. My mind was in the gutter all day, fueling my incessant torment. My daydreams had put me in a certain mood...a mood I hoped Griffin was prepared to accommodate. It seemed wise to prepare him for the duties he was expected to perform when I arrived home, so I pulled out my phone to text him. I clumsily typed out a text with gloved hands and settled into the driver's seat. I turned to place my purse next to me and gasped as my purse slipped through my fingers. A large serrated knife protruded from the passenger headrest, holding up a photo of a woman with a tight black hood stretched over her face, her breasts exposed...my breasts. A dark, thick liquid coated the knife, dripping down and pooling in the seat. I flung open the door and ran as if the car were on fire, glancing over my shoulder to ensure I wasn't being followed. Just beyond my car, at the periphery of the parking lot, I thought I saw a man watching me. I increased my speed and burst through the doors of Higher Yearning, screaming for someone to call the cops.

Meg rushed to my side once she heard the commotion.

I held up my hands to stop her from touching me. I wasn't ready to be touched by anyone.

"Call the cops," I said, before she had a chance to ask any questions.

She nodded and ran back to the counter.

I picked up my phone and shakily dialed Griffin. He answered on the second ring.

"Hey love, I just saw your text. I'm up for the—"

"Need you. Now," I said, barely above a whisper.

"I'm coming, baby. You still at work?" he asked in a calm tone.

"Yeah."

"Good, baby. Stay inside, I'll be there in five minutes. Do you want to tell me what's happening?"

I shook my head and muttered incoherently, desperate to escape the image burned in my mind.

"Okay, love. I'm going to assume that silence was a 'no.' Just listen to my voice until I get there."

I mumbled an inarticulate response to assure him I was still on the line.

"I was thinking about the vacation we've been planning. I think we should go to Turks and Caicos. The beaches are gorgeous, soft white sand and crystal clear, warm turquoise water. We can rent a house on the beach, do nothing but lounge in the sun, swim, and experiment in the kitchen. Just relax, be together. You can read as many smutty books as you want while sunbathing during the day and I'll do my best to recreate your favorite parts every night. I'll even make huge pitchers of strawberry daiquiris and mojitos and bring them to the beach in thermoses. Can you imagine the water lapping at your toes while the sun bronzes every inch of your delicious skin? I promise not to wear a shirt from the minute we arrive at the house until the day we leave—we can even skinny dip if you want, make love with only the fish to witness."

"Mango...mango daiquiris," I said when he paused for breath, having lost myself in the picture he painted.

"That I can do. I'm almost there, love. One more minute."

"Will you bring your guitar...sing to me every day?"

"Anything," he said, a promise.

"I'm scared," I whispered.

"I won't let anything hurt you, baby. Never again."

"I don't want you to get hurt because of me," I confessed.

"Not gonna happen. Nothing can take me from your side," he said. I heard him through the phone and behind me.

He was here. As terrified as I was, the fear ebbed with his nearness. This man would kill before allowing anyone to harm me. I thought him a monster two months ago because of his willingness to protect me with force. Now that same knowledge brought solace.

He scooped me into his arms and cradled me against his chest. I could feel his heart pounding as if he had run a marathon, but his exterior looked as placid as a lake on a still day. Griffin might have been upset, but was not letting it show.

"Tell me, Lo-baby," he commanded gently.

I explained what I had found in my car and he inhaled sharply, his muscles contracting involuntarily. A beat passed before he resumed stroking my back, repeatedly kissing the top of my head. He clutched me against his broad chest as if he were afraid someone might try to snatch me from his arms.

Hunter arrived shortly thereafter and Griffin provided a brief explanation. I watched Hunter flinch before switching into FBI mode. He asked me if I could describe the man I thought I saw, but I'd only seen a dark blur as I ran—I couldn't even be certain it was a man. He nodded before leaving to meet Det. Norse in the parking lot, squeezing my shoulder in a silent show of support as he passed.

Ev arrived a half-hour later; she had no idea what transpired while she was at the accountant's office. After a brief rundown from Griffin, accompanied by a look cautioning her to keep it cool, Ev sat in the chair next to us and took my hand in hers without saying a word. I suspected any words that might have left her mouth would be profane and violent.

It was nearly an hour later when Hunter returned to tell us beyond the obvious. The police had found tracks in the area I indicated, but it was hardly conclusive proof in a public parking lot. When I asked directly, Hunter said he suspected the liquid was blood, most likely animal, purchased at a butcher. He may have been bluffing, but I clung to the explanation as gospel; any other possibility was too horrifying. The computer forensic team would examine the authenticity of the photo. Hunter stressed the possibility that it was not me and that it could have been altered to make it appear to be me, but I knew. In my bones, I knew it was me...that night. I could see the fresh bite mark on my breast, a scar I still carried that would never go away.

After a few questions to clarify the timeline, Hunter sent me home...or more accurately, he sent me to Griffin's house. I could tell Ev wanted us to stay at their apartment so she could be assured of my safety, but there was no way I was subjecting myself to Hunter's pull-out couch-of-pain.

Once at Griffin's, he set me on the couch before activating the alarm and checking every door, window, and closet. Satisfied the house was safe, he carried me upstairs, placed me in a steaming hot bath, and then tucked me into bed. We spoke very little, other than words of love. I fell asleep to the sound of his steady breathing beneath my ear.

Chapter Sixteen

"Courage is resistance to fear, mastery of fear, not absence of fear." -Mark Twain

The next week was a social experiment in the effects of constant companionship on a group of jittery, tense individuals. Griffin and Hunter had ascended to their full Alpha-male glory, their overprotection verging on suffocation. Ev was equally as overbearing in her own way. It was agreed that I would stay at Griffin's house for security reasons, and Ev and Hunter showed up with overnight bags the first night. Between the three of them, the only moments I had to myself were when I went to the bathroom. Even then I didn't get to shower alone, for crying out loud...although that wasn't so bad, seeing as Griffin made sure I cried out loud each time he joined me.

The oppressive concern descended into bickering as to how to best protect me, which I largely stayed out of. Despite the diverging opinions, they managed to agree on several issues, which, despite my protests, included barring me from working at Higher Yearning altogether. I was only *allowed* to work my day shifts at The Stop because Griffin was with me the entire time, except when I was working in the kitchen where Tiny, the head bouncer, had the sudden, mysterious need to pass his days. When I questioned Griffin, he only shrugged with unconvincing innocence.

As scared as I was, their over-the-top concern kept me calm in a strange way. With them worrying obsessively every second of the day, I was forced to be the voice of reason and calm. Who had time to be terrified when I was busy reining in guard dogs 1, 2, and 3?

Hunter hauled the Varbeck family into FBI headquarters and questioned them for hours without success. They maintained ignorance of any threats against me. Neither the police nor FBI had been able to find a significant financial connection between the Varbecks' accounts and the witnesses who dropped out. Hunter had petitioned for a warrant to examine the disbursements from their legal firm's escrow accounts, but the warrant was denied due to insufficient cause.

My deposition was scheduled to take place in three days—we had officially reached DEFCON 1. Hunter wore his sidearm at all times, even in the house, and police cruisers were stationed outside Griffin's house around the clock at the request of the assistant DA.

We were sharing a breakfast of blueberry pancakes when Hunter's phone rang. He excused himself to the office as we continued. When he returned, his face was the definition of shock and relief. He opened his mouth to speak then snapped it shut, shaking his head.

"Well?" Ev and I said in unison.

Ev continued, "You're starting to freak me out...say something."

"That was Det. Norse. He called to tell me...shit, I don't know how to tell you this."

"Spit it out!" Ev, Griffin, and I all snapped at him.

"Heath is dead."

"What?" I asked, while Ev questioned, "How?", and Griff muttered, "Thank God."

"He was beaten to death at Riverhead. They aren't exactly sure how it happened. They were on the way back from dinner and a fight broke out between two gang members. The guards broke it up and when they regained control, Heath was on the ground—dead. The warden believes he was the intended target all along and the fight was a diversion. Heath had lodged several complaints about his treatment by the other inmates and made some vile accusations, but there was no concrete proof that anything non-consensual occurred. He was most likely killed for opening his mouth."

"Holy fuck," I whispered. "I...wow."

We all sat quietly, lost in our thoughts.

"Does it make me a bad person if all I feel is relief?"

"No," all three practically shouted.

Griffin left his seat and squatted before me.

"Love, you're the one he hurt, the one he threatened to hurt again—of course you are feeling relieved. You have nothing to feel guilty about." He wrapped his arms around me, covering my face in consoling kisses. "You're safe now...you are safe."

We spent the rest of the day in a strange fog. It was surreal to have the weight of fear lifted. I hadn't realized how heavy the burden was, how much it influenced my every thought and decision, until I was freed of the anvil sitting atop me. I felt like I could fly.

Griffin opened a bottle of champagne and, despite the early hour, we toasted the end of Heath's reign of terror. Huntleigh left shortly thereafter with promises to come for dinner the following night. I asked Griff if we could finally return to my house and he immediately packed an overnight bag and took me home. We shut out the world, turning off our phones and unplugging the house phone, and spent the night celebrating in a much more intimate way.

The next morning I awoke, muscles aching in the sweetest of ways, and smiled a smile I hadn't felt in nine months. Raising my head from my human pillow, I saw that Griffin was still fast asleep. No surprise there, the man had exhausted himself last night; I even thought he managed to add a few new pages to the Kama Sutra. I was fairly certain a few of his moves defied gravity—what a lucky, lucky girl.

Deciding he needed to sleep, I slipped from the bed and headed down to the kitchen to prep breakfast—something revitalizing would be needed because I planned to continue our self-imposed sequestering for the rest of the day.

The doorbell rang and I hustled to answer it before they rang again and woke Griffin. I swung the door open to a sea of flashes, my name ringing out from several directions above the sound of the shutter clicks.

"Miss Whitney, do you have any comment on the death of Heath Varbeck?"

I slammed the door and slid to the floor in shock.

"What the—" I heard Griffin ask as his footsteps approached. He glanced out the window as he neared me.

"Shit."

He scooped me off the floor and carried me to the family room located in the back of the house, as far from the reporters as possible.

"How did they find out about me? The DA promised my name would be kept confidential until the trial. With Heath dead, there is no trial; no reason to have my name plastered across newspapers."

"I don't know, baby. We'll find out and I'll figure out a way to stop this."

"How did they even get in here? They had to clear the guard booth, right?"

"Another question I intend to have answered very soon," he said, anger straining his words.

He wrapped a blanket around me before walking to the kitchen and returning with our cell phones. The minute he powered mine on, bells and vibrations sounded incessantly to announce a barrage of messages.

"Lo-baby, I'm going to call Hunter and make us some coffee. Don't read or listen to those messages right now...wait until the shock wears off, okay?"

I nodded my agreement, but lifted my phone to call Everleigh—it went straight to voicemail.

Griffin returned a few minutes later with a mug in each hand. After he settled on the couch, he drew my legs across his lap and began to massage my foot. Uh-oh, I wasn't going to like whatever he was about to say.

"Ev's phone has been going nuts since 6 a.m., Hunter's too. Someone, most likely from the DA's office, sold the transcripts of the depositions to the media along with the news of Heath's death. The DA is going to find who did it and they *will* be prosecuted, but there is no way to undo the damage. Ev and Hunter's depositions both referred to you by name, and when reporters realized who your family was, they jumped on it."

Of course they would—old money, a recognizable name in elite circles...it may not be as well-known as the Hiltons or Rockefellers, but there was enough recognition to entice the vultures. I sighed. This was precisely what my parents had feared. I knew the media would be interested during the trial, but I didn't think their attention would be this intense. No doubt Heath's murder while in prison had elevated the salaciousness of the sound bites.

"Hunter is going to have some patrol cars sent over to help us get out of here. We'll head to my house and hide out there. It probably won't hold them off for very long, but it will buy us a little time to figure out how to handle them."

"I have a better idea. Can you take a few days off from The Stop? We won't go too far in case of an emergency. I know it's last minute and you haven't had time to make arr—"

He kissed my lips, smothering my words.

"That's better. Yes, whatever you are thinking—yes. You come first, Lo, always."

I exhaled deeply as warmth and love for this man flooded my every cell.

"Thank you. I was thinking we could head out east to the vineyards for a few days. Let the craziness die down a bit. I heard the Jedediah Hawkins Inn is fantastic."

Griffin chuckled, "I don't suppose the fact that the Jedediah Hawkins restaurant is supposed to be *fantastic* had any effect on your choice."

"Maybe," I said coyly.

"I'll call now and book a room and reservations for dinner. Go pack your bag and we'll leave in an hour."

I kissed him, pulling him against me fully to show my appreciation, before releasing him and dashing to my room.

We left an hour later under police escort. The further east we drove, the more our tension melted away. We both needed this break from the tragedies and worries of the last nine months. We needed time alone to enjoy one another without any threats or work issues looming. We needed time to be Griffin and Sam.

I called Thia during the drive to cancel my appointment for the following day. I briefly explained about Heath's death and the subsequent media frenzy before confessing that Griffin and I were going to hide out for a few days. She granted her therapeutic blessing, after making me promise I would gorge myself on food during the mini-vacation. She also made me promise I would call her if I needed to talk, day or night.

Three days later we returned home rejuvenated; I had never had so much fun in my life. We enjoyed every moment together with the joy of children—walks along the beach, wine tasting, exploring small island towns...it was a dream. We even found a deserted playground to horse around on. We competed on the swings to see who could fly the highest (I totally won if you didn't consider the length of Griffin's legs), after which we attempted to seesaw, an epic failure given our weight and height difference. My favorite part was watching Griffin get stuck in the covered twisty slide when he tried to follow me down. I nearly choked to death I was laughing so hard.

We spent our nights tangled in each other and physically expressing the depths of our growing love. It was magic.

When we arrived at my house, I was relieved to find it was media-free. Hunter had texted us that the guard on duty the morning of our departure had been fired and the complex promised nothing of the sort would happen again. The DA's office had also found the leak and immediately terminated them with possible charges pending. I was still receiving countless voicemails from news outlets requesting comments or interviews, but I deleted them all without listening for more than a few seconds. All things considered, life was shockingly fantastic. I was so happy I barely knew what to do with myself.

I wasn't scheduled to work until Monday, so I stayed home the following day to catch up on laundry while Griffin headed to The Stop. The home phone rang and I reflexively answered without thinking.

"Hello?"

"Hello, Miss Whitney, this is Liz from *60 Minutes*—please don't hang up."

I was about to do exactly that, but something in her voice stopped me.

"Oh, you didn't hang up," she said, surprised.

"You have two minutes."

"Fair enough. We've covered the issue of colleges turning a blind eye to rapes reported by students, as well as the manipulation of crime statistics in the past. We were planning to tackle the topic again, seeing as little has changed, and using the tragedy at Hensley as a cautionary tale. The events were so extreme and the university so negligent, we believe it may inspire viewers to demand changes in state and federal laws governing collegiate reporting. We planned to air when the trial began for maximum exposure, but given *his* death, we are going to air next week. We would like to include an interview with you in the feature."

I noticed and appreciated her discretion in not speaking Heath's name to me. I was also impressed by her passionate explanation of the show's mission for this segment.

"I applaud your goals, but I'm not sure I'm the right person for your interview. I have no direct knowledge of how the university handled previous complaints about Heath."

"You're exactly the right person," she protested vehemently. "Sorry, I'm passionate about this episode; it's sort of my life mission."

I understood immediately. Someone she loved, if not herself, had been raped during college and justice had not been served.

"Why me?"

"You are the heart of the story. It's just another news bite about blah, blah doing something wrong, blah, blah. That is what viewers hear unless we give them something to connect to emotionally—a person with whom to empathize. To succeed, the viewers need to ask themselves—what if that were my child? That is the only way that we can engage them to action."

"That makes sense, but why me?"

"Because your story is one of survival and hope. You're likable and viewers will sympathize with you. Because you are the last victim, and...because you are the only one strong enough to do it. You were the only witness for the DA who was also a victim. I know Miss Carsen had a close call, but her story won't have the same impact. It has to be you. I'm asking you to be the voice for all the other victims. Not just the ones at Hensley, but all girls who have experienced what you have and never had the opportunity to seek justice or tell their story. You can speak for them, and you can inspire them. You are proof that they can survive, overcome, even thrive after what's been done to them. You are the phoenix they need to give them hope."

My eyes welled at the thought of all the others who had suffered in the past and those who would in the future. I thought of the other girls at The Phoenix Centre, as broken as I was, but many already hopeless.

"What would I have to do?" I asked. I couldn't believe I was actually considering this.

"You just need to answer some questions...tell your story. We will email you all the questions in advance, so there will be no surprises. We will even sign an agreement that the show will not air if we ask even a single question not provided to you in advance. We aren't looking to sensationalize the story for ratings—it's already so outrageous that there's no need to create drama."

"I need to think about this before I commit. Send me the questions and I'll look them over. When do you need an answer?"

She cleared her throat nervously, "Well, ideally by tomorrow morning. We need to set the schedule and prepare the promo spots to begin airing."

"No pressure, huh?"

"Sorry, I want to time the airing for maximum impact."

"Email me and I'll get back to you with my decision by tomorrow morning."

"Great. Thank you so much."

After we hung up I sat at the kitchen table, debating. I didn't want to do it. I didn't want to be the spokesperson for every rape victim. I didn't want the whole world to know my name, know what had been done to me. But the guilt of doing nothing gnawed at me.

I grabbed my phone and dialed Thia's cell phone. She answered on the first ring.

"Can you be at my office in fifteen minutes?"

That was quite the greeting, although I would have been disappointed if she'd answered the phone with a typical 'hello.'

"I'll be there."

I called Griffin on my way to let him know I was headed to Thia's and I needed to discuss something with him when he had time. He tried to cover the concern in his voice but failed miserably. We agreed I'd come to The Stop immediately after my appointment.

I arrived a few minutes early and met Thia in the parking lot.

"Sorry, I was coming from the university. My schedule is tight today, so you're only allowed forty minutes to sort out whatever ails you. No niceties or stalling...straight to the point. Got it?"

"You got it, boss lady."

We entered her office, where I immediately recapped the phone call and my hesitation.

"Most sane people wouldn't want to enter the limelight and expose themselves in such a way. I guess that means you're sane," Thia began. "I can't tell you what to decide, Sam. I will say that you have nothing to feel shame about—you did nothing wrong. We can debate whether you are the best representative for the victims of rape until we are both breathless, but it's irrelevant. You are that person. You are a rape survivor, but it's not all you are—you are strong and intelligent, courageous and sensitive. Most importantly, you are the reminder to every other victim that it does get better...whatever imperfections you think you have, whatever flaws you believe remain, you are still worthy of love and happiness...and so are they."

"Aren't you supposed to be impartial? There was a whole lot of 'partial' going on there."

"Sometimes the best way to help a client is to give them the truth. You get to decide how to assimilate that truth into your life, but this is not a matter of opinion."

"I really don't want to do this, Thia," I said, taking a deep breath, "but I will. If the interview could effect change in colleges and prevent future rapes, I have no choice but to go ahead. I owe it to the girls who died, to those who will never have a chance to tell their stories."

"You had already decided to do it. You wouldn't have called me otherwise—you would have called someone who would dissuade you."

"You think you're so clever, don't you?" I asked with mock insult.

"Oh no, I know I'm that clever. Genius, didn't you know?" she said, tapping her finger to her temple.

Well, that explained her eccentricities. Weren't most geniuses eccentrics?

"Time's up. Your homework is to admit to yourself you are going to do this...then call the TV lady and give her the green light. Read the questions she sends and call me if you have any concerns. Now scram."

I rose and trudged toward the door, reluctantly accepting her conclusions.

"And Sam, one more consideration," she paused, assessing me. "When you say 'yes,' you will have a perfectly justifiable excuse to buy a new outfit and shoes."

I gave her a smile as wide as the Grand Canyon. That woman knew the way to turn my frown upside-down.

I continued smiling as I drove to The Stop to share my decision with Griffin. I had just closed my car door when an unnerving thought occurred to me. What if Griffin didn't want me to do the interview? Fuck! I'd never even considered the possibility. What would I do if he asked me not to do this?

I walked into The Stop like a woman heading before a firing squad, fearing the worst. Griffin saw me from behind the bar and immediately came to my side. Without a word, he took my hand and led me to his office.

"What's up?"

I explained about the call from Liz and why I wanted to accept her invitation. He never said a word or gave any indication of his thoughts. He was a disturbingly blank slate. When I finished, I waited for him to respond, but he said nothing.

"Well?" I finally asked when the suspense was too much to bear.

"Well, what? I support any decision you make. If you need to do this, then what is there for me to say other than 'I have your back'? And I do, Sam, I will always have your back."

I threw myself onto his lap, clamping my arms around his neck in a vice-like grip. Then I kissed him like he was the center of my universe...because he was.

"You are perfect," I said, my lips still pressed to his.

"No, Lo, I'm not perfect. I've done things you may not approve of. I've been trying to tell—"

"Okay, close to perfect. Definitely perfect for me," I said, cutting him off. "And I'm going to make you prove how perfect you are for me when you get home tonight."

He groaned as I wiggled my butt on his lap to drive home my point.

"You just love me for my body," he teased.

"No. I dig your pretty face, too."

"Pretty?" he complained while tickling me.

We stayed that way for a while, holding and teasing each other—just being us.

I walked into Higher Yearning to find Meg beaming at me. She was glowing so brightly I was tempted to fish my sunglasses out of my purse.

"Someone's in a sunny mood today," I said after storing my purse and coat in the back. "What gives?"

"Oh, no reason, I just had a great weekend."

"Your date. Shit, I forgot! Tell me everything. Is the mission accomplished? Were you right about the Ph.D.?"

"We didn't get that far. We met in Port Jefferson, then went to a bar and danced for hours. His dance moves were unreal...I was closer to finding my happy ending dancing with him than I've ever been with another person. Mind blowing," she said with a glassy look in her eyes.

Yep, man definitely held a Doctorate in Erotic Fine Arts.

"So there was nothing other than dancing?"

"He kissed me goodnight—again, mind blowing—but I didn't feel comfortable inviting him to my place and he didn't offer his. Total bummer...but he asked me out again for next weekend, so I have my fingers crossed for a more *fulfilling* outcome."

I laughed at her dramatic wink, happy to see her so enthusiastic.

"I'm not looking for a *relationship* relationship, but I think this one has the potential to be just the right balance of exclusive fun without all the emotional entanglements. I could see more than a one-night stand with him."

"Well, if his naked dance moves are as good as his clothed ones, you may want to go back for seconds...and thirds," I said.

"Exactly. We had a great time at dinner. The conversation flowed, he was charming, and we laughed a lot. Casual dating with toe-curling goodnights is exactly what I need. No muss, no fuss—and when it runs its course, there are no hard feelings, just some steamy memories and lingering laughs."

"Sounds like a good plan," I said skeptically. "You sure you can keep emotions out of it?"

"Oh yeah, that's the easy part. And he is definitely not the type to get emotionally attached. Easy-peasy."

Meg believed every word she said, I could tell, but her words revealed a piece of Meg I had never noticed before. She was scarred...someone had hurt Meg—bad. It was easy to miss with her sunny disposition and positive outlook, but it was there. Maybe having my own scars made it easier for me to see...now that I could see beyond just myself.

"Careful, lady. Anyone I knew who ever swore love couldn't touch them got drop-kicked by the bitch."

"Bitch has got to catch you first, and I've learned how to run—fast—like Olympian 50-meter sprint fast," she said with humor, but I thought I caught a flash of steel in her eyes.

"Now you're just tempting fate. Don't say I didn't warn you."

"Lightning doesn't strike the same place twice—even fate isn't that spiteful."

I placed my hand on her arm, wanting to offer her support. It was then that I realized I knew nothing about Meg's past. She seemed so open and warm, but I couldn't remember a single detail about her past outside of references to a typical, happy childhood.

"Meg, you know if you ever need to talk, I—"

"Wes? What are you doing here—miss me already?"

I looked up, horror-struck. Why the hell was Meg calling Westly Black, "Wes," with a smile on her face that promised exactly what I had done to Griffin last night? Holy fuckballs. No, no, no...this could not be happening.

"What happened to Mark?" I snapped at Meg.

Her head spun to me so fast I was afraid she would get whiplash. I guess my tone was even sharper than I had intended.

"Who the hell is Mark?" she shot back.

"The assistant DA you're dating?"

"Um, no. I went out with Wes," she said and pointed to him. Neither of us had bothered to acknowledge him yet.

I turned my deadliest stare on him and pointed, too. "You—go sit in the corner and wait for me there."

His eyes narrowed at me before turning to Meg. "Meg, let me explain."

Meg held his stare. "Did you come here to talk to me or Sam?"

"Miss Whitney," he said flatly.

"And I assume there is something I don't know that I'm not going to like?" Meg asked flatly.

He nodded.

"Thanks for dinner last night. As I said, I had a nice time. Unfortunately, I'm going to have to cancel our plans for this weekend. I don't have time for drama and bullshit. I just wanted to have a little fun. You're not fun anymore, apparently you're just an asshole."

Wes opened his mouth to speak but quickly closed it, shaking his head as he walked to the furthest table.

"Explain," Meg said to me.

"He's the asshole attorney for the guy who hurt me. He's been coming in to bribe or threaten me to prevent my testimony for months."

"That son of a bitch—I sure know how to pick them," she sighed. "At least I found out now," she said casually, but I saw the disappointment in her eyes. "I had no idea, Sam. I would never have accepted if I'd known."

"I know," I said while giving her a quick hug. "Let me go take out the trash."

And with that, I headed in Mr. Black's direction.

"I should kick you in the balls for screwing with my friend's head. Why are you even here? Heath's dead, in case you hadn't heard. There is no trial."

"I never represented Heath. I represent the Varbeck family—"

"Semantics. Let's get this over with and then I never want to see you again. And God help you if you come sniffing around Meg!"

His body stiffened, but it was the only indication he had heard me.

"The Varbeck family asked that I bring you this," he said, extending an envelope in my direction. "They also wanted me to express their sincere apologies for any pain you may have suffered at the hands of their son. They aren't monsters, Sam, even if their son was."

With only a brief glance in Meg's direction, he left, hopefully never to be seen or heard from again.

I sat down and opened the envelope. Inside, there was a check for two million dollars and a hand-written note.

Dear Miss Whitney,

There are no words to convey the depth of our sorrow for your suffering. It is no excuse, but perhaps one day you will be a parent and understand the unconditional love for your child, even when you are horrified by their actions. I have to believe that he was ill beyond his control, no longer the same little boy, because that is a mother's love.

We have decided to divide the trust Heath was to receive on his next birthday amongst his victims. I know restitution cannot undo the damage, and perhaps it will only serve to assuage our guilt.

You will be in our prayers and I hope you can one day find room in your heart to forgive us for defending our child despite his guilt.

Sincerely,

Sandra Varbeck

I wanted to rip the check to shreds like their son had done to my life and send it back to them with a nasty letter, hurling blame at them and accusing them of being responsible for Heath's evil. I was about to do just that when it occurred to me that I was reacting and not thinking. I didn't know if a deep, dark secret lay within the Varbeck family that produced the monster Heath had become, or if pure evil existed in him from birth. It was an answer I would never have. The painful realization that this mother loved and supported her demon son, despite his evil and no matter how absurd it seemed, was truly a testament to a mother's love—and a stark contrast to my parents. For that alone, I decided not to return the check, but there was no way in hell I was accepting a penny of the money intended for him. I was at a loss for what to do with the money until inspiration struck.

I slid my phone from my pocket to locate the number I needed.

"Thank you for calling RAINN, the rape, abuse, and incest national network, how can I help you?" a voice answered.

"Yes, I'd like to make a donation."

Chapter Seventeen

"Nobody ever did, or ever will,
escape the consequences of his choices."
-Alfred A. Montapert

Griffin

I entered the Psychology building at Hensley University where the professors' and advisors' offices were located. I had received a voicemail this morning asking me to come in for a meeting at noon and knew it didn't bode well for me. Knowing what the meeting was likely about did not lessen my apprehension. I was prepared for the possibility of such a call since I went to visit Heath in prison, and when I heard about his death, I expected it.

I walked down the long corridor toward the corner office—the Department of Psychology Graduate Advisor. I hoped she would make this quick and not try and counsel me about my choices...there were none.

I knocked on the doorframe to capture her attention before entering. She nodded to the seat across from her, the smallest chair in the room, and smirked.

"You don't want me to get too comfortable, huh?"

"I think it's appropriate that you feel a bit uncomfortable, don't you, Griffin? We'll call it penance," she said, unreadable. "You know why you're here?"

"I have a guess."

"Heath Varbeck lodged a complaint with the warden prior to his death, claiming you arranged for him to be sexually assaulted by other inmates."

"Did he?" I answered, unwilling to lie, but not planning on volunteering information that could lead to criminal charges.

"Unfortunately, inmate against inmate violence is extremely prevalent in prisons, and the warden found no evidence of any wrongdoing on your part. I'm sure you know all evaluations are recorded."

"I recall hearing that."

She rolled her eyes at me, acknowledging the dance we were engaged in. The warden, police, and university might have suspected I had influenced the abuse Heath suffered, but there was no concrete evidence. I doubt any of them were crying over the death of a serial killer. I was relieved that no charges would be leveled against me, especially while I was still completing my community service for beating the shit out of Robbie. Whatever else came out of this meeting, it was still my lucky day.

"The Varbeck family does not intend to pursue civil action against the State for Heath's death, so other than a mountain of paperwork, the issue is dead."

Knowing her twisted humor, I assumed the pun was intended. I nodded my understanding and appreciation. I had been counting on the Varbecks' desire to avoid further publicity and distance themselves from their son's crimes. I was relieved the risk paid off. I never planned for Heath to be killed, but I couldn't say it was shocking either, nor was I sad at the news. In truth, I would have preferred he suffer the abuse for the next sixty years behind bars. But it worked out for the best; Sam wouldn't have to endure a trial or face Heath again. The latent threat he posed while living was now removed. Already she was lighter—definitely worth any smudges now staining my soul.

"The problem is, you never should have been in that room with Mr. Varbeck. Your clinical hours were completed, and you had a significant conflict of interest."

I raised my eyebrow at her for the last comment.

She stared back, undaunted.

"Yes, it is possible to evaluate and treat clients when there is a personal connection. Many therapists have done so successfully, but it requires compartmentalization and objectivity. Are you going to tell me you entered the eval room to meet with Heath as an objective psychologist?"

"No. I stand by my assessment and diagnosis, but I was not objective where he was concerned."

"Griffin, you abused your access to the prison for your own agenda. You violated several moral and ethical tenets. I am sorry, but I cannot recommend you to the licensing board. You have completed all requirements and as such will receive your Doctoral degree in Clinical Psychology from Hensley; I won't interfere in that regard. You could consider finding another sponsor for your licensing, given time, but I would suggest you prepare yourself to answer several difficult questions before anyone would even consider taking you on."

I nodded.

"You would need to prove to the sponsor you would be able to exhibit better judgment in the future."

"I am not planning to go out and buy a spandex body suit, utility belt, and mask. It may have been vigilante, but my actions were contained to justice for one person. I don't have delusions that I can or should try and rid the world of all evil."

"I'm sorry it has turned out this way. I believe you would be an effective therapist. Are you sure you made the right choice, sacrificing the assistance you could have provided to many others for the benefit of one?"

"Hell yes. If it ensured her safety, I'd do it again without regret, no matter the cost to me."

"Okay." We both rose and she escorted me to her door. "As you are no longer my charge, and you have technically graduated from Hensley, there is one thing I would like to say."

I gestured for her to proceed.

"As a therapist, I am appalled by your behavior. As your advisor, I am disappointed in your choices. As a woman and a friend, I'm glad he got a taste of his own medicine."

I laughed at her candor. I'm not surprised that anyone would be glad to hear that Heath endured the same treatment he inflicted on others without remorse, but I hadn't expected her to verbalize that truth.

"One more thing...if you love Sam and you want to have a future with her, you need to confess your part in Heath's death. The guilt of withholding the truth from her will eat at you, and she may not forgive the betrayal if she finds out. Plus, you are going to have a hard time explaining why you suddenly are abandoning or delaying your licensing."

"I know, but I'm scared she's going to run. Violence is a trigger for her, and while the violence against Heath wasn't done by my hands...I'm not exactly innocent."

"You made the hard choices, now you have to deal with the consequences. You need to tell her, Griffin. There is a chance she can come to terms with your actions if you explain them to her...if she finds out some other way, you're screwed—and not in the good way."

"I know, Thia," I said.

"Take care of my girl," she said with a smile.

"You, too," I returned.

I drove back to The Stop and spent the rest of the afternoon hiding from the world in my office. I knew I had to tell Sam the truth about Heath, even at the risk of losing her. Our relationship couldn't be strong if built on a lie.

In truth, the only thing I risked by punishing Heath was losing Sam; the rest was inconsequential in comparison. Still, even if it cost me a lifetime with her, I wouldn't regret doing everything in my power to avenge and protect her. With enough effort, I could still obtain my State license. It may take a few more years, but it was doable. I was prepared to have Thia withdraw my degree; it was a pleasant surprise to find the last five years weren't wasted. Hell, I was prepared to serve time if it came down to it.

I needed to get this over with before I wound up with an ulcer. I texted Sam to tell her I was on the way over with dinner, throwing up a prayer that I wouldn't lose her again.

Chapter Eighteen

"Rather than love, than money, than fame, give me truth." -
Henry David Thoreau

He was scaring the shit out of me. He hadn't spoken a word since he arrived and handed me the bag with dinner, after which he commenced pacing. Dinner had been plated and on the table for five minutes, and he was still prowling the kitchen like a caged bear. Every time my eyes caught his, I saw wariness before he broke contact.

"Griffin, babe," I said, capturing his attention, "you're freaking me out...big time. Whatever you need to say, just spit it out."

"I have to tell you something," he began, then stopped abruptly.

"Oh my god, you are *not* breaking up with me," I ordered.

He froze in shock. His expression verged on comical, eyes wide and mouth parted.

"Hell no...never. Why would you even say something so ridiculous?"

"I don't know, maybe because you're testing the durability of my kitchen tiles with your pacing? Did you run over my dog?"

He smiled—finally. "You don't have a dog."

"Then we're in the clear. Now tell me what has you acting like a nutcase, so I can tell you how much I love you and we can eat dinner."

"I can't be a psychologist. My advisor won't recommend me to the state licensing board."

"What?" I screamed, enraged for him. "That is complete bullshit. You will be a fantastic therapist, I know it. How dare he...what's his name? I'm going to have a word with him. Who can we appeal to?"

"Whoa, love. Slow down. She's right, I broke the rules...big time. There is no way she can recommend me."

Broke the rules? Oh shit, it must be about the probation for kicking Robbie's ass. Hunter mentioned something like this could happen. But it was one slip-up under extenuating circumstances...maybe if I explained the history, they would reconsider.

"Is this because of the Robbie thing? I'll go talk to them, explain what happened to me. They have to understand."

"No Lo, it has nothing to do with that."

"Okay..." I drew out the word, communicating my confusion and prompting him to continue.

"My clinical hours...I did them at Riverhead Prison, assessing and counseling inmates," he paused, inhaling deeply. "On my last visit I met with Heath. It was a few months ago...before he died."

So Griffin didn't kill him. That was good news, but I still didn't see the problem.

"It was right after I found out about the threats, and I was insanely pissed. Wait, that's bullshit—it's true I was insanely pissed, but I had been planning it since you left for the Phoenix Centre."

"It?"

"I told another inmate he was a pedophile so that he would be abused in prison. I told Heath as much—essentially mindfucked him—and then I left. I made sure he would suffer for the rest of his life for what he did to you and the others. I didn't plan for him to die...I knew it was a possibility, but that wasn't my goal. I'm sorry, Lo, I did it before the Robbie incident," he sighed, running his hands down his face. "I said I wouldn't lie..." he muttered to himself, "honestly, even knowing how much the violence upset you, I still would have done it. The threats...I couldn't risk him hurting you. He needed to know I could get to him if he tried anything."

He turned away without looking at me, his posture rigid, as if bracing himself for my rejection and horror.

"I'm sorry, Lo. I love you so fucking much, I couldn't let it go...he had to pay for what he did, and there was no sentence the courts could have handed down that would have been enough for me. I'm not a homicidal maniac, I swear...except when it comes to someone hurting you."

"You crazy dumbass," I said, the shock beginning to wear off.

He spun to face me, anguish clouding his beautiful features.

"You put your dream of helping others at risk just to punish the asshole that hurt me? I'm not sure if I should punch you or kiss you. And then, to top it off, you think I'm going to leave you for trying to protect me?" I paused to consider. "Punch. I'm definitely going to punch you for being an idiot...then I'm going to kiss you for being my hero."

I rose from my chair, made my way over to him, and punched him in the stomach, which likely hurt my poor hand more than his rock-hard abs. Then I wrapped my arms around his neck and kissed him until my lungs burned for air.

When I pulled back to breathe, I looked up to find him smiling like a doofus.

"I told you most of my reaction to the Robbie beat-down was just from seeing violence, not necessarily that you kicked that dickwad's ass. He deserved it. I've worked through a lot of my issues with the violence, and I can separate past from present now. Actually, there is a twisted part of me that would have liked to see Heath get his...not his death, but his face when you told him what his future held. See, I'm just as messed up as you are...actually, maybe this proves you're just as messed up as I am. You were right—you're totally not perfect and I love you even more."

He grabbed my waist and threw me up in the air before catching me against his chest.

"God, I love you," he said before kissing me senseless. "Are you hungry?"

"For something," I said, nipping his lip and grabbing his ass—and what an ass it was.

"I was hoping you'd say that."

He led me to my bedroom and proceeded to show his gratitude in all of my favorite ways...and some innovative new ones. I loved this man with every tiny microscopic piece of me. Maybe it made me a little crazy, but the fact that Griffin had risked everything he had worked for to protect me and punish Heath was just another reason he was perfect for me. I wanted this man for the rest of my life. There would never be another.

When I awoke the next morning, my head was cushioned on Griffin's chest but something was off. I raised myself and studied my room for a moment—our heads were at the foot of the bed; a few of the pictures on my wall were crooked and the knick-knacks previously on top of my dresser were now on the floor. I smiled, remembering the havoc we wreaked last night. Good times.

I flopped back down on his chest and nuzzled in. The rumble of his laughter shook my head.

"We made a mess."

"We did, and as long as you help clean up, we can make another one tonight."

"Deal."

We lay quietly, enjoying the easy silence of intimacy. Life was so good. No threats, no secrets, no meltdowns—we had found our happily ever after...finally.

"She was right."

"Hmm?"

"Yesterday after she told me she wouldn't recommend my license, Thia said I had to tell you what happened so we could move on. She's nuts, but she's never wrong...it's obnoxious."

"Excuse me?" I said, shooting upright to offer him an incredulous stare.

"I forgot to mention that part yesterday, didn't I? Thia is...was my advisor."

"You've been keeping tabs on me with my therapist," I shrieked, slapping his chest. "You asshole...that bitch! How could you?"

There was nothing I wouldn't have shared with Griffin myself, but knowing he had gone behind my back to garner information about me from my therapist was a horrible betrayal of trust. I moved to leave the bed and storm out of the room, but a massive body tackled me to the bed, pinning me beneath his weight, grasping both of my wrists in one of his huge hands.

"Calm down, Lo-baby. It's not what you think, I swear."

I refused to look at him I was so pissed. He used his free hand to turn my face to him so I shut my eyes, denying him in the only way I could.

"Baby, I—"

"Don't you call me that! I'm furious with you, you oversized snoop. I liked Thia, she was mine. You had no right to take her. Now I have to find a new therapist...start all over. You know how many sessions it's going to take to cover what a jackass you are?" I said hotly, never opening my eyes.

"I knew Thia first; she was my advisor for five years. You don't own her and I hate to break it to you, but I suspect she may be cheating on you...I heard she has other clients," he teased.

I was in no mood to joke, which I illustrated by trying to buck him off me—now that was a joke. I didn't even move him a millimeter.

"I had nothing to do with Ev contacting Thia. I didn't even know she was your therapist 'til that first dinner after you returned from the Phoenix Centre. I'm sure Thia realized our connection when you said my name, seeing as it's not common, but we *never* discussed you. The first time we even acknowledged we both knew you was yesterday, *after* she was no longer my advisor. Even then, we didn't actually talk about you. She just told me that I had to be honest with you if I wanted to keep you. She also told me I better take care of *her* girl."

My anger waned as he spoke, until I was left grinning that Thia had called me *her* girl. I was totally her favorite. I guess I couldn't fault either of them for knowing the other. I believed Griffin when he said they had never discussed me, but I was still pissed. He should have told me sooner. I opened my eyes and gave him a stern look.

"I forgive you, but I'm still pissed you didn't tell me before now. I had a right to know. I wouldn't have stopped seeing Thia, but that was my decision to make."

"You're right, Lo. I'm sorry."

"Fine...and no gossiping about me behind my back."

"We never talked about you other than the brief exchange yesterday."

I nodded, accepting him at his word. There was nothing left for me to say. I wasn't pleased, but I wasn't going turn it into World War III.

In a moment of intense clarity, I recognized our position. He had me fully restrained beneath him. I couldn't move an inch unless he allowed me. Even my face was still anchored in his hand, albeit lovingly.

"Um, babe? You're squishing me."

He studied me without moving.

"And I'm not freaking out. At. All. In fact..." I trailed off, letting him follow my thought to its conclusion.

"Really?" I saw the interest spark in his slate blue eyes.

"Well, we are dressed for it."

He laughed, and I couldn't believe how far I'd come—trapped and defenseless while naked, and the only feeling rising up in me was lust. Amazing.

He released my wrists and braced his weight on his forearms, freeing me. The hand that had been holding my chin to prevent me from looking away moved to caress my cheek as he kissed me tenderly. Every second was breathtaking. As we made love, he possessed me—owning every inch of my body, commanding its response with his words and movement. Sex with Griffin was always out of this world, but this time, it was as if the final piece snapped into place for us. Trusting each other and ourselves with nothing between us.

I arrived at Higher Yearning later that afternoon in the best mood ever. I suspected a trail of rainbows and Carebear-riding unicorns followed in my wake. I may have walked through Hell, but like the phoenix, I had risen from the ashes and now I was soaring. If the trials I had endured were the price of admission for the wonder before me, it was worth the cost. I felt a contentment and peace I had never known—I was blessed.

The only blip of sadness on my radar was Meg. Outwardly she appeared as carefree and open as ever, but I was learning her tells, glimpses of reality beneath her mask.

"Megalicious, want to tell me what's bothering you?"

"Nothing's bothering me," she said unconvincingly. "I'm a little tired, but other than that, everything is great. The semester ends next month and I graduate. I was just accepted to grad school at Hensley. I've got no complaints."

"That scumbag lawyer hasn't been bothering you, has he?"

"Nope. He faded back into the black abyss he crawled out of," she joked, but the laughter was hollow.

"Don't give up, babe. That jackass doesn't represent all men. Forget him, your prince charming is enroute...but you know traffic on the Long Island Expressway, he's just running a little late."

"Thanks, Sam, but my happy ending doesn't include a knight in shining armor. I'm not a Disney princess. My happiness will never be contingent on a man...no offense."

"None taken," I said with a smile.

"My ever after is a fulfilling career, financial security, good friends, and peace. All I want is a drama-free life. That's my dream."

"Alright, girlie. Just make sure you buy a lot of batteries," I teased.

"I splurged on a Costco membership last year. I'm set."

I nearly spit out the coffee I had just sipped.

"You have just officially joined the clan, thanks to that comment. Your induction will take place next Thursday night at The Stop."

"Such a prestigious honor earned so young—I accept."

Oh yeah, she'd fit in just fine.

The rest of my shift passed with our lighthearted banter and smiles. Griffin had planned to swing by and bring me dinner, but he'd gotten hung up at The Stop, so I ran out and bought Chipotle for Meg and I. We were getting ready to close for the night when Griff texted he had just left work, offering to swing by and keep us company until we wrapped up. I told him not to bother because we were almost done and to meet me at my house.

"Want me to wait for you?" I offered, despite my eagerness to get home and watch the second-to-last Project Runway of the season.

"No, you go ahead. I need to use the restroom and grab a sleeve of cups for the front before I head out. I'll set the alarm on my way out."

"Nite, nite," I said while heading to the door.

I walked to my car, mentally reviewing the contestants on the show this season and their successes and failures, trying to guess who was going to show at Bryant Park.

My hand was on the door handle when a body pressed against me, trapping me against the car, seconds before my throat began to sting. I reflexively lowered my chin, but a gloved hand captured it, slamming my head back against a broad shoulder.

"Don't want to leave evidence if I can avoid it. Don't move or you'll slice your throat open before it's time."

I stood, petrified by fear, stunned into silence. I focused on my breathing, calming myself and trying to retrieve my wits. Now was not the time to fall apart. I knew how this story ended if I did nothing. Last time, I never had a chance to fight...this time, odds were not in my favor, but I had a chance and I wouldn't blow it by losing my shit.

The more my reason returned, the more confused I became. This couldn't be related to Heath...he was dead, for God's sake. No trial meant I couldn't testify. Was it possible to have such obscenely bad luck that I could be beaten and raped, threatened with death, and assaulted again in an act of random violence? No way, no one's luck was that bad.

"Who are you? Why?" I asked.

His only response was to press the knife more firmly against my neck, penetrating another layer of skin.

"Seriously? You just admitted you're going to kill me. Is it really such a huge inconvenience to tell me 'why' first—it's not like I can tattle on you if I'm dead."

"Lady, this isn't the movies. You aren't going to talk me out of doing my job, and I'm not confessing to unburden myself."

Job...he was hired for this. But Heath was freaking dead. What the fuck?

"You know, Heath is dead. There is no trial, no reason to kill me. Maybe your boss forgot to pass along the memo, seeing as he's dead."

"No idea who Heath is, but enough talking. We are going to walk nice and slow to the parking lot next door. You are going to get in the van I have waiting without any struggle. If you cooperate, you die quickly with very little pain. You give me a headache and you will suffer in ways you can't even imagine before I kill you."

I know I should be terrified—and I was—but the utter ridiculousness of the situation was distracting. That momentary relief allowed my anger to surge. I clung to the anger like it was a weapon—anger could help me right now, fear couldn't. One thing was for sure... this dipshit was definitely uninformed if he thought there was anything he could do to me that hadn't already been done. He should have done his research if he wanted to deliver effective threats.

I tried to wiggle free, testing his grip, and the knife bit further into my throat. I felt a trickle of wetness down my neck. Great...another freaking scar. This asshole had better kill me before I got the opportunity to gouge his eyes out with my gel-manicured fingernails.

He turned and directed us to the neighboring lot, the knife pressed firmly against my neck. I was running through possible escape scenarios, absorbing as many details as possible in search of an opportunity. We made it about halfway across the lot when his body jerked and the knife fell from my neck, clattering on the asphalt.

"Let her go, asshole," I heard Meg say as his body jerked against mine.

Whatever Meg had done succeeded in getting him to drop the knife, but his arm was still locked around me, his hold unbreakable.

As if in slow motion, he spun us to face her, pulling a gun from god-knows-where in the process. I didn't even have time to call out a warning before the gunshot echoed, causing my ears to ring.

Meg crumpled to the ground as he pulled me backward in a hurry, the gun pressed to the side of my head as he moved away from her body.

"Stupid fucking bitch stabbed me. Motherfucker! Blood is gonna be everywhere. Fuck."

Meg...oh my god, Meg—the stupid, brave idiot. He killed her, my friend...she was trying to save me and he killed her. I dropped my head and vomited. He stopped moving and cursed.

"These are new shoes, you bitch. Christ."

I heard a whoosh to my left where the gun was pressed against my head and braced for the bullet. A loud crack sounded near my ear, different from the shot he fired earlier. Seconds later, he shrieked and released me. I fell forward, crashing to the pavement in a painful heap. I caught most of my body weight with my hands, but the forward momentum still caused me to thump my head against the ground. I lay still for a moment, until I heard a familiar sound—thunk-squish-crack...thunk-squish-crack. I lifted my head to find the most miraculous back facing me. Griffin was on top of the bad guy, beating him like he had Robbie.

I wasn't horrified this time; I wanted Griffin to kill him for hurting Meg. I wanted it so badly, but I couldn't let Griffin carry the burden of taking a life, even in my defense. I sure as hell would let him knock the bastard out, but then I had to stop him.

I crawled closer to him until I could see if the guy was conscious. Nope. Out cold.

"Griffin, love. That's enough. You saved me, he's knocked out. You need to stop now, because I need you to help me. Meg was shot, and I don't know if she's alive...we need to get help."

He turned to face me and blinked twice. I saw the fog lift as he came back to me.

"You okay?" he asked me gruffly.

"No, but I'm going to keep it together until we get Meg help."

"Stay there for a minute."

He grabbed the guy's arm and dragged him carelessly to where Meg was laying. He seemed to fuss with the guy's body for a moment before raising his arm and lowering it quickly. What the hell was he...oh, he'd figured out a way to restrain him. When Griffin backed away, my suspicion was confirmed. The parking lot light reflected off the handle of a long hunting knife that was now imbedded through the guy's hand, deep into the ground beneath. He definitely wouldn't have been able to get free without making noise.

Griffin turned and kneeled next to Meg as I rose, making my way to them.

"She's breathing," Griffin said, his relief evident. "Do you have your phone?"

"No, it's on the ground somewhere with my purse."

"Come here and put pressure on her wound. I'll call for help."

He whipped off his shirt and handed it to me before calling the police.

There was a puddle of blood spreading from beneath her, but I kneeled beside her anyway. I pulled up her shirt and pressed my makeshift bandage to her stomach, where I found the most blood. I prayed with all my heart that she would survive and be okay.

As Griffin ended the call and approached, I whispered, "She was trying to save me. He had a knife to my throat, and she stabbed him so he would drop it. I have no idea where he pulled the gun from, but he just shot her without a second thought."

I heard the sirens blaring nearby before doors began slamming.

"Over here," Griffin called.

He rose slowly with his hands up.

"I have the attacker disabled on the ground. The victim's here; she's been shot."

The officer quickly assessed the scene before speaking, "Get the paramedics in here, the scene is secure."

Moments later, my hands were guided away while professionals assessed her.

"She's breathing, heartbeat's steady," one of the paramedics said to no one in particular.

The officer turned his gaze to the assailant, who showed the first signs of stirring, and smiled when he saw the knife protruding from the guy's hand.

"Man, remind me never to piss you off."

"He had a gun pressed to my girlfriend's head when I got here. He's lucky he's breathing."

"Miss, are you hurt?" the officer asked me.

"I just have a small cut on my throat," I replied.

"Are you able to answer questions or do you need medical attention first?"

"Let's do it now," I sighed, hoping I never had to provide a 'statement' to law enforcement ever again.

After I had given my account of the night's events and answered the officer's questions, he said we were free to go.

"Get it checked at the hospital and have them document the injury," the officer instructed.

I nodded. I was headed there to check on Meg anyway.

When we arrived at the hospital, we checked with the emergency room nurses and found out Meg was in surgery. The nurse promised that the doctor would find us in the waiting room when there was news.

After about an hour, a doctor examined my neck, then decided cleaning the wound and sealing it with some skin-friendly crazy glue would do the trick.

When we settled ourselves in the waiting room, I called Ev and Hunter to explain what had happened. When her shock wore off, Ev promised to meet us at the hospital and Hunter was off to talk to the police.

Everleigh arrived a half-hour later, joining us in the waiting room.

"How is she?" Ev asked with concern.

"In surgery," I replied.

It was four hours later when the doctor finally came out. Meg was doing well. The bullet had perforated her small intestine, but the doctor was able to extract the bullet, repair the damage, and stitch the entry wound. He said she was lucky, all things considered, and that she would need to take it easy for the next six weeks. I knew her family lived in North Carolina and they weren't close. Griffin and I immediately agreed to have Meg stay at my house, where I could assist her for the next few weeks during her initial recovery.

We were finally allowed to visit her when she was assigned a room. She was woozy from the anesthesia, but was happy to see us, me especially. She explained that she saw the man attacking me and grabbed a knife before charging to my rescue. Sheepishly, she admitted it didn't occur to her to call the cops, she was too focused on her rescue attempt.

I explained the plan after her release in two days. She tried to decline my help, but when I pressed her about who would help for the first few weeks, she admitted she didn't have anyone she could ask. My suspicions confirmed, I gave her no choice and she soon relented. We left so that she could rest, but promised to return the following day. Ev had brought her iPad for Meg to use in case she got bored. It was still loaded with books and movies from my stay last year.

Hunter met us as we were exiting. He looked tormented, but said nothing other than to inquire how Meg was doing.

"What's going on? Did the police find out who that guy is?" I asked.

"We don't know anything conclusive yet. I have to head back to the station to coordinate with the police. I should know more tomorrow."

I nodded. We exchanged our goodbyes before heading to Griffin's truck, where I fell asleep before we'd even exited the hospital parking lot. I vaguely remembered Griffin carrying me to bed and stripping off my blood-crusted clothes before joining me.

Chapter Nineteen

"The lack of money is the root of all evil."
-Mark Twain

I entered the kitchen the next morning still dazed after a nightmare-riddled sleep. Griffin had been there each time I woke with soothing words and comforting caresses. Thankfully, these dreams were not like the terrors I used to experience, but they were still unpleasant—my brain painting alternative outcomes to the night before. Griffin was ending a phone call when he noticed me.

"Right, man. I'm going to talk to her now. We'll see you at the hospital. I'll text you either way. Thanks bro, I'm gonna need it."

He ended the call and picked up two mugs of coffee before leading me to the great room. When I was settled on the couch, he handed me my coffee and waited for me to swallow a few sips. Becoming impatient with his lack of explanation, I opened the conversation.

"Who was on the phone?"

"Hunter."

I guessed right. This was not going to be good news.

"Did he get the guy to talk?"

"He did. The attacker was a sub-contractor who rolled on his contact. The police found the guy last night and Hunter went to question him after he left the hospital. It took a little time, but Hunter was able to break him. This contact was actually contracted by someone else who they are still trying to track down, but he knew enough. Hunter had a unit bring in the source...the guy who ordered the hit."

He stopped talking and sat down next to me, moving my coffee to the table before taking my hands in his. His face was completely blank...this was the therapist-Griffin face.

"Lo-baby, it was your father. Hunter arrested him early this morning. After speaking with his lawyer, he confessed. He is being charged with multiple Class A felonies, including conspiracy to commit murder, assault, and kidnapping."

"What?" I had heard every word he said, but their significance was more than my brain could process.

"We all thought it was Heath behind the threats, so the FBI never looked beyond the Varbeck family. They looked guilty as sin because they had been paying off witnesses not to testify, and the fact that the threats stopped after Heath's death seemed like further confirmation. The FBI was still investigating, but it was put on the back burner when the threats stopped—the DA wasn't interested in pursuing bribery charges when the case was dead," Griffin said gently. "After you were attacked, Hunter knew it couldn't be the Varbecks; with Heath dead, they had no motive. Hunter was able to trace the hit back to your father after he interrogated your attacker."

"He actually confessed?" I asked.

"Yes. Hunter thinks your father's attorney recommended he confess. Because of the 'preponderance of evidence,' they will probably try some type of diminished capacity defense. Your father—"

"Don't call him that," I said sharply. "Do not call that man my father—he's a hell of a lot of things, but a father is not one of them."

"You're right, love, he's not."

"Why? Why would he do it? Disowning me was fucked up, but killing me...he paid someone to have me killed?"

"And threaten you...he was behind it the whole time. He admitted he first hired someone to threaten you, and then later contracted the hit. The Varbecks never had anything to do with it."

"So all those ridiculous poetic threats were from my father? I can't see him writing those," I said, confused.

"I doubt he wrote them himself. Your father hired one of his less reputable associates to threaten you; I guess the guy had a flair for the dramatic. When the threats didn't work, he hired a professional hit man to kill you."

"I don't understand. Why was he trying to kill me? There was no trial."

"You are trying to understand something that defies logic, baby. What he did violates human nature on a level no sane person could ever comprehend. He's in police custody now. They will arraign him tomorrow and Hunter assured me he'll be remanded without bail. Hunter also managed to pull some strings if you want to see him. If there's anything you need to say, I can take you."

Did I want to see him? No—I definitely didn't want to see him, but I needed to say my piece, then walk away and never look back.

"He probably won't deign to answer my questions, but there are things I need to say," I said, determined.

Griffin pulled me into his arms and kissed my forehead.

"Okay, Lo. We'll go. Do you want to finish your coffee first?" I shook my head. "I'm too nauseous."

"Go get dressed. I'll make you some peppermint tea to bring in the car."

"Just hold me for a minute first, please."

"Anytime."

I huddled in Griffin's arms for the next ten minutes, absorbing his strength for the impending face-off. He had been my lighthouse, leading me to safe harbor without fail. He'd weathered the storms with me, holding out hope I would find my way to him. His light never flickered, never went out. He was my steadfast beacon—my destination.

"I love you," I whispered, engulfed in emotion and my gratitude, "so damn much. The forever kind."

He lowered his arm, causing me to recline, and lowered his mouth to mine, kissing me sweetly. It was a kiss of appreciation and agreement.

"I love you, Lo-baby—forever. It will always be you."

We arrived at Riverhead Prison at noon—high noon, the classic time for an epic showdown. Yes, I was feeling a tad dramatic. It was like the movies, high concrete walls topped with barbed wire, and a guard booth built on top of the wall. Griffin explained the procedure on the drive out, but entering the jail still alarmed me. Knowing the vast number of criminals contained within the walls—many violent—kept me glued to Griffin's side. This was my first time entering a prison and it would be my last.

"You're not allowed to do anything that gets you thrown in this place, got it?" I ordered him. "I'm totally creeped out."

"Got it. The brochures are pretty accurate, so I wasn't exactly planning our next vacation here," he teased, obviously trying to distract me.

"I can't believe you came here by choice. Now I'm questioning *your* sanity."

"I was on a top secret mission...remember? I had to avenge your honor, right wrongs, be the sword of justice—"

"Stow your shield, Captain America, I understand. I would have been even more appreciative if I'd known you were coming somewhere like this."

"Lo, it's prison...people are incarcerated here. What were you expecting? They aren't doing arts and crafts to decorate the hallways," he said with laughter in his voice.

"I don't know. There's no natural light here. It's worse than the worst dressing room lighting and everything is white except for a few blue accents. Even hospital rooms are stylish in comparison."

"Again, love—prison. This is for the bad guys."

I pressed closer to his side when we passed a group of inmates being led by a guard. Griffin was bigger than most of the prisoners and guards, but I didn't want to risk getting close enough to be shanked.

Griffin chuckled beside me.

"I did it again, didn't I?"

"You did and you're adorable...but less talk about whose ass I can kick and people getting *shanked*," he said lightly but his caution was clear. "We are going into one of the private visitation rooms just around the corner. Are you ready?"

"Just...give me a second," I said, resting my head against his chest.

He wrapped his arms around me as I gathered my courage to face yet another monster.

"Yo, Doc."

"Lionel, how are you?" Griffin responded to the disembodied voice booming behind me.

"A'ight. Lionel don't play. Heard yo boy went down?"

"Yeah, I'd say I was sorry to hear it, but I try not to lie."

"Bitch snitched to da kanga. Backdoor parole."

I raised my head from Griffin's chest to find his eyes, desperate for a translation.

"Do you mind if I explain?" Griffin asked the guy.

"Yo piece?"

"Yes," Griff answered, never looking at me.

"Go."

"Lo, Lionel was one of the inmates I met with while completing my clinical hours. He wasn't a fan of Heath, especially after he complained about his treatment in prison. They aren't mourning his death."

Oh, this must be *the* guy. I felt compelled to say something. I turned until my back was pressed against Griffin's front to address Lionel. Holy shit. This guy made Griff look like a freaking wimp.

Two barks of laughter rang out, drawing the guards' attention.

"Thanks, baby. Every guy dreams of his woman calling him a wimp," he said with a reassuring squeeze.

"Lionel likes. Why she here?"

"Her father's here."

"He need protection?"

"No," Griffin replied sharply. "Let him swing."

Lionel studied Griffin for a moment. "Sup?"

"Put a hit on her, almost got what he paid for last night," Griffin answered calmly, but his body tensed behind me.

"Keep straight. Lionel gots this."

The guys exchanged a chin nod.

"Nice to meet you, Lionel, and...thanks?" I said, sounding like a complete idiot.

"Shorty's too sweet for here."

With that parting comment, he returned to the guard who was waiting discreetly to the side and left.

"Sorry about all that. You *don't* disrespect Lionel, even from prison he can make you pay. He told me you're too sweet to bring here. He's also going to make your father's life hell. "

"Oh, that's...nice of him."

"I think he has a crush on you," Griffin said with a smile. "You ready?"

I nodded and he led me around the corner, opening the door for me. I walked through to find the man I had once called 'father' sitting at a table in the center of the room. The small spark that had hoped to see remorse on his face was extinguished by his obvious revulsion.

Griffin's hand gripped the back of my neck, providing support and warmth, reinforcing me.

I waited long minutes for the man before me to speak, but he said nothing.

"Did Mother know?" I asked in a strong and confident tone, not asking for a reply...expecting it.

"Your mother is overtaxed when we have to fire a maid; I wouldn't burden her with this distasteful necessity."

Griffin's hand tightened on my neck painfully before the pressure receded.

"Why? What would possess you to hire someone to *kill* me? What did I do to you that justified murder?"

"You wouldn't understand the responsibility I have as the patriarch of this family—my obligation to protect the sanctity of the Whitney name at all costs. You never made any effort to understand the legacy of the name, the influence and duty that accompanied the mantle. You have *never* been a Whitney. At one point, I was actually convinced you were the product of an affair. I was actually relieved by the suspicion; it alleviated much of my disappointment. But even there you failed me—the DNA test was 99.9% conclusive that I contributed to your being."

"You didn't answer my question. What did I do that justified murder?"

"I've already told you, Samantha. I warned you, in fact. You were intent on testifying against the Varbeck boy in spite of me, jeopardizing the reputation and character of the Whitney name."

"I was raped," I screamed at him. "Do you understand what that means? Should I get you a fucking dictionary? I did nothing wrong. I had the audacity to attend a review session before finals and walk to my car afterwards. Forgive me for wanting the bastard who took away my choice, broke my body, shattered my spirit, and nearly killed me, to pay for his crime. Forgive me for wanting to speak for the other girls he succeeded in killing who couldn't speak for themselves. You're right...I'm a selfish bitch like that."

"Our ancestors were instrumental in founding this country," he continued as if I hadn't said anything at all. "We have thrived in every pursuit since our arrival, garnered the respect of society, and have consistently been leaders in both business and the community. Do you think sacrifices haven't been made? Do you believe you are the first in our prestigious line to experience tragedy? No, but every member of our lineage who came before had the character to handle their shame privately. Each one protected the integrity of the Whitney brand. For nearly four hundred years, the name has remained unblemished. You, in your small-mindedness, were prepared to throw away four hundred years of sacrifice."

"How can being a victim of rape possibly jeopardize the illustrious Whitney integrity?"

"Who cares about your damned rape? It's inconsequential. What you fail to comprehend is that the moment you exposed yourself to the defense attorney and media, every second of your life would be scrutinized—displayed for public entertainment."

"But I have nothing to hide. I've made a few mistakes here and there, but nothing beyond typical teenage behavior. There was no harm, no deep dark secret in my past that would embarrass the family," I paused, shaking my head at his nonsense. What was he so afraid of? Who cared if people knew that I...

"You...you were worried that the media would turn the microscope on you when my life proved boring."

His icy stare confirmed my accusation.

"You bastard, you disinherited and disowned me. When that didn't work, you sent someone to threaten me. Then Heath died and I got a reprieve, but as soon as I agreed to the *60 Minutes* interview, you hired a hit man. What have you done that is worth killing me to hide?"

He said nothing.

"Tell me. You owe me that much," I demanded.

I snapped, stepping forward to hit him and knock the defiance off his face, but Griffin's arm wrapped around my waist, pulling me against him, restraining me.

"He's not going to tell you, Lo," Griffin said, staring at the sneering man, "but I will."

Well, that knocked the snide look off his pretentious face.

"Mr. Whitney confessed so quickly that Hunter was suspicious he was hiding something. Why else would he risk hiring someone to threaten and kill you? The FBI started digging into your father's financials to track the payment for the hit, and they traced it to an overseas account. That's how they found the secret he was willing to kill you to protect—dumb luck. Your...Mr. Whitney has embezzled billions of dollars; his crimes rival Bernie Madoff's. The Whitneys were bankrupt when you were born. They liquidated everything possible, but it was never going to be enough. He used his business connections to begin an investment group and robbed people blind. No one had a clue. If he hadn't paid for the hit from one of the accounts he used to funnel and embezzle money, who knows how long it would have been 'til someone caught on? He's going to spend the rest of his life in prison no matter what, which is why he was willing to confess to the murder and kidnapping conspiracy charges. He's hoping to have input on where he's imprisoned."

"You really are piece of shit," I said to the stranger seated before me. "I'll be sure to tell the judge to send you to Hell for what you did to those poor people in your greed."

"The FBI seized all of your assets. You don't have a penny," Griffin taunted.

"Come on, babe, I'm done here."

As we turned to leave, Griffin tucked me into his side, supporting me with his strength.

When we reached the car, Griffin called Hunter, who warned us that we would only have a few months before news of Mr. Whitney's Ponzi scheme leaked. The FBI was frantically working to collect evidence for the embezzlement case while trying to keep their efforts quiet. The SEC would certainly get involved, after which the media would find out and evidence would be destroyed.

We drove straight to the hospital to visit Meg, who did her best to hide the excruciating pain she was feeling. It took fifteen minutes of fighting and threats before she finally handed over the keys to her apartment so I could collect the belongings she would need after being released into my care in a few days. Neither Griffin nor I could understand her hesitancy. It became very clear why she was reluctant to have us visit her apartment once we arrived.

Meg's studio was in a dilapidated, one-story building just on the outskirts of the most dangerous area on Long Island. The brick façade was crumbling, the glass panes on the side of the door were broken, and the gutters were overgrown with vines. The building was ready to be condemned.

"What the hell? *This* is where Meg lives? Higher Yearning isn't paying a fortune, but working full-time she should be able to afford better than this place," I said, gesturing to the building. "What gives?"

"I'm speechless, Lo. I have no clue what's going on, but we'll find out."

"Maybe you should stay with the truck while I go inside and pack up."

"There is no way you are going in there without me," Griffin said. His tone left no room for argument.

We entered the building and I was stunned to find the condition of the interior was even worse than the exterior. The smell alone made me want to turn tail and run, and I refused to consider the origin of the myriad stains spotting the walls and floor. Griffin and I took turns muttering our concern and disgust.

When we entered Meg's studio apartment, we were relieved to find it clean. There were safety concerns everywhere we looked: cracks in the ceiling and walls, leaks in the small bathroom, and other various indicators that the structural integrity of the building was questionable, at best. However, Meg had done her best to turn the tiny space into a home. The walls were freshly painted, inexpensive area rugs covered every inch of the floor, and her daybed had a few decorative pillows to add color. What struck me most were the stunning pictures on the walls—they were breathtaking and intimate, but not posed.

"I think we should bring her clothes and a few items to make her feel at home," I said.

We packed virtually all of Meg's personal belongings in less than thirty minutes—she had so little. All of her belongings boiled down to a suitcase of clothes, an overnight bag of shoes, a shopping bag of cosmetics and hair care items, a stack of pictures, and a few throw pillows. The only furniture she had was the daybed, an ancient coffee table, and an even older dresser.

"Griff, I can't stand this...her living this way. She has nothing, and this building is abysmal. She can't stay here. I have plenty of room. She can move in with me, get back on her feet and save some money."

"Lo-baby, you're right, this place isn't safe, but even those with nothing deserve their pride. You can extend the invitation, but be careful how you phrase it. I know you wouldn't judge her character based on where she lives or what she has...but she may be ashamed. Use a soft touch; don't let her see you were horrified by the conditions she was living in. If you tell her that her home is unsafe, she may interpret it as meaning you don't believe she can take care of herself," Griffin said gently.

"Good point, I didn't think of that. I'll tread lightly."

We finished packing Griff's pick-up before returning to my house. Once we had unloaded everything into the garage, Griffin and I made a beeline for the shower to wash off the grime of the apartment building.

Before bed, I washed all of Meg's clothes, hung her pictures, and added her throw pillows and comforter to the bed. I set up the space to suit its intended purpose, not as a guestroom, but as a space Meg could call home...if she chose. She was my friend—a friend who had just risked her life to save mine. There was no way in hell I would let her live in squalor, but I'd have to convince her without wounding her pride.

I headed to Thia's office for our scheduled appointment the following day. She took one look at me and ordered me to tell her what was going on. I recounted every insane detail of the past week without interruption. When I'd finished, she looked thoroughly horror-struck. Wow, I managed to boggle Thia's mind. There was a bizarre sense of accomplishment in that fact.

"Your life is a Hollywood cliché," she said excitedly. "It should be a movie."

"Thia, you're nuts," I said, laughing.

"A Lifetime, made-for-TV movie at the very least. When it happens, I want someone good to play me—Oscar quality. Someone beautiful...Helen Mirren. You don't let them cast anyone other than Helen Mirren."

"You got it. But I think you're too late. I heard WE Network is already working on a TV movie about 'Heath the Hensley Hunter.'"

"Dammit. I should have copyrighted the idea," she said, chagrined.

"They stole it right out from under you," I said, playing along...at least I hoped she was playing.

"How are you feeling?" she asked, resuming full therapist mode.

"Shocked, angry, relieved, happy, grateful...most of all, grateful. Meg will be okay, and Heath is dead. My sperm donor will die behind bars—everyone I love is safe...I'm safe. It's still sinking in, the knowledge that I am truly safe."

"What about your genetic contributor?" Thia asked, honoring my refusal to use any paternal terminology.

"His words cut the way anyone's disdain would hurt, but didn't have the same impact it would have if I still considered him my father. The threads of that bond were severed months ago, something else I'm grateful for. It helped to know that his actions and hatred weren't about me, only the risk I presented in exposing his fraud."

"What about his eventual trial?"

"I have no useful information, so I can't imagine the prosecution will want me to testify. I'm dreading the news coverage...all that attention. I wish I could change my name," I said flippantly.

"Why can't you?"

She was right, why couldn't I? I never viewed myself as a part of that family; I didn't want to be a part of that family. Why should I have to wear a name I hated?

"You're right. Hot damn...I'm going to change my name!"

"Now you just have to decide what name you want. Are you going to go with a generic last name like Smith, or something of significance?"

"Carsen. Meme, Ev's mom, was the only parent I'd ever known. I don't think Ev would mind," I said, my excitement growing.

"I'm sure she wouldn't. What else?"

"I've been having nightmares since the guy tried to take me, but they aren't like the terrors used to be."

"Keep a dream journal so we can track the subject and frequency of the dreams. I suspect they will lessen with time and eventually subside, but we'll keep an eye on it."

"Will do."

"I think we can schedule you for every other week for the next month or so—then reduce your visits to once a month," she said casually, but her gaze was intent.

"You're...you're breaking up with me?" I said, hurt by her abandonment and rejection.

"Don't be ridiculous. I'm not letting go of my cash cow," she said with a wink. "I'll be your therapist for as long as you want or need me. It would be my honor. But Sam, you have made incredible progress. You don't need to see me every week. You are ready to transition from middle to late-stage treatment."

"Okay, it doesn't sound so bad when you put it that way."

"I am so proud of you. You will always be one of my greatest success stories, but that is because *you* were willing to fearlessly confront your past head-on. You will have unexpected flare-ups, moments of struggle, but you will overcome and thrive—I have no doubt."

The *60 Minutes* special about the murder and attacks at Hensley University aired to the highest ratings the show had received in years. As Liz had predicted, the show galvanized the public, who were already demanding legislation to regulate university responses to violent crimes on campus. The interview was difficult for me, but Griffin and Thia were both on-hand to bolster me before and after, which kept me grounded. I was overwhelmed by the outpouring of love and support I received after the airing. Thousands of letters arrived, many from fellow victims who shared their stories and thanked me for speaking for them...for inspiring them. I was humbled by their praise, but the hope they found in my story fueled my soul. It gave purpose to everything I had suffered, as if the fires I had walked through had burned the ground and fertilized the soil, allowing flowers of hope to bloom, bigger and brighter than ever.

We picked Meg up from the hospital a week after her surgery. Griffin carried her to her room and placed her on the bed before slipping out quietly. I fussed with blankets and pillows as she looked around the room, baffled to find so many of her personal belongings.

"Yeah, I brought some of your pictures and stuff to make you feel more at home," I said, trying to answer her unasked question.

"How are you feeling?"

"I'm sore, but it's getting better."

"Good. I wanted to talk to you about something."

"Go for it," she said, watching me carefully to gauge my intention.

"I know you're in school full-time and working full-time at Higher Yearning. You're busting your butt trying to do everything on your own, which I respect. But you're going to be out of work for at least six weeks, which is a major financial hit. So I was thinking...I have more than enough space here, and I'm at Griff's place half the time anyway. Why don't you move in here? It will save you from paying rent, and you could even work on paying off some of the student loans you mentioned earlier than you planned. Besides, I kind of miss having a roommate since Ev ditched me for Hunter. You'd be doing me a favor, really. I know nothing I could ever say or do would adequately express how grateful I am, but I need to do this. Not for you, for me."

She was about to protest but I cut her off, "Please? Before you answer, keep in mind that I have control over your pain meds for the next several weeks."

Meg chuckled then gasped.

"Bitch, don't make me laugh. Damn that hurts. Day one and I'm already questioning your nursing skills. I hope this isn't an example of the type of roommate you plan on being," she said with her usual ease, but I saw the gratitude and embarrassment in her eyes.

"Trying to set the bar low so I won't disappoint. I'm going to warm up some broth for you and get your next round of pain meds."

Meg grabbed my hand when I turned to leave, whispering, "Thank you."

I nodded and continued toward the kitchen. It felt good to focus on someone other than myself, not as a form of escape, but to help another person in need. My past was no longer controlling me; it didn't consume my every thought and emotion. I had finally reached a point in my recovery that I'd healed enough to reach out and support those who supported me...and it felt incredible.

*"I'm an optimist, brought up on the belief that if you wait to
the end of the story, you get to see the good people live
happily ever after."*
-Cat Stevens

It was three weeks post-surgery and Meg was recovering well.
Griffin and I still had to scold her for trying to lift anything heavier
than a mug of coffee, but the doctor was pleased with her
prognosis. I knew she was trying to do everything she was
physically capable of to compensate for the rent-free living
arrangements. I turned a blind eye to her emptying the dishwasher
and wiping down the kitchen counters because I knew she felt she
needed to contribute for the sake of her pride, but I was forced to
lay down the law when I caught her trying to clean the bathroom
two weeks after surgery.

Griffin had been helping in every way possible by refilling
prescriptions, grocery shopping, and getting rid of Meg's old
furniture, with her blessing. We were finally going to spend the
night at his house to enjoy some alone time. I was excited to take
a break and just be us. I didn't mind helping Meg, nor did Griffin.
Both of us were guiltlessly indebted to her—she had, after all, saved
my life—but I was tired of having sex on mute. It was distracting
trying to remain quiet. I was looking forward to a night of
uninhibited wild monkey love at maximum volume.

We were saying our goodbyes to Meg, who was lounging on the couch, when the doorbell rang. Needless to say, we weren't expecting company. Griffin and I both headed for the door, eager to get rid of whatever obstacle dared to threaten our plans. My socks skidded on the wood floors and I crashed into Griffin.

"Whoa, love," he said while steadying me. "In a rush?"

"Like you're not? Please."

With a laugh, he opened the door to Hunter and Everleigh's smiling faces.

"Hi guys, we were driving by on our way home and decided to say 'hi,'" Ev said.

Griffin invited them in and we all exchanged hugs and greetings. I hoped they weren't expecting us to hang around for long...it wasn't gonna happen.

"Did you two have plans for the evening?" Ev asked, while toying with her hair in a very un-Ev-like fashion.

"Actually, we were just headed out. Date night," Griffin replied.

"Babe, we're interrupting their plans," Ev said to Hunter, stroking his chest.

"That's okay, we can hang out for a few minutes," I replied.

What was with her? She was acting like a complete spaz. Beside me, Griffin chuckled. Okay, I was clearly missing something.

"Oh my, I'm so tired," Ev said, covering her mouth for a dramatic yawn.

Holy mother of all that is sparkly! There on her left hand was a gorgeous rock. And not just any rock...an elegant emerald-cut diamond with a simple baguette on each side of the delicate white gold band. It had to be at least two carats—Hunter did me proud.

"Ohmygod!" I squealed.

"I wanna see, too. Don't make the invalid get up...bring the party to me," Meg called from the great room.

I turned to Hunter, grabbing Ev's hand and holding it in front of his face. "This is a job well done," I said, shaking Ev's hand for emphasis. "I'll even forgive you for not asking my permission first."

"Uh, Sam, it's attached and I'm rather fond of my hand," Ev said in defense of the limb I had claimed.

"Sorry, I would have asked your blessing, but you would have blown the surprise," Hunter said apologetically.

"I would not!"

"Lo-baby, you would have," Griffin said as he pried Ev's hand from my clutches.

"Wait a freaking minute...you knew?" I said, turning to Griffin, shocked he'd withheld such huge news from me. "And you didn't tell me?"

"Couldn't break the guy code on this one, love. Besides, you would have slipped and never forgiven yourself for ruining the surprise."

"How did he ask...tell me everything."

Ev opened her mouth to speak when we heard a grunt from the other room.

"One sec, Meg will want to hear, too," I said.

When we entered the great room, we found Meg standing next to the couch, looking breathless and pained.

"Told you it was too soon to stop taking the pain medication," I told her.

"Thanks, Nurse Ratchet," Meg replied testily.

"See what a difficult patient she is...such a grump," I teased. In reality, any display of grumpiness was a rarity with Meg.

A pillow came whizzing toward my face but was snatched from the air seconds before impact. I leaned over and pulled Griffin's mouth to mine, rewarding his heroics with a kiss.

"Okay, spill it," I prompted Ev.

"We found a house we both loved and made an offer a few days ago—which was rejected. I was bummed because the place was perfect...for several reasons. Hunter didn't feel we should increase our offer, so we walked away from it," Ev said, sticking out her lip in a pout. "We agreed only to buy if we both loved it and were comfortable with the price. I was bummed—that house was freakin' perfect—so Hunter took me to dinner last night to cheer me up. Maroni's was incredible, by the way. After dinner, he drove to the house and made me follow him to the porch."

"She kept arguing with me that I was going to get us arrested. I had to remind her that the house was vacant, and I'm an FBI agent," Hunter said, clearly entertained by Ev's concern. "Anyway...he said he just wanted to look in the window. I thought he was reconsidering our offer. Next thing I know he's carrying me through the front door. There were candles and flowers everywhere, and 'When You Say Nothing At All' was playing...the Scotty McCreery and Lauren Alaina version, my favorite. He got down on one knee and took my hands. Then he promised to help fill the house with a lifetime of memories, children, and love if I would agree be his wife."

Tears gathered in my eyes as I pictured the scene. It was the proposal, life, and happily-ever-after she deserved.

"I said yes, of course. Then he explained that our offer *was* accepted and we were officially in contract. He lied to me so he could propose in our future home. He's lucky the realtor and current owners are romantics and accommodated his grand plan."

"This is amazing. You are engaged *and* found the house of your dreams! Griff, grab a bottle of champagne. We have to toast!" I said. "Now, tell me about the house."

Ev and Hunter exchanged a secretive smile.

"It's a colonial, four bedrooms, two-and-a-half baths. The backyard is perfect for kids," Ev said.

"And it's very close to Higher Yearning, which will make it easy for Ev," Hunter added.

"The best part is the neighborhood. All the neighbors seem amazing. We saw a ton of young families when we were there. There's only one house a few doors down from us that seems questionable," Ev added.

Griffin's laughter filtered in from the kitchen.

"What am I missing?" Meg and I asked in unison.

"We're going to be Griffin's neighbors...well, a block away, but still pretty close," Ev said.

Meg, Griffin, and I spent the next hour celebrating with the happy couple, but we eventually made our previously planned escape. Griffin pointed out Huntleigh's new house when we drove past, and I was pleased to see it was as perfect as they had described. We spent the rest of the night privately celebrating all of the joys and blessings life had provided us. We didn't accomplish my goal of destroying every room in the house that night, but we certainly made a good effort.

The next three months passed in a whirlwind of activity—my graduation from Hensley, planning Ev's wedding (a traditional affair at the insistence of Hunter's family), helping Huntleigh move, and my enrollment in culinary school...it's been one event or project after another. Griffin and I stole as many moments as possible, greedy for one another's undivided attention. Without the distraction of serial killers, threats, and hit men, we were able to focus on our relationship, learning all the pieces of one another and how they fit together. I fell deeper in love with Griffin every single day. He never failed to prove his love and commitment to me in both action and words. Each time I swore I couldn't fall any further, a new piece of him would be revealed and I'd plummet deeper, welcoming every second of the free-fall. Our bond, the blend of commitment, respect, and love, was the epoxy Griff had likened us to months ago.

I only saw Thia once a month and most of our sessions were spent catching up and addressing minor issues that arose between sessions.

Meg made a full recovery and became a fully integrated member of our clan. She came to The Stop every Thursday and was always around to grab coffee or dinner. She was not only my roommate, but a dear friend. She made every effort to show her appreciation, despite my assurances that she was not a burden. She never offered an explanation for the hovel she had been living in or her financial difficulties, and I didn't push—she would tell me when she was ready. She was usually so happy and carefree, it was easy to forget the secret we had witnessed.

Hunter came over one day to warn me that the SEC was preparing to announce Mr. Whitney's arrest and forthcoming indictment. It wasn't a surprise; we all knew the time was coming, but I was apprehensive of the media firestorm. I knew I wouldn't escape their attention completely, no matter what precautions I took. Thankfully, my procedural hearing to legally change my name was scheduled for the next week. My lawyer was confident the judge would waive the requirement to publish the name change prior to it becoming official, in light of the circumstances. This time next week, I would be Samantha Melany Carsen. I decided to also forgo my middle names, which were traditional Whitney names, and take Meme's first name instead. Ev was incredibly supportive when I told her about my selected names, reminding me that we had always been sisters and the name change was only an outward symbol of what we already knew. The irony was that we would only share the last name for a few months before Ev became Everleigh Rose Charles.

The media coverage of the-jackass-formerly-known-as-my-father's Ponzi scheme was out of control. For months, I couldn't turn on the TV without seeing his face. Any interest in me faded quickly, until news of his attempt to kill me was leaked. Once again I was thrust into the spotlight and, while it was a nuisance, the coverage provided a platform for me to advocate for reform to protect women on college campuses and increase university accountability. Griffin supported me every step of the way without complaining about the circus my life had become. Eventually, after he was sentenced to life without parole, public interest died down.

Through it all, I never heard from my mother. Not. A. Word. There was a small part of me that had hoped she would approach me to make amends once she was free of my father's influence, but that never occurred. I couldn't bring myself to contact her. While she was innocent of the attempt on my life, her years of abandonment were impossible for me to forget. Maybe one day I would be ready to speak with her, but I was not there yet.

We were lying in bed early one morning, my body draped across
Griffin's as usual, when his sexy voice interrupted my silent
enjoyment of his company.

"You know what I was thinking the other day?" Griffin asked.

"What?" I mumbled into his chest, too relaxed to engage in
guessing games.

"We never made it to Turks and Caicos."

That's right, he had mentioned us taking a vacation months
ago, after I had received the last threat. So much had happened
since then, I'd completely forgotten.

"It's been a crazy six months...we'll get there someday," I said,
glad to be reminded of the dream vacation as something to look
forward to.

"Isn't the Culinary Institute on break next week?" he asked,
trying to sound casual. As if he didn't know my schedule as well
as I did.

"You know it is, but there is no way were are going to find a
decent place to rent this late...it's peak season and last-minute
airline tickets will be through the roof. Why don't we plan
something for after I graduate? We'll have time to make the
arrangements, and it's only five months away."

His body shifted and a paper appeared in front of my face. I
focused on the page; it was an airline e-ticket confirmation in our
names from New York to Turks and Caicos booked for next week.

"You didn't."

"I did."

"When did you book these?"

"When you enrolled. Life was so crazy and I knew school
would be an extra stress, no matter how much you loved it. I
checked the dates and saw you had a break, so I made the
reservations. I figured you were bound to need a vacation by now."

"This is freaking awesome!" I shouted. "We are going on
vacation!"

He squeezed me tighter, appreciating my enthusiasm.

"You are the best boyfriend ever," I said, raising my head to
kiss him.

"I'm not completely selfless. I get to enjoy white sandy beaches, drinks, and, most importantly, you in a bikini."

"Thank you," I said, cupping his cheek in my hand. "You make it so easy to love you, not just because you book us fabulous vacations, but in all the little ways you show me how well you know me and love me."

"Lo-baby, it comes naturally...loving you is what I was born to do. There is nothing I wouldn't do to see you smile or hear you laugh. No distance I wouldn't travel to be by your side, no war I wouldn't wage to protect you. Being with you, loving you, knowing you love me...that's my definition of heaven. I get to spend every day in heaven because of you, so all those little things I do, they're only glimpses of everything you give me."

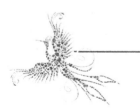

Epilogue

"The phoenix hope, can wing her way through the desert skies, and still defying fortune's spite; revive from ashes and rise." -Miguel de Cervantes

One Year Later...

It was a beautiful summer afternoon when Griffin suggested we pack dinner and head to one of the small north shore beaches. It had been a long week on my feet in the kitchen, though I loved every second. I had finished culinary school in the spring and was now working at a local French restaurant with a stellar reputation. The beach would be quiet on a weekday evening, perfect for a relaxing picnic.

Basket packed and wine bottle in hand, we headed to Cedar Beach. The sun was beginning to meet the horizon, painting the sky with brilliant shades of orange, pink, and purple. The Long Island Sound was calm, only a few boats dotted the sea at this time of night. It was a flawless evening and I absorbed every detail hungrily like food for my soul.

We held hands and walked along the shore in comfortable silence until all signs of humanity faded away, leaving only us and nature's splendor. Ahead I spotted several glowing orbs, almost blending into the sunset, but too bright to be a part of it. As we approached, the orbs became tiki torches. They were positioned to form a perfect circle, the outline completed with crushed stones and bouquets of irises and green orchids. In the center of the circle was a thick beige comforter with colorful accent pillows that matched the bouquets. I stilled to soak in the magic of the scene, afraid it would disappear like a mirage if I blinked. Griffin swept me into his arms, carrying me over the rocks before setting me down on the blanket in the center of the circle. He smiled at me before unpacking our dinner and opening the wine.

"You did all of this?" I asked, still at a loss.

"Most of it. I had a few elves to help and stand guard 'til we arrived."

"Well, Santa, with this setup I assume I've made the nice list, but I have to warn you...I'm going to be *very* naughty in a little while."

"With *this* Santa, that kind of naughty will put you at the top of the nice list," he replied with a panty-melting smile. "Here you go, love," he said, handing me a glass of white wine followed by a plate of cheese, fruit, and French bread.

As I tasted my first sip of wine, music began to play. The song was vaguely familiar, but I couldn't place it. I searched for the source when I heard Griffin's voice singing to me, confused by the fact that he was sitting in front of me, sipping his wine.

"Gotta love Bose portable SoundDocks. The sound quality is amazing," he said nonchalantly.

"Yes, and *your* voice sounds great coming out of it," I teased, hoping for an explanation.

"I heard this song a while ago and it made me think of you. I wanted to sing it for you, but not at The Stop with an audience. You probably know it, but I switched up the arrangement a little to make it work for me."

"Start it over and turn up the volume so I can hear it better," I requested.

He increased the volume and restarted the song before sitting behind me with a leg on each side of mine, providing a backrest for me to lounge against. I listened to the words and recognized the Trisha Yearwood song, "Where Your Road Leads"—Griffin's version was slower and more intimate. I let the words sink in, the commitment, tenderness, and love was so stark. The lyrics were a promise. When the song ended, the guitar accompaniment continued quietly, as if the vow would never end.

"I have something for you...I made it, so don't laugh," he said, a hint of nerves shading his voice.

I felt him reach into his pocket behind me and heard a soft thud on the blanket beside us. He looped his arm around me and let something dangle from his clenched fist. I caught the swinging—I-don't-know-what—between my fingers and examined it in the soft light provided by the torches. It was a strange-looking stone, dangling from a chain. As I examined it more closely, I saw that it was green with varying shades of striations running through the entire stone. I also couldn't help but notice that the stone looked like it had been destroyed and pieced back together. I gasped as the significance dawned. He made me into a stone...or he made a stone into me, and it was beautiful.

"It's called malachite—one of the oldest recorded stones used for jewelry, dating back to ancient Egypt. According to what I read, it's supposed to symbolize protection, love, endurance, and transformation. Kind of perfect, right? I have to confess I learned most of that after I chose it though. Initially I was drawn to it because it matched the color of your eyes," Griffin said, gazing into the eyes in question. "I bought a perfectly round polished stone and shattered it bit by bit, until it was a pile of rubble—then pieced it back together with epoxy," he said with a smile. "But this is only half..." He reached down beside him and raised his other arm around me to show a similar stone dangling from a chain. "Go ahead."

I raised my free hand to grab the other half and moved their jagged sides together—the two halves fit perfectly, creating a whole sphere. You could just make out the scars on the surface of the circle, but it felt solid and whole in my hand.

As I released the pieces, Griffin gently shook them apart and handed me half. I saw that the short chain connected the malachite to a metal circle.

"A key chain?" I asked, surprised by the choice.

He opened his palm to reveal the half he had been holding was also attached to a key chain, but on the end of his was a key.

"I want your ridiculously large wardrobe to move back into my house...permanently. I want to hear you complain about my socks being left on the family room floor. I want your favorite pots and pans in my cabinets. I want to wake up next to you every morning and fall asleep with you on my chest every night. Lo-baby, will you live with me?"

"Hell yes!" I said, turning my head to kiss him. "Can we negotiate who gets which closet in the master bedroom?"

"In a minute, although that seems like a pointless conversation...I know you're taking both," he teased. "Take your key, love."

I placed the empty key chain I had been holding in his palm and reached for the key chain that held my new house key. I grabbed the chain link so I could savor the sight of the Griffin stone next to my key and smiled.

"There's one more thing, baby."

He took my hands in his and stared into my eyes.

"Love, I want you to take my name. I want you to be Samantha Melany Evensen. I want you to be my best friend, my wife, and the mother of my children. I want to love and protect you until the day death parts us...and if by the grace of God I go first, I promise I will be waiting for you to join me in whatever follows this life. I want to be with you for eternity because without you, I am just broken pieces of a whole." He rose on one knee and reached into his pocket, returning with a ring between his fingers. "Will you marry me, my love, and make me whole?"

Tears filled my eyes, spilling over the rim and streaking down my cheeks.

"Yes, yes, yes. I would be honored to be Samantha Evensen. I would be honored to be your wife and the mother of your children. I love you with every broken little shard of me and I always will. There will never be anyone for me but you." I sealed our agreement with a kiss as he slid the ring on my finger. "I'm not ready to be a mother yet, but I think we should practice to make sure we have all the mechanics right for the future."

As the last words left my lips, I flung myself at him, tackling him to the ground. My kiss was hungry and possessive, claiming the man I loved, marking him as mine. He met me stroke for stroke, reciprocating, marking me as his—writing it on my soul.

My hands drifted to the buttons on his shirt and I slid each one through the hole, following the path of exposed flesh with my lips. When I had removed his shirt, I whipped my own over my head, too impatient for his assistance.

His hands traced my ribs around my back as he sat up with me in his lap and released the clasp of my bra to expose me to him. His hands traveled to my breasts as his lips caressed mine, teasing me until I was mindless with desire. As my urgency grew, I rocked against him, longing for the intimate connection that joined us in every way possible. This was the last man I would ever be with in this way—the idea thrilled me.

I reached between us to release the button on his shorts as he rolled me onto my back, sliding my skirt and panties down my legs. He leaned back to appreciate my body, which was fine by me as it gave me the opportunity to examine the merchandise I had just committed to purchasing. God this man's body was spectacular. Every sculpted muscle called for my attention, inviting me to become reacquainted. We hummed our approval in harmony.

I couldn't wait another minute and he was taking his sweet time, so I reached around and grabbed his rock-hard ass, pulling him to me forcefully. I was lucky he braced his weight despite his surprise, but even that brief delay as he adjusted his weight for my benefit was too much. I wrapped my legs around his waist and pulled myself up to him, finding the link I was desperately seeking. His breath rasped out of him in shock. I was never timid in bed, but this was a new level of assertiveness. I took him because he was mine to take. After a beat, his surprise passed and he picked up my rhythm, easily retaking control. He took me as I had him, pushing me higher and higher with every smooth glide. The ocean breeze cooled our damp skin as we both reached for ecstasy. He rose up on his knees, bringing me with him, going deeper than he had ever been. He had me on the brink, but I was clinging to the edge by my fingertips, waiting for him.

"Together," he said, drawing my eyes to his.

As if by his command, both of our bodies tensed and shuddered. I fought to keep my eyes locked on his, wanting him to see my pleasure and love. I was in a state of rapture, blissful shocks traversing every cell in my body.

As my tremors subsided, he lay back, cuddling me to his chest where I could listen to his breath and feel his heartbeat. We snuggled together for several minutes before one of his arms left me and reached to the side. When it returned, he handed me a flashlight.

"What's this for?" I asked, my brain still fuzzy.

He kissed my hand in response and a quick sparkle caught my eye.

I whipped my hand free of his grasp as if on fire and flicked the switch on the flashlight. There on the fourth finger of my left hand was my definition of an engagement ring. It was a fiery round diamond—easily a carat and a half, which looked huge on my tiny hand—surrounded by a halo of smaller diamonds set in white gold. Two diamond-encrusted arms extended from each side of the halo, joining as one before disappearing between my fingers. I could not have designed a ring more perfectly suited to my taste.

"It's perfect."

"It's you," he replied, pleased with my approval.

"I love you, Griffin. You are such a good man—smart, caring, sexy, thoughtful—you make me want to be a better woman. Thank you for loving me."

"Lo, you're impossible not to love. I never stood a chance, not from the first time I heard your laugh."

We dressed slowly, watching each other cover the parts we had just explored.

"I didn't think of it before, but weren't you worried someone may interrupt us?" I asked. It would be very un-Griffin-like for him to be okay with someone intruding on our private moment.

"I posted signs in both directions that said this part of the beach was closed."

"Is that legal? This is a public beach, isn't it?"

He shrugged.

"You went through a lot of trouble, babe," I said, hugging him.

"You're worth it. Haven't you realized that yet? There is nothing I wouldn't do for you. Sam, you are everything to me. All those pieces of me amount to nothing on their own—you are my whole. I was designed to be pieces for you."

Acknowledgements

Life is funny; it puts people in our paths exactly when we need them—even if we weren't looking for them. One of the very first people to read/review *Only For You* was you, CeCe. Who would have thought you would have thought you would wind up being my MOST trusted critique partner. Anyone who enjoys *Pieces For You* should thank you for your contribution to making it the story it is. Without you it would not be nearly as honest and "right." I am honored to call you my critique partner and, even more so, my friend. I can't wait for your book baby's release—I know everyone will love *Tastes Like Winter* as much as I do, and I then will get to say 'I knew her when...'

There have been a number of cheerleaders who have encouraged me since I released *Only For You,* all of whom I adore. But there is one special chica who has been there to encourage, empathize, and make me laugh when I was having moments of self-doubt and self-pity. Jennifer, you can't take a compliment for shit, but you give them beautifully. You ask for nothing, but *'pimp'* my work like a pro. I trust your book whispering, spidey-sense implicitly. Time and time again you've proven yourself to be a true friend, and I am so grateful for you. Besides, who else will laugh about HGSxM with me?

Editors are the unsung heroes of all books, and mine is a freakin' super star. Sheri, you are a dream come true...I am proud to call you my editor and also my friend. Not only is your work impeccable, your suggestions sound, and your speed mind-blowing, but you are a joy in every way. Thank you for making *Pieces For You* shine. If you need an awesome editor, I can't recommend S.G. Thomas highly enough: perfectproofandpolish@gmail.com

I have been blessed with an incredible group of beta readers who shared their honest thoughts and opinions about *Pieces For You*. You have each been a gift to me with both your friendship, critique, and support. In alphabetical order, I must thank...Adrienne, Brandelyn, Hildy, Heather, JJ, Shanny, and my Literati Ladies, too!

As always, I must thank my family, specifically my husband and two boys, whose patience and support make it possible for me to chase my dream and give voice to the stories in my head. Thank you all for being my own personal heroes and cheerleading squad!

To my Momma and Cara, you are my rocks! Thank you for sacrificing your time to help me follow my dream. I love you both more than words could ever express and couldn't do this without you.

Last, but most definitely not least, I have to give a nod to my most bestest best friend, Debbie. Girl, we've known each other forever, plus. We've seen one another through more craziness than any one book could capture (a series maybe). Thank you for being my steadfast friend—accepting and understanding me (better than I do myself at times). If you had laughed in my face when I first told you I was writing a book I probably would have given up without even trying...so you can totally take credit for anything I write. You are definitely one of the graces God has given me that I could never earn but would be lost without! Luv ya so da much. (Does this make up for all the cards I never buy? LOL)

A portion of the proceeds from sales of *Pieces For You* will be donated to RAINN (Rape, Abuse, and Incest National Network) to assist the important work they are committed to in helping rape survivors. I encourage everyone to support RAINN: **www.rainn.org**

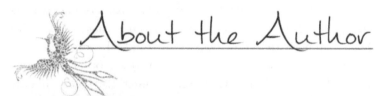

About the Author

Genna Rulon is an up-and-coming contemporary romance author.

During her 15 years in the corporate world, Genna, inspired by her love of reading, fantasized about penning her own stories. Encouraged by her favorite authors, many of whom are indie writers and self-published, she committed to pursue her aspirations of writing her own novels.

Genna was raised on Long Island in New York, where she still resides, surrounded by the most amazing family and friends. She's married to a wonderful man who patiently tolerates her ramblings about whichever book she is currently working on, even feigning interest relatively convincingly! Genna is blessed with two little boys who do their best to thwart mommy's writing time with their hilarious antics and charming extrapolations.

All of Genna's books are brought to you courtesy of coffee and Disney Junior.

You can find Genna online at: www.gennarulon.com

Genna would <u>love</u> to hear from you, and will personally respond to all messages! You can contact her as follows:
Email: genna@gennarulon.com

You can also follow Genna online at:
Twitter: www.twitter.com/GennaRulon
Facebook: www.facebook.com/genna.rulon
Goodreads: www.goodreads.com/gennarulon

Other books by Genna

Only For You
For You Series - Book #1
published: September 17, 2013

All Everleigh Carsen wanted to do was complete her final semester at Hensley University and begin the life she planned.

When a wave of violent crime seizes campus, Everleigh is persuaded by her best friend to attend a school sponsored self-defense seminar, where she meets volunteer instructor, Hunter Charles. After Everleigh's biting sarcasm induces Hunter to eject her from class, an explosive relationship is born.

Everleigh is determined to forget the striking man, but fate—that fickle shrew—continuously intervenes. Unable to escape him, she casts Hunter as her prime adversary. The only complication...Hunter is resolutely pursuing his vindication...by any means necessary. Verbal warfare ensues, and despite Everleigh's ingenious efforts, in Hunter, she has finally found her equal.

Only For You is a compelling tale of friendship, desire, and redemption—brimming with witty characters, intelligent dialogue, unexpected twists, profound sorrow, unfettered hope, and love's unassailable perseverance.

Ever For You
For You, Book #1.5
Expected publication: February 2014

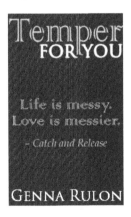

Temper For You
For You, Book #3
Publication date: Sep 24, 2014

Made in the USA
Monee, IL
25 February 2025

12922552R00187